What people are saying about …

FALSE PRETENSES

"Kathy Herman has cooked up a spicy Cajun mystery featuring a likable cast of small-town characters. This intriguing yarn is sure to satisfy the appetites of murder-mystery lovers."

Creston Mapes, author of *Nobody*

"With its perfectly paced suspense, Cajun flair, and riveting look at the high price of deceit, Kathy Herman's *False Pretenses* is a true page-turner. Highly recommended!"

Marlo Schalesky, author of the Christy Award–winning novel *Beyond the Night*

"Kathy Herman has raised her own bar for an action-packed novel with rich conflict and realistic romance. *False Pretenses* is deep and soul-searching with nonstop excitement. It will lead to nonstop reading."

Hannah Alexander, author of *A Killing Frost* and the Hideaway series

"Mysteries abound in Kathy Herman's latest foray into suspense. Though we know some of the characters well, new ones will intrigue readers. The story entwines the secrets of the past with the secrets of today. You'll enjoy this trip to Cajun country. A solid read!"

Lyn Cote, author of *Her Abundant Joy*

"In *False Pretenses,* Kathy Herman has begun a wonderfully intriguing new series set in Louisiana's bayou country—Secrets of Roux River Bayou. *False Pretenses* gets the series off to a fast-paced start filled with suspense, tension, and mystery that will grip readers from the first page."

Marta Perry, author of *Murder in Plain Sight*

"Kathy Herman has written a powerful story of tension, mystery, and danger. Anonymous messages point to a secret from the past that can destroy the future. But there's also a tender love story to challenge that secret."

Lorena McCourtney, author of the Ivy Malone Mysteries and the Andi McConnell Mysteries

FALSE PRETENSES

SECRETS OF ROUX RIVER BAYOU

BOOK 1

KATHY HERMAN

David C Cook
transforming lives together

FALSE PRETENSES
Published by David C Cook
4050 Lee Vance View
Colorado Springs, CO 80918 U.S.A.

David C Cook Distribution Canada
55 Woodslee Avenue, Paris, Ontario, Canada N3L 3E5

David C Cook U.K., Kingsway Communications
Eastbourne, East Sussex BN23 6NT, England

David C Cook and the graphic circle C logo
are registered trademarks of Cook Communications Ministries.

The website addresses recommended throughout this book are offered as a
resource to you. These websites are not intended in any way to be or imply an
endorsement on the part of David C Cook, nor do we vouch for their content.

This story is a work of fiction. All characters and events are the product of the author's
imagination. Any resemblance to any person, living or dead, is coincidental.

Unless otherwise noted, all Scripture quotations are taken from the Holy Bible,
New International Version®, NIV®. Copyright © 1973, 1978, 1984 by Biblica,
Inc™. Used by permission of Zondervan. All rights reserved worldwide. www.
zondervan.com. John 11:25–26 in chapter 36 is taken from the *New American Bible
with Revised New Testament and Revised Psalms* © 1991, 1986, 1970 Confraternity
of Christian Doctrine, Washington, D.C. and is used by permission of the
copyright owner. All rights reserved. No part of the *New American Bible* may be
reproduced in any form without permission in writing from the copyright owner.

LCCN 2010942617
ISBN 978-0-7814-0340-5
eISBN 978-0-7814-0618-5

© 2011 Kathy Herman
Published in association with the literary agency of Alive Communications,
Inc, 7680 Goddard St., Suite 200, Colorado Springs, CO 80920.

The Team: Don Pape, Diane Noble, Amy Kiechlin,
Sarah Schultz, Caitlyn York, Karen Athen
Cover Design: DogEared Design, Kirk DouPonce.
Cover Images: iStockphoto, #10860599 royalty-free; iStockphoto, #9791563
royalty-free; ShutterStock, #4247786 royalty-free; SuperStock, #1525R-116643
royalty-free; 123RF, #1952688 royalty-free; Veer, #PHP2971311 royalty-free.

Printed in the United States of America
First Edition 2011

1 2 3 4 5 6 7 8 9 10

123010

To Him who is both the Giver and the Gift

ACKNOWLEDGMENTS

This is the first time in my writing career that I haven't signed the first book of a new release to my mom. So I'd like to mention her here. My mother, Nora Phillips, closed her eyes and slipped into the arms of Jesus shortly after I started writing this book. Her sudden death was a shock to me but was no surprise to Him, who called her into His presence. I rejoice for Mom, yet I miss her so. She was a close friend and ardent cheerleader. There's just something about a mother's praise and encouragement that is different from anyone else's. Trust me, if there's a library in heaven, she's already trying to get my books added. It's hard letting go of her, but I take comfort in knowing that my loss is temporary. Our joy will be eternal.

The bayou country of southern Louisiana provides the backdrop for this new series and many of the images I describe in the story. But Saint Catherine Parish, the town of Les Barbes, and the Roux River Bayou exist only in my imagination.

During the writing of this first book, I drew from several resource people, each of whom shared generously from his or her storehouse of knowledge and experience. I did my best to integrate the facts as I understood them. If accuracy was compromised in any way, it was unintentional and strictly of my own doing. I also made good use of numerous Internet sites related to the history of the Acadians as well as to idiosyncrasies and customs of the Cajun culture and language.

I owe a debt of gratitude to Retired Commander Carl H. Deeley of the Los Angeles County Sheriff's Department for reading over selected scenes and answering my many questions relating to command posts, containments, and hate-crime investigations; and to Retired Lieutenant Gil Carrillo, Los Angeles County Sheriff's Department Homicide Bureau, for answering my questions about false confessions, bagging evidence, identifying shoes from casts taken at crime scenes, withholding evidence, and dealing with department leaks; and to my brother, Chuck Phillips, for helping me understand the differences in firearms. I love gleaning what I can from experienced individuals who "know their stuff." You gentlemen made my job easy.

I want to thank my friend Paul David Houston, former assistant district attorney, for explaining the steps involved in legally changing a person's name, for researching the statute of limitations on certain crimes in the state of Louisiana, and for helping me to create a believable crime scenario. As always, Paul, you're an absolute joy to work with. Your thorough, concise, and speedy replies to my questions are so appreciated.

A special word of thanks to those whose prayers kept me going, especially through a difficult time of grief: my tenacious prayer warrior and sister, Pat Phillips; my ever-standing-in-the-gap friends Mark and Donna Skorheim and Susan Mouser; my online prayer team—Chuck Allenbrand, Pearl and Don Anderson, Judith

Depontes, Jackie Jeffries, Joanne Lambert, Adrienne McCabe, Deidre Pool, Kim Prothro, Kelly Smith, Leslie Strader, Carolyn Walker, Sondra Watson, and Judi Wieghat; my friends at LifeWay Christian Store in Tyler, Texas, and LifeWay Christian Resources in Nashville, Tennessee; and my church family at Bethel Bible Church. I cannot possibly express to you how much I value your prayers.

To the retailers who sell my books, the church and public libraries that make them available, and the many readers who have encouraged me with personal testimonies about how God has used my words to challenge and inspire. He uses *you* to fuel the passion that keeps me writing.

To my novelist friends in ChiLibris, who allow me to tap into your collective wisdom and experience—what a compassionate, charitable, prayerful group you are! It's an honor to be counted among you.

To my agent, Joel Kneedler, and the diligent staff at Alive Communications. Your standard of excellence challenges me to keep growing as a writer. I only hope that I represent you as well as you represent me.

To Cris Doornbos, Dan Rich, Don Pape, and the amazing staff at David C Cook Publishers for believing in me and investing in the words I write; thanks for all you do to support my writing ministry. I love being part of the Cook "family."

To my editor, Diane Noble, for your abundance of patience and grace when I needed more time (and then some) to finish this book. Your intuitive insights and suggestions added depth to the story. I am so blessed to get to work with you and actually look forward to the editing process!

And to my husband, Paul, the other half of my heart, who is the "guardian" of those long periods of absolute quiet wherein my stories are born, thanks for fielding the phone calls and interruptions and for tiptoeing around the house so that I can be creative. Your sacrifices do not go unnoticed.

And most important, thank You, heavenly Father, for blessing the talent You have entrusted to me so that others might get a picture of Your goodness through the power of story. Let my words glorify Your name.

CAJUN FRENCH GLOSSARY

Ah, c'est bon—	What most people say about Cajun cuisine. It literally means, "Ah, it's good."
Andouille—	A coarse-grained smoked meat made using pork, pepper, onions, wine, and seasonings; spicy Cajun sausage.
Beignet—	A pastry made from deep-fried dough and sprinkled with powdered sugar—a kind of French doughnut.
Benoit—	The last name Zoe chose when she changed her name.
Boudin—	Sausage made from a pork rice dressing (much like dirty rice), which is stuffed into pork casings. Rice is always used in Cajun cuisine.
Bonjour—	Good day. Good morning. Good afternoon.
Broussard—	Zoe and Pierce's last name.
Breaux's—	Cajun restaurant that features live Cajun music.
Capon—	Coward.
Cher—	Dear.
Commes les vieux—	Like the old people.
Courtbouillon—	A rich, spicy tomato-based soup or stew made with fish fillets, onions, and sometimes mixed vegetables.
Couyon—	A stupid person.
Down the bayou—	Cajun way of saying south.
Etienne's—	The Cajun restaurant where Zoe said she gained all of her experience.
Fournier—	Father Sam's last name.
Freesôns—	Goose bumps.
Ils sont noirs—	They're black.
Jourdain's—	The name of the restaurant where Zoe said she worked in Morgan City.

Lagniappe—	A small gift given with a purchase to a customer, by way of compliment or for good measure; a bonus; an unexpected or indirect benefit.
Le Grand Dérangement—	Great Expulsion of 1755–1763, mostly during the Seven Years' War, British colonial officers and New England legislators and militia deported more than fourteen thousand Acadians from the maritime region in what could be called an ethnic cleansing *ante litteram*. Approximately one third perished. Many later settled in Louisiana, where they became known as Cajuns.
Les Cadiens—	Acadians; natives of Acadia.
Make a bahbin—	Pout.
Mal au couer—	Vomit. *I got the mal au couer.* I need to vomit.
Mamere—	Grandmother.
Mère—	Mother.
Mes Amis—	My friends.
Millet—	Jacob's last name.
Monsieur Champoux—	Zoe's first landlord.
Monsieur Hebert Lanoux—	Regular customer at Zoe B's and first customer ever to come to her establishment.
Motier foux—	Half crazy.
Pain perdu—	French toast fried in butter and served with powdered sugar sprinkled on top.
Papere—	Grandfather.
Passing a mop—	Mopping.
Peekon—	Thorn.
Potaine—	Ruckus
Peeshwank—	A little person; runt.
Prejean—	The sheriff's last name.
Propriétaire—	Owner.
P'tit boug—	Little boy.
Rahdoht—	Boring, never-ending conversation.
Rue Madeline—	Madeline Street.

Skinny mullet—	Skinny person.
Slow the TV—	Turn down the TV.
Surette—	Savannah's last name (waitress at Zoe B's).
Un jour a la frou—	One day at a time.
Up the bayou—	Cajun way of saying north.

PROLOGUE

Nothing in all creation is hidden from God's sight.
Everything is uncovered and laid bare before the eyes of
him to whom we must give account. (Hebrews 4:13)

Shelby Sieger sat straight up in bed, clutching her pillow. Trembling. Had she called out again—or imagined it? She clamped her eyes shut and listened. Had she awakened anyone else at the Woodmore House?

An entire minute passed without a sound. She threw back the covers and slid her legs over the side of the bed, groping the nightstand until she found the thin metal chain on the lamp—and pulled it. Sixty watts instantly transformed the room. Why should a twenty-seven-year-old woman feel safer with the light on?

Her three packed suitcases were neatly lined up in front of the white marble fireplace. Maybe once she was away from here, the nightmares would cease. But leaving would be harder than she thought.

Shelby picked up the framed photo of the Woodmore staff taken last Christmas and slowly traced the faces with her finger. Six years was a long time. No one could dispute that Adele Woodmore treated her more like a blood relative than merely a trusted member of her household staff. But hadn't she worked hard for her keep? Adele never ran out of things for her to do. The meager salary she earned in addition to room and board would never have been enough to realize her dream.

She sighed and put the photo back on the nightstand. And why shouldn't her dream come true? Was she less deserving than everyone else?

Her father's words still taunted her. *You stupid, worthless little brat! If I thought someone else would take you, I'd park you on their doorstep. You're nothin'. And you'll never amount to nothin'.*

Shelby blinked several times to clear her eyes. It wasn't her fault that he was a mean drunk guilty of unspeakable acts or that her mother was a blubbering weakling with no backbone. But she wasn't that helpless little girl anymore. Who could blame her for seizing the moment? She'd simply done what she needed to do. Adele had gotten over it; her life would go on as usual.

Shelby slid open the second drawer and took out her wallet to look at the new name on her driver's license and social security card. She had waited an entire year to avoid suspicion. Then, two weeks ago, she gave Adele notice—and managed a sufficient show of emotion to convince her that the decision to leave Woodmore had been prompted by her mother's failing health.

A howling wind caused branches of the longleaf pines to scrape the roof—and cold air to seep through the windows. She shivered and put her wallet back in the drawer, then crawled under the patchwork quilt, content to leave the light on. Soon she would be on her own, self-employed and accountable to no one. Hadn't that always been her dream?

Shelby glanced at the clock. As long as she remained in this house, there was a chance something could go wrong. It would be a huge relief when she could stop worrying that Adele might uncover what the police never did. Six hours from now she would board a Greyhound bus for Lafayette and never look back. And no one would ever know what she'd done or where she'd gone.

CHAPTER 1

As Vanessa Langley stepped gingerly across the creaky wood floor in the empty parlor at Langley Manor, the eyes of the bearded man in the painting above the fireplace seemed to follow her.

A popping noise overhead sent her pulse racing. She looked up at the chandelier. "What was *that?*"

Her husband, Ethan, grabbed her arm, a grin pulling at the corners of his mouth. "Maybe it's the ghost of Josiah Langley." He nodded toward the painting. "He's still *hanging* around."

Vanessa smiled in spite of herself. "I'm sure it's just the house settling."

"Is it?" Ethan lifted his eyebrows up and down. "Or have we traveled back in time—through six generations of Langleys—and entered into ... *The Twilight Zone?* Do do do do, do do do do ..."

"Don't. That's creepy." She shoved him playfully.

Vanessa walked into the dining room and stood at the oblong window, inhaling the pervasive, musty smell of old wood, her eyes feasting on acres and acres of tall green stalks undulating in the summer breeze. "I love the way the cane fields sway in the wind."

"Yeah," Ethan said. "It's like Mother Nature's doing the wave."

"It's amazing to think that many of your ancestors stood at this very window, looking at these same fields. I wonder how much land Josiah Langley owned when he built this place."

"Almost all the land that's now Saint Catherine Parish." Ethan came over and stood next to her. "But the fifteen acres we inherited with the house will be plenty for us to maintain. Be glad my great-grandparents had the foresight to sell the cane fields and use the money to give the house a face-lift. That's going to make converting it to a bed-and-breakfast a lot more doable."

"It'll still be a monumental challenge."

"We can work together on the big decisions." Ethan kissed her cheek. "But I really want to make a go of my counseling practice so you can stay home with Carter and oversee the renovation. You'll be great at it."

Carter Langley darted out of the kitchen and over to her, his mound of strawberry-blond hair falling in a straight line just above his eyebrows, his tattered stuffed beagle, Georgie, tucked under his arm.

"I'm going a-a-all the way up." He pointed to the stately white staircase, his sapphire blue eyes wide with resolve.

Ethan scooped the four-year-old bundle of energy into his arms before he could take off running. "Hold on a second. Daddy will go with you."

"Georgie and me want to see the candy man. He's nice. He gives us lemon dwops."

"I thought we agreed to nip this in the bud," Vanessa said.

Ethan put his lips to her ear. "That's what I'm about to do. Do you really think we're going to find a *candy man* up there?"

"But why feed his imagination when there are so many ghost stories floating around about this house?"

"If we let Carter explore every nook and cranny, he'll see for himself that those spooky stories are ridiculous. The kid's going to live here some day. We might as well dispel this myth up front."

Vanessa tilted her son's chin and held his gaze. "It's important to remember that the man in the closet wasn't real. He was just pretend."

"He let me touch his whiskers," Carter insisted. "They felt pwickly."

"Let's you and me and Georgie go take a look." Ethan winked at her and started up the staircase as Carter let out a husky laugh.

Vanessa bit her tongue. Maybe Ethan was right. But she didn't like it. She pulled up on the window and forced it open about a foot, letting the muggy July air flood the room. Not that it was much of an improvement.

She turned around and brushed the dust off her hands, admiring the spacious dining room, which was trimmed in white crown moldings, and the oval mahogany table with matching chairs, the only furniture still in the house. The red and white floral wallpaper seemed busy and overpowering and was at the top of her list of things to replace. What type of pattern would soften the room? Or should she forget wallpaper and just have it painted a solid color? She had so much to learn about preserving the rich history and yet making the place tasteful and comfortable. Was she really the right person to take the lead on this?

She studied the sepia photograph that hung in an oval frame in the nook leading to the kitchen. Ethan's great-grandparents, Chester and Augusta Langley, were the last to reside in the manor house and chose to demolish all the outbuildings. They recorded in their Bible that those structures were reminders of a time when people had "wrongfully prospered on the backs of slaves."

The plantation house was in remarkably good condition at the time of Chester's passing and five years later when Augusta died. But years of it sitting empty had taken a toll. Though structurally sound, it needed furnishings and a great deal of renovating before it would make a suitable bed-and-breakfast. And what would it take to make their family quarters kid-friendly without spoiling the historic value of this Langley heirloom?

Vanessa turned again to the dining-room window and imagined Ethan and his cousin, Drew, as little boys playing hide-and-seek in the cane fields. How did those two little scamps keep from getting lost in there? She imagined herself surrounded on all sides by cane stalks considerably taller than she and felt short of breath. She heard a car door slam and came back to the present. Who even knew they were out here? She walked through the parlor and opened the front door.

A white Toyota Prius was parked in the driveway, and Pierce and Zoe Broussard were already out of the car and heading in her direction.

"Hey there." Zoe waved. "Hope you don't mind the intrusion. Pierce and I decided to take you up on your offer. We want to see the house before you start renovating." She grinned. "So we can appreciate it afterward."

"I'm glad you did. Come in." Vanessa held open the door and imagined for an instant that she was welcoming the first guests to the bed-and-breakfast. "Don't get your clothes dirty. The maid hasn't been here in years." She laughed.

Pierce followed Zoe inside. "I didn't realize Langley Manor is only three miles from Les Barbes," he said. "For some reason I thought it was twice that far."

Zoe's gaze danced around the room. "It's not as big as it looks from the outside."

"Probably because it's empty. Except for that dining-room table and chairs and a few pictures on the wall, everything else was sold in the estate sale years ago. Great-Grandmother Augusta specified that the table and family pictures were to stay with the house. She probably never dreamed it would be vacant this long. But Ethan's dad and uncles didn't want to leave Tennessee."

"Where are Ethan and Carter?" Pierce asked.

"Upstairs looking for the imaginary fellow in the closet."

"Ah, the candy man." Zoe shot her a knowing look.

"I think once Carter's familiar with every inch of the house, his imagination will take a rest," Vanessa said. "I'm sure it's been hard having his entire world uprooted."

Zoe glanced up the white staircase. "Tell me again how many bedrooms."

"Four up and two down. We plan to knock out a few walls upstairs so we'll have six guest rooms."

"Where will *you* live?" Pierce asked.

"On this level. There's plenty of space in the back of the house to add a third bedroom and make it into our private living quarters."

"So all the guest rooms will be upstairs?"

Vanessa nodded. "The biggest challenge could be adding private baths to each one. People who routinely stay in B and Bs have probably shared a bathroom with other guests at some point. But I never liked it."

Pierce shot her a crooked smile. "I know bed-and-breakfasts are really the *in* thing, but I find it amusing that people actually pay to sleep in an old house and share the toilet with strangers."

"It's about the ambiance, *cher*." Zoe poked him with her elbow. "It's a little slice of history and a lot more romantic than staying at a motor inn."

"Well, if at all possible," Vanessa quickly added, "the guest rooms at Langley Manor will have private baths. Thankfully the house has been updated over the years and has indoor plumbing and electricity and modern conveniences. But it's been empty a long time, and it needs a complete makeover."

"Who's going to do the work?" Pierce asked.

"We've contracted Southern Pride."

He nodded. "I've heard they're the best. When do they start?"

"The plans are being drawn up now. We're hoping to see blue-prints sometime next week."

"So how much longer will you be renting the apartment from us?"

"Oh, I don't see us moving in here for at least eighteen months," Vanessa said. "Probably closer to two years. Even if our private quarters are finished before that, I have no desire to move in here until all the remodeling is finished. I wouldn't do well with the mess or with the workers traipsing in and out."

"Not that I want to lose you as tenants, but I can hardly wait to see this place done over." Zoe smiled, her intriguing blue-gray eyes looking as big as quarters, framed by her dark, chin-length hair. "It's one of the few plantation houses in Saint Catherine Parish that survived the Civil War. The locals are proud of that—even if the Langleys were British."

"I've read some of Augusta Langley's diaries," Vanessa said. "It really bothered her that the British mistreated the Acadians."

"Mistreated?" Pierce raised his eyebrows, his voice an octave higher. "The British ordered the forced removal of every last Acadian from what's now Nova Scotia—because they wouldn't renounce their Catholic faith and become Protestant. And wouldn't swear allegiance to the British flag and take up arms against France. A third of the Acadians died in the process. I'd say *Le Grand Dérangement* was more like ethnic cleansing than mistreatment, wouldn't you?"

Vanessa felt embarrassment scald her face in the awkward silence that followed. "Yes, I suppose it was," she finally said. "What the British did to the Acadians was similar to what the U.S. government did to the Native Americans. It was shameful."

"Yes, it was." Pierce turned his head, his prominent nose suddenly reminding her of Charles de Gaulle. "Louisiana may have been a safe haven, but life in the bayou was totally foreign. Summers were stifling. And I'm sure alligator and crawfish weren't all that appetizing at first. They learned to make do with whatever they could find. But it's not like they had a choice."

"And think of the delicious cuisine that just keeps evolving." Zoe put her hand on his back as if to calm him down. "Our entire Cajun culture has evolved into something unique in all of America. We can be proud."

"I *am* proud. Just not of the way it all came about." Pierce was quiet for a moment, and the tautness left his face. "Sorry for getting on my soapbox, Vanessa. I used to teach history and have strong feelings about the plight of *les Cadiens*. Some Acadians were my ancestors who settled here long before that fat cat Josiah Langley bought up the land. No offense."

"None taken."

"Langley didn't even try to adapt. He clung to everything British, right down to the name he gave this place. He chose manor instead of plantation—his way of flaunting his British superiority. The Cajuns resented it."

"Were any plantations owned by Cajuns?"

"Not around here. French Creoles, not Cajuns." Pierce's dark eyes matched his mood. "Back then most Cajuns barely had enough to live on. Look, no one can change what happened, but outsiders should understand how and why the Acadians settled here—and what was taken from them. It drives me crazy that most everything associated with the word *Cajun* has been reduced to a tourist attraction or a souvenir."

So Pierce regarded them as outsiders? Vanessa was relieved to hear footsteps coming down the staircase and turned just as Ethan and Carter reached the bottom.

"I thought I heard voices. Hey, guys." Ethan walked over to Zoe and hugged her and shook Pierce's hand. "What's up?"

"Just came to get that tour you offered us," Pierce said. "Maybe Carter would like to show us around."

"Yay!" Carter threw Georgie up in the air and then caught him.

"Looks like the yays have it." Ethan smiled. "He knows his way around as well as I do."

"And what about the candy man in the closet?" Vanessa raised an eyebrow.

"No sign of him or his lemon drops." Ethan winked. "I guess he's moved on."

"Maybe he went a-a-all the way up on the roof." Carter stood on his tiptoes, his hands stretched toward the ceiling. "Like Santa Claus!"

"Are you old enough to show Mister Pierce and me all the rooms in the house?" Zoe asked.

"I had my birfday. I'm four." Carter proudly held up four fingers.

"Well, that's certainly old enough. Where should we start?"

"There's a big, big, big, *big* fireplace—bigger than Daddy. Big as a giant!" Carter took her hand. "I'll show you."

"Okay, I'm ready."

Zoe reached for Pierce's hand and let Carter lead them toward the back of the house.

Vanessa met Ethan's gaze and wondered if even he could love that child as much as she did.

"This place is going to make a wonderful bed-and-breakfast," he said. "I can picture us living here. What a great way for Carter to grow up. He'll charm the guests and learn some important people skills in the process. I can hardly wait to see the blueprints."

"Me either. But the more I think about it, the more convinced I am that all the guest rooms should have a private bath."

"I agree…. Honey, what's wrong? You look flustered."

"I am."

"What happened?"

Vanessa fanned herself with her hand. The heat was suddenly oppressive. "Oh, I mentioned something I read in Augusta Langley's diary about her feeling bad that the British had mistreated the Acadians, and Pierce went off." She told Ethan everything she could remember about the uncomfortable exchange. "I totally agreed with

Pierce about how awful it was. But I was floored at how prejudiced he is toward the British. I didn't see that coming."

"I haven't noticed it."

Vanessa arched her eyebrows. "You will if you ever get into a discussion about Cajun history. Be forewarned."

"The last thing we need is a Cajun landlord who resents us. It's going to be a long time before we move in here." Ethan looked over her shoulder, seemingly distracted by something. "Is that a marble on the floor?"

He walked past her to the dining-room table, got down on all fours, and stretched out his arm underneath it until he had something in his hand.

"No way," he said. "You're not going to believe what this is."

"Tell me."

Ethan crawled out from under the table and rose to his feet, holding a tiny yellow object between his thumb and forefinger, his eyes wide. "It's a lemon drop."

"Very funny."

"See for yourself."

Ethan walked toward her, the object in his open palm.

"It's obviously a lemon drop," she said. "I just think you put it there."

"*What?* Why would I do that?"

"As a prank. To make me think Carter actually saw some guy in the upstairs closet. I don't think it's funny."

"Neither do I. And I'm not into cruel pranks. I have no idea where it came from."

She studied his stony expression, half expecting him to break into laughter at any moment. "Well, I'm sure Carter didn't put it there."

"Honey ..." Ethan gently gripped her wrist. "*I* didn't. I promise."

"We had all the locks changed. No one else has a key to the house."

"Well"—Ethan pursed his lips and looked up the white staircase— "if Carter did see a man up there, the guy got in without a key."

"How? The doors are all locked. Windows, too."

Ethan shrugged. "I don't have an explanation. Yet. But it wasn't the ghost of Josiah Langley. Besides, I doubt they had lemon drops in 1839."

"Don't kid around, Ethan. This is creepy. How will we ever be safe here if someone can get in and out without a key?"

"Take it easy, honey. There has to be an explanation."

"It terrifies me that Carter might actually have been close to this ... this ... trespasser." Vanessa glanced up at the oil painting, a chill crawling up her spine. "Let's not say anything to Zoe and Pierce. I don't want anything else added to the ghost stories about this place."

"Agreed. We need to talk to Carter again and start taking his description of this character seriously. And we need to report it to the sheriff."

CHAPTER 2

The next morning, Zoe Broussard hurried down the stairs from her apartment above Zoe B's Cajun Eatery and walked through the alcove and into the cozy dining area. The aroma of warm beignets, oven-hot bread, and freshly brewed coffee filled her senses.

The place was starting to fill up with customers, the hum of their voices the perfect background music. Could it really have been a decade ago that she opened this place? Little had changed, other than the size, the color scheme, and the addition of a few oil paintings from local artists. The same French country furnishings still flavored the ambiance.

Two of her longtime customers sat at the table next to the window, where she'd hung her prize fern. She unfolded a red and gold fleur-de-lis print tablecloth that matched the curtains, shook it, then spread it evenly across the table, smoothing out the wrinkles.

"There you go," she said. "Still warm from the dryer. And don't worry about the coffee spill on the other one. There's almost no stain I can't get out."

"Aw, you take such good care of us." Tex Campbell's bushy silver eyebrows shifted as he winked at his tablemate. "What would we do without you?"

"You mean, *besides* starve?"

Father Samuel Fournier shot her a knowing look, his hazel eyes magnified by his thick lenses. "There's more truth to that than I'd like to admit."

Savannah Surette's petite frame whisked past the table in the direction of the kitchen, her ponytail swaying. "I'll bring you more coffee. Hebert called in his breakfast order and is on his way."

"I wonder what's keeping him?" Father Sam said. "He's usually the first one here."

Zoe shook her head, her arms folded. "Hebert shouldn't be living alone. One of these days someone's going to find him dead in his sleep."

"Would that be such a bad way to go?" Father Sam pushed a lock of white hair off his forehead. "But that skinny mullet will make ninety-five on his next birthday and hardly ever sees a doctor."

"He still needs looking after."

"That's what he's got us for," Father Sam said. "And he seems just fine to me."

"Shoot"—Tex waved his hand—"he shamed us at checkers the other night—*again*. All his burners are still lit."

"That's beside the point," Zoe said. "He's an old man."

"Old is as old does." Tex sat back in his chair, his thumbs hooked on his suspenders, his bald head shiny under the overhead lights. "Hebert's mind is sharp as a tack."

"He's old enough to be your father."

"Impressive, don't you think?" Tex flashed a grin as wide as the

Rio Grande. "I suspect that ornery Cajun is gonna be around for a while yet."

Savannah stopped at the table, filled two cups with coffee, and set the white thermal pitcher on the table. "Your orders are up next."

The tinkling of the bell on the front door caused Zoe to turn just as Remy Jarvis shuffled in the front door, a red cap backward on his head and two copies of Monday's *Les Barbes Ledger* in his hand.

"Happy day, everybody," Remy said. "I am late. My bike got a flat tire. Mister Ives fixed it for me. It cost fifty cents. That's two quarters." Remy's eyes were wide. "And I had two quarters!"

"Ives is a good friend, isn't he?"

Remy bobbed his head, shifting his weight from one foot to the other. "Mister Ives is my friend. I brought two newspapers, Miss Zoe. Sorry I am late."

Zoe took the papers and patted Remy's cheek. "You're not that late, and it couldn't be helped. I knew you'd be here."

Remy beamed, a seven-year-old in a grown man's body. "Bye. Happy day, everybody." He turned and left the eatery.

"That was sure kind of ol' Ives," Tex said. "Wanna bet he asked Remy how much money he had on him and acted like two quarters was exactly what he charges to fix a tire?"

"Ives would do just about anything for Remy," Zoe said, scanning the front page. "I'd like to think we all would."

A few seconds later the front door opened again, and Hebert Lanoux stepped inside, dressed in too-short khaki pants, a wrinkled yellow shirt, and socks that didn't match.

"There you are," Zoe said.

Hebert, his mass of mousey gray hair sticking up in the back where he'd slept on it, shuffled over to the table and kissed Zoe on the cheek, then sat next to Father Sam. *"Bonjours, mes amis.* And how's everybody dis fine day?"

"Couldn't be better," Tex said.

"I'm feeling great." Father Sam took a sip of coffee, looking authoritative in his black and white cleric shirt. "How come you're late?"

"Oh, I made da mistake of listening to da news and lost consciousness." He laughed, exposing a row of discolored teeth. "So much of what dey call news is *rabdobt.*"

A row of lines appeared on Tex's forehead. "What's raw dot?"

"Boring talk dat goes on and on and on," Hebert said. "Can't get jus' facts anymore. Now we got to listen to everybody's opinion. And den somebody's opinion of everybody's opinion."

Zoe nodded. "That's why I prefer the newspaper. Pierce listens to cable and tells me what I absolutely need to know." She handed one copy of the newspaper to Father Sam and tucked the other under her arm.

"But isn't it great we live in a country where we're allowed to speak our minds?" Tex took his red kerchief and dabbed his forehead. "No one's forcin' us to watch the tube."

"Good point," Father Sam said. "We can always slow the TV. Or just turn it off."

Savannah came out of the kitchen, her smile infectious, her right hand balancing a round tray almost as wide as she was tall. "Here we are, fellas."

Zoe studied the breakfast entrees as Savannah served them. Pain perdu for Father Sam. Eggs benedict for Tex. Beignets and a side of andouille sausage for Hebert. Beautifully arranged on the plates. A slice of orange and a sprig of mint. Pierce always made such a nice presentation.

"Will that do, everybody?" Savannah said. "Or is there something else I can bring y'all?"

"I think we're good," Tex said. "Still got half a pot of coffee."

"Uh, since you asked"—Hebert picked up his knife and fork—"I could use a little o' dat citrus marmalade on dese beignets."

"Done. Anybody else?"

Father Sam smiled sheepishly. "More milk for my coffee?"

"Coming right up."

Zoe heard a child's voice and turned, surprised to see Vanessa and Carter Langley coming in the door.

"Miss Zoe, guess what?" Carter raced toward her, Georgie tucked under his arm. "Mommy said I could have cwepes!"

Zoe crouched next to Carter. His round eyes looked like big blue buttons, and his dimpled cheeks were flushed with sheer delight.

"Which flavor crepes would you like?" she said. "Blueberry, strawberry, banana, or apple?"

"I want apple!" Carter glanced over at his mother and then added, "Please." He cupped his little hands around her ear and whispered, "I don't like peelings—just the goodest part of apples, like the kind in apple pie."

"Well, you're in luck because that's the kind we have. I'll tell Mister Pierce to be sure to get *all* the peel off."

"Where do you want us?" Vanessa glanced around the room. "How about that corner table, where you-know-who's mess won't be so obvious?"

"Oh, he's fine. Sit wherever you're comfortable. Breakfast is on the house."

"You don't have to do that," Vanessa said.

"It's the least I can do after Pierce's blunt and unsolicited history lesson yesterday." Zoe stroked Carter's thick straight hair. "I hope you know he's excited about you renting the upstairs apartment. We wouldn't have rented it to just anybody. Y'all are so nice, and we know you'll take care of it. How's the back entrance working out for you?"

"It's perfect. And with Carter in tow, it's nice that our parking spots are close. Ethan and I love the apartment. Thanks for letting us share the balcony—I mean the gallery. We love to be out there in the evenings and watch the people on the sidewalks—and listen to the band playing at Breaux's."

"You like Cajun music?"

"*Very* much." Vanessa's face was suddenly animated. "Ethan's grandfather grew up here and learned to play the accordion, banjo, and mandolin. He moved to Alexandria after he got married and for years played in a band called the Bayou Boys. Later on he learned to play the guitar and fiddle, too, and taught Ethan's dad and uncles to play all of those. They still do."

"Really?"

"They're good, too. The band at Breaux's reminds me of them. Ethan's family has strong Cajun ties. I had intended to mention it to Pierce yesterday before he—"

"Insulted you?"

Vanessa's cheeks turned as pink as her blouse. "I didn't take it as an insult, but it was awkward. Maybe once he realizes that not everyone with British ancestry is the enemy, he'll see that we can love and appreciate all the unique things about the Cajun culture."

Zoe sighed. "Pierce needs to be around more people like you and Ethan. Ever since he quit teaching and became the chef here, he spends so much time back in that kitchen that he's hardly ever exposed to anyone who isn't Cajun. His world has gotten much too small. Please don't judge him too harshly. He's really a sweetheart."

"I can see that. I was just caught off guard by his resentment of the British. Ethan and I will have to prove to Pierce that we're all on the same side. I'd like us to be friends."

"Me, too," Zoe said. "Actually he's fond of you. And he's nuts about Carter. His issues with the British go back generations in his family. It's not personal."

Vanessa held out her hand to Carter. "Sweetie, we'd better go find a table and let Miss Zoe get back to work."

"I want to sit *there!*" He pointed to a table against the brick wall and took off running.

"Carter, wait …" Vanessa sighed and looked at Zoe apologetically. "He hasn't quite learned his restaurant manners yet."

"He said *please* without being told. I thought that was very polite for a four-year-old. Relax. Just enjoy your breakfast."

Zoe watched Vanessa get Carter situated at the table, at the same time admiring how the newly refinished oak floors accentuated the tan and ruddy tones in the brick. And the red and gold in the new tablecloths.

Hebert tapped her arm. "Who dat *p'tit boug?*"

"Carter Langley. Isn't he adorable?"

"Dat beautiful lady his mama?"

"Uh-huh." Zoe studied Vanessa: a perfect size six with long, dark hair and striking blue eyes. She felt a tinge of jealousy and dismissed it. "Her name's Vanessa Langley. She and her husband, Ethan, inherited Langley Manor. They're renting the apartment upstairs while the house is being renovated and converted into a bed-and-breakfast."

"Where dey from?"

"East Tennessee. Ethan's a psychologist and just got hired by a Christian counseling firm in Lafayette."

"Dat's real nice. Hope dey work out."

"Me, too." Zoe lowered her voice. "I just hope the folks in Les Barbes will accept them."

"They accepted me," Tex said. "What's the difference?"

"Da difference"—Hebert licked the powdered sugar off his finger—"is dat it weren't your uppity British kin who looked down dere noses at da Cajuns."

"But that young lady over there and her husband had nothin' to do with that," Tex said.

"No, they didn't." Zoe shook her head. "And they're not the least bit uppity."

"Good." Father Sam wiped his mouth with a napkin. "So there's no reason to punish them for the faults of their relatives. The plantation house has been vacant so long that most people here have never even met a Langley."

Hebert smiled, powdered sugar dusting his chin. "Guess dey will now."

CHAPTER 3

Early Monday evening Vanessa Langley waited with Ethan and Carter in the dining room at Langley Manor while sheriff's deputies searched the premises. Through the window, beyond the live oaks draped with Spanish moss, she could see a hawk soaring above the cane fields and a huge billowy thunderhead forming in the eastern sky.

"I wonder what's taking so long." Vanessa turned to Ethan, who was sitting next to her at the dining-room table. "At least they're being thorough."

"We'll eat out when we're done here," he said. "Don't worry about making dinner."

Carter sat on the floor, creating something yet undefined with his building blocks. "I want a giant hot dog—with lots of pickle welish."

A grin spread across Ethan's face. "I love it. We finally move to Louisiana, where we can order any delectable Cajun dish in the known world, and our son wants a hot dog."

The sound of footsteps echoed from the staircase, and then sheriff's deputies Stone Castille and Mike Doucet came into the dining room.

"We're finished," Stone said. "We'd like to visit with you for a few minutes. Is it all right if we sit here at the table?"

"Of course. Tell us what you found."

"That's just it"—Stone glanced over at Mike—"Deputy Doucet and I didn't find anything that suggests forced entry. Or even a *port* of entry, for that matter. Your doors and windows seem to be secure."

"They should be," Ethan said. "We recently had the locks changed. So how could someone get in here?"

"We do have a growing number of homeless in the parish." Stone pursed his lips. "And it's a well-known fact that the place has been vacant for years. It's always possible someone saw you and Mrs. Langley enter the house and sneaked in while you were looking around, hid in the house, then stayed after you left."

"On the other hand," Mike said, "if a squatter had been in here, there should be trash, a blanket, bucket, candles—some telltale sign. But except for the dusty footprints on the wood floors, it's hard to tell anyone's been in the house at all."

"A lot of those footprints are ours." Vanessa tented her fingers. "And the contractor's people."

"Would you mind if we spoke to your son?" Stone said.

Ethan motioned for Carter to come sit in his lap. "Carter, this is Deputy Stone and Deputy Mike. They'd like to ask you some questions about the man you saw upstairs. I want you just to tell the truth."

Carter nodded, clinging tightly to Georgie. He held up one hand, his thumb tucked behind his fingers. "I'm four."

"My little boy is four"—Stone put on a pair of nose glasses—"and he's really smart. I'll bet you are too. Can you tell me about the man you saw?"

"He was nice. He gave me lemon dwops. And his face was whiskery."

"By whiskery, do you mean he had a beard?"

"No, he had white pwickles on his chin—like a cactus."

"I see. And what color was his skin?"

"Bwown." Carter smiled. "He said he was chocolate, but he was just being silly. People can't be chocolate. He looked like Doctor Ben."

"Doctor Ben was Carter's pediatrician before we moved here," Vanessa said. "He was African-American."

"Good, this is very helpful. Carter, what color was the man's hair?"

"Black. He had itty bitty curls like Gi Gi. That's my gwandma's poodle."

"Was the man skinny like Deputy Mike? Or was he rounder like me? Or was he just medium, like your daddy?"

Carter shrugged. "He wasn't fat."

"Was he young like your daddy or older like me, or did he seem like a grandpa?"

Carter cocked his head and looked at Stone questioningly.

"Deputy Castille," Vanessa said, "Carter's grandfathers are youthful-looking and fit as a fiddle. I'm not sure he knows how to gauge young and old that way."

"Let's skip that. We already know the guy had white stubble on his chin. Carter, can you remember anything else the man said to you?"

"Uh-huh. He said"—Carter put his index finger to his lips—"'Shh. I'm the candy man.' Then he showed me his pocket was empty ... but then out came the lemon dwops. It was funny."

"Is there anything about his voice that you remember?"

"He whispered all the time."

"What else did he say?"

"He said if I didn't tell I saw him, he would give me more candy next time. But I told Mommy and Daddy anyway. I'm not supposed to talk to stwangers."

"Do you remember what the man was wearing?"

"Um ... his shirt was blue. It had a pocket where all the lemon dwops came from."

"Do you remember anything else about him?"

"He wasn't pwetend."

"Can you tell me the difference between real and pretend?"

Carter paused for a moment and then set Georgie on the table. "Georgie's a pwetend dog. He can't bark or wag his tail. I have to do it. If he was a weal dog, he could do it all by hisself."

"I'd say you definitely know the difference between real and pretend." Stone wrote something on the clipboard. "I think we're finished. Carter, you've been very helpful. But your mom and dad are right about not talking to strangers—or taking candy or anything else from them. If you see this man again, don't even talk to him. Run straight to your parents or a grown-up you know and tell them."

"We should have taken Carter seriously," Ethan said. "We just thought the upheaval of moving here had caused him to create a fantasy world. But Vanessa and I never buy lemon drops, and there's no other explanation for our finding one on the floor right after

Carter told us about the man giving him some. I suppose he could have sneaked in here while we were in another part of the house. It wouldn't be that hard to do."

"There is a possibility we haven't addressed." Mike folded his arms on the table, his gaze moving from Vanessa to Ethan and back to Vanessa. "I assume you're aware of the reports of paranormal activity at Langley Manor over the years?"

"Who isn't?" Vanessa said. "But since there's no such thing as ghosts, those stories are all hype. Even Carter knows that."

Carter nodded. "Ghosts are just made-up stories. Mommy and Daddy and me looked everywhere in this whooole house, and we didn't find any ghosts."

"You're absolutely right, but some people believe they're real. In fact"—Mike's gaze seemed probing—"I just saw a TV program about haunted houses being big business. If a place can practically guarantee that their guests will bump into a ghost, it'll stay booked all the time."

Vanessa tapped her fingers on the table and tried to hide her indignation for Carter's sake. "Deputy Doucet, do you think we're making this up as some sort of stunt to rouse curiosity and drum up business?"

Mike sat back in his chair, his arms folded across his chest. "A harmless ghost story on the record certainly couldn't hurt future business."

"That's ridiculous," Ethan said. "But if we *were* going to make up a ghost story, we could've come up with someone a lot more convincing than an unshaven African-American man who told a four-year-old he was made of chocolate and gave him lemon drops.

Give me a break. There're plenty of ghost stories about Josiah Langley wandering the halls. That would've made a lot more sense if we were trying to draw curiosity seekers."

Stone put down his pencil. "Mr. and Mrs. Langley have a good point."

"Actually what we *have*," Ethan said, "is an unwanted intruder and no explanation for how he got in or what he wanted. Our four-year-old might understand the difference between what's real and what's pretend, but he's not so discerning between who's dangerous and who isn't. We want to make sure this man doesn't get back in here. What do you suggest we do?"

"You might consider having security lights installed," Stone said. "Motion detectors would be even better. An alarm system would be better yet."

Ethan sighed. "We'd be throwing away money if we sank it into security measures when we know the renovation crew is going to be in here, knocking out walls."

"How soon do you anticipate the work starting?"

"We still have to approve the blueprints," Vanessa said. "But sometime in the next few weeks."

Stone put his reading glasses back in his pocket. "Since this plantation house has historic significance, I doubt we'd have trouble convincing Sheriff Prejean that a temporary patrol check a couple times a day would be in order. Once the renovation starts, the constant flow of trucks and workers will be all the deterrent you'll need."

Zoe walked up the stairs from Zoe B's, went in the apartment, and closed the door. She picked up the mail on the breakfast bar and went through the arched doorway into the living room. She set the mail on an end table and went out on the gallery, one of many that extended out over the sidewalk on either side of *rue Madeline.*

The evening air was thick with humidity and the faint scent of mesquite smoke coming from the Texas Cajun Grill on the corner. Swirls of blazing orange and purple painted the western sky. She stood at the wrought-iron filigree railing, savoring the evening breeze just beginning to stir, and watched the tourists stroll the sidewalks where dozens of shops and eating establishments vied for their business.

She smiled. Had business at Zoe B's ever been better? She went inside and sat in the overstuffed chair, propping her feet up on the ottoman, and started looking through the day's mail. The electric bill. The water bill. The cell phone bill. A credit card solicitation. An envelope with her name typed on the front. This didn't come through the mail. Was the Merchant's Association trying to save postage again?

She slit open the envelope and unfolded a piece of white 8 ½ x 11 paper, on which letters had been cut from a magazine and glued to form five words: *I know what you did.*

Zoe stared at the words, her mind racing with the implication. Was this a prank? How could anyone know what she had done? And why now, after ten years—

"I thought I heard you come in."

Her pulse quickened. She turned to see Pierce's tall frame filling the arched doorway. "You startled me, *cher.* I thought you were taking a nap."

"I couldn't sleep." Pierce yawned. "I'm starved. Dempsey's over-seeing the kitchen tonight. I thought maybe we could walk over to Market Street and eat at Louie's. Don't tell anyone, but your number-one chef is craving a big juicy cheeseburger and fries."

"All right. Let me change into something cooler." Zoe fumbled to get the paper back in the envelope and quickly slipped it on the bottom of the stack.

"Anything interesting in the mail?"

"Just bills. I'll keep them with the others and pay them all next week."

"I don't know why you don't learn how to pay them online and save yourself the trouble."

"Do we have to have this conversation every other week? I like writing them out! Okay?"

"I'm just trying to save you time." Pierce's thick, dark eyebrows formed a bushy line. "Would you rather not go out for dinner? I can make us something here."

"Actually I'd like to go out." She shot him an apologetic look. "I didn't mean to bite your head off. I had another run-in with one of the waitresses for coming to work with cleavage showing. Why don't these girls understand what's appropriate attire for work and what isn't? I'm fed up with having to police them." *Nice save!* "Anyhow, I didn't mean to take it out on you. Let me go change. It'll just take a minute."

Zoe went into the bedroom and flopped on the bed, her gut already starting to churn. Was she jumping to conclusions about the meaning of the note? Did it matter? The statute of limitations had run. The law couldn't touch her.

So what might the bearer of the note hope to get from her—money? Was she willing to pay for someone's silence? Could she afford to? Then again, could she handle what it would do to Pierce if he learned the truth about her? The thought of losing his love and respect terrified her. And so did the thought of losing her business and her reputation. If she agreed to pay money, would that be the end of it? Or would she be trapped into paying someone for the rest of her life? This was never supposed to happen!

She closed her eyes and willed away the fear. How she loved this quaint community of Les Barbes. Its French name translated as "beards"—which perfectly described the Spanish moss that hung from the live oaks and cypress trees. Before she moved here, had she any concept of what it was to really *belong*—to be part of something bigger than she?

People here had roots. Proud roots soaked with the tears of their Acadian ancestors and transplanted deep in this foreign land that had received them with open arms when no one else would. *Les Cadiens* made Louisiana their home and evolved into a new people—Cajuns—never wavering in their Catholic beliefs, but with a language, music, and cuisine uniquely their own. Cajuns had not only survived; they had redefined themselves and thrived. Isn't that what she had done? Wasn't she a perfect fit here among them—as one of them—even if her name wasn't really Zoe Benoit and she didn't have a drop of Cajun blood in her veins?

Suddenly she was aware of the music playing at Breaux's. How long had she been sitting there?

She got up and took a light blue sundress from her closet and put it on, then sat on the bed and slipped into her most comfortable sandals.

Pierce appeared in the doorway. "About ready?"

Zoe nodded, aware that her heart was racing and that she was perspiring.

"You sure you're up to this?" Pierce came over to the bed and sat beside her, his arm around her. "Your face is flushed. That must've been some run-in."

"Well, it's the last one. Tomorrow I'm going to pick out uniforms." She laid her head on his shoulder, glad to avoid eye contact. "I should've done it before now. Today's low-cut fashions are inappropriate for the workplace—at least Zoe B's."

"There you go, Mrs. Broussard. Problem solved. See how easy that was?" Pierce got up and pulled her to her feet, his expression completely guileless. "If that's the worst challenge we face, babe, I'd say life's pretty good."

And what if it isn't? she thought. *What if life as we know it is about to end?*

CHAPTER 4

Vanessa sat with Ethan and Carter at a cozy table at Zoe B's, finishing her dinner.

"I love this place." Vanessa pushed the last bite of corn bread into her mouth. "Too bad Zoe and Pierce aren't working tonight. I'd like them to know we're *paying* customers. I don't want them to feel obligated to let us eat here free of charge."

"We definitely need to get that straight," Ethan said. "I have a feeling we'll be eating here often. The shrimp gumbo was to die for, and number-one son devoured that pig in a blanket." Ethan tickled Carter's ribs, evoking a giggle.

"It's a hot dog, Daddy."

"I need to be more like you," Ethan said to Vanessa, "and exercise some restraint with the bottomless bowl selections and the corn bread that comes with it. I really didn't need that order of boudain."

"I have no idea where you put it all. See that old gentleman sitting with the priest?" Vanessa nodded toward two customers occupying a nearby table. "The one with the untamed hairdo?"

"Uh-huh."

"His name is pronounced Ay-bear and spelled H-E-B-E-R-T."

"I've seen that name a lot down here," Ethan said. "I would've gotten it wrong."

"Zoe introduced me to him this morning. He's going to be ninety-five on his next birthday. The white-haired man with him is Father Sam Fournier."

"I didn't catch Father Sam's last name."

Vanessa smiled. "It's French. Four-nee-ay. He's retired now, but he was rector at Saint Catherine's for thirty years. That's where Zoe and Pierce go. We really need to consider the churches we've visited and get serious about committing to one ourselves."

"All three of us seem drawn to Grace Creek Bible Church. It's small enough to be friendly and big enough to have lots going on. Sunday school was great. And Ben Auger's a good preacher." Ethan turned to Carter. "Remember the church with the big cross out front?"

"I liked the puppets. And the pwayers. And when we singed 'Jesus Loves Me.'"

"Would you like it if we went there again?"

Carter gave a hearty nod. "Georgie wants to go too."

"I'm sure Georgie is welcome there," Vanessa said.

She sipped her iced raspberry tea and looked outside at the scores of tourists on the sidewalks along *rue Madeline*. "It's seven o'clock. Time for the police to close the street and let the tourists take over."

"And time for a certain little boy to take a bath." Ethan tickled Carter's ribs. "Are you looking forward to going to summer preschool again tomorrow?"

"Yes! Me and Georgie like Miss Pamela."

"That's good, because Mommy and I do too. Honey, you ready to head upstairs?"

"Whenever you are." Vanessa folded her napkin and set it on the table. "I hope there's a breeze so we can sit out on the gallery and listen to the band at Breaux's. It's relaxing."

Ethan put his hand on hers. "You feeling any better about the situation out at the house?"

"Not really. The sheriff deputies didn't have any answers, and I got the feeling they think it was you-know-who's imagination talking. I'm glad they're going to patrol the area a few times a day. But it's not like the intruder is driving a car and parking it out front."

Zoe strolled along *rue Madeline*, hand in hand with Pierce, the street still radiating warmth from the afternoon sun. The delicious aroma of caramel corn flavored the night air and might have made her mouth water had she not eaten her fill at Louie's. She had a flashback of Vanessa Langley's hourglass figure and suddenly felt chagrined that she no longer had a defined waistline.

"I've never seen so many tourists," Pierce said. "The numbers are always more noticeable this time of night, when the street's closed off. I sure hope we're getting our fair share of business."

Zoe surveyed the row of quaint shops on the south side of *rue Madeline* and the people waving amidst a garden of blooming plants on the galleries above. She moved her gaze to the building painted deep gold and trimmed in black and read the matching sign suspended from the gallery just above the entrance:

Zoe B's Cajun Eatery
Pierce and Zoe Broussard, owners

Would the excitement of owning the eatery ever wear off? Wasn't it her dream come true, even more today than ten years ago when she started out by renting just half of the first floor from Monsieur Champoux? Even then she was persnickety about the whole dining experience, scraping up every cent she could to ensure that the ambiance as well as the food was something people would talk about. She refinished the wood floor herself, painted the walls, found a fantastic closeout on French country tables and chairs, and made tablecloths and curtains to match. She had an up-to-code kitchen installed and hired a worthy chef to prepare a collection of Cajun recipes she'd fallen in love with and perfected. And hadn't it paid off? Zoe B's was an instant hit in Les Barbes.

She smiled, remembering the sweet elderly customer who first walked through her door ...

"Ah, dis is nice," the old man said as his gaze flitted around the room. "So you da *propriétaire?*"

"Yes, I'm the owner, Zoe Benoit." She shook his hand, careful not to let her elation overpower her professional demeanor. How long had she waited to say those words? Not bad for poor white trash from Devon Springs, Texas. As far as anyone here was concerned, she was as Cajun as the crawfish étoufée on the menu. "Welcome. And what is your name, *Monsieur?*"

"Da name's Hebert Lanoux."

Zoe smiled. "Please come in."

She made sure Monsieur Lanoux was seated, and she watched from a polite distance, pleased that he seemed to savor every bite of the étoufée and then ordered bread pudding. She expected him to eat only half the entrée and take the other half home with him. But he ate every bite of it and his dessert, too!

Finally he wiped his mouth and put his napkin on the table and motioned for the waitress to bring him his check.

Zoe sauntered over to the table. "And how was your dinner, Monsieur Lanoux?"

"*Ah, c'est bon.*" He grinned, his hands patting his lean middle. "I tink dat was even better dan *mamere's* cooking. And please call me Hebert. You'll be seeing a lot of me—"

"Zoe …? Have you heard a word I've said?"

Pierce's resonant voice brought her back to the present.

"Sorry, *cher*. My mind was wandering."

"Where were you?"

"Oh … standing at the door at Zoe B's on opening day. Do you realize that Hebert has come in almost every day—at least once—for the past decade?"

Pierce smiled, wrinkles of annoyance gone from his forehead. "What in the world made you think of that?"

"Seeing our new sign sent my mind in reverse, that's all."

"The new building colors sure make the place stand out." He squeezed her hand. "Come on, babe, let's go home."

Home. What a different meaning that word had taken on since she married Pierce. In five years of marriage he had rarely raised his voice and never his fist.

Zoe walked with Pierce toward the alley behind the row of buildings that lined the south side of *rue Madeline.* Her life was good. After all these years, was God finally going to punish her for what she'd done? Was that what the note was about? Or was she worrying for nothing?

A man bumped into them, the jolt causing Zoe to drop her purse on the ground.

The man bent down and picked it up, brushed it off, and handed it to her. "I'm so sorry. I was watching the people. Guess I should've been watching where I was going. What a klutz."

"No harm done. I'm Zoe Broussard, and this is my husband, Pierce. I don't think we've met."

"Angus Shapiro from Dallas, Texas. I'm staying in Lafayette on business and drove down to Les Barbes to look around, maybe find souvenirs for my kids."

Shapiro? Zoe smiled to herself at how odd that sounded, given the number of the Cajun French surnames in the area.

She shook hands with Angus. A respectable handshake, though his hand felt calloused and clammy. He wasn't wearing a wedding ring. Single dad? "Pierce and I own Zoe B's Cajun Eatery. If you haven't eaten yet and are looking for some authentic Cajun food, you should give it a try. We're known for our crawfish étoufée —thanks to Pierce. He's the head chef."

Pierce shook the stranger's hand, eyeing him cautiously. "Actually I'm a former-history-teacher-turned-chef. It seems I've found my calling. Or it found me, I'm not sure which."

"Too bad I've already eaten," Angus said. "I need to drive over here again and try your place."

Zoe took a coupon out of her purse and handed it to him. "We're offering two-for-one on any of our dinner entrees until the end of the month."

"It says here you're on *rue Madeline.*" Angus's Texas twang gave the street name a whole new sound. "Isn't that where I am?"

"Yes, Zoe B's is that dark gold building over there." Zoe motioned with her hand. "Phone number's on the coupon if you want to call ahead and make a reservation. It's a good idea after five."

"Thanks. I guess it's good that I *bumped into you*—so to speak." A smile appeared under his mustache. "I'll make it a point to come back sometime this week. You folks have a nice evening."

"Yeah, you, too." Pierce stood silent and watched Angus's tall, lanky frame blend into the crowd.

"He seemed nice," Zoe said.

"A little old to have hair down to his collar. And did you notice he didn't look you directly in the eye?"

"What I noticed was a nice guy who was a little embarrassed and who was also a potential customer." Zoe pushed her shoulder against his. "Why do you always assume people can't be trusted?"

"Because most of them can't. I trust my family. And Dempsey and Savannah." He pulled her closer and kissed her cheek. "And I trust you with my life. I don't need to trust anyone else."

Zoe's guilt taunted her. She had worked hard to earn Pierce's trust. It wasn't as though she had deceived him about her love for him or anything regarding their relationship. What transpired before they met didn't concern him—as long as he had no knowledge of it.

But if someone else did and intended to make sure Pierce found out, she could lose everything she had worked ten years to build. Then again, maybe the anonymous note wasn't referring to the past. For now she just needed to stay calm and keep a clear head. If someone intended to blackmail her, she hadn't heard the end of it.

"You look pale, babe," Pierce said.

"I think the humidity's getting to me." She put the back of her hand on her forehead. "I'll feel better once we get back in the air-conditioning."

CHAPTER 5

Zoe locked the door to the apartment and went down the stairs. She passed the office and the customer restrooms in the alcove and walked out into the dining room at Zoe B's. The hot pink sky was visible through the blinds where Father Sam, Tex, and Hebert sat at the table by the window.

Zoe picked up Tuesday's edition of the *Les Barbes Ledger* from one of the empty tables and handed it to Hebert. "Have you seen this yet? Pierce said the news is mostly good."

Hebert tore off a piece of beignet and popped it into his mouth. "Dats why I live here and not in New Awlins." He opened the newspaper, and an envelope fell out on the table. "Oops. Dis is yours."

Zoe's heart sank. She saw her name typed on the front of the envelope. Was this another anonymous note? She pasted on a smile and snatched it from Hebert. "Thanks. Is everybody's breakfast okay?"

The three men nodded in unison.

"That's what I like to hear. I'll tell Savannah you need more coffee."

She walked into the kitchen and stood off to the side by the freezer. She tore open the envelope and pulled out a piece of paper with the same five words cut from a magazine and pasted on: *I know what you did.*

She stared at the words, her mind racing in reverse. Was that possible? Certainly no one could prove it. Or could they? Why else would they go to all this trouble to make her squirm?

She heard Pierce talking to the kitchen staff and stuffed the note back in the envelope, then pushed open the swinging doors and nearly ran headlong into Savannah.

"There you are! The guys need coffee!"

Savannah's nose twitched the way it did when she was annoyed. "I was just coming to get a fresh pot."

I can't believe I snapped at her. Zoe sidestepped around Savannah and left the dining room. She ran upstairs and into the apartment, putting her back against the door. Her hand was shaking. What if she was wrong about the statute of limitations? What if she could still be prosecuted?

But even more was at stake than legalities. If the truth got out, Zoe B's would be history. And so would her acceptance in the community. And what about her marriage? Was Pierce's love for her solid enough to weather what would surely be perceived as betrayal?

She hurried into the bedroom and opened her lingerie drawer and put today's note on the bottom with the other one. It was too soon to panic. She needed to stay calm and keep a clear head. Maybe the notes meant something else.

"You okay …? Zoe …?"

Zoe heard the voice but didn't realize for a second where she was or who was talking.

She blinked and looked up into Pierce's questioning eyes.

"You've been standing here at the stove for several minutes," he said, "looking as if you're in a daze. Is something wrong?"

"I'm just tired. I didn't sleep well last night. I skipped breakfast and shouldn't have. I came to get something to eat."

"You still bothered by your run-in with the new waitress yesterday?"

"I guess. I should probably go choose the uniforms before I change my mind."

"Or go take a nap."

Zoe raised an eyebrow. "I have to turn in the food order by four o'clock, or we're going to run short. I'll be fine. I just need a quick lunch and a cup of coffee."

"Taste the gumbo, babe. It's extraordinary today."

"It's always extraordinary."

"Not like this." Pierce flashed an uncharacteristically boyish grin, his face beaming. "I added an ingredient. Now it's even better than Marie Nadeau's. If I can duplicate this, and I'm pretty sure I can, I might surprise everyone and win the Gumbo Classic. That would sure be good for business."

"And an incredible honor. So what's the special ingredient?"

Pierce kept smiling and said nothing.

"You're not going to tell me?"

He shook his head. "It'll be more fun if you don't know. And it'll add to the intrigue if you get asked." He took her hands in his. "Zoe, I think I finally nailed it. Come on, taste it."

Had she ever seen him this confident before? This delighted with himself? He was almost giddy.

She took a tasting spoon out of the drawer, dipped it into the pot of simmering gumbo, and blew on it for a few seconds, then slowly sipped the gumbo and savored it. "Oh my ... this is *amazing!*"

"Then you can taste the difference?"

"Definitely. I can't identify what it is, but it's distinct. And wonderful. I think Marie Nadeau is about to be dethroned, and I'm not just saying that. This is the best gumbo I've ever tasted."

Pierce picked her up off the ground and spun her around. "I'm so excited, babe. I always dreamed of being a chef, but winning the Gumbo Classic and getting to display the Copper Ladle on the wall—well, that would be more than I ever dreamed possible. But whether I win or not, thanks for believing in me. You always have, and it means everything. You, Madame Broussard, are the other half of my heart. You know that, right?"

She did know that. And it worked both ways. Each had so much invested in the other. What if her deception had put all that in jeopardy?

"You know I feel the same. You've always been there for me, too." *Always.*

God, I know what I did was wrong, but I had to keep it from Pierce. Please don't let him find out. It'll break his heart.

Vanessa parked her Honda Odyssey in front of Langley Manor and rolled down the windows, taking in the humid summer breeze thick

with a sweet fragrance she had noticed before but couldn't identify. Glints of sunlight filtered through a basket weave of live oak
branches. And somewhere in the forest the jackhammer-like sound
of a busy woodpecker echoed off the trees.

It was peaceful out here—so peaceful it seemed almost ridiculous
to believe that a strange man had gotten into the house uninvited.
Or that a sole lemon drop should be sufficient grounds for a sheriff's
investigation. Could Carter have imagined the man in the closet? It
was certainly possible, but she had no intention of going inside the
house by herself.

The mansion's stately pillars were stained with two decades of
mildew, but it wasn't hard to envision how magnificent this family
heirloom would be after it was washed down with bleach and given
a fresh coat of white paint. How much more difficult would the
refurbishing task be if Ethan's great-grandparents hadn't replaced the
columns or the exterior wood? Or if Ethan's dad and uncles hadn't
seen to it that the exterminators came out four times a year, even
when the house sat empty? Replacing the roof would be the easiest
task, remodeling the interior the most creative.

Vanessa sighed. With so much to look forward to, why was she
longing for Sophie Trace and the tree-covered foothills of the Great
Smoky Mountains? Was it the absence of family and close friends
that weighed heavily on her this morning? Or was it that she had
nothing to do while Carter was in preschool two days a week? She
missed teaching first grade, but it was impractical for her to go back
to it with this renovation about to start. Ethan was counting on her
to juggle the details and oversee the process, and she was eager to do
it. So why was she feeling this way?

Vanessa folded her hands on the steering wheel and rested her chin on them. Perhaps it was because she felt like an outsider here. As nice as Pierce and Zoe were, they and the entire Cajun community in Les Barbes were a family unto themselves. Could she and Ethan ever hope to be regarded as anything other than descendants of the British Langleys, who had looked down their noses at the Cajuns?

She could still see the indignant expression on Pierce's face when he spoke of how the British had abused the Acadians. In spite of his apology, hadn't his offensive posture revealed his resentment? What would it take to reverse his unfounded core belief that no person of British descent was worthy of his trust?

Vanessa wiped the perspiration off her upper lip, finally realizing how hot it was getting outside. She suspected that Zoe agreed with Pierce but was too polite to admit it. If she and Ethan were ever going to belong here, they had to make sure they weren't permanently labeled.

A twig snapped. Her pulse quickened. She moved her gaze across the weed-covered grounds and glanced in the rearview mirror.

"Hello?" she heard herself say. "Is somebody out there …? Hello …?"

Suddenly everything was still, even the breeze.

Vanessa started the car and quickly rolled up the windows, making sure the doors were locked. A chill scurried up her spine. She scanned the trees along the forest's edge. Was the intruder out there? Was he watching her?

Zoe walked out of the dining room at Zoe B's and into the alcove, holding tightly to the weekly food order she needed to call in. She unlocked the door to the office, flipped the light switch, and let the door close behind her. On the floor was an envelope with her name typed on the front. Her heart sank.

She stared at it for a moment, her pulse racing, then reached down and picked it up. Who had pushed it under the door? Why hadn't she paid more attention to the people coming into the eatery?

She grabbed the letter opener, slit the envelope, then pulled out a sheet of white paper, on which the same five words had been cut and pasted: *I know what you did.*

She slid down into the desk chair, filled with dread, her thoughts racing back ten years—to the scheme she had devised so she could get out on her own and support herself. She had executed each step with great care and without anyone realizing what she was up to. Or so she thought. Why would someone wait an entire decade before coming forward? Was it to extort money from her? Was she willing to get caught in that trap? And what if this person knew the truth about her family?

She looked up at the framed photo of Pierce and her, enjoying the dance floor at their wedding reception. Nobody seemed hung up that none of the bride's relatives were there. All that mattered was that Pierce loved her and she was now a Broussard. How could anyone know what taking his name meant to her? Any children born to them would have a Cajun heritage with strong family ties, free from the shame she left in Devon Springs and without any knowledge of it.

Zoe tucked the note in her blouse and ran the envelope through the paper shredder. No way was she going to be the victim in this.

She knew how to diffuse this situation before it had the power to undo everything she held dear. Did she have the courage? It was risky. But if it worked, whoever was sending these notes couldn't hold the past over her head.

Vanessa set the well-read copy of *The Velveteen Rabbit* on the nightstand, kissed Carter on the forehead, and whispered, "Mommy loves you. Sleep tight."

She turned off the lamp and tiptoed out of Carter's room, through the living room, and out onto the gallery, where Ethan stood leaning on the ornate wrought-iron railing.

"That didn't take long," he said.

"I think preschool wears him out." Vanessa linked arms with Ethan, noting that the muggy air hadn't cooled much since the sun went down. He seems to love it."

"So … the men in your life are adjusting well. You haven't said much about your day. Did you do anything special?"

"Not really. I drove out to the manor house. I had no intention of going inside," she quickly added. "I was just feeling a little lost with Carter in school and was trying to get revved up about the renovation." Vanessa held her gaze on a man in a blue ball cap walking by himself. "A weird thing happened. I was sitting in the car, listening to the quiet, and I heard a twig snap. I called out, but no one answered. I had the creepiest feeling I was being watched, so I started the car and made sure the windows were up and the doors locked. It was probably a deer or something. I didn't wait around to find out. I just wish I felt safe going in the house. I need to get in there and make some notes."

"I'd change the locks again if I thought it would do any good," Ethan said. "But the sheriff's deputies didn't see any sign the locks had been tampered with."

Vanessa felt her skin turn to gooseflesh. "We know Carter didn't see a ghost. So how did the man get in?"

"Maybe there was no man, except in Carter's imagination."

"Why are you hedging? We can't just blow off the lemon drop."

Ethan pushed his glasses up higher on his nose, his dark hair curlier from the night's humidity. "I've been thinking a lot about this, honey. A number of people have been in the house. Any one of them could've set down a package of lemon drops and not remembered where. Isn't it possible that Carter found them and incorporated them into his imaginary story?"

"Ethan, if you really believed that, you wouldn't care if I went out there alone."

"The truth is I don't know what to believe, other than it's not smart to take chances."

"I didn't. But how long are we supposed to live like this?"

CHAPTER 6

Sheriff Jude Prejean folded Wednesday's edition of the *Les Barbes Ledger* under his arm and pushed open the door at Zoe B's, the jingling of the bell causing a number of folks to look up. He recognized most of the faces. Too early for tourists.

Jude nodded a few hellos while he waited for Savannah to come seat him. The healthy green plant hanging from the ceiling above the window gave the eatery a homey touch.

"Hey, Sheriff. Table for one?"

Jude smiled. "Not today. Two of my deputies will be joining me."

Savannah picked up three menus. "Right this way."

He followed her to an empty table in the corner. Outside, the glowing pink sky formed a worthy backdrop for the row of historic buildings across the street. No clouds. It was going to be another scorcher.

"I'll bring your coffee," Savannah said. "Are you going to wait to order until your deputies arrive?"

"Yeah, thanks. Shouldn't be long."

Jude turned over his cup. Half a minute later Savannah came back to the table and filled it with coffee.

"Pierce is cranking out the beignets this morning," she said. "Why don't I bring you some—on the house? You can enjoy them while you're waiting."

"That'd be great. Thanks."

Jude blew on his coffee and took a sip. Best coffee in Saint Catherine Parish. And he'd probably tried them all.

He glanced over at Hebert Lanoux, who was having breakfast with his cronies. Had it really been thirty years since this sweet old gentleman had given him a job stocking shelves at the corner grocery after school? Monsieur Lanoux had outlived his wife and his son and lived a fuller life than a lot of guys twenty years his junior.

Savannah hurried past his table, her brown ponytail swaying, her right hand balancing a large round platter filled with orders. How did such a tiny woman do that? She couldn't weigh more than a hundred pounds.

The door opened, and Deputy Chief Aimee Rivette and Chief Detective Gil Marcel came inside.

Jude raised his hand, and the two walked in his direction, their boots clicking on the wood floor.

"Good morning, Sheriff," Aimee said. "That's some sunrise."

"Yep. Enjoy it. Once that sun's up high, the thermometer will follow."

Savannah came over to the table and set down a white carafe of coffee and a plate of beignets. "That should get y'all started. I'll be back to take your order in a few minutes."

"Help yourselves," Jude said. "A little *lagniappe* on the house."

Gil rubbed his hands together. "Nothing can compare with homemade beignets."

Aimee laughed. "Is that why you spend half your paycheck on Krispy Kremes?"

Gil tore off a piece of beignet and stuffed it into his smile, powdered sugar falling on his chin. "These are too messy for the squad car. I'd eat them every day if I could. Justine makes them on holidays, but that's about it."

"Judging by that roll hanging over your belt," Jude said, "she's doing you a favor."

Gil wiped his mouth with the napkin. "We only go around once, Sheriff. Gotta grab a little gusto."

"Oh, I see. You grab the gusto"—Jude winked at Aimee—"so Justine can grab those love handles."

"Aw, come on." Gil tried to look hurt, but his smiling eyes betrayed him. "I passed my physical agility test in spades. Surely you called this meeting for some reason, other than to harass me about my doughnut addiction?"

"Actually I did. I wanted to commend you two for the way you handled the investigation of illegal dumping. You got the local stations behind us and raised awareness. Thanks to your efforts we're finally going to get the support we need to get this parish cleaned up. That's no small feat."

"I was just the mouthpiece." Aimee's twinkling blue eyes drew attention away from her dark roots, which seemed to beg for a touch-up. "It was Gil who rattled the chains out there and kept the pressure on."

"Don't forget it took the whole team to rummage through the garbage and figure out who's doing the dumping," Gil said. "Prosecuting those responsible and naming names will make people think twice before trashing the parish."

Jude took a sip of coffee. "Mayor Blanchard is so encouraged by the progress that he called a meeting with the other mayors in Saint Catherine Parish. He wants us to show them what we did here. The governor got wind of it and is really impressed. I wouldn't be surprised if all the parishes end up following our lead."

Aimee smiled. "Makes all that hard work seem worthwhile."

Gil took another bite of beignet. "I never considered that what we did would catch on."

"I'm proud of the job you did," Jude said. "I'm going to recommend you both for a Distinguished Service award and wouldn't be surprised if—" His phone vibrated. He glanced at the screen. Why was Stone Castille calling his cell phone so early? "Excuse me. I'd better take this … Sheriff Prejean."

"We've got a problem," Stone said.

"I'm holding a breakfast meeting with Aimee and Gil. Can't it wait?"

"No, sir. I'm looking at a dead body. And y'all need to see this one before I call it in. I don't think you'll want the media all over it."

"Where are you?"

"At the old Vincent farm—just down the bayou from Langley Manor."

"Nobody's lived out there in years."

"Nobody's *living* here now. Trust me, sir. Y'all need to see this."

Jude sighed. "We'll be right there."

Jude drove his squad car across a rickety wooden bridge and turned left at the faded mailbox marked *Vincent* onto a gravel road. He glanced in his rearview mirror at the cloud of white dust and the blazing red ball that hung in the eastern sky. He passed by a row of cypress trees draped with Spanish moss and spotted the stained roof of the dilapidated farmhouse about fifty yards ahead.

He slowed and pulled up behind Stone Castille's squad car. He got out and stretched his lower back. The dawn air was warm and heavy and smelled like wet earth.

Half a minute later Aimee and Gil pulled in behind him, and the three of them trudged through the weeds toward the house.

Stone waved and met them half way. "That was quick. This way. Get ready for a jolt. You're not going to believe who it is."

Jude followed Stone through the high weeds toward a row of massive trees on the edge of the sugarcane fields. There it was.

Jude stopped, sickened at the sight of a Caucasian male, noose around his neck, hanging from a live oak. And even sicker when he recognized the man's face—and the red ball cap on the ground. "Aw, Remy. Why? Why'd you do it?"

"Sheriff, this wasn't suicide," Stone said. "I believe he may have been lynched. Someone left a note under my wiper blade when I was in Crawfish Corner, having a cup of coffee. The exact words were, 'A white man is hanging from a tree at the old Vincent farm. How does it feel?' The word *white* was underlined."

"How long ago was that?" Jude said.

"Less than thirty minutes. When I found the note, I drove out here to look around. I didn't bother calling for backup. I figured it was another hoax."

"Where's the note?" Jude said.

"I bagged it and put it into evidence. It's just a sheet of white paper with the message in bold type printed off a computer. I'm hoping we'll get fingerprints off it."

Jude took out his handkerchief and wiped the perspiration off the back of his neck. "Why would anyone want to hurt Remy Jarvis?"

"Remy was an easy target. They probably grabbed him while he was out delivering newspapers. I found at least three sets of shoe prints. Come take a look."

Jude followed Stone to where the body dangled and saw overlapping shoe prints in the mud beneath.

"Make casts," Jude said. "That'll give us something to go on. People will be screaming for justice when they find out a white man was lynched."

"Especially someone as gentle and trusting as Remy," Aimee said. "So much for racial harmony."

Jude folded his arms across his chest. "There's no proof that whoever did this is African-American. Anyone could've written that note."

"That's true," Stone said. "But we can't afford to blow off the Langley boy's allegation that he saw a black man in the manor house. That's less than two hundred yards from here."

"But you didn't find any evidence of forced entry—or any entry."

"Maybe we should take a closer look," Aimee said.

"Maybe we will. But for now let's keep the note confidential. Let's just call this in and investigate it by the book. When the media finds out, our investigation will be under a microscope. The whole country will be watching. Let's make sure we don't miss a step."

⚜

Zoe sat in her office and downed a cup of lukewarm coffee she didn't remember pouring. It wasn't even noon, and she'd already talked herself out of doing anything about the notes. Why act in haste and admit to something that would have life-changing consequences?

She needed to wait. To see if things escalated. Wasn't it possible someone was playing a joke on her? Was that any more far-fetched than the notion that someone had figured out what she'd done?

There was a knock on the door, and then a muffled female voice.

"Zoe, it's Vanessa. Can I talk to you?"

"Hang on. I'm coming."

Zoe walked over to the door and looked through the peephole, then unlocked the dead bolt.

"Sorry. We keep this door locked for security reasons. Few people even know this is the office. Come in."

"I can't." Vanessa glanced up the stairs. "Carter's watching cartoons. I need to be within earshot. I just wanted to know if you heard about the lynching."

"Pierce mentioned something about a murder, but I was a little preoccupied at the time. What happened?"

"Early this morning a man was found hanging from a live oak on the property adjacent to Langley Manor. Can you believe it?"

"Good heavens!" Zoe paused to let the gravity of the situation sink in. "Do they know who it was?"

"His name hasn't been released yet."

"Pierce and I have black friends," Zoe said. "I sure hope it wasn't someone we know. This is horrible. I didn't even know lynchings happened anymore. I can only imagine how upset and scared the black community must be. I should probably make some calls and see what I can find out."

"Zoe, the victim was white."

"White? I've never heard of a white man being lynched."

"The authorities aren't calling it a lynching, but someone phoned the radio station and claimed that a note was left on a deputy's windshield that proves it was racially motivated. The sheriff didn't deny it, but he can't comment during an open investigation."

"He's going to have to tell us something! It's not like murders happen here every day. I'm sure people are scared."

"He really can't, Zoe. I've been through this with my mother. She's a police chief, remember? She never talks about cases when an investigation's in progress." Vanessa glanced up at the open door to her apartment and then dropped her voice to just above a whisper. "I have a bad feeling about this. What if the black man Carter saw in the closet was involved? What if he was hiding at our place, planning the whole thing? The timing fits."

"Whoa, girl. Slow down. You don't even know for certain that there *was* an intruder. You said the sheriff's deputies didn't find anything to suggest it."

Vanessa blew the bangs off her forehead. "I know. It's perplexing. But the man Carter described is obviously African-American. And now a white man is lynched right next door to Langley Manor. How can that be just a coincidence?"

"Sweetie, your imagination's on tilt. You need to take a deep breath and think about this."

"I haven't *stopped* thinking about it. Something happened I haven't had a chance to tell you yet. I drove out to the manor house yesterday when Carter was in preschool. I didn't go in. I just sat in the car with the windows rolled down. I heard a twig crack somewhere close by. I called out and no one answered. But I felt someone watching me. It made my skin crawl, so I left."

"But you didn't see anyone?"

"No. That's what made it so creepy. I knew someone was there, but whoever it was didn't answer me."

"It could've been an animal. The woods are full of them."

Vanessa grabbed a lock of her dark, shiny hair and began twirling it. "Maybe I'm overreacting. But it's frightening that someone was murdered so close to Langley Manor. It makes Carter's story about the man in the closet all the more unsettling."

"I'm sure it does. But don't jump to conclusions. There's probably a logical explanation."

"I'm not so sure. There's something else you don't know. We found a lemon drop on the floor at the manor house."

"You're kidding. When?"

"When you and Pierce were out there and Carter took you on a tour."

"Why didn't you tell us?"

Vanessa tucked her hair behind her ear. "We were a little freaked out and didn't want to say anything about it in front of Carter. But we're also trying to keep any more ghost stories from circulating."

"Pierce and I wouldn't have told anyone. I can't believe you didn't trust us."

Vanessa sighed. "I'm sorry. We should have. We were trying not to add to the gossip about paranormal activity at Langley Manor. Even one of the deputies who did the trespassing report questioned whether Ethan and I might have planted the lemon drop because a good ghost story could be great for B-and-B business."

"After what you just told me, you have to pursue this. At least tell the sheriff your concern that there could be a connection between the black man Carter saw and the hanging."

Vanessa arched her eyebrows, her clear blue eyes the color of her tank top. "I'm sure he's already thought of it. My mom's mind works like that. But I think I will call and express my concerns. I need to get back upstairs before number-one son gets into mischief. Thanks for listening. I needed to talk to someone and didn't want to bother Ethan at work."

"I'll be upstairs after five," Zoe said. "Knock on our door and let me know how it went."

CHAPTER 7

Zoe walked into the dining room at the eatery and saw Savannah replacing candles in preparation for the dinner hour. She took a slow, deep breath and then walked over to her.

"How's it coming?"

"Almost done. I'm ready to get off my feet."

"I see you put daisies in the bud vases, too. Looks nice."

"They're really fresh today," Savannah said flatly.

An awkward moment of silence prodded Zoe to do what she came to do.

"I owe you an apology, Savannah. I probably sounded as if I were scolding you this morning about Hebert and the guys needing more coffee. Actually I was upset and preoccupied about something totally unrelated. I'm sorry I was short with you."

"You don't have to apologize."

"Why, because I'm the boss?" She reached over and squeezed Savannah's hand. "That's not the way we do things around here. I didn't want you to go home for the day without my having explained myself."

"It's okay. I could tell something wasn't right." Savannah put a fresh candle in the glass holder. "Actually nothing about this day seemed right.

Everyone who came in was talking about the lynching, even the tourists. I've grown up here and heard stories about the way things *used* to be. I never thought it would happen now. And never to a white man."

"Are the authorities actually calling it a lynching?"

"Of course not." Savannah rolled her eyes. "But the sheriff didn't deny that someone left a note on a deputy's car that suggested it was. He just won't comment on it."

"Have the authorities released the name of the victim?"

"Not yet. Everyone's wondering who it is, but they have to notify the next of kin first."

"I wonder what's taking so long." Zoe smoothed a wrinkle out of the tablecloth. "Wasn't the body found early this morning?"

"Yes. And I'm pretty sure the call came in when the sheriff was sitting right here with two deputies. They left without ordering and said they needed to go take care of something. That was at sunup."

"I can't imagine why they haven't released the victim's name."

"I sure hope it's not someone I know."

"And who would that be?" Zoe said. "You know just about everybody in town."

Vanessa sat with Sheriff Jude Prejean and Deputy Stone Castille at the kitchen table in her apartment.

"Sheriff, I never expected you to come over here personally," Vanessa said. "I just felt compelled to report my concern about the hanging—and the fact that it happened on the property adjacent to Langley Manor. Do you have any leads?"

"We can't discuss the details of the investigation," Jude said. "We haven't even released the victim's name yet."

"Are you aware that just a few minutes ago, a man called the radio station again, this time revealing exactly what was in the note?"

"What he *claims* was in the note."

"So there was a note?" Vanessa studied the sheriff's expressionless face. "Look, I understand you can't give details, but can't you just say whether or not this was racially motivated?"

"We can't rule it out."

"Then shouldn't we rethink the validity of my son's story," Vanessa said, "now that there's been a murder in close proximity— one that might've been racially motivated?"

"Yes, I think we should." Sheriff Prejean cleared his throat and seemed to be thinking. "For starters I'd like to go ahead and run DNA testing on the lemon drop. It's a bit of a long shot that we'll get viable DNA, but the sugar coating is gone, which suggests it had been in someone's mouth before it ended up on your floor." Jude rubbed the sandpaper shadow on his chin. "If your son really did see a man in the closet, we need to discover who that individual is and if he was also at the scene of the hanging. It's certainly suspicious."

Vanessa brushed the hair out of her eyes. "I'm just so confused why your deputies didn't find any evidence that the man broke in."

"That was baffling to us, too," Jude said. "Have you noticed anything that suggests this intruder might have come back?"

"I haven't gone inside the house since your deputies did the trespassing report. Something did happen yesterday morning that didn't feel right, but I almost feel foolish mentioning it."

Vanessa told the sheriff and the deputy about hearing a twig crack while she sat in the car, outside the house.

"It could have been a stranger lurking about," Vanessa said. "Or it could've been a deer or something. But I didn't imagine it. I felt as if someone were watching me. It was creepy. I finally left."

"Gave you the *freesôns*, did it?" Jude seemed to read her blank look, then quickly added. "That's what folks around here call the goose bumps. What time was that?"

"Around ten o'clock."

Stone wrote something on his tablet. "Why didn't you report it?"

"Report what—that I heard a twig snap? I didn't actually see anything. And it's not like I knew there was going to be a lynching next door."

"Of course you didn't, ma'am. Just don't hesitate to call next time something doesn't feel right. It could be important."

Vanessa moved her gaze to the sheriff, who looked to her like an older version of Matt Damon. "So do hate crimes happen often around here?"

Jude pursed his lips. "There hasn't been a lynching in this parish since 1975. And as far as I know, it's never happened to a white man."

"But you *do* have racial problems."

"Some racial *tension*, I suppose. But problems?" Jude shook his head. "Not that I can see. Whites and blacks have learned to respect each other, including in the workplace. Just haven't had problems on my watch."

Vanessa looked at Stone and then at Jude. "I keep wondering what it is you're not saying."

"Excuse me?" Jude shifted in his chair and scratched his ear.

"Look," Vanessa said, "my mother was on the Memphis police force the whole time I was growing up, and now she's the police chief in Sophie Trace. I know that authorities typically withhold something vital to a case, something only the guilty person could know. Since I'm in the middle of this, Sheriff, I think I have a right to know if my family is in some sort of danger."

"If we thought you were"—Jude's round, hazel eyes were truthful—"we would say so. We released all the information the public needs to know."

"Do you have any suspects?"

"Not yet. But after what you just told me, I'd like to go back to the manor house and inspect the grounds and the closet for trace evidence. If anything matches what we found at the murder scene, then we can assume your intruder was involved. And if he's in the system, we'll know who he is."

Vanessa nodded and rose to her feet. "I'll get you the key."

Zoe walked across *rue Madeline* and down a block to Cypress Park. She sat by herself on a wrought-iron bench, her body finally thawing out from the air-conditioning. Would they ever be able to regulate the temperature in their building so that the office wasn't freezing?

She set her gaze on a Louisiana heron that high-stepped ever so slowly in the shallow water along the bank of the pond, watching for an unsuspecting minnow. Some of its blue-gray plumage had a peachy cast and looked almost iridescent in the bright sunlight.

A flock of white ibis squawked overhead and then landed on the grassy terrain on the other side of the pond and began the dinner march across the grounds, foraging for insects or frogs or whatever else could be stirred up.

The bells of Saint Catherine's started to toll. Zoe glanced at her watch and smiled. Five o'clock straight up. She closed her eyes, the resonant sound still stirring her soul after all these years. How she loved Les Barbes! It was here, as a young entrepreneur, that she finally tasted the American dream—so palatable after the bland years that were seasoned only with the salt of her own tears. Every ingredient that went into making her new life pleasant was carefully chosen. She broke a few rules getting what she needed, but no harm had come to anyone because of it.

She would have been content just to own Zoe B's. Falling for Pierce had been both an inconvenience and a gift. Never had she imagined she could trust a man, let alone love one. Yet hadn't the past five years been the best of her life? Wasn't she secure enough with Pierce to want to have his children?

I know what you did. Fear gripped her as she considered again the implication of the notes. Was someone about to wreck everything she'd worked for? What did he or she want from her—a confession? Retribution? Hush money?

Even if she could scrape up the money, was she willing to be blackmailed? A demand for money would likely result in another and another. And how long could she keep it from Pierce?

God, I know what I did was wrong. But what choice did I have? I would never have gotten out any other way. How else was I supposed to support myself?

Maybe she should just tell Pierce the truth and trust that his love for her was stronger than the shock and disappointment he would feel. But was it? How would he react when he found out that she wasn't the person he thought she was? Would he doubt that her feelings for him were authentic when everything else about her had been fabricated, including her happy childhood and the death of her parents? Would he still want to start a family when he found out she didn't have a drop of Cajun blood in her ancestry—and what her family was *really* like …?

The sound of fist hitting flesh and her mother's crying sent terror through her.

"Shelby! Michael! I know you can hear me!" Her father's voice was earsplitting, his speech slurred. "This is your mom's fault! She brought it on herself! I didn't want to hurt her! You know that!"

Her father ranted for quite some time. Then things got quiet. Too quiet. Was he coming for her now?

Shelby pulled the covers over her head and hugged her doll. She learned early on it was useless to fight him. She just closed her eyes and hoped he would pass out.

Why couldn't she have been born in a different family …?

"Excuse me, ma'am. Are you Zoe Broussard?"

The young male voice startled her. She looked up and saw a freckled boy of about ten or eleven, holding a skateboard under his arm.

"Yes. Who are you?"

"Jacob Millet. I'm supposed to give this to you." The boy handed her an envelope with her name typed on the front.

Zoe felt as if her heart were falling down a well. "Who's this from?"

"The man didn't tell me his name," Jacob said. "He was in a hurry. He gave me ten dollars to bring it to you."

"How did you know where to find me?"

"He pointed to you from the parking lot."

Zoe's heart sank. The guy had been following her? "What did he look like?"

"I couldn't really tell. He was on a motorcycle and wore a helmet with an eye shield. He said you were expecting this envelope—that it was very important and you would *know* who it was from."

"Where is he now?"

"He had to leave. He said he'd be in touch."

"How long ago was that?"

"Just a couple minutes."

Zoe locked gazes with Jacob and saw a polite young boy who thought he had done a good deed. She softened her tone. "Didn't your parents ever tell you not to talk to strangers?"

Jacob's cheeks turned bright pink. "Yes, ma'am. But the man didn't seem dangerous, and lots of other people were around. I can sure use the ten bucks. I'm saving to buy a new skateboard."

"All right, Jacob. Thanks for delivering the envelope."

"You're welcome. Have a nice day."

Zoe stared at the note in her hand and then tore it open. The same five words were cut from a magazine and pasted on a sheet of white paper: *I know what you did.*

How could he know? Who was he? And what was his next move?

Zoe felt sick to her stomach. There was only one way to fix this. It wouldn't be easy. But how could it be any harder being blackmailed?

CHAPTER 8

Zoe opened the door and stepped out on the Broussards' half of the gallery that jutted out over the sidewalk at Zoe B's. The sun had disappeared beneath the horizon, leaving the western sky ablaze with streaks of orangey pink and purple.

She clutched the portable phone so hard her knuckles were white. Could she pull this off? She waited until she heard Pierce's footsteps coming in her direction, then put the phone to her ear.

"No, I'm glad you called," she said louder than she intended to. "I-I'm just so shocked. Tell her husband how sorry I am. I'll see y'all tomorrow. Bye."

Pierce came up behind her and put his arms around her, his cheek next to hers. "I didn't hear the phone ring. What's wrong, babe?"

She paused, her palm so sweaty she thought the phone might slide out of her hand. "My friend Annabelle—the gal I roomed with when I worked for her parents' restaurant in Morgan City—died Monday night of viral pneumonia. Her funeral's tomorrow after-noon. I just can't believe she's dead. She was only thirty-seven, same as us. She had a husband and two little kids. It's just awful."

"I'm so sorry," Pierce said. "Who called to tell you?"

"Her brother, Wyatt." She turned around in Pierce's arms and gazed into his trusting brown eyes. She had to make him believe her. "He spent a lot of time trying to find me. He knew I'd want to know."

"That was thoughtful. I heard you say you'll see him tomorrow. Are you going to the funeral?"

"I think I should. It's at eleven at Holy Cross Catholic Church in Morgan City. Wyatt asked if I could come out to the house afterward and spend some time with the family. Could you cover for me tomorrow? I know it's your day off. I hate to ask."

"Of course I will." Pierce kissed her cheek. "Do what you need to do. I can handle things here."

"Thanks. I don't deserve you."

"Hey, we're a team, remember? My turn to carry the ball."

Zoe blinked the stinging from her eyes. If things went the way she hoped, maybe it would be the last time she had to deceive Pierce like this.

"I hear someone in the hallway," he said.

"It's probably the Langleys. They said they'd knock on our door after they got Carter to bed. I want to know what the sheriff had to say."

Zoe sat next to Pierce on the couch in their apartment and took a sip of sweet tea, listening to Vanessa retell the details of her late-afternoon conversation with Sheriff Jude Prejean and Deputy Stone Castille.

"That's about it." Vanessa turned her ear toward the open front door as if she were listening for Carter. "I gave the sheriff the key to Langley Manor, and they were supposed to go out and investigate and get back to us. I'm sure we'll hear something tomorrow."

"Did you get the impression," Pierce said, "that Jude thinks there's a connection between the intruder at the manor house and the hanging?"

"He wouldn't say." Vanessa glanced over at Ethan. "We're still not sure there even *was* an intruder at our place. I'm eager to know whether they found DNA on the lemon drop or collected any trace evidence from the closet. I'm more and more suspicious that someone was in the house."

"I don't know what to make of the twig incident." Ethan took Vanessa's hand. "But I think having the sheriff investigate further is important if we're ever going to have peace of mind."

"So do I," Zoe said.

"Let's not forget the bigger issue." Pierce leaned forward, his hands clasped between his knees. "The note on the deputy's windshield was obviously put there to rile the white community. Why? We haven't had any serious racial unrest in years."

"The sheriff hasn't actually confirmed there was a note," Vanessa said.

"He didn't deny it either, and he certainly could have—if it wasn't true."

Zoe was vaguely aware of Vanessa commenting and Pierce replying, but how could she worry about a lynching when her very future was hanging in the balance? Who was the man following her, and what did he really know? Would she be able to leave town without him following her? If so, would her plan work? What if it backfired and her secret was exposed? Would she be able to face Pierce? Would he even want to see her again—ever?

"Zoe ...?"

She heard Pierce saying her name and looked up into his questioning face and realized three set of eyes were on her.

"Sorry, *cher*. I was thinking about Annabelle. Were you talking to me?"

"I just asked if you wanted more tea." Pierce's dark eyes were wide with compassion. He glanced over at the Langleys. "Just before you knocked on the door, Zoe got a call that her friend Annabelle had died. It was quite a shock."

"I'm so sorry," Vanessa said. "Why didn't you say something? We can talk about this later."

"Don't feel bad. I really did want to hear what the sheriff had to say."

"Well, now you and Pierce know everything we know." Ethan stood and pulled Vanessa to her feet. "Let us get out of your hair and give Zoe a chance to absorb the shock of her friend's death."

"Did Annabelle live in Les Barbes?" Vanessa asked.

"No, she and her family live in Morgan City. I'm going to drive down for the funeral tomorrow. I still can't believe she's gone."

"How did she die?"

"Viral pneumonia."

"That's too bad. People usually recover from that." Vanessa's eyebrows came together. "Did Annabelle have complications?"

"I don't know the details. I'll find out more tomorrow." Could she remember what she'd said long enough to write it down so she could keep her story straight?

Vanessa put her arms around Zoe. "If there's *anything* we can do, we're just next door."

Late that night Jude Prejean sat at the table in his office and looked over the facts they had so far in the lynching case, dreading the interview with Remy Jarvis's father, whom his deputies finally reached just after dark, when he returned from a day's fishing on the Roux River.

Jude heard footsteps and looked up just as Deputy Chief Aimee Rivette came to a stop in the doorway.

"Emile Jarvis just arrived," she said. "I got him a cold drink and seated him in the first interview room. I smelled whiskey on his breath."

"It's going to take more than booze to stop the kind of pain he's in." Jude took off his reading glasses and rubbed his eyes.

"Now that we've released the victim's name, Sheriff, the media's anxious to hear from you."

"They can wait. I want to talk to Emile first."

"This is sad for more than just the obvious," Aimee said. "Remy was everybody's brother or son or grandson. He touched us all on some level."

"We're not resting until we find out who's responsible." Jude stood, the worn cartilage in his basketball knees feeling the effects of having trudged over uneven terrain at the Vincent farm and again at Langley Manor.

He followed Aimee down the hall and into the first interview room, where Emile Jarvis was seated, his arms folded on the table.

Jude squeezed the man's shoulder. "I can't even imagine what you're feeling, Emile. I'm so sorry about Remy. We're going to get whoever did this."

Emile nodded but didn't say anything.

Jude walked around to the other side of the table and sat next to Aimee. When was the last time he dreaded an interview this much? An awkward silence followed.

Emile seemed to stare at nothing, his wavy salt-and-pepper hair pulled back in a ponytail, his unshaven face red and swollen. It was hard to tell how much color was sunburn and how much was the result of tears spilled over his son's murder.

Finally Jude said, "Everyone in the department is outraged over what happened to your son. We are committed to bringing the guilty parties to justice."

"Why'd dey kill him?" Emile said softly. "Remy wasn't a *couyon*. He wasn't stupid. He was slow, dat's all."

"Everyone knew that," Jude said. "This crime was about blacks and whites. The victim could've been anyone. I doubt it was personal."

"It was to me." Emile lifted his gray, bloodshot eyes. "My boy, my own flesh and blood, strung up like a side o' beef...." A tear dripped down his cheek.

"Judging by the time of death," Jude said, "Remy must've been grabbed while he was out delivering newspapers. The coroner said he died from a blow to the head before he was hanged."

Emile sobbed into his hands and shook his head. "Remy never hurt anybody. He had a heart o' gold."

"I don't mean to minimize your loss in any way," Aimee said, "but you can take comfort that Remy was unconscious and didn't know what was happening to him."

"But *I* know. I loved dat boy. It's been him and me since his *mere* died. Remy was special. Had a sweetness 'bout him only his kind has. He couldn't defend hisself. How could dey hurt him dat way—" Emile clamped his hand over his mouth, his eyes suddenly wide and frantic, and jumped to his feet—"I got the *mal au couer....*" He turned and ran out of the room and across the hall to the men's restroom.

Jude started to follow him, but Aimee grabbed his arm. "He can throw up without you. Maybe he'll feel better. It's probably a combination of booze and shock."

Jude sighed. "Truthfully I can't get the image of Remy hanging from a tree out of my mind. I'm glad Emile was on the river when it happened. No father should have to witness that."

"He had to identify Remy's body," Aimee said. "I'm sure he's imagined the whole thing a hundred times over."

"I'll never forget it." Jude's mind flashed back to the red cap on the ground—and the shocking realization that followed. He replaced the image with one of Remy crossing the finish line at the Special Olympics.

"People will be up in arms," Aimee said. "Not just because Remy was the victim, but because a white man was targeted. The media is calling it a lynching, even if we're not."

Jude drew a circle on the table with his finger. "I didn't deny it was racially motivated. But the word *lynching* never crossed my lips. And I didn't confirm the note. It's all speculation."

"Sheriff, the man who called the radio station knew what was in the note word for word. We've got the recording of his voice, but he called from an untraceable cell phone." Aimee sighed, fatigue making her look older than her thirty-nine years. "The public believes the caller. Maybe it's time to confirm it and make an appeal for people to use restraint. We don't have enough manpower to keep the peace."

"Fair enough. I'll go public with it. Police Chief Norman has already borrowed officers from Lafayette and New Iberia PDs. If we work together, we'll be ready, whatever the response."

Jude took his phone off his belt clip and scanned through his messages until Emile came back and resumed his place at the table.

"Sorry," Emile said. "My stomach's in a wad."

"No need to apologize," Jude said. "This has to be a nightmare for you. We promise not to keep you long. We just need to ask a few questions. Did Remy have any close friends?"

"Jus' me and his kin. Other folks took a likin' to him though. He couldn't go anywheres widout someone strikin' up a conversation."

"Were the exchanges always positive?" Jude said. "Or did some people talk down to Remy because he was slow?"

"Most folks were kind. Sometimes kids laughed at him or got scared o' him because he was different."

"Could you walk me through a typical day in Remy's life?"

Emile stared at his hands. "I got him up at four. Put his bike in my truck and drove him down to da *Ledger* building. He rolled his papers and delivered 'em, den rode his bike home and was back by seven. I cooked us breakfast. Remy did chores around da house and played video games while I did woodworkin' in da garage. He rode wid me when I made deliveries. Lots o' times, before we called it a day, we went to Cypress Park and fed da ducks. We did most everything together."

"But not today?"

Emile's eyes brimmed with tears, and he waited until he regained his composure before continuing. "Remy was supposed to ride his bike over to his aunt Sue's and stay put while I went fishin' on da river. I took him wid me when we fished for fun, but I needed to do some serious catchin' today to fill up my freezer. Dat's a long day for Remy."

"Your sister, Sue Fontaine?"

Emile nodded. "At first when Remy didn't show up, Sue thought we got our wires crossed and I'd taken Remy wid me. She tried callin', but dere's no cell signal on da river and she couldn't get through. When she heard about da hangin', she got scared and reported him missin'."

"I'm glad she did," Jude said. "I recognized Remy as the victim right off but had no way of getting in touch with you. Thank the Lord your sister knew you were on the river and would be home by dark. I'm sure your heart sank when you saw my deputies waiting in front of your house when you pulled up."

"Broke my heart when dey told me what happened. I took da hosepipe and a bar o' soap and cleaned up on da patio, den put on dry clothes and went wid 'em over to da morgue and identified my son's body." Emile wrung his hands. "Dat's as bad as it gets."

"Yes, it is, Emile. I'm so sorry. Can you recall if any black person ever threatened you or your son?"

"Nah. We got along wid everyone."

"Any African-American who might want to get back at you—a dissatisfied customer? A disgruntled neighbor? Anyone?"

"Not dat I know of."

"Did Remy ever make remarks about black people—something that could be misconstrued as racist if someone didn't know Remy thought like a child?"

Emile shrugged. "News to me, if he did. I know what you're gettin' at, Sheriff, but dose folks accepted my boy. We fished off da bridge wid 'em all da time. I don't look at any person as better dan another, and dat's how I taught Remy...." Emile's voice cracked. "Lot o' good it did me."

"Did Remy work with any blacks at the *Ledger?*"

"Didn't work wid anybody. Took care o' his own route. Dere's a supervisor, but she's Hispanic."

"Could there have been an African-American who felt he got aced out of the route they gave to Remy?"

"I don't see it. Remy had da same route for eleven years. Folks at da *Ledger* made up a simple route he could remember, but dey treated Remy like everybody else. He earned his money. Did a real good job for 'em."

"I know he did," Jude said. "I was down at Zoe B's many times when he brought the paper in. Remy took pride in his job."

"Dat he did." Emile wiped a tear off his cheek with the back of his hand. "He was a good boy."

"Remind me how old Remy was," Aimee said.

"Thirty-two. O' course in his head he was still a little boy. His mind jus' never grew up. Made things harder for him, but dere was somethin' real special 'bout him too."

Aimee nodded. "Yes there was, Emile. His death is a loss to everyone in Les Barbes. We all feel it."

"Don't know what I'm gonna do now." Emile's lip quivered. "Remy's all I had."

"We released his name to the media just a few minutes ago," Jude said. "And I'm going to have to go back out there and confirm the content of the note we found on Deputy Castille's squad car. Unfortunately that means you're going to get swarmed by people wanting to ask you questions. I imagine the networks are already setting up outside your house. Do you want to give a statement?"

Emile shook his head. "I jus' wanna go home and close da blinds and let it all sink in. I need to sit alone wid my thoughts."

Jude glanced over at Aimee. "Deputy Chief Rivette will escort you home and make sure the media stays out of your face. But I have to tell you, Emile, hate crimes like this draw national attention. Life's going to get even tougher for a while."

CHAPTER 9

The next morning, Zoe stood at the bathroom mirror and fastened the strand of pearls that seemed to be the perfect accessory for the only black dress she owned. When was the last time she wore it—when Pierce's uncle Gaston died last year?

She saw Pierce's reflection in the mirror and felt his arms slip around her, his newly shaven cheek next to hers, the spicy, woody fragrance of his Tuscany cologne unmistakable.

"You look much too pretty to be going to a funeral," he said. "But I know you're hurting. You shouldn't have to face this alone. Maybe I should go with you."

"I'll be fine as long as I know you're watching things here. We can't both be gone."

"Actually we can. I trust Dempsey to do the cooking and run the kitchen. And Savannah could coordinate things in the dining room and would jump at the chance to make some overtime."

Zoe held his gaze in the mirror. He could *not* come with her. She had to sound believable. "You are incredibly sweet to want to be with me today. And I love you for it." She turned around in his arms and cupped his face in her hands. "But I need to be present, really present, for Annabelle's family. I know myself. Unless I'm confident everything is operating smoothly at the eatery, I won't be able to turn loose of it."

"I see."

"Pierce, you're the only person I trust to run Zoe B's. I really need you here."

"All right, babe. I want to do whatever I can to make things easier for you."

"Thanks." She combed her fingers gently through his hair. "And don't worry about me. The long drive will give me time to gather my thoughts and think of what I want to say to Annabelle's family."

"Well, you of all people understand what it's like to suddenly lose someone you love. I can tell the death of your parents still plays on you."

The lie plays on me, she thought. *I've told you so many I can hardly keep them straight.* "I definitely won't have trouble empathizing. I imagine I'll be late getting home."

"How late?"

"I don't know, but I'll probably spend the whole afternoon with the family. Don't plan on me for dinner."

"Do whatever you need to. I'll hold down the fort." He kissed her forehead. "Relax, will you? I've got you covered. I don't want you worrying about anything here. Just go pay your respects and spend as much time as you need to with Annabelle's family."

"Thanks, *cher*. I appreciate you being so understanding."

She started to turn back to the sink, but Pierce didn't loosen his embrace. Why was he looking at her so strangely?

"Zoe, I've got bad news. I've been debating whether to wait until you get back to tell you this, but you're bound to hear it on the radio."

"What is it?"

"They released the name of the man who was hanged." Pierce fingered her pearl necklace. "It was Remy Jarvis."

"*What?*" It took several seconds for his words to register. "I-I can't believe it." Remy's childlike countenance flashed through her mind as Pierce's image blurred. A tear spilled down her cheek. "Why would anyone want to hurt such a gentle soul? This is devastating."

"I'll say. I can't even imagine the backlash when word gets out."

"Savannah will be crushed. Hebert, too."

"Everyone will." Pierce plucked a tissue from the box and handed it to her. "I'm sorry to add this to the burden you're already carrying, but I didn't want you getting caught off guard. I'm sure it's all over the radio."

Zoe dabbed her eyes. "Poor Emile. He must be inconsolable. Are there any suspects?"

"Not yet. The sheriff is sorting through evidence taken from the crime scene. Babe, you have to try and put it out of your mind for now. You've got another death more pressing at the moment."

Zoe saw the mascara all over the tissue. So much for looking nice. Could this day get any more complicated?

A loud clap of thunder shook the building and reverberated for several seconds.

"You're going to need your umbrella," Pierce said. "It's supposed to rain all day."

"That's all I need." Zoe was suddenly aware of raindrops pelting the window.

"It's a result of the tropical depression," Pierce said. "I just listened to the weather report. The rain is supposed to get heavier between here and the gulf as the day goes on. They're saying to allow extra time if you're driving down the bayou. Traffic could be backed up."

"Okay, I'll leave as soon as I'm ready." *But I'm headed north on I-49.*

Vanessa sat in the rocking chair in Carter's room, the same chair Ethan's parents had used to rock him when he was a baby, and watched as Carter finished building a tower out of plastic blocks.

"Wow, that's amazing," she said. "Just one more."

Carter picked up the last block with both hands, giggling all the while. He placed it carefully on the top of the tower, which swayed ever so slightly, and then let go, his eyes wide with anticipation. It didn't fall.

"You did it! Good job!"

"I want to keep this so Daddy can see it."

"He'll love it. I'm so proud of you. It's not easy building a tower as tall as you are without it falling over."

"I'm a good builder."

"Yes, you are. And you're Mommy's sweet boy. Come give me some of that sugar."

Carter ran over to her, hugged her tightly, then climbed into her lap and nestled in her arms. Was her baby really four already? How much longer would he allow her to engage him in this tender ritual?

"Is the sheriff coming here again?" he asked.

"I don't know. Maybe. He's checking on some things at the manor house."

"He's looking for the candy man, but I don't think he's going to find him."

She combed his mound of thick hair with her fingers. "Why do you say that?"

"Because the candy man can dipsappear."

Vanessa smiled at her son's mispronunciation. "How do you know he can disappear?"

"He told me."

"Did you see him do it?"

"He was *in* the closet. And then he was *all gone*." Carter pushed back and looked up at her, his eyes sparkling, his cheeks dimpled. "It was a magic twick."

"It's okay for you to have a friend that's make-believe. But it's important not to pretend when the sheriff is trying to find him. Sweetie, are you absolutely sure the man you saw in the closet is real and not make-believe? I won't be mad. I just need to know the truth."

Carter sighed. "Mommy, I alweady told you."

"I just need you to be absolutely sure because it's very important to the work the sheriff is doing."

"Is the candy man bad?" Carter ran his thumb and forefinger along the hem of her tank top.

"No one said that. But the sheriff needs to find him and talk to him."

"Well, maybe if we call him, he will come out of the closet."

Vanessa picked up Carter's hand and studied his little fingers. If only it were that simple. How would she ever feel safe at Langley Manor until this mystery was resolved?

"Mommy, what is lynching?"

How had he overheard Ethan and her talking? They had tried to be so careful.

"It's a mean thing some people do to hurt someone else. It's a word for grown-ups, not little boys."

Vanessa held her son snugly and rocked him in silence, her arms around him like a soft blanket. His innocent little mind didn't need to know details, didn't need to see that horrible image.

She still wondered if he'd been affected on a subconscious level when Ethan's cousin, Drew, was shot. Could a ten-month-old be just feet away from the blood spatter and see his mother's frantic response and not be traumatized?

Vanessa sighed. Could people in heaven see what was happening on earth? Did Drew know that his dad and uncles gave the deed to Langley Manor to Ethan and her as a wedding gift—and the money in Drew's trust fund for the refurbishing? At least something good had come out of Drew's senseless murder. She hoped he knew.

The last thing she wanted was for the lynching to be in any way associated with Langley Manor. Didn't the locals have enough generational resentment toward the Langleys without adding this to the mix? Vanessa sighed. *Lord, please don't let the Langley name get pulled into this terrible hate crime.*

Carter looked up and held her face in his hands. "Don't be sad, Mommy. Jesus is your fwend."

She smiled. "Yes, He is. Thank you for reminding me."

"Can I go play now?"

"Of course you can." She gave him one last hug and then helped him down. "I love you so much."

"I love you, too. Bye. I have to go find Georgie."

Zoe drove north on Interstate 49, a downpour impeding her vision. She stayed focused on the taillights of the car about fifty yards in front of her. Remy Jarvis's murder weighed heavily on her, but could she allow herself to deal with that reality before she finished what she had come to do? Wouldn't whatever happened today impact the rest of her life?

She glanced at her odometer. She had about forty miles to go before she arrived in Alexandria. For a split second she was tempted to withdraw all the money from savings and disappear. But how could she walk away from her marriage? From the only man she had ever loved?

No. She had to do this. She had to set the record straight. Wasn't Adele a merciful person—and religious? Surely she could convince the woman that desperate people do desperate things. Surely she could work something out with her so that Pierce never had to know.

God, if You'll just help me get through this, I promise never to tell another lie.

She remembered the first serious conversation she'd had with Pierce shortly after they met, and the lies that had rolled off her tongue....

"So, Zoe Benoit, are you ever going to tell me about yourself?" Pierce had said. "Where are you from? You're no Looziana Cajun. You sound Texan."

"Good ear. I'm impressed. I was born and raised in Dallas." She studied his expression. Would he be able to see through her? "My parents moved there from New Orleans after my dad got a promotion with Kidwell Meat Company. Turns out a number of families who attended Saint Bartholomew's Church with us were Cajun, and we sort of adopted each other and became a community unto ourselves. It was a great way to grow up preserving our Acadian roots. We were close—like family." Whatever *that* meant.

"What brought you to Les Barbes?"

Zoe put on her saddest expression and paused for half a minute. "It's a long story. I-I'm not sure I can talk about it."

"Okay." Pierce placed his hand over hers. "I didn't mean to pry. I'm just so taken with Zoe B's and wonder how you got the idea to open this place. If it's too painful to talk about, I completely understand."

Zoe tingled at his touch. No man had ever caused her to respond that way before. "No, it's okay. Actually I feel more at ease with you than I have with anyone in a long, long time."

"Well, don't feel like you have to tell me anything unless you want to."

Zoe slipped her hand into his. "I really want to. Just bear with me. I get a little emotional." She had wondered about this moment since she changed her name. Would the story she had fabricated about her family hold up? Could she remember all the facts? She had to start somewhere. Pierce was a good person to practice on. "I can't remember a time when I didn't want to open my own eatery. In fact I opted not to go to college so I could work at Etienne's, this incredible Cajun restaurant owned by a couple at church. I learned everything I could possibly take in, including how to make authentic Cajun food and what makes it taste really good."

"How long did you work there?"

"A couple years. The time flew by. I never stopped learning new things."

"So why'd you leave?"

"Something awful happened." Zoe stared at the wall without blinking until her eyes had watered sufficiently. "Our house burned down. My parents were killed. The fire marshal said it was arson, that someone had doused the outside of the house with gasoline. But the police never discovered who was responsible or why they did it."

"Where were you when this happened?"

"At the restaurant. We didn't close until eleven, or I would've been home. Maybe if I had been, I could've warned them and gotten them out. Maybe they'd still be alive."

"Or maybe you would all be dead, Zoe." Pierce gently squeezed her hand. "I can't imagine how horrible it must've been to lose your family like that."

"The worst part"—Zoe made her eyes water until a single tear trickled down her face—"is wondering why I lived and they died." Was she really telling him this pack of lies without even flinching?

"You'll drive yourself nuts trying to figure that out. Maybe God has something special for you to do."

Zoe looked into his compassionate dark eyes and continued the story, almost believing it herself. "I moved in with the Thibodeaux family next door, and they treated me like a daughter. But after a few months I couldn't bear to be in that neighborhood anymore. Everything and everyone reminded me of what I'd lost. After my parents' estate was settled, I moved to Morgan City and went to work at Jourdain's, a really upscale Cajun restaurant. I made friends with the owners' daughter, Annabelle, and eventually we rented an apartment together. I worked at Jourdain's a couple years until I discovered Les Barbes. From the moment I set foot in this gorgeous little town and the Roux River Bayou, my Cajun roots went down, and I knew it's where I belonged."

"It must have been great to feel at home again. So how did Zoe B's come about?"

She took a slow, deep breath. Pierce was such a nice guy. How could she tell him such blatant lies? "I had tucked my inheritance away, hoping someday I'd open my own eatery. I started looking around and saw a sign that this building was for rent. Monsieur Champoux let me sign a lease to rent just half of the first floor and remodel it the way I wanted." At least that part was true.

"It looks great," Pierce said. "Very inviting."

"Thanks. I did the painting and refinished the floors myself. I made the curtains and the tablecloths and found an unbelievable closeout sale on the French country furniture. It took everything I had to get Zoe B's going. And all those years of restaurant experience paid off. The place was a hit and just took off. The locals love it, but I get a lot of tourist business, too."

Pierce moved his gaze slowly around the room. "I just live a couple miles up the bayou, but I didn't realize Zoe B's was here until a month ago. Discriminating Cajun that I am, I'm impressed with the cuisine. Your crawfish étoufée is the best I've tasted. You're doing a great job here. I admire you for following your dream. I love to cook and have always wanted to be a chef, but I have neither the credentials nor the experience. The fact that I've taught history at Roux River High School for seven years means nothing on a résumé for a wannabe chef."

"Pierce, for heaven's sake, you're only thirty-one," Zoe said. "Don't give up on your dream...."

A screechy, scraping sound brought her back to the present, and she realized the rain had stopped and her wipers were still on. She turned them off and backed off the accelerator. All she needed was a ticket stamped with the date and location.

The one thing she had never lied about was her feelings for Pierce. How could she have known when she lied to him about her background that he would win her heart and she would fall head over heels in love with him—and become his wife? Until she met Pierce, hadn't she found men to be despicable and untrustworthy? Could it be any more ironic that now it was she who could not be trusted?

She hated the lies! But what was she supposed to do after the fact? If Pierce ever found out she could rattle off falsehoods like a mantra, would he even be able to stand the sight of her?

God, I'm not a bad person. You know I didn't set out to hurt anyone. I was just trying to survive.

She saw a green highway sign. Only twenty-five miles to Alexandria. She suddenly felt light-headed and queasy. Nothing in her wanted to go through with this.

CHAPTER 10

Pierce Broussard stood next to the table by the window at Zoe B's, missing Zoe and commiserating with Hebert, Father Sam, and Tex about Remy Jarvis's murder.

"Pierce, I hope you don't mind us occupying this table so long," Father Sam said. "Normally we'd have been out of here an hour ago."

"You're fine. Nobody's having to wait to be seated." Pierce put his hand on the priest's shoulder. "You gents stay as long as you like. I'll have Savannah bring you more coffee."

"I tink we're all shell-shocked," Hebert said. "Hasn't been a lynching on da bayou in decades."

Pierce nodded. "So why now? And why Remy?"

"Guess all we can do is surmise," Father Sam said, "until the sheriff catches the lost souls who did this."

Pierce looked out the window as two doves landed on the balcony railing above Sole Mates, the women's shoe store across the street and three doors down. "I know I sound like a stuck CD, but I don't understand why there wasn't a whisper of this beforehand."

"Not everyone carryin' a grudge speaks up before he blows," Tex said.

Father Sam took his glasses and began wiping the lenses with his napkin. "I'm encouraged that Reverend Isaiah Rhodes from Praise Tabernacle expressed his outrage and asked whites not to retaliate, but to wait for the authorities to sort this out. He's a well-respected clergyman. People will listen."

"Reasonable people will," Pierce said. "All we need is for a few *un*reasonable folks to let their anger turn physical. We're liable to have race riots on our hands."

Half a minute of silence went by.

Finally Hebert said, "Did I tell y'all I knew Remy when he was jus' a little *peeshwank?* Kids called him Runt till one year he shot up like a weed and towered over all o' dem."

Tex raised his bushy eyebrows. "I can't picture that Texas-size boy ever bein' a runt."

"Dat was a long time ago." Hebert traced the rim of his coffee cup with his index finger. "I'll tell you sometin' 'bout Remy Jarvis: What he lacked in his brain, he made up for in his heart. Emile loved on him, and it showed."

"I wonder how Emile's doing," Pierce said.

"Da man's brokenhearted." Hebert shook his head. "He's gonna need his friends to hold him up."

"And we will," Father Sam said. "Did I tell you Emile and Remy went to Mass at Saint Catherine's when I was the rector there? I feel like I've lost family."

"We all do." Pierce felt emotion tighten his throat as Remy's daily salutation, "Happy day, everybody," echoed in his head. "I just can't believe such a gentle, decent human being came to the end of his life, hanging from a tree."

⚜

Zoe turned at the open wrought-iron gate, and as she drove toward the grand entrance of the Woodmore House, her gaze took in its grandeur: the huge magnolia trees lining either side of the circle drive, the sweeping lawns dotted with weeping willows, dogwoods, crepe myrtles, and the white gazebo at one side of the flower garden. Had it gotten more beautiful in the past ten years? Or was it just that she had taken it for granted when she worked for Adele?

A silver-haired man wearing a charcoal gray uniform opened her door and tipped the rim of his hat. She immediately recognized him as Julien Menard, Adele's chauffeur.

"Hello, Shelby. Mrs. Woodmore told me you were coming. I'm so glad to see you. You look lovely. The shorter haircut becomes you."

"Thank you." Zoe got out and faced her old friend. She took his hands. "It's great seeing you, too, Julien. You just get more handsome with age. I'm surprised you're still here."

"To tell you the truth, I don't understand it myself. Mrs. Woodmore doesn't go many places these days. She doesn't need a chauffeur. It'd be cheaper for her to call a cab. I'm just grateful. I'd like to put in a couple more years before I retire."

"How's your family?"

"Oh, my sweet Marie is walking the streets of gold. I miss her sorely. But my kids are all married now, and I've got seven grandchildren. Can you believe it? Tell me about yourself." He held up her left hand. "Is that a wedding ring?"

Zoe smiled. "Yes, I'm married to the proudest Cajun you'd ever want to meet. Five years now." *Please don't ask his name.*

Julien's face beamed. "Do you have children?"

"Not yet. One of these days, though."

"What does your husband do?" Julien stole a glance at the sporty blue BMW coupe she was leasing.

"Goodness, look at the time." Zoe stared at her watch. "Mrs. Woodmore expected me five minutes ago. I probably should go inside. Maybe we can talk later."

"Yes, of course. I'll park your car around the side until you're ready to leave. The butler's name is Edward, by the way."

"Thanks."

"It's great seeing you, Shelby. It truly is."

Zoe smiled at her Julien, then straightened her dress and walked up to the front door. Before she could ring the bell, a middle-aged African-American man in a dark suit opened the door.

"Edward, I'm Shelby Sieger," she said. "Mrs. Woodmore's expecting me."

"Yes, ma'am. She's waiting in the sunroom. She said you'd know how to find it."

"Thanks."

Zoe took a slow deep breath, then walked past the polished oak staircase, through the elegant blue and white parlor, and down a long hallway painted deep yellow and trimmed with white crown moldings.

She stopped in the doorway of the glass room, rendered speechless by the splendor of the massive live oaks that formed a basket weave of shade over the exquisitely manicured grounds.

"Heart stopping, isn't it?" Adele's voice had aged, but her southern drawl was a dead giveaway. "Hello, Shelby."

"Hello, Mrs. Woodmore." Zoe turned her gaze to her former employer, who was seated on the gold, blue, and green floral print love seat. Adele's hair was snow white now, and she was too thin, but her charming smile was as disarming as ever. She still wore a simple gold cross around her neck.

"Come here and let me look at you, hon."

Zoe went over to Adele and extended her hand. "I appreciate your agreeing to meet with me on such short notice."

"I was thrilled when you called. I've been praying for you all these years. And your family. I know your mama's health was failing when you left here. Did she pass?"

Zoe's heart began to pound. Was she crazy to think she could do this? How could she undo all those lies—or even remember them all? How could she tell Adele the truth about why she left? What if Adele had her arrested?

"Oh, hon, you're all flushed and perspiring. I didn't mean to upset you. I've just wondered about how things turned out, that's all. Please sit wherever you like. That white chair behind you is luscious."

Zoe took two steps back and sank into the chair.

"Would you care for a glass of iced raspberry tea and some homemade butter cookies? I know how much you like them."

"I'd love some," Zoe said, before she had time to consider whether or not she could keep anything down. "I'm amazed you remember after all these years."

Adele laughed. "I still have my mind, even if the rest of me's withering away." The elderly woman folded her hands in her lap, her faded blue eyes seeming to probe Zoe's thoughts. "I must say I was shocked when you called. I didn't expect to see you again. You said there was something real important you needed to discuss with me."

"There is," Zoe heard herself say. "I-I'm just not sure where to begin."

"Well, start at the beginning, hon. Take all the time you need."

The beginning? Perhaps it was better just to give her the bottom line. If Adele was going to call the authorities, why waste time agonizing over the litany of lies she had told? Her heart nearly pounded out of her chest. How could she have allowed herself to get trapped this way? Was it too late to just get up and run out to her car? It wasn't as though Adele could find her. She didn't even know her legal name.

"Shelby, are you feeling all right, sugar? Your face is a peculiar shade of gray. Let me ring for Edward and have him turn the air conditioner down some. It's awful muggy today, what with the tropical storm carrying on down the bayou and all."

Zoe felt as if her mouth were stuffed with cotton. No words would come out. She had imagined this moment almost every day for the past ten years. Could she actually do it? Did she want to? What had she gotten herself into?

"Shelby, say something, hon. You really look ill...."

She was vaguely aware of Adele's voice and the woman's hand grasping her wrist. Suddenly she was clammy cold and perspiring. Dizzy. What was happening? All she could see was gray fuzz, and it seemed as if one side of the floor had been raised at an angle, and she was slowly sliding off ... falling ... falling ... into nothingness.

Pierce walked slowly through the kitchen at Zoe B's, admiring the way Dempsey Tanner had laid out the buffet of sauces, spices, and ingredients he would need to prepare orders during the lunch rush.

"Very efficient." Pierce patted him on the back. "I'm anxious to see if we get comments on the seafood gumbo."

"We should. It's incredible." Dempsey looked up, his red eyebrows looking shiny under the florescent lights. "Are you ever going to tell me what you added?"

"Are you kidding? Then I'd have to kill you." Pierce laughed. "It's going to remain my little secret as I cling to the hope of surpassing Marie Nadeau in the Gumbo Classic."

"Seriously, boss. This is superb. I realize I'm partial, but I recognize perfection when I taste it."

"Well, I've played around with it for years." Pierce picked up the big spoon and began moving it slowly back and forth in the gumbo. "Marie is probably trying to improve hers, too. Let's just hope she hasn't discovered something that makes hers even better. I really want to win first place—just once. Not that I haven't enjoyed second place. But I feel like I've finally cinched it."

Dempsey wiped his hands on his apron. "Heard anything from Zoe?"

"No. And I'm concerned about her ability to focus on her driving, especially in this heavy rain. She wanted me to stay here and manage things, but I should've insisted on going with her."

Dempsey shook his head. "Zoe would've worried about the eatery. You know how she is."

"I do. That's why I agreed to stay. I hesitated to tell her the news about Remy before she got behind the wheel. But I didn't want her finding out on the radio."

"What'd she say?"

"She cried. She was so fond of Remy. They go way back. But more than anything, she seemed concerned about Emile."

"I know some workers at the sugar refinery who say there's going to be retaliation. It only takes a few angry loudmouths to stir things up."

"I hope not," Pierce said. "This seems to be an isolated incident. We haven't had racial problems in a long time. And leaders in the black community have condemned it."

"That won't bring Remy back."

"No, but it says something about the mind-set of African-Americans here. I don't think anyone believes this was justified. Striking back blindly in a fit of outrage is the wrong response. And that won't bring Remy back either."

"Agreed." Dempsey folded his arms across his chest, his freckled face solemn. "But whoever picked Remy as the victim knew it would shake this community to the core."

Zoe opened her eyes and saw faces peering down at her. Adele. Julien. Edward. What happened? She remembered talking with Adele and feeling sick and dizzy.

"Shelby, you passed out, hon," Adele said. "I need to go call Doctor Willis."

Zoe reached out and took Adele by the wrist. "No. Please. I'm fine. I just skipped breakfast and shouldn't have. I'm a little shaky. My blood sugar is probably low."

"You gave us quite a scare," Julien said.

"I'm fine. Really. I just need to eat something high protein."

"Goodness, now *I'm* feeling a little puny." Adele fanned herself with her hand. "Why don't I have Laura Beth bring you a smoked turkey and cheese sandwich and a glass of milk? How's that sound?"

"Perfect. I'm really sorry to be so much trouble." Could she keep anything down? She had to force herself to eat so she would feel well enough to finish what she had come to do.

"For a moment, hon, I thought I was going to have to contact your husband to authorize medical treatment. I looked through your purse … and got your home phone number off your checks."

The intensity of Adele's questioning gaze caused Zoe to look away, feeling at the same time terrified, embarrassed, and strangely relieved. It was too late to turn back. Adele knew she was not going by the name Shelby Sieger.

"Julien. Edward. You can leave us now," Adele said.

Both men gave a slight bow and quietly left the sunroom, their footsteps echoing in the long hallway. What now? Was Adele going to interrogate her?

Adele pushed the intercom. "Laura Beth, I'm going to have lunch in the sunroom with my guest. Would you please make us turkey and cheese sandwiches on that delicious sourdough? I'd like a bowl of fresh fruit with that. And milk … Yes, that's all for now."

Adele took the lid off a copper box on one of the end tables and reached inside. She took out a couple packages of something wrapped in cellophane and handed them to Zoe. "You probably should eat these cheese crackers right away, hon. You'll feel better."

"Thank you, Mrs. Woodmore. I'm sorry to be so much trouble." *You don't know the half of it.*

Adele resumed her place on the floral love seat, her thin white eyebrows furrowed, her hands folded in her lap. "After you're feeling better, I expect you to tell me why you're *really* here, Shelby—or whatever your name is now. I'm a straightforward person. I know a lot more than you give me credit for."

CHAPTER 11

Zoe looked into Adele's questioning eyes and took in a slow, deep breath and let it out. And then did it again. She just wanted to come clean without being questioned by the police—and without causing the woman any more pain than was necessary. The turkey sandwich had made her feel much better. Why couldn't she find her voice?

"Take your time, hon. If there's something else I can have Laura Beth bring you, just ask. But we're going to sit right here until we clear this up."

Zoe's pulse raced. She could do this. She had to do this. "I-I *want* to clear this up, Mrs. Woodmore. The name you saw on my checks is my married name, Zoe Broussard. I changed my name to Zoe Benoit right before I stopped working for you."

"Whatever for, hon?"

"I wanted to divorce myself from my family and blend into the Cajun culture. I lied to you about my parents. My father was a mean drunk—a real loser. My mother was weak and never lifted a finger to protect herself—*or* me. Not from the beatings. And not from"—Zoe looked at her hands and swallowed the anger that formed a knot in her throat—"not from his inappropriate advances. My brother left home at seventeen and toured with a rock band. I almost never saw him after that. I didn't want the name Sieger, and I didn't plan on ever having a married name since men repulsed me and I planned to be single the rest of my life."

There, she said it. Probably the truest statement she'd ever made. What must Adele think of her?

"I can understand that, hon." Adele's voice was gentle. "But you were in my employ for six years. Why did you wait all that time to change your name?"

Zoe blinked the sting from her eyes. "Partly because I didn't want to have to tell you *why* I was doing it. I couldn't stand the thought of you knowing the ugly truth about my family. I hated feeling like I was trash. I hated the disgusting memories. Sometimes … I even hated my parents. But that's not the only reason I changed my name."

Adele cocked her head. "Oh?"

Zoe felt a hot tear trail down her cheek. "When I gave you notice, I told you I was going back to Devon Springs to take care of my sick mother. That was a lie. Almost everything I told you was a lie. I even lied to cover the lies. I honestly don't remember half of what I did tell you about my family." Zoe took the napkin off her plate and dabbed her eyes. "I just wanted to get away from all that."

"But you were away from it, hon. You were here with me."

"I know, but that's not what I mean." Zoe sighed. "No offense, Mrs. Woodmore, you treated me well, and I appreciated the room and board. Working here got me away from my parents, but I was dependent on you. That's not the future I had in mind."

Zoe looked into Adele's eyes and saw only kindness. Could a distinguished lady like her, a woman of means, ever understand how diminished she had felt by the abuse? Or how desperate she had been for a new life?

"Well, did you find what you had in mind?"

Zoe chewed her lip. "Yes, I did. But I made some … compromises. *That's* why I came here to talk to you."

"Go on."

"Actually what prompted this visit is that I recently started receiving anonymous notes, each with only five words: *I know what you did.* That can only mean one thing, and my life will be ruined if it comes out. What I'm about to tell you is what I think that person knows, and what I believe he wants to hold over my head. I'm not proud of what I'm about to tell you, but I hope you can forgive me and allow me to make things right."

"I'm listening, hon."

Zoe wiped the perspiration off her lip. Once she admitted the truth, she couldn't take it back. What choice did she have now? She'd come too far to shut down.

"Mrs. Woodmore … I-I deceived you. I'm the one who stole your diamond ring. I took it off your finger while you were sleeping. I'm so ashamed. I knew you trusted me, and I took advantage of it."

Adele looked out the window and seemed to stare at nothing. Finally she said, "I'm not surprised."

"You're not?"

"I suspected as much. You were different after that."

"Yet you never confronted me."

"Child, you looked me straight in the eyes—and the police and the insurance company—and said you knew nothing about it. I couldn't prove otherwise. But regardless, it wasn't worth ruining your young life over. I'd grown very fond of you. I suppose I wanted to be wrong."

Zoe felt the heat color her cheeks. "How come you didn't make up a reason to get rid of me? How could you trust me if you thought I stole from you and lied about it?"

"I didn't trust you, but I trusted God. I knew He had a plan in all this. I prayed and prayed that you'd tell me the truth and unburden yourself." Adele folded her hands in her lap. "Took you a while, hon. But here you are."

"Ten years is a lot more than a *while*," Zoe said. "I'm sorry for what I did. I was raised Catholic. I knew it was wrong to steal. But I wasn't going to get ahead unless I got a break—and there it was. I couldn't resist." Zoe wiped a tear off her cheek. "I justified my actions by convincing myself that your insurance would cover it."

"Well, you were right. But that's not the point now, is it?"

"No, ma'am."

"I'd like to know what happened after you took my ring, Zoe."

"I hid it in my closet, in the zippered pocket of a jacket I never wore. Six months later, I found someone in New Orleans who paid me fifteen thousand for it. I opened three bank accounts there and deposited five thousand dollars in each. Then, to avoid suspicion, I waited almost a year before I changed my name. Once it was legal, I gave you notice."

"You're even more resourceful than I thought." Adele's eyes turned to slits. "Why did you choose Les Barbes?"

"I fell in love with the place the first time I laid eyes on it—the live oaks draped with Spanish moss, the old-world architecture, people who seemed connected to each other. I did some checking, and according to the chamber of commerce, the tourist trade would easily support another eating establishment. I picked the surname Benoit so I could pass for Cajun. It worked. The community accepted me with open arms. I can't tell you how much better it felt to be Cajun than poor white trash."

Adele stared out the window. Finally she said, "How did you use the fifteen thousand dollars? That doesn't seem like enough to fund a business."

"I started small, and I worked hard. I signed a lease to rent half an old building in the downtown. I lived in the apartment upstairs and opened the eatery downstairs. I painted the walls and refinished the floors by myself. I bought used tables and chairs and furnishings. I made curtains and tablecloths. It was darling."

"I see. And what name did you give it?"

"Zoe B's. I read everything I could get my hands on about Cajun culture and cuisine. I'm a pretty good cook, and I experimented with recipes until I perfected a few. I hired a chef for several years. And after I married Pierce, he became the chef. We make a good team. I didn't even have to change the name Zoe B's, since my married name is Broussard."

"So you were able to make a go of your business?"

Zoe nodded. "Finally. We're doing really well, but I'll be ruined if the people in Les Barbes find out I acquired the eatery with dishonest money. And my husband, Pierce, can't know. He just can't. It'll break his heart, and it'll be the end of my marriage. That's why I

came here today. I figure whoever left those notes will have nothing
to hold over me once I confess everything to you and work out a plan
to pay you back."

"You make fixing it sound so simple." Adele's chin quivered.
"Did you know my late husband, Alfred, had the ring specially made
for our fiftieth anniversary? It was a surprise. He had gone all the way
to South Africa to find a perfect diamond for the solitaire. He died a
few months later. That ring was the most precious possession I ever
had. It was worth twice what you got for it, but no amount of money
could ever replace the sentiment."

Zoe's heart sank. Could she feel any lower? But would it really
have stopped her from stealing it, had she known Adele felt that way
about it? "I'm sorry. I was only thinking of myself and what it would
take to be out on my own. I never meant to cause you pain. Let
me make this right without involving the police and without Pierce
finding out. I'd die if I lost him. I never thought I could love or trust
a man, but he's more important to me than anything."

Adele was quiet for a moment and seemed to be pondering
something. "So you think the person who left you the notes knows
how you got the money to start Zoe B's and plans to extort money
from you to keep quiet?"

"Sure looks that way. There's nothing else for anyone to hang
over my head."

"Do you have any idea who it might be?"

Zoe shook her head. "Absolutely none. But it's irrelevant if I can
square things with you, without involving the police. Please, could
we just have your attorney draw up papers with a schedule for me
to pay back the money? The statute of limitations has run, and the

police wouldn't be able to make any charges stick. There's no reason for Pierce to know."

"Haven't secrets caused you enough pain?" Adele said. "Wouldn't it be better all the way around if you just told your husband the truth?"

"I can't do that. He loves Zoe Benoit, not Shelby Sieger."

"But she's one and the same, hon."

"Not to Pierce. He thinks I'm Cajun. That means a lot to him. He can't know I lied about that. Or that I stole from you. It'd break his heart. I just want to pay back the money and put all this behind me."

Adele traced the flowers on the arm of the love seat. "Assuming I'm willing to go along with some sort of repayment, don't forget I collected thirty thousand dollars from the insurance company. I'll need to give that money back. There will be questions, hon. And another thorough investigation. All this will come out. They may decide to file a civil suit of some kind."

"That's why you can't tell them I stole the ring." Zoe suddenly felt hot all over. "Please, Mrs. Woodmore. You don't have to give back the money until I pay you in full. I promise I'll give you every penny. I've thought about this, and I can come up with a thousand a month. I'll have you paid back in thirty months. Let's do this quietly so Pierce doesn't find out. Just have your attorney draw up the papers."

Adele twirled a white curl on her temple. "I forgive you for stealing from me, Zoe. And I'm open to your paying me back by the month. But I don't want to be a party to deception."

"The insurance company has already been deceived. After I pay you back, you can return the money to them. They'll be shocked that you're so honest, and I doubt they'll care *why* you returned it."

"But you're deceiving your husband, hon."

"I've never had the courage to tell him about my father's abuse. I told him my parents died in a house fire. He thinks it was my inheritance money that bought Zoe B's. He'll be devastated if he finds out the truth."

"Not if he loves you. It'd take time and effort to regain his trust, but you'd be free of the lies."

"Pierce and I never talk about my past. I lied to him way back in the beginning of our relationship. But it's history. It's not worth risking what I have now to dredge all that up. Please, Mrs. Woodmore. Can't we work out a payment plan and keep it between us? That's the only way I know to stop whoever is sending me the notes."

Adele fingered the gold cross on the pendant around her neck and seemed miles away. Finally she turned to Zoe. "I'll talk to my attorney about drawing up the papers. But I'm going to talk to God about your dilemma. Paying me back is merely a Band-Aid, hon. You're never going to be free as long as you're living a lie."

CHAPTER 12

Vanessa Langley leaned on the filigree iron railing on the gallery outside her apartment, observing the diversity of tourists milling about on the street on a Thursday night.

A kaleidoscope of creative neon signs and the smell of mesquite wood, popcorn, and homemade fudge gave *rue Madeline* a festival-like atmosphere. Near the outdoor tables at Breaux's, children waltzed to the sound of the fiddle and accordion that were as much a part of the Cajun culture as beignets and étoufée.

On the other side of *rue Madeline*, a sleek black horse, its hoofs clicking the pavement, pulled an open carriage filled with T-shirt-clad tourists. From the galleries neighbors watched and waved, some nearly hidden by the abundance of lush greenery and flowering plants. And on the sidewalks scores of buyers and browsers ambled from one shop to another, toting everything from camera bags and kids to plastic bags and cotton candy. Two little boys were marching in place in a puddle left by today's storm.

Les Barbes was fascinating—such a quaint, engaging community with a distinctive old-world charm. Could she have ever imagined when they moved here that they would end up in the middle of another murder investigation? What if the sheriff discovered the mysterious intruder at Langley Manor was involved in Remy Jarvis's hanging? What if they never figured out how the man got in or out with dead bolts in place? How could she ever feel safe there?

She felt Ethan's arms slip around her as he placed his cheek next to hers. "A penny for your thoughts, Mrs. Langley."

"I was just reveling in the festive spirit of *rue Madeline* after dark," she said.

"And …? Maybe wondering whether Sheriff Prejean is going to discover something that will complicate our lives?"

"You know me too well. But even if he can't connect our intruder to the hanging, Ethan, we still have to deal with the fact that this man got in and out when we had the placed locked up tight as a tick."

"Or accept that he doesn't exist and is merely the figment of our son's vivid imagination. Carter's going through a huge adjustment not having his grandparents and Aunt Emily doting on him all the time. We've both heard him talking to imaginary characters."

Vanessa sighed. "But he seems very sure this man is real and not pretend."

"Honey, he's four. Unless the sheriff finds something, I think we have to go on the premise that Carter's 'candy man' isn't real—unless you believe in ghosts."

"Of course I don't. The paranormal thing is ridiculous. But I know I didn't imagine that someone was watching me when I went back out there."

Ethan brushed the hair away from her eyes. "Vanessa, there's so much going on in your head, it's hard to gauge whether the threat was real or whether you were reacting to past traumas."

"My struggle with your cousin's murder has absolutely nothing to do with this."

"Actually it does. We both know that my dad and uncles wouldn't have given us the deed to Langley Manor if Drew were still alive—or the money from his trust fund to help with the renovation. Ever since we moved here, Drew's death has been on our minds, especially when we're out at the house. That has to have an effect on you."

"For heaven's sake, Ethan. I heard a twig snap, and it scared me. That doesn't equate to post-traumatic stress disorder."

"No, but wouldn't you agree that your reaction to speed away from there was extreme? All I'm saying is that our moving here has brought the reality of Drew's murder full circle. And it's possible that you're reacting to it on a subconscious level."

"You're psychoanalyzing me."

He smiled and kissed her forehead. "Just don't be surprised if your PTSD rears its ugly head. Even though Carter can't remember Drew's murder or your panic afterward, at least not on a conscious level, I think that may be why he creates these imaginary characters—nice men who make him feel safe. Especially now, since his environment has changed."

"Why are you just now telling me this?"

Ethan pushed his round glasses up higher on his nose. "I didn't really consider PTSD until you overreacted to hearing the twig snap. You fled—like you did when Drew was shot and you were trying to protect Carter."

"You're right." She put her hand to her chest. "I can feel my heart racing, just thinking about it. That was the most horrible thing I've

ever been through. I was terrified the shooter was coming after us. I
don't know that I'll ever be completely over it."

"Maybe not completely, but you haven't had any anxiety epi-
sodes in the past year. That's why I'm saying that moving here has
brought back memories of Drew's death, and you may be reacting to
things that wouldn't normally evoke that kind of fear."

"That's not what this feels like."

"Honey, I'm not sure you'd be able to tell, if it was. But it's the
best explanation I have for what's happening."

"Well, if Sheriff Prejean doesn't call tomorrow to tell us what
he found, I'm going to call him and push for answers. If he can
match DNA on the lemon drop to anything at the murder scene,
we'll know Carter and I are not imagining things."

Ethan turned and paused. "I heard a door close in the hallway. I
wonder if Zoe made it home."

Zoe no sooner stepped inside the apartment than Pierce was at the
door, putting his arms around her.

"I'm so glad you're home, babe. Thanks for calling when you left
Morgan City. I didn't think you'd be this late."

"I didn't want you to worry," she said. "What a day. I'm spent."

"Want to talk about it?"

Zoe buried her head in his chest. "Not really." *Not ever!* "There's
not much to tell. The priest said a funeral Mass, and the church had
a nice luncheon afterward. Shelby's ashes will be put in the family
mausoleum with her husband's grandparents."

"Shelby? You mean Annabelle."

Slow down, Zoe, before you blow it. "Uh, yes, Annabelle. Sorry, it's hard to think clearly right now. Shelby is Annabelle's cousin, and she sort of took me under her wing for most of the day."

"That was nice of her. Was Annabelle's family glad to see you?"

"They seemed to be. But being with them was a bit sobering. Her death was such a loss to her husband and two children. It was hard to know what to say."

"I'm sure you could've done without the tropical storm. I heard it rained five inches in New Orleans with sustained winds of forty miles per hour."

"It wasn't that bad in Morgan City, but the weather was definitely a pain." Zoe left his arms and flopped on the couch. "How'd it go at the eatery?"

"Fine."

Pierce sat next to her. At least she didn't have to look into his eyes. She hated lying to him.

"Hebert and the guys stayed most of the morning," he said, "rehashing the details of Remy's murder. Even though the coroner says the blow to the head would have killed him almost instantly, it hurts us all to think of how Remy might have suffered before he died. He had to have been terrified."

Zoe shook her head, anger heating her face. "Poor Emile. He must be heartbroken. I can hardly wait until they arrest whoever did it."

"There's talk of retaliation."

"By whom?"

"I don't know, but Dempsey knows some guys out at the sugar refinery who told him there might be trouble."

Zoe turned to Pierce, his prominent nose a reminder of his French heritage. "Did he call Jude's office and report it?"

"No, but I did. I called the police, too. Chief Norman has asked for reinforcements from the Lafayette and New Iberia PDs."

"Good heavens, all we need is for someone to strike a match in this racial tension and set off a firestorm. That won't bring Remy back."

"Well, the police chief and sheriff have cruisers everywhere. Any trouble that starts will be ended quickly."

Zoe's eyes brimmed with tears. "I can't bear to think of Remy being hanged. He was like a child. Why would anyone want to hurt him?"

"The authorities haven't released any more details, other than to say they think he might have been chosen at random in the predawn hour when he was delivering papers. But the media hasn't reported that any witnesses have come forward. As far as I know, no one saw or heard anything—except the creep who called the radio station, and nobody knows who he is."

"For some reason Remy's death hit me a lot harder than Annabelle's. I just can't believe he's gone." Zoe wiped a tear off her cheek.

"His obit was in today's paper. No funeral date was given, since the autopsy isn't completed yet and Remy's body hasn't been released to his dad." Pierce took Zoe's hand and held it. "This was a double whammy for you, babe. Sorry I told you right before you left this morning, but you would have been even more devastated to hear it first on the radio."

Zoe nodded.

"Is there anything else about the funeral or your time with Annabelle's family you want to talk about?"

No! "Honestly, Pierce, there's nothing to tell, other than I'm glad I went and paid my respects. But I couldn't get Remy off my mind. I'm exhausted."

"Why don't I crank down the air conditioner so you can take a nice hot bubble bath?"

A great place to hide! "That sounds wonderful, though I may never cool off again. I think it's still ninety outside with a hundred-percent humidity."

"I'll crank it way down," Pierce said. "It'll help you relax."

Zoe eased into the warm bath and stretched out under a thick blanket of white bubbles scented with honeysuckle. She closed her eyes, aware that her heart was beating too fast.

Why didn't she feel relieved, now that she had confessed everything to Adele? Was it because their agreement wasn't a "done deal" until the papers were signed? Or because the man who had left her the notes still had to be dealt with? Or was it because Adele might be right, that Zoe would never be free as long as she was living a lie? What difference did it make? Hadn't she been living with secrets for as long as she could remember? Wasn't there a point of no return when it came to lying—a point when telling the truth would do more harm than the cover-up?

She'd imagined dozens of times how betrayed Pierce would feel if he found out she'd been lying to him from the beginning. He was a proud man. Would he be able to forgive her—ever? And what if he knew that the woman who took his name, who was going to bear his children, wasn't Cajun after all—and that her own father had sexually abused her? What if he saw her as she had seen herself all those years—defiled and unworthy of love? Would she be left with only lies and brokenness?

Zoe blinked to clear her eyes. Hadn't she cried enough for one day? Shouldn't she be satisfied that Adele had agreed to let her discreetly pay back the money—and without involving the insurance company until after the debt was paid? Thirty months was a long time to be taking that kind of money out of the eatery's income. But how many times in their marriage had Pierce even looked at the checkbook? She would just have to rely on his trusting her to handle the finances and hope she could find ways to cut expenses so the bottom line still showed a substantial increase. Wasn't it ironic that now, when the eatery was finally making a healthy profit, she literally had to *pay* for her mistake?

She closed her eyes and leaned her head back on the foam bath pillow. How different might things be now if she hadn't lied to Pierce when they were just getting to know each other. But would she, even in her most vulnerable moment, have had the courage to tell him about the abuse she suffered? Her father had stolen more than her innocence; he had stripped away her dignity and self-worth. Pierce's love and acceptance helped to silence the taunting fear that somehow the abuse had been her fault. She couldn't lose Pierce. She just couldn't.

CHAPTER 13

Zoe sat at the window table at the eatery, next to Father Sam and across from Tex and Hebert. She knew the morning rush was about to hit and was grateful for a few minutes with her friends to commiserate about Remy. Not that there was much left to say. The mood was grim.

Outside, life went on as usual. Friday's sky blazed lava pink, a gorgeous backdrop for a flock of white ibis flying just above the tree line.

On the gallery above the Coy Cajun Gift Shop, Madame Duval, dressed in a floral shift and clutching what appeared to be a coffee mug, stood at the railing between two overgrown potted plants, waving to someone on the sidewalk.

The bell jingled on the front door, and a young man came in and placed two newspapers on the counter in front of the cash register, and then left without saying anything.

Happy day, everybody! Remy's voice echoed in her heart. Could he really be gone?

"Who's the new guy?" Tex said. "He was here yesterday, too."

"I don't recognize him." Zoe sighed. "He sure isn't friendly."

Father Sam patted her hand. "Maybe he's just a temporary until the *Ledger* finds someone new to take Remy's route."

"Maybe," Zoe said. "But I think this route was tailor-made just for Remy. I have a feeling it'll be absorbed by one of the other route people—maybe even Mr. Congenial there. It's depressing that our sweet, gentle Remy's never coming back."

Savannah brought a fresh pot of coffee to the table and poured refills all around.

"Your orders are up next," she said. "Y'all look miserable. You're going to have to do better than that when I bring your breakfast, or people will think I accidentally served you lemon juice instead of orange."

No one smiled at Savannah's attempt to lighten the mood.

Hebert blew on his coffee. "Dere's no easy way to accept dat Remy's life was stolen from him. Dose swine who did dis are sick *capons.*"

"Sick cowards and then some," Savannah said. "I have a more descriptive name in mind, but it would be unladylike to say it out loud." She clamped her hands over her mouth and walked toward to the kitchen.

"I wonder when the funeral's going to be." Father Sam moved a spoon slowly back and forth in his coffee. "Saint Catherine's isn't big enough to hold the kind of crowd Remy's funeral will draw, especially if it gets national coverage."

"It's already gettin' that," Tex said. "I saw a CNN van parked out at the Roux River Inn. I suspect a lynchin' is big news in this day of political correctness and hate crimes."

Zoe looked out at the morning sky, hot pink quickly fading to pastel. "I wonder if *any* of the networks are brave enough to step up and demand justice when the killer might be black. Everyone's so worried about being politically correct."

"Justice is justice," Tex said. "Who cares what color the jerks are?"

"You're preaching to the choir," Zoe said. "Regardless of what the media does with it, no one here is going to let this go until Remy's killer is brought to justice. I just hope there isn't trouble. All we need is for a bunch of hotheads to take this into their own hands."

"Young lady," Father Sam said, "we've been so busy talking about Remy's situation, you didn't finish telling us about your friend Annabelle's funeral."

"There's nothing more to tell. It was a traditional Catholic funeral Mass." *So now I'm lying to a priest, too?*

"Musta been a mess at da cemetery," Hebert said, "wit da heavy winds and rain down da bayou."

"We didn't go to the cemetery. Annabelle was cremated. The urn with her ashes was put in the mausoleum owned by her husband's relatives." Isn't that what she told Pierce? Suddenly it didn't sound right. "Listen, guys, I need to get to work." Zoe rose to her feet. "Maybe if we talk through our feelings together, we'll figure out how to deal with Remy's murder while we're waiting for the authorities to solve it."

"Let's hope they do," Tex said. "Doesn't sound like they have any leads yet."

"Well, I know sometin' fuh shore." Hebert stared at his hands. "No red-blooded Cajun is goin' to hold his tongue after one o' his own got strung up like a feral hog and left to die...." His voice trailed off, and a runaway tear trickled down his cheek. "Dis town owes it to Emile to make shore Remy's killer don't get away wid dis."

Zoe felt as if her heart were in a vice. In all the years she'd known Hebert, this was the first time she had seen him cry.

Vanessa sat at an oblong table in one of the interview rooms at the sheriff's department, holding Carter in her lap and waiting for someone to talk to her about the results of their investigation at Langley Manor.

"Mommy, why do all the deputies have real guns?" Carter sat Georgie upright on the table. "So they can shoot the bad guys?"

"They don't want to shoot anyone, but the guns are to protect nice people from bad guys who want to hurt them."

"Is the candy man a bad guy?"

Vanessa brushed her hand through his bangs. "We don't know, sweetie. That's what we have to find out. We still don't know for sure there is a real candy man."

"Mommy, I alweady told you he was *weally* in the closet."

Vanessa kissed his soft cheek, which smelled faintly of peanut butter. "I know you did, and the sheriff's deputy wrote it down, remember?"

Carter gave a nod. "Good. How long do we have to stay here?"

"Just until Mommy talks to one of the deputies." She glanced at her watch. It was already after one. What was taking so long? "Why don't you sit over at the little table and put your ABC puzzle together?"

"Okay." Carter slid off her lap and went over and sat at a child-sized table in the corner.

She heard a knock at the door, and then Sheriff Jude Prejean and Deputy Stone Castille stepped into the room.

"Sorry to keep you waiting, Mrs. Langley," Jude said. "We've been inundated with calls and emails and media questions related to the hanging, and I wanted to be in on this."

"Thanks. And please call me Vanessa."

Jude pulled out a chair and sat across the table, Stone next to him. "All right, Vanessa. We'd like to go over what we found."

"*Found?* So there was something?"

Stone opened a file and spread out the contents. He picked up two photographs and handed them to her. "Understand, this isn't something we're releasing to the media, and it's important that you keep it between you and your husband for now. We found three distinct shoe prints on the ground underneath Remy's hanging body. And a fourth in close proximity, which is what the photograph in your right hand shows. The photograph in your left hand shows a shoe print we found at the edge of the woods near the manor house. Notice the distinct shape. It's a match."

Vanessa's pulse raced. "So you're saying at least one of the people involved in the lynching had also been on the grounds at Langley Manor?"

"Not exactly," Stone said. "Keep in mind the shoe prints don't prove any of these four were involved in the hanging. It merely proves they had been at the scene sometime recently—and that one of them had also been on your property. But we did find other evidence that's disturbing."

"What?"

Jude locked gazes with her. "The DNA we found on the lemon drop matches a piece of chewed gum we found near the scene. The person is not in our system, but it is a male."

"Good heavens." Vanessa glanced over at Carter and lowered her voice to just above a whisper. "You're saying this man *was* in the manor house and at the scene of the lynching?"

"No doubt about it."

"Then you have to take my son's description of the man seriously."

"We are," Jude said. "But a black man with white stubble on his face and a pocket full of candy isn't a lot to go on. We're hoping the FBI lab in New Orleans will be able to identify the brand and style of shoe he's wearing. We're already questioning some people in the know in the black community, trying to find out if anyone fitting that description stands out. But I have to tell you it's a long shot."

Fear seized her as she processed the implications. "But how did this man get *in* the house?"

"We think we know." Jude's hazel eyes widened. "We found a door in the back of the closet. It leads to a wooden staircase that descends below ground level to a tunnel that comes out at the edge of the woods."

"What do you mean, 'comes out'?" Vanessa said.

"There's a door, much like a cellar door, that's hidden under some brush. The lock was broken. Anyone who knew it was there could come and go at will."

Vanessa combed her hands through her hair. "Why would the Langleys have built a tunnel? And who would even know it was there? None of the blueprints I saw of the house showed the stairs or the tunnel."

"I couldn't tell you that, ma'am," Jude said. "But we've nailed the trapdoor shut from the inside. I promise you no one's going to get in now."

"Thank you. That part's a relief." Vanessa put her hands around Georgie, a cold chill crawling up her spine. "It's just so scary to think this alleged murderer was in our home—inches away from my son, who can identify him. And that he's still out there."

Zoe sat on the couch in her living room and waited until the hands on the clock showed two o'clock, then keyed in Adele Woodmore's phone number. What if Adele wasn't willing to work with her—what then?

"Woodmore residence."

"Edward? This is Zoe Broussard. May I speak with Mrs. Woodmore, please?"

"Yes, Madame is expecting your call. Hold please."

Zoe jumped to her feet and paced in front of the window, every second that went by sheer agony. All she needed was a little mercy on Adele's part. She would gladly pay her back to stop this blackmailer in his tracks.

"Hello, Zoe."

"Hello, Mrs. Woodmore. Have you had time to have your attorney draw up the papers?"

"He's agreed to get it done by closing time today, hon." She sighed. "I don't mind telling you I'm greatly bothered that we're leaving your husband out of this. Just seems wrong to me."

"It's the lesser of two evils. Pierce just can't find out about this. It'll ruin our lives."

"Are you sure, hon? I just have to believe that your being honest with him can only strengthen your marriage in the long run."

"Not if it destroys it in the short run. Mrs. Woodmore, he has no idea about my sick family or how I got the money to start Zoe B's. What good would it do to tell him now? Please, just work with me."

A long stretch of dead air made her wonder if the phone had gone dead.

"Mrs. Woodmore, are you there …?"

"Yes, I'm here, hon. I'm going ahead as we agreed. Where do you want me to send the papers?"

"Don't send them! I'll drive to Alexandria and sign them—just as soon as they're ready. I'll check back on Monday, how's that?"

"That'll be fine. Listen, Zoe … I just want you to know that I've made this a major prayer concern of mine. I know God doesn't want you to live with this cloud of dishonesty hanging over your head. I've asked Him to intervene."

"Define *intervene*." She knew God listened to Adele. What was she asking Him to do?

"I just want the Lord to make an honest woman out of you, hon, and help you break this cycle of lying. You'll never be free as long as you're living a lie. There I go repeating myself. I've already said what I have to say. It's not my style to coerce you to confess everything to your husband. It has to come from the heart, and that is most definitely your personal business."

"I appreciate that. So just to be clear: You're fine with me discreetly paying you back in monthly installments of a thousand a month?"

"Yes. I'm glad you told me the truth and unburdened yourself. I just hope that sometime soon you'll have the courage to end the deception by telling Pierce the whole truth. I'm sure you were afraid of my reaction, too. But see how it's working out?"

"Trust me, Mrs. Woodmore. It wouldn't work out with Pierce. So I have your word you won't tell him?"

"Oh, you have my word, hon. But I'm not going to stop praying that God will intervene and make this right. It's not going to be over just because you sign the papers."

CHAPTER 14

Zoe sat on a wrought-iron bench in Cypress Park, basking in the warmth of the afternoon sun and bemoaning that Pierce and his kitchen staff felt compelled to keep the eatery feeling nearly as cold as the deep freeze.

At least she had a viable excuse to leave the building so she could get quiet and relish the relief of having squared things with Adele. What was there left to do? Hadn't she confessed every detail of her deception and agreed to pay Adele the thirty thousand dollars over the next thirty months? Adele wouldn't accept any interest. Could the woman have been any kinder? Any more forgiving? So why had she insisted that it wouldn't be over when Zoe signed the papers? Of course it would be over. It was as though a giant boulder had been lifted off her shoulders. What difference did it make now if this mystery man attempted to blackmail her? Or threatened to go to Adele with what he knew? Zoe had beaten him to it.

She breathed in ever so slowly and exhaled, imagining all the tension of her ordeal with Adele leaving her body. She turned her gaze on a handful of white-faced ibis picking through the grass between the pond and the amphitheater. About ten yards directly in front of her, three roseate spoonbills, their feathers two different shades of vibrant pink, sifted the shallow water around the perimeter of the pond. A group of preschoolers occupying a nearby picnic table sang "Happy Birthday" to a little girl with blonde pigtails. Out in the open, about fifty yards from where she sat, two teenage boys took turns throwing an orange Frisbee for a golden retriever.

She heard someone call her name and looked up just as Vanessa Langley let loose of Carter's hand and sent him running toward her.

"Miss Zoe! Miss Zoe! Did you see the pink birds?" he shouted.

Carter came to an abrupt halt directly in front of her, his dimpled cheeks flushed, his eyes bluer than the summer sky.

"They're in the pond," he said, sounding out of breath. "Thwee of them!"

"Aren't they beautiful?" Zoe brushed his thick bangs off his damp forehead. "They're called roseate spoonbills. I know those are hard words for a little boy to say."

"Wosy spoonbells," he said proudly, clutching Georgie to his chest.

Close enough. Zoe smiled and gave him a hug, then looked up at Vanessa. "Fancy meeting you here."

Her new friend looked lovely in a yellow sundress and designer sandals, her long dark hair pulled back and tied with a matching scarf. Did she even sweat?

"I wouldn't normally go walking in the heat of the day," Vanessa said, "but Carter was such a good boy while we waited to speak with the sheriff that I took him out for ice cream and let him play on the playground. We were on our way back to the apartment when we spotted you."

"I'm just out here thawing out," Zoe said. "It's hard to regulate the air-conditioning in our building. And in order to keep the kitchen comfortable, Pierce has to crank it down lower than I would like. At least customers don't complain."

"Always feels comfortable to me," Vanessa said.

"Good. So did the sheriff have anything more to say about the investigation at the manor house?"

"Actually he did." Vanessa tilted Carter's chin upward. "Sweetie, would you like to play on the slide a few more minutes?"

"Yay! Come on, Georgie."

Vanessa smiled as Carter raced toward the slides, Georgie tucked under his arm. "He's hardly turned loose of that stuffed beagle since we left Sophie Trace. I'm surprised he didn't go back to sucking his thumb."

"It was a big adjustment moving here, wasn't it?"

Vanessa nodded. "Exciting though. We're all looking forward to the renovation process at the manor house. We just never expected to be in the middle of a murder investigation."

"Did the sheriff find something?"

"Actually he did. I haven't even told Ethan yet. It's a lot to process."

"Well, if you want to process out loud," Zoe said, "I'm a good sounding board."

"The sheriff asked me to keep it between me and Ethan. Can you keep a secret?"

"Absolutely."

Vanessa sat on the bench, her arms folded, and seemed lost in thought for a moment. Finally she said, "We know for sure there was an intruder at the manor house."

"How?"

Zoe listened intently as Vanessa told her about the matching DNA on the lemon drop found at Langley Manor and chewing gum found at the crime scene. And about the staircase and secret tunnel.

"Good heavens," Zoe said. "So Carter *didn't* imagine the man in the closet."

"Looks that way. The same shoe prints were cast at both places, but that doesn't really prove the intruder was involved in the lynching, so the sheriff isn't releasing the information to the media. Other than Pierce, you need to keep this to yourself."

"I will." Zoe studied Vanessa's profile and her long eyelashes. "Did you and Ethan know about the tunnel?"

"No. And my curiosity's on tilt. I'm sure the blueprints don't show a door in the back of the closet or the stairs and tunnel. I wonder if Ethan's great-grandparents even knew about it. They were the last to live in the house. They did a lot of renovating, but never knocked out walls."

"I'm curious too," Zoe said. "At least the trapdoor is locked from the inside so you don't have to worry about the intruder anymore."

"But he's still out there. That gives me the creeps. Especially the thought that he might have been involved in the lynching." Vanessa twirled a lock of her hair. "Pierce told me the victim was a friend of yours."

"He was. Remy delivered newspapers to Zoe B's every morning for the past ten years. He was like a little brother. So innocent. He was thirty-something but with the mind of seven-year-old. Killing him was no different than killing a child." Zoe blinked away the sadness. Where was she going to get the strength to grieve Remy's death when she had just invested every ounce of emotional energy into cleaning up her past?

"I'm really sorry," Vanessa said. "Such a senseless crime."

"Remy was well-loved in Les Barbes. Let's just hope his murder doesn't trigger violence before the authorities figure out who did it."

"I'm on overload. My head is spinning." Vanessa rose to her feet. "I hate to run, Zoe, but I've been gone all afternoon. I need to get my pork chops in the oven. Ethan will be home soon."

Vanessa took of sip of sweet tea and glanced over at the open door, watching Carter playing with his toy submarine in the bathtub.

"I'm anxious to find out if your dad or uncles knew about the tunnel," Vanessa said.

"My guess is they didn't." Ethan pursed his lips, his eyebrows arched above his round glasses. "I want to know *all* the secrets of that old place and write them down before they're lost forever."

"Me, too. I'm going to dig out the rest of Augusta Langley's diaries. Maybe something she wrote will give us a clue."

"Well, before we start knocking out walls, I'd sure like to know the significance of the tunnel. It might be worth preserving. Josiah Langley went to a lot of trouble to put it in. The least we can do is find out why."

"I'd like to walk through it. Maybe the reason for it being there will become obvious."

"I'll go with you." Ethan took off his glasses and rubbed his eyes. "This is intriguing. How do you suppose the guy Carter saw in the closet found out about the tunnel? Maybe he just discovered the trapdoor at the edge of the woods? Then again, how likely is that when it was hidden under brush?"

"Not very. And right now he's our biggest problem. He's still out there. When he can't get the trapdoor open, he might break in."

"Honey, why would he do that? He has to know the police are investigating. If he's smart, he'll get as far away from here as he can."

"What if he's not smart?"

Ethan took her hand in his. "Then he'll get caught even faster. Every law-enforcement agency in the state has been alerted. He, or the other persons involved, are bound to do something suspicious. He'll be caught eventually. We just need to trust the Lord and try not to worry."

"I'm angry that he's defiled your family's heirloom."

"The crime didn't happen at Langley Manor, Vanessa. Why does the fact that he was in the house have to taint the family heirloom?"

"I don't know. It's creepy to think he was in there. Maybe they were *all* in there."

"Maybe. The house is just rooms and doors. The fact that these guys might have slept there and the fact that there's a secret tunnel just adds mystery and intrigue to the history of Langley Manor and could be just as fascinating to our B-and-B guests as ghost stories."

Zoe walked into the office and flipped the light on, then let the door close and lock behind her. She realized she had stepped on something and looked down. Under her shoe was an envelope.

"I wondered when I'd get the next one," she said out loud. "It doesn't matter what you know. I'm one step ahead of you." She reached down and picked up the envelope with her name typed on the front. She slit it open and unfolded the note, which had the same type of letters cut from a magazine. But the message was longer this time: *I know what you did. It's going to cost you. We need to meet. Tell no one. Wait for instructions.*

Zoe's neck muscles tightened. How dare he tell her what to do? Who did he think he was? Should she save this note with the others, or shred them all? She read it again, her mind racing in reverse, trying to figure out who could be doing this. A number of men worked for Adele in the six years Zoe did, but most of them worked outdoors, and she couldn't even remember names and faces. How could one of them know that she had stolen the ring—especially when the police finally dropped the matter? And how did he figure out where she relocated—and her married name? And why wait ten years to blackmail her? None of it made sense.

Zoe exhaled and stuck the note in her pocket. He could make all the demands he wanted. But the threat to her had been over the minute Adele knew the truth and agreed to let her pay back the money. Zoe was eager to meet with this creep and tell him herself—and before Pierce accidentally intercepted another of his notes and started asking questions.

CHAPTER 15

The next morning, Zoe walked into the dining room at Zoe B's and spotted Savannah in the waiting area, a bucket on the floor and a mop in her hands.

"There you are," Zoe said. "What are you doing?"

"I spotted footprints over here and thought I'd pass a mop. We still have a few minutes before we turn on the Open sign."

Zoe glanced outside at the gray dawn, her thoughts turning to Remy. How many times had she turned on the Open sign and unlocked the door, only to find Remy standing outside with the newspapers?

"Okay, that's better," Savannah said. "I'll go plug in the coffee-makers. Let the Saturday morning rush begin."

"Wait, I need to ask you something. Did you notice a new male customer that came in alone a few times this past week?"

"Define new."

"Just someone you're not used to seeing who kept coming back all week."

"Not really. A Mr. Shapiro who's staying in Lafayette on business has been in several times—but always with another man. He said he ran into you and Pierce the other night and you gave him coupons and invited him to try us." Savannah smiled. "He's hooked."

"Anyone else?"

Savannah shrugged. "Not at the moment. I'd have to think about it. You looking for someone specific?"

Just the creep who keeps slipping notes under my door. "Not really. I've given out a lot of coupons to men and was just curious if they're using them."

"By the way," Savannah said, "did you ever pick out a uniform?"

"I found something I like, but I'd like to know what *you* think. I thumbed through the catalog a hundred times, and I'm still inclined to go with a black skirt and white blouse. I really don't want them to look like uniforms, and it's unfortunate I have to do this at all. But I've had it with being the bad guy when one of the waitresses comes to work dressed inappropriately—present company excluded—and I have to send her home to change. Would it bother you to wear the same thing every day?"

"Not at all, especially if it's stylish. It'll be a relief not to buy so many clothes."

"Actually the blouse is girly. It's short sleeve with a sweetheart neckline and looks nice tucked in or left out. The skirt is straight and I want it just below the knee. I honestly think the outfit's flattering."

"So when do I get to see it?"

"I'll bring samples in next week and let you try them on. You wear a size two, right?"

"A two or a four, it depends."

"I'll bring both. All right, you go plug in the coffeemakers. And

I'll plug in the sign and unlock the front door. I don't think I'll ever get used to Remy not being on our doorstep when we open."

Zoe unlocked the door, surprised when Hebert opened it and came in. He was dressed in too-short khaki pants and an unironed blue shirt. At least his white socks matched today and went with his athletic shoes.

"Well, aren't you the early bird? How are you feeling?"

Hebert kissed her on the cheek, his whiskers chaffing her face. "*Commes les vieux.*"

"Like the old people? What makes you say that? Aren't you feeling well?"

Hebert put his hand on his heart. "Dis ting dat's happened to Remy makes me feel all ninety-four years. I was wid Emile last night. He can barely speak."

Zoe stroked his back. "Come in and have some coffee. Being with friends will help."

She led Hebert to the table next to the window. "We'll help each other through this. We're not going to let whoever killed Remy kill our spirits. We have to be strong and keep going. It won't always hurt this much."

Hebert's eyes brimmed with tears, and he looked outside. "I know dat in my head. Just doesn't feel dat way right now."

Zoe, overwhelmed with empathy, fought not to cry and was relieved when the front door opened and Father Sam came inside.

The priest, his full head of white hair neatly combed, walked over to the table and sat across from Hebert. "Hello, friends." He shot Zoe a questioning look. "Rough morning?"

"Hebert was with Emile last night," she said.

Father Sam put his hand on Hebert's. "I wasn't as close to Remy and Emile as you were. But I'm sad too. And angry. I want the authorities to find the person responsible and punish him for this horrendous crime."

Hebert nodded. "Dey will. Folks won't let dis go. Did you see all dose media vans parked outside da courthouse?"

"I sure did," Father Sam said. "I've never seen such a sight here before. You'd have thought we had a terrorist attack or something."

Zoe raised her eyebrows up and down. "Didn't we? A hate crime *is* terrorism, even if the terrorists are homegrown. And just because only one man was targeted doesn't make it less vicious."

Tex came in the front door and raised his hand. "Mornin', everyone." He walked over to the table and settled into the chair next to Hebert. "We've got us a little media madness out there—all the major cable channels plus Lafayette, Houma, and New Orleans—as far as I could tell. Could be more. Things are heatin' up, and the sheriff still isn't sayin' whether they have any suspects. But I'm not sure how much he can say durin' an open investigation either."

Savannah came to the table and started filling cups with coffee. "Well, he'd better say *something,* unless he wants folks to start reading between the lines. It's better if they know he doesn't have anything so they don't start speculating. That's how rumors get started."

Zoe was tempted to tell them about the shoe prints, the DNA, the secret tunnel, and the suspect's connection to Langley Manor, but Vanessa had made it clear she couldn't say anything.

"My guess," Zoe said, "is that Jude's working every possible angle. He's got to do everything right. The whole world is breathing down his neck."

Hebert picked up his cup and blew on his coffee. "Dat's fuh shore."

Zoe walked into the office for the fourth time that morning, hoping to find an envelope with "instructions" on how to make contact with the man who intended to blackmail her. What was taking so long? She could hardly wait to see his face when she informed him that Adele knew everything and he wasn't going to get a nickel from her. It was time to end this before it went any further.

She glanced at her watch. Noon. She was sleepier than she was hungry. Why not go upstairs to her apartment and put her feet up—catch a power nap to help offset her restless night?

She left the office, then walked up the stairs and unlocked the door to her apartment. On the wood floor in the entryway was an envelope with her name typed on the front! She picked it up, her heart nearly pounding out of her chest. She grabbed the letter opener and slit the envelope, then pulled out the note—more letters cut from a magazine and pasted on: *Roux River Park. Landry Trail. 5:00 p.m. Wait at the first turn. I'll find you. Tell no one.*

She knew the exact spot. Not that she was entirely comfortable meeting the mystery man in those dark woods. But it made sense he didn't want to be seen with her. Would she recognize him? It almost had to be someone who had worked for Adele.

She was curious to find out how much he knew—and how he had come to know it. Hadn't her clandestine meeting with the jewelry dealer been off the books? Hadn't he paid her with cash? Hadn't the money been deposited in three bank accounts in the name of Zoe Benoit? Shelby Sieger no longer existed. How could anyone have figured that out—and that she had moved to Les Barbes? She had left no forwarding address.

Zoe flopped on the couch and stretched out, every muscle in her body begging for rest. Hadn't she been smart to go to Alexandria and confess everything to Adele? No way was she letting this guy turn her life upside down. All she had to do now was meet with him, tell him why he was wasting his time, and walk away.

Jude Prejean sat at the old oak desk in his office, his hands clasped behind his head, his gaze set on the round, white columns of the Saint Catherine Parish courthouse across the street. The fresh white paint made the historic building seem to glow in the hot July sun.

At the corner of Courthouse and Primeaux a vendor stood on the sidewalk, selling andouille corn dogs.

Jude glanced at his watch. Noon. He listened intently. Now he could hear them. Not far away, the bells of Saint Catherine's rang out, announcing it was time for the noon recitation of the Angelus. An old man sitting on the courthouse steps took off his hat and bowed his head.

Jude bowed his head in kind and folded his hands as he had done at noon for as long as he could remember. How much longer would the bells be tolerated in Les Barbes? How long before some secular progressive who had no respect for this sacred tradition argued that ringing the bells violated the separation of church and state?

He silently recited the words to the Angelus. *The angel of the Lord declared unto Mary, and she conceived by the Holy Ghost. Hail Mary, full of grace, the Lord is with thee....*

"Sheriff?"

Blessed art thou among women, and blessed is the fruit of thy womb, Jesus....

"Sheriff, I'm sorry to interrupt, but there's been a new development."

Jude opened his eyes and tried to hide his annoyance. "What development?"

Aimee Rivette stepped into his office, the dark roots in her bleached hair taking away from her otherwise professional image. "We have an African-American male in the first interview room who has confessed to hanging Remy Jarvis. I thought you'd want to sit in on this."

"You thought right." Jude stood and followed her out into the bustling detective bureau, then kept stride with her as they walked down the hall. "What do we know about him?"

"He came in on his own and doesn't want legal counsel," she said. "Name's Marcum Terrell. Age forty-two. Lives out on Roux River Road, near the sugar mill. Divorced. Currently unemployed. No criminal record. Has ties to a black pride group in New Orleans called BAD—Blacks Against Discrimination."

"Did you ask the New Orleans PD about this group?"

Aimee nodded. "The group spews a lot of anger toward police. A number of their members and organizers have been arrested for disorderly conduct. Their aim is to draw attention to racial profiling and police brutality against blacks."

"Are they known to be violent?"

"That's the thing. Not really. They're more mouth than muscle. I guess Mr. Confession took it to the next level."

Jude opened the door to interview room one and let Aimee go in first. "Mr. Terrell, I'm Sheriff Jude Prejean, and this is Deputy Chief Aimee Rivette." He sat at the table opposite Terrell, next to Aimee. "I understand you have something to tell us."

"I hanged Remy Jarvis," Terrell replied. "From a big live oak at the old Vincent place."

"I see." Jude tented his fingers and paused for half a minute, letting his authority fill the room. "Why would you do that?"

"He was white. That's all the reason I needed."

"Hanging a white man was a pretty bold move."

"So was hangin' a black man. How many black men have been lynched in Saint Catherine Parish?"

"None in the past thirty years," Jude replied. "So why did you just now get motivated to do this? Did your involvement with BAD play into this? We understand you've been to a few rallies."

Terrell's eyes narrowed. "BAD had nothin' to do with it. I did this on my own."

"Why'd you come forward?"

"It was just a matter o' time before you found me. I hate lookin' over my shoulder. I'd just as soon get it over with."

"All right. Let's talk about the murder. Where was the scene in proximity to the farmhouse?"

"Fifty yards up the bayou. Why're you askin' me what you already know?"

"What kind of rope did you use?"

"Just plain hemp rope from my shed."

"What was the victim wearing?"

"I didn't pay attention. I was kinda busy."

Jude leaned forward on his elbows, his jaw set. "How could you hang a man and not notice what he was wearing?"

"I'm pretty sure he had on shorts and a T-shirt. Yeah, that's it. I think the T-shirt had somethin' written on it."

"Where'd you kill him?"

Terrell's eyebrows came together. "I hanged him where you found him at the Vincent place. Watched him struggle and kick and choke." He laughed. "Kind of beats all, don't it? A black man lynchin' a white man?"

Jude wanted to grab the guy by his collar and slap the smug grin off his face. Instead he breathed in slowly and counted to ten and then exhaled. "I'm curious how you single-handedly restrained a guy who outweighed you by sixty or seventy pounds, got him to the Vincent farm, and then strung him up."

Terrell shifted in his chair. "I held a gun on him. He was scared and beggin' for his life. It was funny. And pathetic."

"Really?" Aimee pursed her lips. "Because Remy had the mind of a seven-year-old child. A child might beg to go home—or to see his mom or dad. But a child wouldn't beg for his life. He doesn't understand death."

"Well, that's what happened. You weren't there."

And I'm beginning to think you weren't, Jude thought. *This isn't adding up.* "Mr. Terrell, where's the gun you held on Remy?"

"I panicked and threw it in the river. That was before I decided to confess."

"What kind of gun?"

"A Glock .45."

"Let me make sure I understand this," Jude said. "You never fired it, and there's no way we could prove you used it in the commission of the crime, and yet you threw a fine gun like that in the river?"

The expression left Terrell's face. "I said I panicked. Look, I just confessed that I hanged Jarvis. You have to tell the media. People want the truth."

"Then you're going to have to plug up the holes in your confession."

"What holes? I did it. What more do you need to know?"

Aimee folded her arms across her chest. "There's an aspect of Remy's death you're leaving out. Tell us what it is, and we'll go straight to the media. Every cable channel in the country is on pins and needles, waiting for us to release the name of the killer."

"I told you I hanged the guy. What more do you want from me?"

"The truth," Jude coaxed. "So why don't you stop playing games and just admit you slit his wrists and let him bleed out?"

"Oh, thaaat." The corners of Marcum's mouth curled up. "I only did it to tranquilize him so I could get the noose around his neck. It was fun, like killin' him twice. But I didn't have any help. I did it all myself."

"What did you use to slit his wrists?"

"My pocket knife. But I washed it in Clorox. You're not going to find blood on it."

"That's enough." Jude shot Aimee a knowing look. "We're done here. Deputy Chief Rivette will see you out."

"Come on, Marcum." Aimee stood. "Looks like you're not going to make headlines after all."

"But I just confessed *everything!* I'm guilty of a hate crime. You have to arrest me."

Aimee took him by the elbow. "You're not the killer."

"But I *am* the killer. I did it. I hung Remy Jarvis. What part of my story doesn't fit? Maybe I just didn't say it right. Ask me again. Let me prove it to you."

Jude shook his head. "You're not our guy, Mr. Terrell. There are details we tried to get you to supply. It's obvious you don't know. We're looking for a killer, not someone who's craving media attention."

Aimee walked out with Marcum Terrell, and Jude folded his hands on the table and let out a loud sigh. They were right back where they started.

CHAPTER 16

Zoe leaned against the trunk of a massive live oak that shaded the concession patio at Roux River Park. An elderly man, his arms folded and head bowed, was asleep in a white plastic lawn chair next to a picnic table where a woman and three school-age children were eating snow cones. The parking lot was filled with cars, and the swimming pool was packed, but she didn't see many people walking in the park. Probably too hot.

Zoe came dressed in capris and a tank top and a comfortable pair of walking shoes. She glanced at her watch. *4:50.* Time to get this over with. She breathed in slowly and let it out, then began walking toward the woods and the sign that marked the starting point on Landry Trail.

She wondered if the mystery man was already waiting for her at the first turn. She hadn't seen anyone enter or leave the trail in the ten minutes she'd been standing near the concession patio. Her stomach felt as if an army of tiny soldiers were marching on it. Was it over-the-top reckless, meeting a stranger at a secluded place? She reached into her pocket and felt the mini can of pepper spray. There wouldn't be a whisper of a breeze in the woods—should she need to

take aim. Why was her heart beating so fast? All she had to do is tell
the truth for a change.

Zoe stopped in front of the attractive cement marker trimmed
in red brick.

Landry Trail 2 1/4 miles

Children under 16 must be accompanied by an adult

Stay on designated pathway

Could she go through with this? An image of Pierce popped
into her mind. She had to do this. If he found out she'd lied to him
from the beginning, how could he ever believe anything else she told
him—especially that she loved him with all her heart? And who would
patronize Zoe B's once word got out that she was a thief and a liar?
They would both lose everything. It was too late to turn back. She had
to silence this man. Or be ruined.

Zoe walked past the marker and onto the trail, instantly hit with
the scent of damp earth and the noticeably cooler temperature of dense
shade. If she remembered correctly, the first turn was about fifty yards
ahead. She walked slowly on the uneven earthen path, glad that she had
thought to wear walking shoes, listening for footsteps behind her or any
sign that someone might be following her from behind the trees.

She felt a sharp prick on her neck and slapped the spot. Why
didn't she think to put on insect repellent? Though the chances of
her getting West Nile virus were slim compared to the harm this man
could do with what he knew.

Zoe stopped and breathed in slowly and then exhaled slowly. She just needed to stay focused and look confident. Tell him that she had confessed everything to Adele, that the law couldn't touch her because the statute of limitations had run, and that there was nothing he could hold over her head. Then hope he believed her and would leave her alone.

Jude went into the conference room and looked down at the table, facts and photographs from the Jarvis case spread out from one end to the other. His eye fell on the photos of the shoe prints cast at the scene.

He took his cell phone off his belt clip and punched in the speed-dial numbers for Chief Detective Gil Marcel.

"This is Marcel."

"When are we supposed to get the analysis of the shoe impressions?" Jude said.

"It'll be at least Monday, Sheriff. Maybe longer. I told them to put a rush on it, and that if they didn't believe it was high priority, to turn on CNN, Fox, and every other cable channel."

Jude sighed. "Yeah, okay. Thanks."

"Sorry our suspect turned out to be a fruitcake with a pathological desire for notoriety."

"I'm sorry too. What else have you learned about him?"

"Terrell worked at a food chain warehouse until a year ago. He got into an altercation with black coworkers who said he wasn't doing his share of the work. He left and never went back. He's definitely unstable, but nothing leads us to think he's capable of murder. We're looking into who Terrell's been talking to and where he spends his time. If there's a connection to the case, we'll find it."

"We don't have time for *ifs*. Race relations in this town just got shoved back thirty years! There's no way Marcum Terrell did this, so find out who did. I want his head on a stick!"

There was a long moment of dead air.

"Yes, sir," Gil finally said. "We're on it."

"Gil, wait …" Jude switched the phone to his other ear. "I didn't mean to bark. I'm just feeling the heat. The governor called a few minutes ago—right after the mayor called—right after Police Chief Norman called. In fact the phone hasn't stopped ringing."

"I know there's a lot of pressure to make an arrest, sir. And we're working around the clock and using every available resource to find whoever's responsible. We don't owe anyone an apology for doing our job."

"No, we don't. Is anyone in the black community talking?"

"Not really," Gil said. "I haven't sensed people holding out. It seems to me that they genuinely don't know who's responsible. They'd have to be nuts not to share information with us when there's talk that angry whites are about to march across the railroad tracks."

"We need to partner with Chief Norman's officers and make sure that doesn't happen."

"We are, sir. But it's hard to do anything about rumors."

Zoe stopped on the earthen trail, the forest denser than she remembered it, the canopy tighter. She listened carefully, but the only sound was birds chirping. Perspiration rolled down her back. Had the walk required that much effort? Or was it just that, without a breeze, even the shade was stifling in this humidity?

She fixed her gaze on the bend in the trail up ahead and couldn't seem to move her feet. What happened to the confidence she'd brought with her? Was this insane? Was it too late to turn back? Her heart began to pound and then pound wildly, like the rhythmic beating of a tribal drum. How did she talk herself into this? Suddenly it seemed like a very bad idea.

She started to turn around and go back, but in the next instant was in a choke hold with something sharp pressed against the side of her neck.

"Make a sound and you're dead," said a male voice. "Keep your hands where I can see them and move forward nice and slow. I'll guide you where I want you to go. Got it?"

Zoe nodded and put her hands up. He grabbed her hair from behind and pushed her forward. She took a step and then another and another. Why the show of force—to intimidate her? To establish the upper hand?

When she got to the bend on the trail, which angled left, he yanked her hair and forced her to the right and off the path, deeper into the woods. The ground beneath her was soft and muddy. Mosquitoes swarmed around her and lit on her exposed skin. She endured the bites, not daring to move her hands to swat the culprits—or to reach in her pocket for the pepper spray.

Finally the man pulled back on her hair until she stopped, the knife blade now pressed between her shoulder blades.

"I'm not resisting," she said. "There's no need to bully me."

"I'm going to turn you around. If you make a sound I don't like,
I'll push this blade all the way through you. Is that clear?"

"Yes."

He spun her around, his hand holding tightly to her wrist, and
she looked up into the face of—Angus Shapiro. "*You?* It was you who
left the notes? Why? What do you want from me?"

"Oh, I think you know."

"Is this about the ring? Because I told Adele the truth. She knows
everything."

"I don't know anything about an Adele or a ring. I want my
money."

"Money?"

He laughed. "Don't play dumb with me. You pulled a fast one
when your parents died. You collected the inheritance money and
split before I got paid. But I always knew I'd find you one day."

"What are you talking about? My parents aren't dead. Frank and
Raleigh Sieger live in Devon Springs, Texas."

"Nice try. But your maiden name was Benoit, and your parents
were Pierre and Violet Benoit. You grew up in Dallas. Your parents
made their living trafficking heroine. They owed me almost a hundred grand when they died in the house fire. You should've paid me
before you pocketed the inheritance money and split."

"No, you've got the wrong person. I changed my name from
Shelby Sieger to Zoe Benoit. The real Zoe Benoit is out there
somewhere. Their daughter is out there. It isn't me! I didn't inherit
anything."

Shapiro rolled his eyes. "Give me a little credit, will you? I just
happened to be in Lafayette a couple weeks ago and read a feature

story in the Sunday paper about an eatery called Zoe B's that was celebrating its tenth anniversary."

Oh no, she thought. *Why did I let Pierce talk me into doing that interview?*

"What made my ears perk up," Shapiro said, "was that the young entrepreneur's parents died tragically in a house fire in Texas. And that she took her inheritance, moved to Les Barbes, and started an authentic Cajun eatery called Zoe B's. How she went from the name Zoe Benoit to Zoe Broussard when she married her husband, Pierce, and never even had to change the name of the eatery. Any of this sound familiar?"

Zoe locked gazes with Shapiro. What could she say? Was she finally caught in her own web of lies?

"Cat got your tongue, Zoe?" He tightened his grip on her wrist and held the knife blade to her cheek. "Okay, this is what you're going to do. You're going to wire the hundred grand your parents owed me to my offshore account. This is your lucky day. I've decided not to charge you interest or carve you like a totem pole—*if,* and *only* if you do what I say."

"Please, you've got the wrong person," Zoe said, her voice quivering. "Years ago I-I read about the Benoits dying in a house fire and their daughter, Zoe, surviving. I grew up with an abusive father, and I'd been planning to change my name and start a new life. I liked the name Zoe Benoit and I wanted to pass for Cajun, so I changed my name to that and kept the story about my parents dying in the fire. That's the truth. I swear."

"Don't insult my intelligence. You knew your parents owed me money. You wanted to keep it for yourself." He pushed the tip of the knife into her cheek, and she felt the sting as it pricked her skin. "You skipped out and stuck me with a debt that almost got me killed. Now you're going to pay that debt." He touched her bleeding cheek, then wiped his finger on her tank top. "Or you're going to die."

Zoe felt light-headed and wondered if she was going to faint. What had she gotten herself into?

"Believe me, you don't want to mess with me. I've got a real mean streak."

"If I cashed in everything we have, I couldn't come up with a hundred thousand dollars. I'm not even sure I can borrow that much. We just took out a business improvement loan so we could repaint the building and update our kitchen."

"Figure out something. You have until the banks close on Monday. Just be sure it's ready to wire."

"What account number?"

"You'll hear from me again before then."

"There's no way I can get that much money without my husband knowing about it, especially if we have to sign something."

"So tell him. But I'll be watching and listening. If either of you goes to the cops—or tells someone else who does, I'll know. And it'll be the last thing you ever do. Oh … did I mention I'm really good at disguises? And accents. Angus Shapiro isn't my real name either. So going to the cops won't get me caught. It'll just get you killed."

"You're actually threatening to kill me if I can't get the money?"

"It's not a threat. It's a promise."

He shoved her to the ground, and she noticed a handgun tucked into his waistband. In the next second he disappeared into the woods.

Zoe got up off the soggy ground, her shoes and clothes damp and soiled, blood trickling down her cheek. She was vaguely aware of mosquito bites that itched and burned. How was she going to explain her appearance to Pierce? How was she going to tell him that she had lied to him from the beginning? And because of her deception, everything they valued was in jeopardy—maybe even their lives?

She brushed her hands together and trudged back to Landry Trail and started walking back to the starting point. What if she ran into someone she knew? What would she say? That she fell on the trail? Cut her face on a rock? She probably looked as though she'd been attacked.

Terror seized her. How was she going to get a hundred thousand dollars? What if that didn't satisfy him? Or what if he planned to kill her anyway? She had seen his face. Even if he was a master of disguises, she had heard his voice. Would he really let her walk away?

Losing her life seemed less frightening than losing Pierce. Would he even speak to her again when he found out she'd deceived him? And that the only reason she was telling him anything was because she was forced?

Zoe started to cry. *God, what have I done? I've ruined my life. I've wrecked my marriage. All I ever wanted was a normal life. I never meant for any of this to happen. I'm so tired of living a lie. But what kind of life will I have if I tell the truth?*

Maybe the best thing she could do was disappear. But what if Shapiro was watching her? What if he had a way to track where she was? If she tried to run, would he come after her and kill her—especially since he was convinced she had run once before?

Did she dare go to the authorities despite his threat to kill her if she did? Was she ready to face Pierce and confess the whole ugly truth and accept the consequences, no matter how painful? The Catholic Church wouldn't sanction a divorce, but didn't Pierce have grounds for an annulment? Was there anything to stop him from walking away and leaving her to fix this herself?

God, I can't fix this. I need help. I don't want to lie anymore. But if I tell Pierce the truth, I'm going to lose him. Yet if I don't, I'll never get the money and Shapiro will kill me. Show me what to do.

CHAPTER 17

Zoe slipped in the back door of the building and ran up the steps to her apartment. Pierce was in charge of the kitchen tonight and wouldn't come upstairs until after eleven.

She started to put the key in the lock when a voice startled her and she dropped the key on the floor.

"Zoe! There you are." Vanessa stepped out of her apartment. "Ethan and a colleague went to a seminar in New Orleans today and won't be back until late, and I know Pierce is cooking tonight. I wondered if later you might want to go out with Carter and me and get ice cream. What happened? You've got mud all over you."

Zoe bent down and picked up the key without looking at Vanessa.

"Zoe, you're bleeding. Are you all right?"

"I lost my footing on a walking trail and fell. I just need to get cleaned up. My ego hurts worse than the rest of me." She turned the key, her hand shaking, and pushed open the door. "I'll take a rain check on the ice cream. It's been a hectic day."

"You sure you're all right?"

"I'm fine. Just ready for some down time." *Leave me alone, Vanessa.*

"If you change your mind, we'll probably go out around seven and walk over to Scoops. They have the best peanut-butter cookie dough ice cream on the planet."

"Thanks. But I'm in for the night."

Zoe went inside and quickly closed the door. Vanessa was only trying to be a friend. Did she have to be so abrupt? She looked at her reflection in the entry-hall mirror and did a double take. Her face was pale and streaked with blood and sweat, her tank top smeared with blood where Shapiro had wiped his finger. No wonder Vanessa was concerned.

She started to walk toward the bathroom when she heard a knock on the door. *Go away, Vanessa.* She tiptoed to the door and looked through the peephole.

Vanessa knocked again. Shouldn't she answer the door, rather than taking a chance she might raise suspicion?

Zoe sighed. She pasted on a smile and opened the door. "I was just about to take a shower. Can I call you later?"

"I'm concerned about you. You look upset."

"You'd be upset too, if you tripped on a rock and fell on your face."

"Is that all? Because I'm really getting some funny vibes."

Vanessa's bluntness marched right through her defenses, and Zoe felt her face turn hot. "I'm fine. I just need to clean up."

"Did someone hurt you?" Vanessa gently gripped her wrist and lowered her voice to a whisper. "Were you attacked? Look at you. Your clothes are muddy and torn. You're bleeding. You're visibly shaken."

"Mind your own business." Zoe pulled her wrist free. "I told you, I fell."

"I'm thinking maybe you had a little help falling."

"Don't make this into something it's not, Vanessa. I'm fine. I'm just a major klutz. It's embarrassing."

Vanessa's gaze seemed to probe her conscience. "I can't just walk away, Zoe. Something's terribly wrong. Why don't I go get Pierce?"

"No! He's the last person I want to talk to right now." *Why did I tell her that?*

"Then talk to me. I'm a good listener, and you can trust me. But don't expect me to walk away and pretend I believe you're fine."

Zoe's heart beat so fast she was sure they could hear it downstairs in the dining room. "It's not something I can talk about in front of Carter."

"He won't hear us. He fell asleep. I'll probably have to wake him to go out for ice cream. Come over to my apartment and tell me what happened. Let me clean up that cut on your face."

Almost robotically, Zoe shut the door and followed Vanessa next door and into the Langleys' living room, where the aroma of fresh-baked cookies was pleasantly pervasive. She considered what she was about to do. Once she told Vanessa what had happened, she could never take it back. Was she ready to do that? Shouldn't she take time to think first? Then again, if she thought too hard about it, would she have the courage to tell anyone?

Vanessa took her by the arm and seated her on a wood chair, then looked carefully at the cut on her cheek. "Good, it doesn't look deep. I'll be right back."

Zoe sat in the quiet, studying the framed photos that graced the Langleys' bookshelves. Such happy faces. Did Vanessa have any idea how blessed she was to come from a normal family? The only pictures Zoe had of her parents and brother were in a sealed envelope at the bottom of a shoebox, her only memory of them locked away in the basement of her mind, along with the disgusting odor of whiskey and the sounds of yelling and slapping and crying—and of unwanted footsteps creeping in the darkness toward her bed.

Vanessa came back in the living room. "Why don't we do this in the kitchen? It'll be easier."

"All right." Zoe rose to her feet and followed Vanessa into the kitchen.

She stood at the sink and closed her eyes, trying not to think about how much it was going to sting.

"I'm going to pour some hydrogen peroxide into the cut," Vanessa said, "and then dab around it with clean gauze. It's going to hurt like nuts for a minute, but if I can get it cleaned out, I doubt you'll have to worry about infection. Okay?"

Zoe nodded, her eyes clamped shut. A few seconds later, she felt the cold peroxide saturate her cheek and a stinging so intense it made her eyes water. She sucked in a breath.

Vanessa held a towel under her chin and let the peroxide run down her face. "Exhale, Zoe. The worst is over. I'm going to do it again, but it won't sting nearly as much this time. Ready?"

"Go ahead."

Vanessa repeated the process and waited half a minute, then dabbed around the cut with clean gauze and handed Zoe the towel. "Wipe your chin. But don't touch the cut."

"Thanks." Zoe opened her eyes. "How bad is it?"

"Really not bad. I'm putting a little antibacterial ointment on it now … and a Band-Aid to keep the germs out. There. That should do it. All right, let's sit at the table. Tell me what happened."

"I don't even know where to begin."

"Try the beginning."

"We don't have that much time."

"Then give me the short version, Zoe. Come on, five minutes ago, you were ready to talk. Don't shut down now."

"I'm not sure I can do this. Really. This is a bad idea."

"No, what's a bad idea is your trying to deal with whatever happened all by yourself. Were you attacked? Is that why you don't want to tell Pierce? Talk to me. I'm listening. And if I don't wake Carter up, he'll sleep till morning. Take your time."

Zoe thought back to the day she told Mrs. Woodmore the truth. Hadn't that worked out? If she didn't talk to Vanessa, would Vanessa go to Pierce? Or Ethan? Would either of them go to the police? Was it too late to handle it herself? But did she dare involve Vanessa? Would it put her at risk?

"I honestly don't think you want to get pulled into this. It could be dangerous."

"I'm *already* into it. Just talk to me."

Zoe sighed. "I don't know where to begin, Vanessa. So I'm just going to give you the bottom line first: I've been living a lie for ten years. And it's finally caught up with me."

Pierce turned the kitchen over to Dempsey and walked out to the dining room at Zoe B's, instantly spotting Hebert, Father Sam, and Tex sitting at the table in front of the window.

"Hey, guys," he said. "How's it going?"

Hebert shook his head. "Emile got da results of d'autopsy. Remy's skull was crushed on one side wid sometin' metal, possibly a tire iron. Dey say he died right off, but who can know dat fuh shore? Oh, dey say dey can, but Emile doesn't believe it. Dat's eatin' him up."

"I'm sure it is," Pierce said. "Has he decided when he's having the funeral?"

Father Sam cleared his throat. "Tuesday afternoon at one. Emile asked *me* to say the memorial Mass, and Monsignor Robidoux at Saint Catherine's has graciously agreed to step aside and let me officiate for an old friend. It'll be in the obits tomorrow. Remy's being cremated, and there won't be a burial. Emile's going to spread his ashes along the Roux River—privately, when he's ready and after the media's left him alone."

No one said anything for half a minute.

Finally Tex said, "Hope y'all don't mind if I change the subject before Pierce has to get back to the kitchen. I just wanted to say how tasty the seafood gumbo was tonight. I've always enjoyed it, but there was just somethin' extra good tonight."

Pierce smiled. "I'm glad you noticed, Tex. I've been experimenting in preparation for the Gumbo Classic."

"Well, that was as good as it gets." Tex put his hands on his middle. "I ordered the bottomless bowl and had to make myself quit eatin' after the third refill. Mighty good."

Pierce patted Tex on the back. "Glad you approve. How was everything else?"

"Da red beans and rice hit da spot." Hebert gave him a thumbs up. "Corn bread was my weakness tonight. I can never get enough o'dat."

"I had the crawfish étoufée," Father Sam said. "My compliments to the chef."

"And the chef thanks you. Okay, fellas. I'd better get back before Dempsey thinks I've abandoned ship."

"What's Zoe doin' tonight?" Tex sat back, his thumbs hooked on his suspenders.

"I'm not sure. I noticed she left a little early, but she hasn't come down for dinner. I think she enjoys the evenings I work late." Pierce smiled. "Gives her a chance to do whatever she wants."

Zoe stared at her hands folded on Vanessa's kitchen table. Had she ever felt more vulnerable than she did at this moment?

"So now you know everything," she said. "My marriage was founded on false pretenses. And so was Zoe B's. I can't imagine what you must think."

"What *I* think," Vanessa said, "is that you need a friend, not a judge. You can't change the past. What matters now is what you decide to base the future on."

"Pierce won't see it that way."

"Maybe not at first. He'll be disappointed."

"More like devastated."

"But he loves you, Zoe. It's so obvious that he does. Surely he'll have some compassion for the abuse you suffered and at least some understanding of *why* you stole the ring. I certainly do."

"Even if he does, it won't matter. He'll never forgive me for lying to him all these years. Or for letting him believe I'm Cajun."

"You don't know that."

"Yes I do. Nothing is more important to him than his Cajun heritage. That's part of what he thought we shared. I'm going to lose him over this."

"I hate to say it, but better Pierce than your life."

"Pierce *is* my life...." Zoe let out a sob and then stifled it.

Vanessa put her hand on Zoe's. "I'm so sorry. I can only imagine how painful this is. And I wish you had time to figure it all out before you take the next step, but you don't. You have to tell Pierce everything you told me about your past and about your meeting with Shapiro. And then you've got to go to the sheriff with it, whether Pierce supports you or not."

"But Shapiro promised he'd kill me if I do that."

Vanessa held her gaze. "Zoe ... trust me, Shapiro's planning to kill you as soon as he gets his money. The only leverage you have is he wants his hundred thousand."

"I'm so scared, Vanessa."

"I know. But you have to tell Pierce—the sooner the better—and then tell Sheriff Prejean."

"I can't go to Jude with this. He's a longtime friend. I'd have to tell him everything. I'd be humiliated all over again. And once it's on the report and everyone in town knows about it, Zoe B's will be history. I'd rather go to the police. At least it'll be less personal."

Vanessa shook her head. "It won't matter. You were accosted outside the city limits. That's Sheriff Prejean's jurisdiction."

"How do you know that?"

"My mom's a police chief, remember? The police have jurisdiction in the city. The sheriff has jurisdiction in the county—or in this case, the parish. I know you're embarrassed and don't want Sheriff Prejean to know all these personal things about you, but, believe me, he's heard a lot worse. The important thing is that he knows Angus Shapiro—or whatever his real name is—is trying to extort money from you and has threatened your life. If Pierce is too upset to deal with this, I'll go with you to talk to the sheriff."

"You would do that?"

"Of course I would. But don't count Pierce out. First you need to get honest with him."

Zoe studied Vanessa's expression and saw only compassion. If she made it through this alive, and Pierce left her and Zoe B's went bankrupt, at least she would have one friend in town who didn't abandon her.

CHAPTER 18

Zoe lay in bed, listening to the *click click click* of the ceiling fan and the *drip drip drip* of condensation trickling down the eaves and onto the barbecue grill outside her window. She'd already taken one of the muscle relaxants the doctor had prescribed Pierce for his occasional bouts with back pain. Why didn't she feel any more relaxed? She glanced over at the clock: *11:04*. How much longer until Pierce would be home and she would have to tell him that the Zoe Benoit he married was a fabrication—a fraud?

How would he react when he realized she had deceived him, that her given name was Shelby Sieger, and that she was the daughter of a pathetically passive mother—and an alcoholic father, who abused her and whose only French relative was the murdering thief who had married his cousin?

Would it matter to Pierce that she truly loved him? Or would he believe even that now? Could he comprehend that she never had the courage to reveal the truth about herself, or how she acquired Zoe B's, because she was afraid of losing him?

Vanessa's advice echoed in her head. *God hasn't abandoned you, Zoe. He just wants you to come to Him and admit the truth.*

He'll forgive you, if you ask Him. That's really where you need to start.

Zoe slid out of bed and onto her knees, her hands folded, all too aware that Vanessa's assurance that God would forgive her didn't include any encouragement about Pierce.

God, I'm sorry for everything—for stealing, for lying, for deceiving everyone, especially Pierce. I know I don't deserve it, but please forgive me. Help me know what to say to Pierce so he'll at least understand why I—

She heard the key in the lock and the front door open. Fear seized her. She climbed back in bed and hugged her pillow, as if that could somehow muffle the sound of her thumping heart.

Pierce's footsteps moved down the hall toward the bedroom. In a few minutes, life as she had known it would cease to be. And unless she did exactly as Shapiro had instructed her, so would she.

Vanessa lay in Ethan's arms, her mind racing faster than her pulse. The neon lights were still flashing along *rue Madeline,* but the band at Breaux's had stopped playing. She heard a door open at the Broussards' a few minutes ago, and now water was running in the bathroom. She didn't hear voices.

"Honey, try to relax," Ethan said. "You did everything you could."

"I should've offered to pray with her."

"Zoe knows how to pray." Ethan pulled her closer. "Nothing's going to change in her life until she tells the truth—to herself, to God, and to Pierce. Let's hope that's what she's doing."

"I can see why she's concerned about Pierce's reaction. I remember that day out at the manor house when he went off about the plight of the Acadians. It's obvious his heritage is incredibly important to him. Maybe Zoe's right. Maybe part of his attraction to her is the fact that he thought she was Cajun too. Maybe he'll never forgive her for lying to him about that."

"Maybe not," Ethan said. "But her only way out of this pit is to tell the truth. I'm sure she realizes that, since she gave you permission to tell *me* everything."

Vanessa sighed. "I can only imagine how horrible it would be to have a sexually abusive father."

"Are you sure she's not lying about it to get sympathy?"

"As positive as I can be. It was very hard for her to talk about it, and I doubt she could fake blushing. But her pain seemed real to me. My parents are so wonderful that it's hard to relate to her violent upbringing. She refers to herself as white trash. The shame goes really deep."

"It certainly would explain why she felt safe with Mrs. Woodmore for so long. And how she justified stealing the ring in order to achieve independence. Do you think she was sorry for lying? Or just sorry she got caught?"

"I don't know. Maybe both. She knows it was wrong, that's for sure. She hated lying to Pierce. She's afraid that now he won't believe how much she loves him. That he'll think it's just one more thing she lied about."

Ethan raised his eyebrows. "Well? Could you blame him?"

"No. But if he really stops to think about it, what did Zoe have to gain by marrying him? She didn't marry him for his money. She owned her own business, albeit wrongfully. And she didn't need to change her name. She'd already done that and had been well received in the Cajun community. She had what she wanted. Getting married was never part of her plan. With her abusive background, she didn't even trust men. But she fell in love with Pierce. That's the *only* reason she would've married him."

"It's a wonder she didn't choose a man just like her father." Ethan kissed her forehead. "I'd be honored to think *you* did. I have the utmost admiration for your dad."

"Me, too. I'm just so sorry Zoe's dad hurt her."

"It's sad and, unfortunately, more common that most people realize. It's estimated that at least one in four women and one in six men have suffered some form of sexual abuse. I hope now Zoe will seek counseling and try to work through the bad memories, the anger, and self-loathing. Keep in mind none of this is an excuse for stealing and lying. But it does make it easier to understand."

"Let's hope Pierce thinks so."

Ethan traced her eyebrow with his finger. "Zoe has a more immediate issue. I wonder if she and Pierce will go to the sheriff yet tonight."

"I don't know. I'm so scared for her, Ethan. Shapiro said he'd kill her if she did. She's convinced he means it."

"You said yourself he's probably planning to kill her either way. At least with the authorities on her side she stands a good chance of coming out of this alive."

"What if Shapiro put a listening device in her apartment? What if he knows she's decided to go to the sheriff? What if he knows she talked to *me?*"

"Don't look for trouble, honey." Ethan brushed the hair out of her eyes. "He doesn't sound that sophisticated. You've been watching too many cop shows."

"Maybe." She sighed. "But after Drew was shot and killed in front of me, then you nearly died trying to expose why, it's hard for me not to think worst-case scenario. People always think something *that* awful will never happen to them. But now I know it can."

"*Can*. But only if God allows it. And if He allows it, He supplies the grace to walk through it." Ethan kissed her cheek. "We have to trust Him with this."

"I know. I'm just not so sure Zoe does."

Jude sat at his computer, reading through the Jarvis murder file. How could they have no leads in the case? Why hadn't someone in the black community come forward quietly and fingered the guilty parties—or at least offered a clue? Law-abiding African-Americans could not be happy with the media hype surrounding this case. Why wouldn't someone talk? Surely there was some sort of scuttlebutt concerning who might have done this.

His mind flashed an image of Remy, stripped of dignity and hanging from a tree like some ghoulish Halloween decoration. As if the poor guy hadn't struggled enough with the mental challenges he faced.

Jude blinked away the intrusive image and pushed back his chair and stood, hands on his lower back. He stretched until he felt the tightness relax, then stepped over to the window and looked out at the parish courthouse, illuminated and stately, and the streets emptied of the day's throng of tourists. What was he doing here this late on a Saturday night, reviewing the same unyielding information on the Jarvis case, while Colette curled up on her side of the bed, lost in a novel? Wasn't it time to go home and get some rest before Sunday Mass, lest he embarrass his family by falling asleep again during Monsignor Robidoux's sermon?

He felt his cell phone vibrate. *Yes, Colette, I'm on my way.* He took it off his belt clip, surprised to see the call was from Stone Castille.

"Yeah, Stone. What's up?"

"We've got a situation boiling at Roux River Park."

"Talk to me."

"A bunch of teenagers—blacks and whites—spouting racial slurs and threats. It's getting ugly. Apparently a fistfight broke out earlier, and someone broke it up. Details are sketchy. I'm pretty sure alcohol's a factor. A few of them seem eager to go at it again, so I've called all units to assist. Six deputies are here, and the others are en route, including some of Chief Norman's officers. I thought you'd want to know, especially since one media van has arrived—and others are bound to follow."

"How many teens are involved?"

"I counted twenty-nine. Only ten are black."

"I'm heading your way."

"We've got it under control, Sheriff. I just wanted to give you a heads up."

"I was just leaving the station to go home," Jude said. "The park's on the way."

⚜

Jude spotted a sea of flashing colored lights and turned into the parking lot near the concession patio at Roux River Park. He pulled up behind Deputy Chief Aimee Rivette's squad car and got out.

Stone Castille waved and hurried to meet him. "I think the worst is over, Sheriff."

"Fill me in on what happened."

"We're still trying to put it together, but it appears that two groups of teens, one African-American and the other Caucasian, got into an altercation that escalated into expletives and racial slurs and then a fistfight. According to one of the black teens, at least four white males overpowered him and started dragging him away, threatening to hang him. The white kids claim they were just clowning around."

Jude glanced over at the detainees. "Wanna bet the black kid didn't think they were clowning around?"

"You got that right. He was pretty shaken."

"What were they doing out here this time of night?"

"All of them flunked the breathalyzer."

"Well, if they violated the no-tolerance policy regarding alcohol consumption in the park, each of them is going to get slapped with a five-hundred-dollar fine on top of disorderly conduct, public intoxication, minor in possession, battery—and possibly a hate crime. This is going to be a serious wake-up call for these kids—especially if they've never been in trouble before."

"Judge Dufour sure won't make it easy for them," Gil said. "He's one tough—"

Something flashed, and then a loud popping noise echoed in the darkness. And then another. And another. A black detainee let out an agonizing cry and grabbed the back of his thigh. For a split second, it seemed as though the earth stood still, and then people starting scrambling in all directions.

Jude drew his gun, his heart nearly pounding out of his chest, and hunkered down behind a trash barrel.

Stone dropped down behind him. "All three shots came from the tennis courts on the north side of the park."

"Yeah, I saw the flash. Help me get that kid out of the open— over there, behind that bougainvillea bush. Let's go."

Jude rose to his feet and scurried, stooped over, to where the wounded teen lay on the ground.

"We're going to get you out of the line of fire, son." Jude holstered his gun and took the boy's wrist as Stone grabbed his ankles. "Ready?"

Stone nodded.

The two of them lifted the boy about a foot off the ground. They carried him ever so gently and set him on the ground behind the bush, then slowly rolled him over on his stomach.

Jude spoke into his shoulder mike, "We have shots fired at Roux River Park. One civilian down. Three gunshots from the north end of the park. Type of firearm unknown. No suspect description or vehicle at this time. All available units roll to the park Code 3 to assist with containment and evacuation. Use south entrance unless given specific perimeter position. Request any help the police department can spare. Have paramedics roll to the south end of the park. Tell them not to enter until requested. Repeat: Paramedics are not to enter until requested."

Jude held up a tiny LED flashlight and looked carefully at the boy's wound and glanced up as several deputies attempted to herd the drunk teenagers behind the concession building. He saw Gil Marcel and whistled, motioning for him to come.

In the next instant, Gil knelt next to him and Stone. "Yes, sir."

"Gil, I want *you* to coordinate the perimeter. I'll secure the park and set up the command post. Chief Norman's officers should be here soon. Go."

"Stone, I need you to stay with the boy and control the bleeding until the paramedics arrive. Have you got a clean handkerchief?"

"Yes, sir. I think I do."

"Here, take mine, too." Jude took a clean handkerchief out of his pocket and handed it to Stone, then looked into the wounded boy's eyes. "What's your name, son?"

"Deshawn … Macey." The kid lay with his head turned sideways and resting on his hands.

"How old are you?"

"Sixteen."

"You're going to be all right. Deputy Castille is going to apply pressure to the wound to help slow the bleeding until the paramedics arrive. It's going to hurt a little, okay?"

Deshawn nodded, his eyes narrowed, his lips tightly pressed together.

Stone placed the folded handkerchiefs, one on top of the other, over the gunshot wound, then knelt over the boy and pressed down on the handkerchiefs with his palms.

Deshawn whimpered as the white handkerchiefs almost instantly turned red. "Will someone call my mom?" The young man was panting, his eyes wide with fear.

"Sure we will." Jude peeled off his uniform shirt, then pulled his T-shirt off over his head and handed it to Castille.

"My m-mom's a nurse," Deshawn said. "At Hargrave. She's on duty tonight."

"Then she'll probably want to meet the ambulance." Jude made sure his voice sounded reassuring. "Deshawn, try to relax. Deputy Castille is going to have to press harder to get the bleeding under control." *God help us if he can't.*

Jude gave a nod, and Castille bore down harder, the T-shirt quickly soaking up the blood.

Deshawn winced. "I-I know your son. Saul. We were in the same science class. He's cool."

"Thanks. His mother and I think he's pretty special." Jude buttoned his uniform shirt and avoided looking into Deshawn's eyes. He could only imagine how he would feel if it were *his* son lying there, dying. He glanced over at Castille. "Keep pressure on the wound. I'm going to go make sure the paramedics are cleared to get in here and then set up a command post. Let's hope Chief Norman sends enough extra personnel to help process twenty-nine drunk teenagers. And that we get the shooter before he strikes again."

Deshawn took hold of Jude's wrist. "Am I going to die? I just want to know."

The boy's bluntness cut through all his defenses. Jude shook his head. "Not if I can help it, son." *But it's really out of my hands.*

CHAPTER 19

Zoe heard the bathroom door open and Pierce's footsteps moving down the hall in her direction. She clutched tightly to her pillow, her heart banging so hard she felt as if it might explode. How did she even begin to tell him the truth about herself?

God, help me, or I'm going to die of a heart attack before I can say anything.

Pierce crawled into bed and draped his arm over her. "Are you awake?" he whispered.

"Yes. I've been waiting for you. There's something we need to talk about."

"Oh?" He gently stroked her hair. "Am I in the doghouse?"

"No, *I* am."

"You?" He sounded amused. "Why?"

Zoe wiggled out of his embrace and sat up on the side of the bed. She turned on the lamp, her back to Pierce. "Before I tell you, I just want to say that I love you with all my heart. What I'm about to reveal will be easier to handle if you can remember that."

Zoe turned and pulled her legs into the bed and sat with her back against the headboard, her pillow held tightly to her chest.

"Good grief, what happened to you?" Pierce raised himself up on one arm. "Did you wreck the car?"

"No. Just hear me out. I've tried to imagine how this conversation should go. There just isn't an easy way to deliver this news."

"For crying out loud, Zoe. You're my wife, the other half of my heart. You can come to me with anything. What is it?"

"I've lied to you ... all these years."

"About what?"

"For starters, the name you knew me by, Zoe Benoit, wasn't the name my parents gave me. I was born Shelby Sieger. And my parents aren't the deceased Pierre and Violet Benoit of Dallas. They are the probably-still-alive Frank and Raleigh Sieger of Devon Springs, Texas."

Pierce got up on his knees and looked into her eyes. "Why would you lie to me about something that important?"

"I-I was ashamed. I couldn't bear for you to know the truth about me, that my father was a mean drunk ... who abused me ... every way you can imagine ..." Zoe choked on the words and wondered if she had the courage to continue. Finally she added, "My mother knew but was too afraid of him to do anything about it."

Pierce leaned back against the headboard, his gaze straight ahead, his arms folded across his chest. "I'm sorry, Zoe. That's horrible. But you should've trusted me with it."

"If that was the whole story, I might've. But there's more. It's all connected." Zoe hugged her pillow tighter. "After I graduated from high school, I worked two jobs—one for a housecleaning service and the other for Walmart. I put as much space between me and my parents as I could for a couple years. The sexual abuse happened less frequently, but the violence escalated. I wanted to move out, but I couldn't afford a car *and* rent. My friend Hannah knew the situation and let me move in with her without paying rent until I could get my finances worked out. But my dad went ballistic. He wanted me to come home. He came to the apartment drunk and carrying a ball bat. He threatened to hurt us. Hannah got scared and called the police."

"Did you tell them he'd been abusing you?"

"No. I was too scared. And embarrassed. I didn't want to end up in court, having to describe the awful things he'd done to me. But after that, Hannah said I needed to find somewhere else to live. So I looked for jobs out of state and took one in Alexandria, Louisiana as a live-in maid for a woman named Adele Woodmore. She was a widow with a huge estate. The position included a nice room, all meals, and a small salary. I was safe there. My parents had no idea where I was."

"Did Adele know you by your real name?"

Zoe nodded. "My work references were good. I worked three years for the same two employers, and neither knew anything about my home life. It wasn't until later I decided to change my name. I worked for Adele for six years. She treated me well and would have been happy for me to work there the rest of my life. But I was totally dependent on her. The small salary I made went mostly for a car and incidentals, and I would never have been able to save money to get out on my own. I really couldn't support myself. It was depressing."

"Are you rabbit tracking, or is this relevant?"

"It's totally relevant. Adele wore a diamond ring—more like a rock—that her late husband had given her. One day when she was napping, I-I got the idea to take it off her finger and let her think she had misplaced it or dropped it. I knew she trusted me and would never suspect me. I couldn't believe I was doing it. But I did. I took the ring."

"Good grief, Zoe! What were you thinking?"

"That she was rich and would never miss it. And I could sell it and use the money to start a new life. I saw a chance to change my circumstances, and I seized it."

Pierce shook his head, but didn't say anything.

Zoe told him how she had convinced the police she knew nothing about the ring. How she had hidden the ring for six months in the pocket of a jacket she never wore, then sold it to a jeweler in New Orleans for fifteen thousand, split the money into three bank accounts to avoid suspicion, and waited almost a year to change her name.

"Why did you choose the name to Zoe Benoit? That seems a little random for a Texan."

"It wasn't random at all. I didn't want to feel like white trash anymore." Zoe felt her face burn, even now. "I wanted roots I could be proud of, and passing myself off as Cajun seemed perfect if I planned to stay in Louisiana. The first time I ever laid eyes on Les Barbes, I knew it's where I wanted to live. And start my own eatery. It was a dream that kept building over time. So before I changed my name, I started reading everything I could get my hands on about the Cajun culture. I even learned a little Cajun French. One day I read an article in the newspaper about a Dallas couple who died in a house fire."

"Let me guess," Pierce said sarcastically. "Violet and Pierre Benoit?"

Zoe nodded. "They had one child, a surviving daughter, Zoe, who was my age. I saved the newspaper article and decided to change my name to Zoe Benoit and say that my parents had died in a house fire. That way I never had to acknowledge my real parents or my upbringing."

"But you told me all kinds of stories about your happy childhood days."

Zoe's eyes turned to pools, and tears trickled down her face. "I made them up. I almost believed those stories after a while. I wanted it to be true."

Pierce bit his lip and wouldn't look at her. "I don't get it. Why are you telling me this now—five years into the marriage? Why didn't you just let me live with my illusion. *Why*, Zoe? Nothing can ever be the same now! You're a liar and a criminal! What am I supposed to do with that? Tell me! Because I don't know!"

"Pierce, please don't yell." Zoe covered her head the way she used to do when her father was about to hit her.

"Oh, spare me the drama," he said. "Who *are* you? Do I even know the real you? Sieger? Were you just going to lie to our kids about being Cajun? Make up names and dates of births and deaths for grandparents, too? Were you just going to hope and pray we never pursued our family tree? How far were you willing to go?"

Zoe reached over to the nightstand, plucked a Kleenex from the box, and blew her nose. "There's more."

"You've got to be kidding."

"I would never have had the courage to tell you the truth. But something's come up in the past couple weeks. I started to receive anonymous notes with just five words: *I know what you did.*

I thought for sure someone figured out I stole the ring and wanted hush money not to go to Adele with the information. That's when I decided to go to Adele and confess everything. So I made up the story about my friend Annabelle dying. I needed a reason to leave town that day so I could drive to Alexandria and face Mrs. Woodmore."

"So you lied to me about *that*, too?"

"I'm sorry, Pierce. I just wanted to fix things. I hated lying to you again, but I kept thinking it would be the last time."

Pierce threw his hands in the air. "Why stop when you're so good at it? I never suspected a thing. I prayed for your safety while you were driving down the bayou in that tropical storm, for heaven's sake. How can I trust anything you say?"

"I don't blame you for being mad. Or for wondering if you can trust what I say. But this is the gospel truth. Why would I hurt you like this and risk our marriage by telling a lie?"

"What happened when you went to see Mrs. Woodmore?"

Zoe told him everything that had happened the day she went to Adele and confessed to stealing the ring, how Adele agreed to let her pay back the thirty thousand dollars, and how the notes became threatening after that, leading up to tonight's meeting with Angus Shapiro or whatever his real name was.

"So what *does* he want, Zoe? I assume you told him you confessed everything to Adele about the ring?"

Zoe started to cry. "He doesn't know anything about Adele or the ring. He was looking for Zoe Benoit, the daughter of Pierre and Violet Benoit, who died in a house fire in Texas."

"Did you tell him you're not that person?"

"He didn't believe me. He said my parents were involved in trafficking heroine and that they owed him a hundred thousand dollars when they died. He thinks I'm their daughter, Zoe, and that I skipped out with the inheritance money so I wouldn't have to pay their debts."

"So he wants a *hundred thousand dollars* from you? How can he just march into your life and make this demand without any proof you're the daughter he's looking for?"

"Pierce, please don't yell. This is hard enough."

"Maybe I want to yell! How in world did Shapiro even find you?"

"He was in Lafayette on business and read the feature story they did on Zoe B's. He put two and two together and figured I must be the Zoe Benoit he'd been looking for all these years."

"That is just great! I hope you told him you're not paying him a nickel! That he's got the wrong person!"

Zoe felt sick. Was she going to throw up? "I tried."

"What's that supposed to mean?"

"He held me at knifepoint and told me to get the money by the time the banks close on Monday or he'd kill me. And if I went to the cops or told anyone else who did, he'd know. And he'd carve me like a totem pole and then kill me. He cut my cheek to prove he was serious."

Pierce's face went from flushed to ashen.

"I would never have had the courage to confront my deception unless I was forced." Zoe put her hand over her mouth and willed away the nausea. "I'm not half as worried Shapiro's going to kill me as I am that this is going to kill *us*—our marriage."

"What marriage? It's all a lie!" His voice bounced off the walls.

"You're the one who killed us, Zoe! You just took away everything I believed about you! What do you want from me? You broke my heart and stole my future...." Pierce bit his fist, his chin quivering. Finally he lowered his voice and said, "You're not considering trying to come up with the hundred thousand?"

"No. He's probably planning to kill me either way. Vanessa convinced me that I have to go to Jude with this. It's my only chance to stay alive."

"*Vanessa* knows about Shapiro?"

"She saw me when I came in this evening. I was sweaty and bloody and my clothes were torn. She thought I'd been raped. If I hadn't told her what was going on, she would've gone downstairs and gotten you. That wasn't the right time."

"And this *is?*" Pierce got up and flung his pillow into the door. "I can't believe what a dupe I've been."

Zoe winced. Had she ever seen him so mad? "I wouldn't blame you if you hate me right now. But I need you to help me figure out how to talk to Jude without Shapiro finding out."

"Oh, so *now* you decide to involve me in your life. Well, guess what? If Shapiro is watching you like he said, there's no way we can go to Jude without the guy knowing. He's probably listening in to our phone calls. For all I know, he's got our room bugged." Pierce picked up a hardback book from the nightstand and slammed it on the floor.

"Calm down," she said. "You can hate me later. Right now, we need to think."

"Why bother? We're dead, Zoe! There's no way out of this! Once Shapiro knows you've gone to the sheriff, he's going to come for us, whether it's tomorrow or the next day or the next! Drug dealers are thugs. They get even."

"Have a little faith that Jude might catch him. If I give him the hundred thousand, he *will* kill me for sure. And you, too, since you've seen him and heard his voice."

Pierce flopped on the bed and lay flat on his back, his eyes closed, his fists clenched, tears trickling down the sides of his face.

Zoe's heart sank. The only other time she had seen him cry was when his grandfather died. "You have every right to be furious with me for deceiving you. But you have to believe I never meant to hurt you. I just didn't want to lose you."

"And how did that work for you, Zoe?"

His sarcasm was biting. Was he trying to say she *had* lost him? Was he just speaking out of anger? Or was he too devastated by her betrayal to ever recover? Did she dare allow herself to give in to the fear and sorrow?

"Pierce. I love you. That's not something I can fake. In your heart, you know it's the truth. I don't want anything to happen to you. Or me. Before we're both too depressed to think straight, we need to decide what to do."

CHAPTER 20

Vanessa lay in Ethan's arms, praying, aware that it had been almost five minutes since she had heard any shouting or door slamming coming from Zoe and Pierce's apartment.

Lord, help them get through this. Don't let it destroy their marriage.

"Ethan, are you awake?" she whispered.

"I keep dozing off. Is it still quiet over there?"

"Yes, for about five minutes now. Do you think we should knock on the door and let them know we're here, in case they need us?"

Ethan stroked her hair. "No. Zoe knows that. We don't know whether or not she told Pierce about your earlier conversation. It's better if we stay out of it."

"We can't stay out of it. What if Shapiro knows she talked to me? We're in this, whether we like it or not. At some point, we're going to have to talk to them."

"Well, not at two in the morning."

"I hope Pierce doesn't walk out on her," Vanessa said. "No matter how wrong it was that she lied about her past, I know Zoe didn't lie about her feelings for him."

"Victims of childhood sexual abuse are so used to living with secrets," Ethan said, "that lying becomes second nature. Maybe now that she's had to confront the truth, Zoe will be able to move past it."

"She may not get the chance unless the sheriff apprehends Shapiro," Vanessa said. "I'm really scared for her. I wish I knew what she told Pierce."

"Judging from the shouting, probably the truth."

"I'll never be able to sleep with this up in the air." Vanessa sighed. "I was looking forward to going to church at Grace Creek in the morning, but now I'm thinking we need to stay home and help Zoe and Pierce."

"I was looking forward to it too. I'm so ready to join a church and get involved again. But I guess we can put that on hold for a week. Pastor Auger will understand." Ethan pulled her closer. "If we're going to be of any help to Zoe and Pierce, we need to stay strong and not get paralyzed by fear."

"Easier said than done."

"I never said it was easy. But we've been through worse."

Vanessa's mind flashed back to the terrifying moments after his cousin, Drew, was gunned down, and the agonizing hours when Ethan was being pursued by the men responsible.

"The faith you showed in going to the police when Drew's killers tried to shut you up amazed me," she said. "You said if right is right, it's right all the time and not just when it's convenient."

"It is. But it's important to use wisdom in *how* you go to the police. It's not like I went down to the station and wrote out a statement."

"I know, Ethan. I just wish I had your faith. So how do we help Zoe and Pierce do the right thing without endangering their lives—or ours?"

⚜

Jude Prejean leaned on the hood of his squad car, which had been moved to the south parking lot near the main entrance of Roux River Park and set up as a command post.

Gil Marcel paced nearby, cell phone to his ear, checking in with his people, who had been assigned to specific areas of the perimeter.

Stone Castille was in charge of making sure the intoxicated, restless teenagers were not only segregated, but also unable to talk to each other before they could be questioned by authorities. To ensure their safety while the shooter was still at large, Stone coordinated the shuttling of the teens by police to several indoor facilities in the park.

Jude turned around and looked across the street from the main entrance of the park, where media and parents waited. The tension was almost tangible as authorities worked to contain the shooter and determine what, if anything, was known about him.

Police Chief Casey Norman was using the hood of another squad car to keep a log of his officers and where each was being utilized. He looked over at Jude. "You really know how to throw a party on a Saturday night, Sheriff."

"Beats staying at home in the air-conditioning with my beautiful wife and three adoring children, enjoying a home-cooked meal and a great movie."

"If you're like me, you haven't been home except to sleep since Remy Jarvis was murdered." Casey wrote something on his log. "So what's your assessment of what happened here tonight?"

Jude spotted the headlights of more vehicles arriving on the north side of the perimeter. "We haven't been able to determine whether the shooting and the fighting were related. What we do know is that the fighting and the threat to lynch the black kid resulted from anger over Remy Jarvis's murder."

"Remy's murder was a travesty," Casey said. "I'm surprised we haven't had a race riot on our hands."

"Well, I'd say that's a real possibility, now that the news is out that a black youth was shot following a violent clash between white and black teenagers."

"Any word on Deshawn Macey?"

"Not yet. He sustained a nasty gunshot wound. Lost a lot of blood. It could go either way. I don't need to tell you what could happen if that kid dies."

"If we could arrest the shooter, it would go a long way in easing the tension." Casey took a handkerchief out of his pocket and wiped the perspiration off his face and neck.

"There's little chance he's going to slip through the perimeter," Jude said. "If he's out here, we'll find him."

Pierce lay on the sofa, a bed sheet draped over him, and stared at the ceiling fan going round and round in the dark. He felt as if his head would explode. He was sure his heart already had—his hopes and dreams blown to smithereens, nothing left but devastation and the lingering stench of betrayal.

How could he not have seen through Zoe's lies? Why didn't he question her more about her parents? Didn't he sense she was holding something back? Didn't it seem odd that she didn't have contact with anyone from her past?

Pierce sighed. The sadness that overtook her any time he brought it up was more troubling than his unanswered questions. But how could he have known she was hiding dark secrets from him—secrets that could put her life in jeopardy?

Pierce threw back the sheet and got up. He opened the door to the gallery and stepped outside, the first gray light of dawn visible in the eastern sky. He stood leaning on the wrought-iron railing and looked down on *rue Madeline.*

How serious was the threat to Zoe's life? Was this Shapiro character really capable of murder? Would he have put himself at risk by accosting her, cutting her face, and scaring her half to death if he didn't intend to follow through?

Pierce shuddered. He saw the newspaper van go by and thought of Remy. If harm could befall an innocent guy like that, was it so far-fetched that Zoe, with her deceptive baggage, could end up as the victim of mistaken identity? What did they have to do to ensure they didn't end up as murder victims? Or was their fate sealed the minute Zoe passed herself off as Zoe Benoit in that feature story?

Pierce gripped the railing and shook it, silently shouting at the top of his lungs. *Zoe, what have you done?*

Vanessa sat in the living room with the lights out. Out of the corner of her eye, she saw something moving outside and could make out the silhouette of someone standing at the railing on the gallery next door. She realized it was Pierce. He took the bottom of his T-shirt and wiped his eyes.

Vanessa's heart sank. *Lord, please help him. He must be devastated.*

Unless he and Zoe could find a way to tell Sheriff Prejean about the situation without Shapiro knowing, the state of their marriage was the least of his worries. Was Shapiro capable of listening in on their conversations? Could he track their whereabouts? Or was he bluffing?

And if Zoe and Pierce did tell the sheriff their circumstances, could he protect them from Shapiro? Would he? Could he even spare the manpower while he was investigating Remy Jarvis's murder?

Ethan came in the living room and sat next to her on the sofa. "I couldn't sleep, so I turned on the TV. Someone shot a black teenager at Roux River Park last night. Apparently there was some sort of racial incident with a group of teens prior to the shooting. The sheriff and the police chief have been on the scene all night and have sealed the park, hoping to catch the shooter."

"Do they think it's a payback for Remy's murder?"

"The news commentator posed the question, but the sheriff wouldn't comment. I wonder how long he's going to be out there. I'm not sure Zoe and Pierce would feel comfortable talking to anyone else."

Vanessa glanced outside and saw that Pierce was no longer standing at the railing. "If Sheriff Prejean has been out there all night, he's not going to be available to take on anything else. He might even go home to get some rest."

"Of all days for there to be another crisis," Ethan said. "Zoe and Pierce can't put off talking to the authorities. They've only got until tomorrow when the banks close before Shapiro figures out they didn't do what he said."

CHAPTER 21

Jude put on his dark glasses as the sun cleared the top of the tree line on the east side of the park. It was going to be another cloudless scorcher. He turned to Gil Marcel and caught him in the middle of a yawn.

"Sorry, Sheriff," Gil said. "It's been a long night."

"Have some more coffee. We're just getting started. Tell your people on the east and west sides of the perimeter to search the woods again. The sun's high enough now that they should have sufficient light. Chief Norman's officers will sweep the park grounds. I want this shooter in custody or we'll have to keep the park closed and deal with hundreds of disappointed and angry folks who made plans to come here."

"Yes, sir. We're on it."

Jude heard Casey on the phone, telling his officer in charge to begin a thorough search of the park property and facilities.

Stone Castille got out of his squad car and walked over to Jude. "Deshawn Macey's out of recovery, but he's still critical. The surgeon said if he pulls through, he's going to need more surgeries and extensive rehab. It's too soon to know if he'll regain the use of his leg."

"He's lucky he didn't bleed out at the scene."

Stone looked down at the ground and moved a rock with his boot. "Sir, we have a bigger problem. A couple dozen African-Americans are marching in front of Hargrave Medical Center, carrying placards and claiming Deshawn Macey was targeted by whites in retaliation for the lynching of Remy Jarvis."

"We don't know that."

"These folks aren't exactly in the mood to listen. It's getting ugly."

"I don't blame them for being upset." Jude tore a paper towel off the roll and wiped the sweat off his forehead. "But we need to put a stop to the speculation before it gets out of hand. I'm putting you in charge, Stone. Organize a team and get over there. Manage the crowd and tell them exactly what we know. Assure them that we're on their side and want the shooter caught and brought to justice. See that the situation doesn't escalate."

"What should I do about the teenagers we didn't arrest? I'm having them brought back over here so we can release them to their parents."

"I'll have someone else take care of it. I want you at the medical center. Find a way to keep the peace. I'll go to the media again. I'll assure people that justice will be done and convince them that they need to show restraint."

Zoe sat at the kitchen table, picking at a half-eaten bagel, studying Pierce's demeanor, trying to decide which emotion seemed more pronounced: anger or fear.

"Have you thought any more about what we should do?" she said.

"You think I could *stop* thinking about it?"

"I guess not. I sure haven't. I've been racking my brain, trying to figure out a way to talk to Jude without Shapiro finding out."

"Well, save your brainpower," Pierce said. "You can't get to Jude anyhow. A black kid was shot at Roux River Park last night. That's where Jude and most law-enforcement personnel are right now. Looks like they might be there for some time. They've closed the park and a search is underway."

"Where did you hear that?"

"It's all over the news."

Zoe felt her neck muscles tighten. What were they going to do? She didn't feel safe confiding in a deputy.

There was a knock at the door.

"Stay put." Pierce got up and looked out the peephole. "It's Ethan and Vanessa." He opened the door. "I'm surprised you're still speaking to us."

"Of course we're speaking to you," Ethan said. "May we come in?"

Pierce held open the door and let them pass. "Where's Carter?"

"We arranged for him to stay with a friend from his preschool," Vanessa said.

"You two really shouldn't get involved. This Shapiro's dangerous."

"We're already involved." Ethan put his hand on Pierce's shoulder. "Let's put our heads together. There has to be a solution."

"I can't think of one."

"Come out to the kitchen," Zoe said.

Vanessa and Ethan walked into the kitchen and sat across from her at the table. Pierce remained standing.

"I'm so sorry," Zoe said. "If I thought I could get away from Shapiro without putting any of you at risk, I'd just get in the car and start driving." She glanced up at Pierce and wondered if he would just as soon she did.

"There's no way out of this." Pierce went over and stood in front of the window, his arms folded. "Shapiro's planning to kill us either way. We might as well go to Jude and tell him everything—and hope he can find Shapiro before Shapiro finds us."

"We all agree you need to tell the sheriff what's going on," Ethan said. "But if Shapiro is watching you, you're putting yourselves in grave danger the minute you walk in and out of the sheriff's department."

Zoe sighed. "He said he'd know if we went to the sheriff or told someone else who did. So he must have a way of monitoring our phone calls, too."

"He's probably bluffing," Ethan said. "But why take a chance when there may be a way around it?"

"What way around it?" Pierce came over and stood next to the table.

"We need to throw him off his game." Ethan pushed his glasses up higher on his nose. "There's more than one way to go to the sheriff."

Jude glanced at his watch. How much longer was he willing to tie up all this valuable personnel when trouble was brewing at the medical center?

He saw Police Chief Norman put his cell phone back on his belt clip and walked over to him.

"How long before your officers will be done with the sweep?" Jude asked.

"I'd say within the hour." Casey stuck a pencil behind his ear. "They just recovered the third .357 shell casing in close proximity to where the others were found at the south end of tennis court A. But they also discovered shoe prints in the damp grass, leading from the tennis court to the parking lot. A man's size eleven. Might mean something. The sprinklers were on in that area of the park from nine thirty to ten p.m. These would've been made after that. The timing's right."

"Good work. My teams are finished searching the woods. No sign of the shooter. But we did find beer cans and whisky bottles in a small clearing in the west woods. We'll dust them for prints. Might yield something. It's time to make a decision whether we want to maintain the perimeter a while longer or give it up."

"It's your call," Casey said, "but since the containment's not getting us anywhere, maybe we should put our efforts into maintaining order. What's happening at the medical center is bound to happen somewhere else, too. We need to be ready. And a number of my officers pulled a double shift and need to go home and get some sleep."

"I think the two of us could use a little of that ourselves."

Casey looked pensive and seemed to be lost in thought. "I keep asking myself what kind of heartless loser could use that kind of firepower on unarmed teenagers."

Jude's mind flashed back to those terrifying moments after the shooting, when he thought Deshawn Macey was bleeding out.

"Since both sets of kids claim they ran into each other by accident, I'm thinking it was one of the teenagers. The odds are pretty slim that someone else just happened to be in the park packing a .357 Magnum and decided to open fire."

"I agree. So why didn't at least one of the kids give up the shooter?" Casey said.

"I can only think of two reasons. Either they really didn't know who did it. Or we didn't lean on them hard enough." Jude took off his dark glasses and wiped the sweat off his eyelids with the back of his hand. "The kids we arrested for threatening to hang that African-American kid deny knowing anything about it, even after we offered a deal to the first one who gave us the shooter. Maybe their lawyers will get them to wise up. Being charged with a hate crime is serious, and none of them have any priors."

Zoe glanced over at Pierce and tried to look past his stony expression. She didn't dare think about how she had broken his heart or the fact that they had no future together. All she could allow herself to think about was surviving this ordeal.

Did Pierce seem willing to go along with the plan Ethan suggested? What if it backfired? What if Shapiro could somehow track what they were doing? What if he had some sophisticated technology they didn't know about? He was a serious drug dealer with a serious grudge he'd been nursing for a long time. What was to stop him from executing all four of them when he realized he wasn't getting his money?

She thought back to the dreadful moments in the woods when he held a knife to her cheek and cut it ever so carefully, just to make his point. Was that the action of a man who was bluffing? She shuddered.

"Look, I know we're all scared," Ethan said. "I think this plan will give you a way to stay under the radar until the sheriff can advise you what to do. If we do it right, I don't see how Shapiro could know where you are. It'll buy you some time."

"Or we could just go to the sheriff and trust him to protect us." Pierce folded his hands on the table.

"For how long?" Vanessa said. "The authorities are focused on the hate crimes. I'm not sure they have the personnel to protect you—or even to look for Shapiro, since he claims that's not his real name."

"Do you have a gun?" Ethan said.

Pierce shook his head. "I've never even fired one."

"I've got pepper spray," Zoe said.

Ethan leaned forward on his elbows and moved his gaze from Pierce to Zoe and back to Pierce. "You need to decide if you want to do this or not. I can borrow the van until five. I probably should go get things ready."

Vanessa put her hands on Zoe's. "I know it's not foolproof. But it could be the last thing Shapiro's expecting you to do. If we act quickly, we might pull it off."

"It's the *might* part that worries me," Pierce said.

Vanessa glanced over at Ethan. "We aren't without help. I think we should pray."

"God isn't going to bail us out," Pierce said. "It's Zoe's lies that got us into this mess."

"Well, the Lord specializes in messes," Ethan said. "It's when we're rendered helpless that we can really see His power at work. When we can't, He *can*. I say we ask Him."

Vanessa and Ethan held hands and extended their free hands to Zoe and Pierce.

"Father," Ethan said, "You are mighty and powerful and stronger than anyone who would seek to hurt us. We feel scared and vulnerable. And yet we know that we're never out of Your sight—not for a second—and that Your plan for us cannot be thwarted. Mistakes have been made, Lord. We admit that and know those things will need to be dealt with later. But right now we need Your help. Father, guide us. Protect us. Give us wisdom to act responsibly—to be gentle as lambs and shrewd as serpents. Let Your power be made evident in our weakness. Let there be no doubt that You are Lord of everything, even our messes, and will use even those to accomplish Your purposes. We pray these things in the name of Your Son and our Savior, Jesus Christ. Amen."

Zoe opened her eyes, aware that Pierce instantly let go of her hand. She looked over at Ethan and Vanessa, more curious than embarrassed. She had never prayed like that before—not holding hands, and certainly not as if she actually expected God to act.

"All right," Ethan said. "To borrow a now-famous phrase from a brave American: 'Let's roll.'"

CHAPTER 22

Pierce went downstairs to the kitchen at Zoe B's, where Dempsey Tanner was focused on finishing up the last of the Sunday brunch orders.

"What are *you* doing here?" Dempsey said. "I thought you and Zoe were dealing with a family emergency."

"We are. I just wanted to come tell you how much I appreciate your taking my shift. It's no easy task taking on the Sunday brunch crowd. I owe you one."

"Or *two*." Dempsey flashed a crooked smile. "You know I'm glad to help. What's the plan?"

"I've arranged for Benson Surette to cover my shift in the morning."

"*Savannah's* husband?" Dempsey glanced up, his hands still arranging food on the plates. "He hasn't worked here in over a year. Are you confident he can handle the kitchen?"

"I don't really have a choice. Needless to say, I'm more comfortable with you back here, but I can't expect you to work a double shift today *and* tomorrow."

"How long did you say you'll be out?"

"I didn't." Pierce popped a mushroom into his mouth in an effort to look natural. "We'll get back as soon as we can. And,

Dempsey"—he waited until Dempsey paused and caught his gaze—
"I don't want you discussing this with anyone. If someone asks where
we are, just say we're out on personal business."

"All right, boss. Is there anything else I can do?"

"Not really. Zoe asked Savannah to take charge out front. I'm sure
you'll do fine." Pierce glanced at his watch. "I've got to get going."

"Is there a number where you can be reached?"

Pierce shook his head. "No. But I'll check in from time to time.
Hopefully we won't be gone long. If you have questions or concerns,
direct them to Savannah."

He turned and hurried out of the kitchen, through the dining
room, and out into the alcove. He waited a full minute to be sure he
wasn't followed, then went out the back entrance and walked briskly
toward the rendezvous point.

Ethan's simple solution suddenly seemed absurd, but did he have
a better idea? The most important thing to consider was safety. Until
they were inaccessible to Shapiro, talking to the sheriff wasn't a viable
option.

Pierce crossed First Street, wondering how Jude would respond
when he found out his longtime friend Zoe Benoit Broussard was a
fraud.

Zoe waited until two thirty, then slipped out the back door of Zoe B's
and jogged over to First Street, then turned north on *rue Evangeline,*
looking over her shoulder every so often. Had she even considered
how vulnerable she would feel without her cell phone? Ethan's plan

was so simple that, had the circumstances not been life threatening, it might have seemed almost comical.

Out of the corner of her eye, she noticed that a blue car to her left had slowed to a crawl. Her heart nearly pounded out of her chest. Finally she got up the courage to look over at the driver, a man—not Shapiro—who seemed to be looking for an address. She remembered Savannah telling her that Shapiro had come in to Zoe B's several times with a male client. Zoe had never seen him. Would she even know if this supposed client were following her? Didn't she have to be sure before she met up with the others at the rendezvous point—or risk ruining everything?

Zoe began to run and then run faster and faster, glad when she looked back and saw him make a U-turn. Was he following her and trying to make it look as though he wasn't?

Shapiro's words came rushing back. *Did I mention I'm really good at disguises? Angus Shapiro isn't my real name either. So going to the cops won't get me caught. It'll just get you killed.*

She made a sudden turn and cut through the side yard of a light-blue two-story house that backed up to a red brick house on the next block. She crossed Vaughn Street and cut through two more yards until she came out on the sidewalk along Gabel.

The digital sign at the bank flashed the time: 2:56. She still had four minutes. The others might not even be there yet. She turned into the narrow alley between Belle's Beauty Shop and Renee's Alterations, her hands on her knees, and tried to catch her breath.

Was this attempt to keep Shapiro from knowing their whereabouts going to work—or was it just plain silly? Then again, without the ability to track them electronically, how would he have a clue how to find them?

Vanessa pulled into Rouses Market and looked in the rearview mirror for any sign of another car entering the lot right behind her but saw only a Ford pickup pulling out. She drove to the back row and parked under the shade trees, then locked the car and went inside the store. She strolled up and down the produce section, then slipped through the swinging doors and into the warehouse, where the customer restrooms were. She leaned on the wall next to the ladies' room and pretended to be waiting for someone to come out.

Three young men were clowning around as they loaded boxes of produce onto plastic carts. She smiled at them and glanced at her watch.

Hurry up, she thought. *Or I'm going to be late.*

When the workers walked away from the loading dock, she quietly made her way over to the back exit, pushed open the steel door, and skipped down the steps. She ran down the alley and out to the sidewalk, then headed toward the rendezvous point.

A police car sped past her, lights flashing. Vanessa thought about her mother and wondered how disappointed she would be when this was all over and she realized that Vanessa and Ethan had not called her and asked for advice. Vanessa already knew her mother would insist they go to the authorities rather than attempt to outsmart a dangerous criminal. But conventional protocol didn't apply here, and they had to act swiftly.

Vanessa picked up her pace as if that would somehow erase her doubts that this was the wisest decision. Wasn't it a moot point anyway? She had left her cell phone locked in the glove box as Ethan had instructed her. Two minutes from now, everything would be set in motion.

Zoe stood behind a huge live oak, one of many that shaded the grounds of Grace Creek Bible Church. She spotted the blue and white van with the church logo on it. She glanced at her watch, her heart thumping so hard that her arm shook. It was three o'clock. She didn't see Ethan behind the wheel of the van—or any sign of the other two. Had something gone wrong? Had she misunderstood what she was supposed to do?

"Zoe ... over here."

She jumped, her hand over her heart, and turned toward the familiar voice. Pierce waved at her from behind a tree about twenty yards away.

"Have you seen Vanessa or Ethan?" he said.

Zoe ran over to him. "Not yet. I just got here. Isn't that the van over there?"

"I think so. I wonder what's keeping them." He looked around nervously. "Did you have any problems?"

"Not really. Some guy in a blue car pulled up next to me and seemed to be looking for an address. I didn't recognize him, but I ditched him immediately. I cut through some yards and ran over a couple blocks. I'm sure he didn't follow me. I'm probably being paranoid anyway."

"With good reason."

She looked into his eyes and saw fear—and pain. "Pierce, I—"

He put his hand to her lips. "There's nothing left to say. Let's just do what we have to do to keep from getting our throats slit."

Nothing left to say? Was he unwilling to let her explain herself? Did he think she had no remorse?

The sound of feet pounding the ground caught Zoe's attention, and she spun around just as Vanessa came to a stop.

"Sorry I'm ... a little ... late," Vanessa said, sounding out of breath.

"Actually it's right at three." Pierce glanced over at the church van. "I wonder what's keeping Ethan?"

Vanessa started to reach into her pocket and then stopped. "I'm not used to not having my cell phone. I'm sure he'll be here any minute. Did either of you see anyone suspicious?"

"I didn't," Pierce said. "Zoe ditched some guy in a blue car who appeared to be looking for an address."

"Did you see his face?"

Zoe nodded. "It wasn't Shapiro. And the guy made a U-turn and headed the other way. I cut through some yards and never saw him again."

"There's Ethan." Vanessa's eyes grew wide as she pointed to the van. "Let's go."

Zoe climbed into the backseat of the Grace Creek Bible Church van, glad that the tinted windows made her feel invisible. Pierce came in and sat beside her. Vanessa sat up front with Ethan.

"Thank you, Lord, that we all made it okay." Ethan buckled his seat belt. "Please get us there without incident."

Zoe liked the way Ethan talked to God as if He were right there with them. She noted how tenderly Ethan held Vanessa's hand—and that Pierce's hands had turned to fists, his arms tightly folded across his chest. Didn't his body language say more than the harsh words he was holding back?

Zoe willed away the tears. If she started crying, would she ever be able to stop? Pierce would never forgive her. How was she going to let go of her best friend—her partner—her lover? How ironic it was that the lies she told in order to keep Pierce were now the very reason she had lost him.

Ethan started the van and drove slowly to the exit, then pulled onto Grace Creek Boulevard and headed west out of Les Barbes.

No one spoke for perhaps an entire minute.

Finally Ethan said, "In case you haven't heard, they called off the search for the shooter. But now there's trouble at the medical center. A group of African-Americans are marching outside with placards, claiming that the shooting was a payback for the lynching. And a group of whites are taunting them, saying they had it coming. It's getting ugly. That's probably where the sheriff is. And the police chief. And the media."

"Then let's hope we don't need help," Pierce said. "Did you get us a prepaid cell phone?"

Ethan nodded. "Yes, it's been activated. You have five hundred minutes. That should give you more than enough to contact the sheriff and tell him everything. Just remember, you can't call Vanessa or me at home or on our cell phones, just in case Shapiro has the

capability of listening in on *our* calls. If he knows we've been in contact, he might try to force us to tell him where you are."

Vanessa turned and looked over the seat. "Maybe it'll be over
before he even realizes you're gone."

"Wouldn't *that* be nice?" Zoe said. "I just hope he doesn't try to
pry information out of our staff. We didn't tell any of them what was
going on—just that we're dealing with a family emergency."

"I doubt he'll draw attention to himself," Ethan said, "especially
if he's able to track your cell signal—again, assuming he really does
know how to do that. I'm not so sure that he's not bluffing. But why
chance it?"

Zoe nodded. "Pierce and I turned our cell phones on and left
them in the apartment."

Ethan pulled down the visor and looked at them in the mirror.
"Good. At least your signal will be emitting. Maybe by the time he
realizes you're not there, you will have been able to get through to
Sheriff Prejean."

Sheriff Jude Prejean, eyelids heavy, stood outside Hargrave Medical
Center, a few yards from where black activists carried placards and
shouted accusations that whites were taking justice into their own hands,
without any proof that it was blacks who murdered Remy Jarvis.

Jude heard static coming from his walkie-talkie and then a male
voice.

"Sheriff, this is Castille. Do you read? Over ..."

"Affirmative," Jude said. "What's up?"

"Four Trojan horses are in the corral south of HMC. Over ..."

"Copy that," Jude said. "How big is the herd?"

"I see thirty-two. *Ils sont noirs*. Repeat: *Ils sont noirs*. They're hoofing it to the watering hole. Should be in your sights shortly. Over ..."

"Copy that." Jude glanced over at the deputies who were standing between the two groups hurling verbal insults back and forth. "Have the cowboys arrived from Lafayette or New Iberia?"

"Negative. We're standing by, saddled up and ready to go."

"Let me know when they're here."

"Will do, Sheriff. Out."

Jude squinted and looked beyond the crowd to the next block and saw the new arrivals walking toward him. How long would his crowd-control team be able to maintain order?

Deputy Chief Aimee Rivette walked over to him, a row of lines on her forehead. "Four vehicles with thirty-two black activists? We're stretched thin as it is." She shook her head. "Some of our people have been on the clock for over twenty-four hours. Focus is becoming a problem."

"You're reading my mind." Jude glanced over at a media crew doing a live broadcast. "Get with Chief Norman and find out when he expects those reinforcements to be here."

CHAPTER 23

Zoe stood next to the church van, under the shade of a huge live oak, and looked up at the stately pillars that graced the front of Langley Manor. Under different circumstances, camping here with Pierce might be an adventure—perhaps even a romantic one. Could she ever have imagined there would come a time when she dreaded being alone with him?

"That's everything," Vanessa said. "Why don't you come take a look?"

Zoe followed Vanessa inside the old plantation house, instantly hit with the smell of old wood and the stark realization that whoever hung Remy Jarvis had probably hidden here too.

Vanessa led her to the back of the house, to the bedroom nearest to the kitchen, where Ethan and Pierce were inflating two air mattresses.

"I went by the storage locker and dug out our camping gear," Ethan said. "I brought sleeping bags to put on these air mattresses. Also flashlights, a fan, and a lantern—all battery operated. Plus plenty of extra batteries. There's a camping toilet and paper supplies over there in the bathroom."

Zoe perked up. This might not be so bad.

Ethan stood and brushed his hands together. "I stopped at Crawfish Corner and got that Styrofoam ice chest and filled it with bottled water, orange juice, smoked turkey, and cheese. There's bread, peanut butter and jelly, cereal bars, pretzels, and chips in the sacks. Also trash bags, paper towels, plastic utensils, and a package of moisturizing cloths to sponge off with. I know it's hot in here, and there's no running water. Hopefully the fan will help. Did I forget anything?"

"Are you kidding?" Pierce said. "I can't believe you went to all this trouble to make us comfortable. Write down what we owe you, and I'll pay you as soon as we get back."

"Just talk to the sheriff and stay safe." Ethan gave Pierce a pat on the back. "That'll be payment enough. Remember not to go in the front part of the house with flashlights. The sheriff is having a patrol come by a few times a night. He can't see the light on back here. If he sees light, he'll call for backup and investigate, and you'll be anything but under the radar."

Zoe eyes clouded over. Did she deserve their kindness? Would anyone else they knew have taken this kind of risk to help them? "I-I'm so sorry for creating this mess."

Vanessa put her index finger to her lips. "We've already determined who is Lord of our messes. No more apologies."

"It's probably a little scary being out here by yourselves," Ethan said, "especially after the incident with the 'candy man' in the house and the lynching on the property next door. But the outside door to the secret tunnel has been nailed shut. You're safe here. If I didn't feel sure of it, I'd never suggest it. But just so you don't feel defenseless ... I left my Louisville Slugger behind the door."

Pierce shot him a knowing look. "Thanks, man."

Zoe reached in her pocket and felt the can of pepper spray.

"If the sheriff wants you to stay in hiding while he looks for Shapiro," Vanessa said, "we can borrow the van and bring you more supplies. But there should be enough for several days. Shapiro doesn't know about this place. It's probably the safest place you could be."

Ethan glanced at his watch. "I hate to run, but I promised to get the van back by five. It was generous of Pastor Auger to let us borrow it. Vanessa and I have gone to his church several times, but we're not officially members yet."

"What did you tell him?" Zoe asked.

"Just that we had some friends who were in a little trouble and needed to move some things this afternoon—which wasn't a lie. He didn't push me for details." Ethan patted Pierce on the back and shook hands with him. "Remember, unless it's an emergency, don't call us on our cell phones or our home phone. Vanessa and I will call you from a pay phone and check in."

Vanessa put her arms around Zoe and whispered, "Don't be scared. God is right here with you. Even if Pierce shuts you out, God won't."

Jude keyed in the auto-dial number for Colette's cell phone. Had she seen his news conference with the media? Was she aware of the escalating situation? The phone rang only once.

"There you are," Colette Prejean said. "I was hoping you'd call. What a messy situation you've got going on."

"So much for a relaxing Sunday at home."

"Saul wants to know how Deshawn Macey's doing."

"Still critical," Jude said. "But holding his own."

"Saul said he's a good kid. Why was he mixed up in all that?"

"From what we can determine, he was just in the wrong place at the wrong time. Have you been watching the news?"

"Actually I have. CNN did a short sound bite of you talking to the media. I was so proud of you. You sounded professional. Calm. Articulate. Certainly not the stereotype of the southern sheriff."

"My Cajun accent wasn't too much?"

"I can't say *fuh shore.*" She laughed. "The news anchor didn't seem to have any problem understanding you."

"Good," he said. "So is the phone ringing off the hook?"

"And then some. I finally unplugged it. You shouldn't have to spend an hour playing it all back. I decided anyone who needs to talk business can contact you through proper channels. Our close friends and family have our cell numbers."

"Thanks. Of the messages you listened to, could you tell if the comments were generally positive or negative?"

"Why, Sheriff, I only listened to the positive comments. I don't want to hear anything negative about *my* man."

He chuckled. "You don't, huh?"

"Heavens no. You're already working more hours than you should, trying to find Remy's killer and this shooter. The last thing you need is people second-guessing your efforts. I have no patience with that."

"Spoken with conviction."

"We're in this together. I take it personally when folks start coming down on you when they don't know what they're talking about. It's like a *peekon* sticking in my heart. It's all I can do to respond like a lady."

He smiled. But she was *all* lady. How did he ever win her heart? He definitely married up. "Let's talk about something pleasant. So has Saul decided he's ready to go take his driver's test tomorrow?"

"Oh, he's ready." Colette lowered her voice, the way she always did when she spoke seriously about one of the kids. "I'm not sure about Mama. Just think, Jude. Our baby's old enough to drive. Before we know it, we're going to have an empty nest."

"Why don't we just concentrate on how nice it is to have Raymond and Bridgette home from college? We've only got them for another couple weeks before they have to head back."

"Oh, I am. I made *courtbouillon* for them tonight. I sure wish you'd been here to share it."

Jude winced. "Aw, did you make homemade corn bread, too?"

"Of course I did. Don't worry. We saved you some."

"You're a saint."

"My halo's a little tarnished for thinking ill of those who don't appreciate the sacrifices you're making to solve these cases."

"I think the Almighty will forgive you for coming to my defense. But there will always be those who don't agree with or understand the way I do things."

"Well, I'd prefer they move to another parish."

"I'm an elected official. They have a right to question what I do."

"Maybe so. But *I* can unplug them." Colette giggled. "I don't know why I find that so amusing, but I do."

"Sweetheart, I've got to get back to the front lines."

"You sound exhausted."

"That about sums it up. As soon as I feel sure things are secure here, I'm coming home. I'll call and tell you when to heat up the *courtbouillon.*"

Zoe wandered around the first floor of Langley Manor, watching the last vestiges of dusk slip away through the trees. Pierce didn't want to talk—fine. She'd stay out of his way. She wished the windows had drapes she could pull. At least no one could see in unless she turned on a flashlight.

The rear of the house was another story. Once it was dark, wouldn't the lantern-lit room make them visible to anyone or anything prowling out back? She considered the food Ethan brought and wondered whether bears inhabited the woods and might be drawn to it. Then again, this plantation house had been here since 1839. If bears were a threat, wouldn't everyone in Les Barbes know those stories—just as they knew the ghost stories?

She shuddered and dismissed the ghost stories Hebert had told her about Josiah Langley wandering the halls at night, calling for his stillborn son, William. She became aware of a presence behind her and sucked in a breath—

"The phone is working." Pierce's resonant voice echoed in the empty room.

Zoe exhaled, her hand over her pounding heart. "You scared me to death." *Maybe that's what you wanted to do.*

"I called the sheriff's department and was told Jude is in the field and unavailable. I tried reaching Colette at home. For some reason, the phone rings and rings without an answering machine picking up."

"This cell number won't be recognizable on their caller ID," Zoe said. "She'll probably think it's one of those annoying marketing calls and just ignore it."

"That's just great. It's obvious we're not going to reach Jude tonight." Pierce threw his hands in the air. "Why are you standing out here in front of those windows when Ethan told us *not* to?"

Zoe cringed at his harsh tone. "Ethan said not to turn on the flashlight out here, and I won't. I'm just antsy and wanted to walk around. I don't want the sheriff's patrol to know we're here anymore than you do."

"And I don't want to be forced to call 9-1-1 because you fall and break your neck while walking around in the dark!" Pierce's voice went up a decibel. "Let's just try to get through this in one piece, okay? For once, will you just do what you're told without adding your two cents?"

Zoe bit her lip. How was she supposed to reply to such an irrational outburst? She didn't want to make him any more agitated that he already was. "All right," she said calmly.

She turned on her heel and walked slowly toward the light in the back of the house, trying not to show how hurt she was. Did she even have a right to be hurt? If it weren't for her lies, none of this would be happening. But was she going to let Pierce bully her the entire time they were confined together? Did she really have a choice? He had to let go of his anger and disappointment and fear somehow. Could she really blame him for taking it out on her?

She walked into the back bedroom and lay on her air mattress. It was only nine o'clock. She was too wired to be sleepy. Was she just supposed to lay here in silence and stare at the ceiling?

Zoe thought of Adele Woodmore and how kind the dear woman had been in the face of her startling confession. Hadn't Zoe promised to call her tomorrow to see if the repayment agreement was ready and when and where she should go to sign it? If Pierce decided to split up, was she capable of operating Zoe B's? Without Pierce's partnership and support and culinary abilities, did she even want to? Did it matter what she wanted? She had agreed to pay Mrs. Woodmore a thousand dollars a month for the next thirty months.

What if their breakup caused their steady customers to stop coming? What if their friends felt allegiance to both of them and weren't comfortable supporting Zoe as long as Pierce and she were at odds? Unless Zoe B's continued to make a healthy profit, how could she come up with the extra thousand a month? Would she go bankrupt? Would she end up right back where she was ten years ago—without a family? Without enough money to take care of herself?

She was aware that Pierce had stretched out on the other air mattress, his hands clasped behind his head. A scowl distorted his classic French profile, his distinctive nose protruding from his taut face like that of a fairy-tale villain. She could only imagine the angry thoughts bouncing off his brain. How quickly his love had turned to disdain. Instantly their history had been rewritten. She was not the woman Pierce thought he married, and yet he was, and would forever be, everything her heart desired. How cruel was that reality; how befitting its irony.

Zoe wished she'd never been born. Emotion tightened her chest. She closed her eyes, salty tears soaking the sides of her face. She turned on her side, her hand clamped over her mouth, stifling the sobs until she felt as if her head would burst. She'd been alone before. But having experienced the joy of being truly loved—after the dysfunctional relationships she grew up with—could she survive without it? Then again, had Pierce loved who she really was, or who he *thought* she was? Would he have loved Shelby Sieger? If she had come wrapped in that package, with all the baggage that went with it, would he have felt the same?

Zoe sat up and grabbed the roll of paper towels and tore off a piece, then lay down again and blew her nose. In spite of misrepresenting herself, had she ever lied about her feelings for him? Hadn't she been a good wife? Wouldn't she have been a loving mother?

It was irrelevant now. Motherhood was one more dream crushed by the weight of her deceit. The family they were ready to start would never come to be. The son and daughter whose faces she had imagined and whose names she had practiced a hundred times would never exist. There would be no Callie Jeanette Broussard or Tory Pierce Broussard. Because of her lies, she would be left with no one—not even herself. Zoe Broussard was a fraud, every area of her life exposed and laid bare. All that was left was the pathetic truth of who she really was and the lengths she had gone to conceal it.

CHAPTER 24

Vanessa stood at the railing on the Langleys' half of the gallery above Zoe B's, watching the horizon blaze pink on the first day of August. The morning breeze, lukewarm and almost damp enough to wring out, was scented with the delicious smells of coffee, warm beignets, and something spicy.

She wondered if Zoe and Pierce had reached Sheriff Prejean and told him about Shapiro's threat and the frightening case of mistaken identity. How had they fared through the night—were they able to sleep? Were they talking to each other? Had they decided to split up? Had they called a truce?

Ethan came up behind her and put his arms around her, his cheek next to hers, the leathery scent of his aftershave overpowering the breakfast smells.

"Thinking about Zoe and Pierce?"

Vanessa nodded. "I hope they had a restful night, but I doubt it."

"I'll give them a call before I get to the clinic. There's a pay phone at the convenience store on the corner. Maybe you can check in with them too, before you pick up Carter."

"I will." Vanessa smiled. "I sure miss our little guy."

"Me too."

"Something tells me he's ready to come home. Four is young to handle a sleepover. I'm just glad he seemed enthusiastic about it since we needed the space to deal with the Broussards' situation."

"It worked out perfectly." Ethan kissed her cheek, then moved over next to her at the railing and looked down on *rue Madeline*. "I imagine they're pretty scared, now that they've had time to think about it. There's a lot more at stake than just their physical safety."

Vanessa sighed. "I can't imagine how hard it's been for Zoe, living with the deception and all those secrets."

"Or for Pierce, who's now looking back on his entire married life as a lie."

"It's so sad, because they really do—or at least did—love each other. If only Zoe hadn't lied to him."

"She learned to lie to cover her shame," Ethan said. "She'd been doing it so long, it became second nature. I doubt it was a difficult decision to steal the ring and lie to Mrs. Woodmore. Zoe felt justified because she saw it as her way out. She's responsible for that. But this thing with Shapiro really isn't her fault."

"Do you think Pierce will ever be able to understand why she made the choices she did?"

Ethan shrugged. "I don't know, honey. He may not care *why* she did it, especially when it's impacted him so deeply. If they're going to make it through this, they're going to have to look beyond themselves for the strength to forgive—Pierce to forgive Zoe, and Zoe to forgive herself and the parents who abused her. I've never seen forgiveness on that level come from human nature. It takes God."

"They go to church, but I don't get the sense that Zoe and Pierce really *know* the Lord or make Him a part of their everyday lives. Did you see how they looked at us when we joined hands and prayed?"

Ethan slid his arm around her. "Yeah, I think they were uncomfortable with it. But if they ever needed to know that God's there for them, it's now. They were probably more receptive than they let on."

"I know Zoe's afraid Pierce will leave her. Or worse yet, try to have the marriage annulled."

"We know God doesn't want their marriage to end over this," Ethan said. "But it's going to take Him to keep it from happening."

Zoe sat at the antique table in the dining room at Langley Manor and looked out over the green cane fields, hoping the cereal bar and orange juice she'd consumed a half hour ago would stay down.

Why was she thinking of her mother? She had put the woman out of her mind for more than a decade. Was it because she was afraid? Almost as afraid as she'd been all those nights when she had clung tightly to her doll and waited in the dark, hoping her father would pass out before he made it to her bed? Why didn't her mother ever try to stop him? That haunting question still angered her. Zoe had vowed way back then that if she ever had a daughter, she would never allow anyone to hurt her that way.

She sighed. What difference did it make now? She would never have a daughter. She and Pierce weren't going to start a family. Or even start over. They were done.

Zoe heard the wood floor creaking and then footsteps moving toward her. She held her gaze on the cane fields.

Pierce came into the dining room and remained standing. "I called Jude again—at home and at the sheriff's department. The answering machine didn't go on at the house. But I got through to his office. He's due in this morning, but they aren't sure when. I'll have to try back later."

"Shapiro said he'd contact me again before the deadline and tell me where to wire the hundred thousand. He's probably getting suspicious because I'm not answering my home or cell phone."

"Probably so, Zoe! And he'll only get more suspicious as the day wears on. That's why I didn't leave my name and number at the sheriff's department. I don't want there to be any written record of my call. For now, Shapiro probably thinks we're out scrambling to get the money. But once the banks are closed, and he hasn't been able to contact you, he's going to make good on his promise to kill us. It's just a matter of when."

"Maybe Jude will find him," she said.

"How? Since you don't know his real name or what he really looks like. You just double-crossed a drug dealer—who believes it's the second time you did it. He's not going to let this go."

"I'm scared," she said, barely above a whisper.

"Well, you're not the only one."

An unexpected tenderness in his tone led her to think that he might be more concerned for her than for himself.

"I'm sorry," she said. "I know being sorry doesn't change anything."

"You're right. You should've trusted me, Zoe."

"Really?" She turned and looked into his sad, dark eyes. "If I had told you how I got the money to start Zoe B's, wouldn't you have stopped seeing me? Maybe even felt compelled to go to the police—or to Mrs. Woodmore?"

Pierce didn't say anything.

"I shouldn't have lied to you. It was wrong. But from my perspective at the time, it was less wrong than destroying the good thing we had going. I was falling in love with you—something I didn't even think was possible, given my childhood abuse. I knew telling you the truth wouldn't undo the past. What it *would* do was wreck any chance we had for a future. It was self-serving not to tell you. I don't deny that. But I never, ever intended to hurt you."

"Did you really think that letting me fall in love with a fraud would not hurt me?"

"Yes, because I tried to be the person I led you to believe I was—the person I wanted to be." Tears ran down Zoe's cheeks. "I thought I could make you happy. You have to believe me."

"Believe you?" Pierce rolled his eyes. "You've got to be kidding. And if you think you can manipulate me with your tears, forget it. I don't feel sorry for you. What you did was beyond the pale. I don't even have a word for that kind of deceit."

Desperate, she thought. *Desperate people do desperate things.*

Zoe felt as if her mouth were stuffed with cotton. What could she say in her own defense? The very shame she worked so hard to hide had been laid bare, all her secrets exposed. Pierce knew she was a thief. And a liar. He knew she'd been sexually abused. And that she wasn't Cajun. And her family was dysfunctional. Somehow his knowing the truth made her feel repulsive.

Pierce sighed. "I'm going to go clean up the best I can. And then I'll try calling Jude again."

Vanessa inhaled the delicious aroma as she drizzled warm syrup over the top of her pain perdu, at the same time observing Hebert, Father Sam, and Tex, who occupied the table next to her.

Savannah poured Vanessa a coffee refill and then moved over to the table with the three men.

"Tell me again where Zoe and Pierce are today," Tex said.

"They had some personal business to take care of." Savannah put some tiny tubs of creamer on the table in front of Tex.

"So Dempsey's running da kitchen?" Hebert asked.

"Not this morning." Savannah's voice sounded playful. "Benson is."

Tex snapped his suspenders. "Whoa. Your hubby's back? Where've I been?"

"He's not *back*, Tex. Just covering for Pierce."

"Surely Zoe and Pierce are planning to attend Remy's funeral Mass tomorrow?" Father Sam said.

"I didn't ask. But knowing how Zoe felt about Remy, I'm sure they are."

Vanessa took a sip of coffee, wondering if Zoe had given much thought to Remy since Shapiro threatened her—or had even heard that his funeral was Tuesday. Should Vanessa remind her? If the sheriff advised her to stay in hiding, would knowing she was missing the funeral just add to her stress?

"I'm going wid Emile today," Hebert said, "to pick up Remy's ashes. Maybe we can avoid da media since everybody's distracted wid dat *potaine* at da medical center."

"I'm afraid it's turned into more than a ruckus," Savannah said.

"She's right," Tex leaned forward, his elbows on the table. "I heard on the news that some black activists arrived from Baton Rouge and have been exchangin' unpleasantries with white workers from the sugar refinery."

Father Sam shook his head. "All we need is troublemakers from the outside stirring things up. We can work out our own problems. People are understandably upset and scared after Remy's murder and then this senseless shooting. But getting groups from outside Les Barbes involved will just turn this town into a powder keg. And a media circus."

"Oh, I think we're already there," Tex said.

Hebert swatted the air and said something in Cajun French that the others seemed to understand.

Vanessa took a bite of her pain perdu and pretended to be oblivious to the conversation at the next table. She and Ethan had been so consumed with Zoe and Pierce's problems that they hadn't even listened to the news to check the status of the racial tension that had been building outside Hargrave Medical Center.

The bell jingled on the front door, and a forty-something man came in and smiled at Savannah.

She grabbed a menu. "Right this way." She seated him at a table next to the brick wall.

Zoe B's was bustling this morning. At least things seemed to be running smoothly.

Vanessa finished her breakfast, eager to check in with Zoe and then go pick up Carter. She wiped her mouth with the napkin, aware that the man seated next to the brick wall had been staring at her for quite some time. She was used to getting double takes—but this was downright annoying.

She looked up and locked gazes with him, thinking he'd be embarrassed and look away. He didn't flinch. Suddenly her heart was pounding so loudly that she was sure it was audible to everyone. Why did she have such a bad feeling about him?

She tried not to react and motioned for Savannah to bring her check.

"Here you go," Savannah said. "Anything else?"

"No, breakfast was great." Vanessa pasted on a pleasant look, then put a tip on the table and walked over to the register to pay her bill. All she wanted to do was get out of there.

Jude sat at the desk in his office, having his first cup of coffee before the day went into high gear. He had checked with Deputy Castille the minute he arrived at work and was advised that Deshawn Macey was still in critical condition and the situation at the medical center had intensified. The number of demonstrators, black and white, continued to increase—as did the media presence. Several white demonstrators had pelted police with produce and were charged with disorderly conduct, and two black youths were arrested after a tire-slashing spree in the medical center parking lot.

Officers arrived earlier in the morning from the Lafayette, New Iberia, and Morgan City PDs to help maintain order. The Franklin PD was sending officers tomorrow to assist in keeping the peace during Remy Jarvis's memorial Mass at Saint Catherine's, which was also being televised on a large screen in the Saint Catherine's High School gym.

Jude glanced out the window. The traffic was bumper-to-bumper on Courthouse Boulevard. The media was a big pain in the neck that only added to the traffic congestion caused by the high volume of tourists. It wasn't as though the media came to report the news. Reporters seemed more interested in human-interest stories that reinforced their opinions of the situation, their preconceived notions.

His intercom buzzed, followed by his administrative assistant's voice.

"Sheriff, there's a call for you—a Pierce Broussard. Says it's urgent, but he won't say what it's about. I tried giving him to Deputy Chief Rivette, but he insisted on speaking to you."

"It's okay, Lisa. I'll take it."

"He's on line one, sir."

"Thanks."

Jude took a sip of coffee. What was so urgent that Pierce wouldn't talk to anyone else? He put the receiver to his ear and pressed the flashing button. "Hello, Pierce."

"Jude! Thank heavens. I've been trying to reach you since yesterday afternoon."

"Really? I didn't see any messages."

"Actually, I didn't leave messages."

"How can I help you?"

Pierce exhaled into the phone. "Zoe and I are caught in a dangerous situation, and we're not sure what to do. We've been hiding since yesterday afternoon."

"Hiding from whom?"

"It's so complicated. I hardly know where to begin."

"Start at the beginning. Tell me everything."

"I need to tell you the ending first," Pierce said, "and then I'll back it up. A drug dealer named Angus Shapiro—that's not his real name—accosted Zoe. He claims her parents owed him a hundred thousand dollars before they died, and he's come to collect."

"And they didn't?"

"No, her parents are alive. He's got the wrong person. Zoe changed her name ten years ago from Shelby Sieger to Zoe Benoit. This guy thinks she's the daughter of Pierre and Violet Benoit, who were heroine dealers. He wants her to have a hundred thousand dollars ready to wire to his account by the time the banks close today—or he's threatened to kill her *and* me. He said if we went to the authorities or told someone who did, he would know, and it would be the last thing we ever did. So we found a place to hide out and have been trying to get in touch with you on a prepaid cell phone. There's no way he's going to let us live, whether we pay him or not—"

"Pierce, wait. Slow down. Where are you?"

"I don't think it's safe to tell you that. Just hear us out. I'm going to put Zoe on and let her tell you the whole story."

CHAPTER 25

Vanessa walked out the front door of Zoe B's and leaned against the building, the traffic along *rue Madeline* surprisingly heavy, even for the morning rush hour. She keyed in the fast-dial number for Ethan's cell phone. It rang once. Twice. Three times.

Come on, pick up!

"Hey there," Ethan said. "I was just about to call you before I begin my first counseling session. I talked to Pierce about an hour ago. He still hadn't reached the sheriff. He sounded stressed. I can only imagine how hard it is for him being confined with Zoe under these circumstances."

"No kidding. Did either of them sleep?"

"Off and on. They appreciate the air mattresses and the fan. At least they're as comfortable as they're going to get under these circumstances."

"I'm glad for that. I'll call Zoe from the pay phone at Rouses Market before I pick up Carter. I'm going to be a nervous wreck until this is over."

"Well, I don't see any way it'll be over today. Zoe and Pierce might have to stay put for a while."

"Let's hope not. Maybe the sheriff has an idea we haven't thought of."

"Honey, are you okay? You sound funny."

"I'm fine. I just had a creepy thing happen." Vanessa glanced over at a family of tourists dressed in Roux River Bayou T-shirts, walking into Zoe B's. "I was having breakfast at the eatery, and a man at another table kept staring at me. It was so annoying that I finally stared back, thinking he would get embarrassed and look away. He didn't."

"I'm sure he thought you were attractive. You should be used to that by now."

"No, this was different. It almost felt threatening."

"Threatening? Did he say anything?"

Vanessa sighed. "No. This sounds pretty silly, now that I say it out loud. He just gave me the creeps, that's all. I'm probably overreacting."

"Don't be so quick to blow off your instincts. Where are you?"

"Standing in front of Zoe B's. I think I'll walk around the building to my car so I don't have to go back in."

"Good. Make sure he doesn't follow you. I'll stay on the line until you're inside your car."

"All right. I'm walking. I can't believe how hot it is already."

"I know," Ethan said. "I thought Tennessee summers were hot. But the humidity is something else."

"I miss having a place to take Carter swimming."

"Maybe we should consider buying a family pass to the pool at Roux River Park. I heard it's nice."

"I'd love that. It would give me something to do outside with Carter when it's so hot."

"Why don't you find out what we need to do to buy a pass? It can't be that expensive. Let's just do it."

"Sounds like a plan." Vanessa stopped at the car and glanced over her shoulder. "Okay, I'm getting in my car now. I love you."

"I love you, too. Let me know if you find out anything after you talk to Zoe."

"I will."

Vanessa slid in behind the wheel and locked the car. One quick stop at a pay phone to talk to Zoe—and then she would pick up Carter. She could hardly wait to see him.

She started the car and glanced in the rearview mirror, surprised to see the back door of the building left wide open. How did that happen? Weren't she and Ethan the only two besides Zoe and Pierce who had keys to that door?

She heard a rustling sound in the backseat, then felt something tighten around her neck, closing off her windpipe. She tried to grab the cord or strap or whatever it was but it seemed to tighten like a vice as she screamed without a voice and clawed frantically at the hairy wrists and the hands of the attacker who held it there. She heard herself making choking sounds and wondered if she was about to be raped or killed—or both.

Lord, help me! Help me!

"Stop fighting!" he ordered. "And I'll let go. Make any attempt to scream or call for help, and we'll hurt your kid. You don't want to test me on this. I've got a real mean streak and zero tolerance."

Vanessa felt the pressure subside and began to gasp, desperately trying to inhale. After several tries, she sucked in air, then began to cough violently for what seemed an eternity, finally able to catch her breath—and a glimpse in the rearview mirror of those same creepy eyes she had seen in Zoe B's.

"Don't … hurt … my son," she begged. "Please."

"Well now, that's entirely up to you—and whether or not you're willing to tell me what I want to know."

⚜

Jude listened to every word Zoe Broussard told him and then turned off the recorder and sat back in his chair.

"Did you get all that on tape?" she asked.

"I did. Is Pierce still there?"

"I'm here."

"I don't need to tell you two how serious this is. You were smart to hide." Jude glanced at his watch. "I imagine this guy has already figured out you've pulled a fast one. He's going to do everything he can to find out where you are. Does anyone know besides the Langleys?"

"No," Zoe said. "And if he's monitoring our phone calls, he won't find any calls made to us by Vanessa or Ethan."

"But if there isn't *any* activity on your cells or your land line, that alone will be red flag."

Zoe sighed. "I didn't think of that."

"Since he doesn't know where you are, my guess is he's going to try to force your whereabouts out of someone."

"But that's why we didn't tell anyone!" Zoe said. "Not even our staff."

"He doesn't know that." Jude shook his head. "The timing on this couldn't be worse. With all that's going on with the hanging and the shooting and Remy's funeral tomorrow, I simply can't spare the resources to protect you."

"We understand," Zoe said. "Vanessa told us you probably wouldn't. That's why Ethan thought we should hide before Shapiro got suspicious. We figured we'd be safe here for a few days."

Jude raked his hands through his hair. Of all times to be stretched to the limit. "Are you going to tell me where you are?"

"Can you promise us there's no way Shapiro can find out?" she said.

"Absolutely."

"We're out at Langley Manor," Pierce said. "Ethan set us up in the back bedroom on the ground level—we've got sleeping bags, food and water, even a battery-operated fan. No one can see the light on from the front of the house. Not even your patrol."

"Which I've had to temporarily suspend," Jude said. "Every available officer is needed to keep the peace and help investigate."

"What do you suggest we do?" Pierce said.

"Stay put and lay low. Zoe, the clothes you had on the night Shapiro threatened you ... have you washed them?"

"No, they're in the laundry hamper in our bathroom."

"Good. I'd like your permission to go in and retrieve them. We might find valuable DNA on them that could tell us who this guy is."

"All right. I was wearing red capris and a red-and-white floral tank top. You can't miss them. There's mud all over the back. And Shapiro smeared my blood across the front of the tank top with his finger. My Nikes are in the closet. The soles have mud caked on them."

"What about the notes Shapiro left you?"

"They're stacked neatly in my lingerie drawer. Take those, too. Jude, come to think of it, he might have touched the door to the office when he slipped a couple of the notes under the door."

"We'll dust for prints, but our best chance of getting usable DNA is your clothes and those notes."

Vanessa broke out in a cold sweat, her heart pounding with raw terror. She finally stopped panting and tried to breathe normally.

"We haven't officially met," the man said. "The name's Shapiro."

"What do … you … want?"

"Tell me where I can find Zoe and Pierce Broussard."

"They've been gone … all weekend," Vanessa said.

"Why didn't they take their cell phones?"

"I don't know. Maybe they wanted … some time alone."

"Well, the weekend's over. Why aren't they back?"

"You should ask the people who work for them."

"I'm asking *you*." Shapiro grabbed her by the hair and held her tightly against the headrest, pressing a knife blade to her throat. "I promise you, you do not want to mess with me. If you want to see your kid alive, you'd better start talking."

How could he know where Carter was? Should she give up Zoe and Pierce, just like that, knowing he would kill them? The image of Zoe's bleeding face popped into her mind and made her shudder. Would he cut her, too, until she talked—and then kill her the minute she told him what he wanted?

Lord, please help me! I don't know what to do!

"Well?" She felt a sting and realized he was cutting her neck ever so slightly with the knife blade. She felt as if she were going to lose her breakfast.

She clamped her eyes shut. "Please ... I can't tell you what I don't know."

"Then tell me what you *do* know." His voice was deep and raspy. No hint of the Texas accent Zoe described. "Where did the Broussards go? If you want to go on living and get your kid back unharmed, tell me now!"

Vanessa trembled, a drop of perspiration trickling down her temple. There was no way Shapiro knew where Carter was. Wouldn't he have had to follow Ricky's parents home after they picked him up on Sunday? Why would he do that before he even had a reason to suspect Zoe and Pierce weren't going to give him the money? Surely he was bluffing.

"Where *are* they?" Shapiro said. "I'm running out of patience!"

"The Broussards are my landlords. I've only known them a few weeks. Why would they tell *me* their plans?"

"You live across the hall from them. People always tell a neighbor when they're going to be out of town."

"I hardly know them." Could he tell her heart was nearly pounding out of her chest? "If I knew where they were, why would I risk my son's life—or mine—by not telling you?"

"Beats me. But you're lying."

"Why would I lie?" *You'll kill us all, that's why.* "It makes no sense! Please, I'm begging you—you're making a huge mistake. I can't tell you something I don't know."

"Have it your way, Vanessa. This is going to get very unpleasant. But you *are* going to tell me where they went. Hand me your cell phone."

Vanessa picked up her cell phone, her hand shaking, and passed it back to Shapiro. Would he figure out the anonymous caller number she entered in the directory was the Broussards' prepaid cell number? Would he think to look for that?

"Now start the car!"

"Where are we going?"

"Shut up. Just do what I say."

CHAPTER 26

Zoe sat on her air mattress, hugging her knees, wishing Pierce would say something about the phone call they'd just had with Jude.

Finally she said, "Thank you for staying calm. I know it was humiliating telling Jude our personal business."

He lifted his gaze and shot her one of his classic you-got-that-right looks.

"At least Jude knows everything now," she said. "Maybe he'll get DNA evidence off the clothes and shoes I was wearing when Shapiro assaulted me."

"We can only hope."

The disgust in his voice made her want to cry. Could she blame him for feeling repulsed by the whole drama?

"When Vanessa calls," Zoe said, "we need to fill her in on everything so she won't be alarmed if she sees deputies in our apartment."

Pierce stretched out on his air mattress, his hands behind his head. "You'd better hope they find something that tells them who this Shapiro creep is, or we're going to live in fear until he finally kills us. Drug dealers are ruthless. They settle every score. I still can't believe you got us into this."

Zoe wiped away the tear that trailed down her face. Did it even matter that there was no way she could have seen this coming? None of it would have happened if she hadn't tried to be someone she wasn't.

A dull thud came from upstairs. Zoe froze.

"What was *that?*" Pierce jumped to his feet and grabbed the ball bat from behind the door.

For a split second she was a child again, staring up at her drunken father.

Pierce gripped the bat with one hand and put his index finger to his lips with the other.

She listened intently for footsteps moving across the ceiling, but the only sound she heard was the thumping of her heart. Had something fallen? There was no furniture upstairs and nothing hanging on the walls that she could recall.

Neither of them moved for several minutes. Had Shapiro found them? Had he forced Vanessa or Ethan to tell him where they were? Fear seized her. What if they were going to die?

God, when Ethan prayed, he said we're never out of Your sight—not for a second. That means You see us right now. Help us! Don't let Shapiro hurt us!

"We need to get out of here," Zoe whispered.

"And go where? We're sure not safe outside this house." Pierce stuck his head out in the hallway and then turned to her. "I'm going upstairs and take a look. It's probably nothing."

"It didn't sound like nothing."

"Every door and window is locked," he said. "There has to be an explanation for the sound. Wait here."

"Are you kidding?" Zoe scrambled to her feet. "I'm not staying here by myself. I'm coming with you."

"Suit yourself. Stay right behind me."

They crept down the hall to the back stairs and slowly climbed, one cautious step at a time, to the next level.

Despite the massive live oaks that shaded the house, enough light came through the window at the end of the hallway for them to see where they were going. Zoe stayed right on Pierce's heels, clinging to the hem of his shirt, half expecting the ghost of Josiah Langley to jump out at them at any moment.

Pierce entered the first room, looking and listening intently before moving on to the next. Except for the sound of their breathing, it was absolutely still.

When they came to the last bedroom—where the deputies had found the door to the secret tunnel—Zoe stopped and clung to the door frame, her pulse racing so fast she feared she might faint.

Pierce crept over to the closet and gingerly tapped the walls with the bat. "I see the door to the tunnel."

"Isn't it behind the bookshelf?"

"No, the bookshelf's next to it. The deputies must have left it there." He turned the knob and pulled open the door, jumping back as if he were expecting someone to lunge at him.

"Do you see anything?" she whispered.

"Not really. It's dark. I can't tell where the stairs are."

Pierce backed up and turned around, then prodded her out into the hallway. "We've been through every room. There's nobody up here."

"No*body*. But what if the stories about Josiah Langley's ghost aren't so far-fetched after all?"

Pierce rolled his eyes. "I don't see anyone, do you?" He made a sweeping motion with his hand. "There's no one here but us. Let's go back downstairs."

Pierce moved toward the big staircase that led down into the formal entryway.

Zoe started to follow him and stepped on something hard. She stopped and picked it up. "I don't believe this."

"What now?" Pierce sighed and turned around.

"I just stepped on a lemon drop." She walked over to him and put it in his hand. "Explain how *that* got here."

"Don't overreact. I'm sure it's left over from when the intruder was here."

"Funny the deputies didn't see it."

"Zoe, it's not that light up here. It wouldn't be hard to miss. You didn't see it until after you stepped on it. We just searched all the rooms on this floor. There's no one up here. It was probably just the house settling."

"It sounded like something fell on the floor."

Pierce handed her the bat. "Fine. Search it again, if you want. And search the secret tunnel while you're at it. And the basement. And the attic. I'm going downstairs and wait for Vanessa's call. If you run into Josiah Langley, tell him hello for me."

Zoe's eyes clouded over, and she blinked away the tears. Wasn't it hard enough being confined here without Pierce's sarcasm?

Jude stood in the living room of Zoe and Pierce's apartment and waited while Stone Castille and Mike Doucet went to retrieve the clothes Zoe was wearing the night she met with Shapiro—and to find the notes he left her. He glanced around the apartment. What a cozy place it was. Their French country furnishings captured the old-world charm that was also pervasive at Zoe B's.

He spotted the Broussards' wedding picture on the bookshelf and went over where he could see it better. Had it really been five years since Zoe and Pierce got married? He remembered their wedding like it was yesterday—especially the reception. Zoe and Pierce had cooked the food themselves ahead of time. He had never seen a more delicious, authentic spread of Cajun food. Several cousins got together and played zydeco and contemporary Cajun music. It was one, big happy party that went on for hours. Why hadn't he given a second thought to the fact that Zoe's family wasn't there? Now that he knew the truth about her, shouldn't it have given him pause?

Jude looked at the framed picture of Pierce's family. The Broussards were a proud lot. Even if Pierce somehow weathered the betrayal he must be feeling, would his family? Would they be able to accept Zoe after this?

Stone came out of the bathroom, wearing plastic gloves and carrying paper bags. "I've got the shirt, capris, and shoes. I hope we get DNA—and that this jerk is in the system."

"That makes two of us."

Mike came out of the bedroom. "I found all five notes, right where Mrs. Broussard said they'd be." He held up a small bag. "I'll get these sent to the lab."

"Good work. Put a rush on it. Gil's got one of the detectives dusting the office door for prints. There's got to be something usable in all this."

Jude's phone vibrated. He took it off his belt clip, read the display, and put the phone to his ear. "Yeah, Aimee. What's up?"

"Sheriff, we got a break in the Jarvis case. The lab discovered a spot of blood on Remy Jarvis's shirt that didn't belong to Remy. They did a DNA analysis and found the guy in the system—name's Reagan Cowan, age thirty-nine, of New Orleans. He was arrested in 2001 on cocaine possession. The case was thrown out on some kind of technicality. Cowan's wanted in Texas on aggravated assault and trafficking charges. We've got an APB out on him. I just sent his mug shot to your phone."

"Good work, Aimee."

"Also, we just got the report on shoe impressions we cast at the scene of Remy's murder. I put the report on your desk but thought you'd want a heads up."

"Give me the bottom line."

"Using their SoleSearcher database," she said, "the FBI was able to identify three distinct shoe impressions on the ground directly under the place where Remy was found hanging. The size twelve Converse high-top was Remy's. They also found a men's size eleven North Face summer sneaker, and a men's size ten and a half Columbia Newton Ridge hiking boot. Can't get any more specific than that."

"Good," Jude said. "All we need now are suspects."

"Also, the fourth shoe impression we cast on the Vincent farm and also on the grounds at Langley Manor fit a Sears and Roebuck loafer sold in 2001 and 2002. They noted the soles were extremely worn."

"That's interesting," Jude said. "Seems an odd shoe to wear when traipsing around the two properties."

"That's what I was thinking. Not exactly a hiking boot."

"No, but it's not something we're going to find in everyone's closet either. Okay, Aimee, thanks."

"Are you finding everything where Zoe said it was?"

"Yeah, it's all here. We should be done shortly. I was about to check with the team at Roux River Park and see if they found anything near the first turn on Landry Trail where Shapiro threatened her. I really can't afford to pull our people off the other details to get this done. But I don't want to be investigating another murder either. Let's find this guy."

Vanessa drove west on Grace Creek Boulevard and out of the city limits of Les Barbes, Shapiro now holding a gun on her.

"Where are we going?" she asked for the third time, hating that her voice was shaking as much as the rest of her.

Was his silence a ploy to intimidate her? How much longer could she pretend not to know where the Broussards were before Shapiro starting hurting her? Did he really believe she knew—or was he just fishing? How far was he willing to go to find out?

At least her gut feeling that he didn't know where Carter was seemed to be correct. Why else would he have stopped threatening to hurt her son if she didn't talk? But did that make the situation any less dire? If she gave in and told Shapiro where Zoe and Pierce were, wouldn't he dispose of her—and then go after them? And if she didn't tell, wouldn't he try to force it out of her? Her only way out of this alive was to catch him off guard and make a run for it the first chance she got.

Lord, show me what to do. I need wisdom. And angels!

"Turn right on Plantation Highway," he ordered.

"Why won't you tell me where we're going?" she asked, not expecting a response.

Vanessa turned on her blinker and exited at Plantation Highway. She stopped at the stop sign and made a right turn as she was told. Why did he make her take *this* exit? Langley Manor was only another mile on this road. Did he know Zoe and Pierce were there? Had he been playing her all along?

She stole a glance at Shapiro in the rearview mirror. His eyes laughed at her mockingly. She shuddered, her heart hammering so wildly that she felt light-headed and wondered if she had any business driving.

"Slow down and get ready to turn," he said.

"Where? There's no cross street for several miles."

"Shut up and just do it."

At least he wasn't going to Langley Manor. Vanessa slowed the car. "Do you want me to pull over?"

"No. There's an unmarked road up ahead."

The Vincent place? Did he know?

"There—on the right. Turn."

Vanessa turned onto the road, feeling the same panic she did after Drew was shot and she thought the killer was coming back for her. The last thing she wanted was to be alone in that farmhouse with Shapiro.

If she were going to survive this, didn't she have to be smart? Didn't she have to win his confidence? Didn't she have to make her move at just the right moment?

Lord, make me gentle as a lamb and shrewd as a serpent. I belong to You. You live in me. Don't let him desecrate this temple.

"There's a wooden bridge up ahead. Turn left at the mailbox just beyond it. You'll see the name *Vincent* on it."

Vanessa did as she was instructed, more panicked by the minute. Why was he bringing her out here? Did he even know Remy Jarvis had been murdered here? She glanced in the side mirror at the cloud of white dust behind her.

"There's a farmhouse up this road," Shapiro said. "That's where we're going."

Vanessa resisted the urge to jump out of the car and run. Wouldn't he shoot her—even if just to disable her? But if she waited for "the right moment," would she still have the courage to seize it? How long could she refuse to give in to the fear that threatened to steal her hope?

She spotted the mold-stained roof of the farmhouse up ahead. Everything in her wanted to flee. Images of Ethan and Carter popped into her mind. How would they deal with losing her? She had to make it through this alive. She had to keep a clear head.

"Pull up in front of the house and kill the motor."

Kill the motor? How she wished that was all he wanted killed. She did what he said, her stomach feeling as if it were falling down an elevator shaft.

"Now slowly hand me the keys."

Vanessa took the keys out of the ignition and passed them over the seat to Shapiro.

He got out of the car, then opened the driver-side door. "Get out. I want to see your hands."

Vanessa got out of the car, her hands up, and avoided eye contact with Shapiro.

"Well, aren't you the pretty one?" He stroked her hair with the barrel of his gun. "I'll bet your husband would hate to see that sweet face rearranged. You won't like it either." He laughed mockingly. "This is your last chance to tell me where Zoe and Pierce Broussard went—before things get very unpleasant."

Terror seized her. *Lord, what do I do? If I go in there, he's going to hurt me until I talk—then he'll kill me and go after Zoe and Pierce.*

Shapiro opened the hood of the car and tinkered with some wires, keeping the gun pointed at her.

"There. The car won't start until I put everything back where it belongs—just in case you were entertaining the idea of stealing the keys and taking off."

Vanessa glanced up at the dilapidated farmhouse and realized it was boarded up.

Shapiro grabbed her arm and turned her around. "Walk."

"Where?"

"Toward those trees."

Vanessa high-stepped through the high weeds toward a horizontal row of massive live oaks. Beyond them she saw a broad expanse of cane fields, the stalks tall and green and swaying in the breeze. On the other side was the Langley property.

A bumblebee buzzed around her head, and she swatted at it without even thinking.

Shapiro grabbed both sides of her neck and squeezed. "Keep your hands up and keep walking."

"Where are you taking me? I don't know anything."

"Shut up." He stuck the gun barrel flush against her back and nudged her forward.

Vanessa spotted a shed about thirty yards in front of her, and her knees nearly dropped her. Is that where he was taking her?

"You should know this farm is a crime scene," she blurted out. "A man was murdered on this property. The place is crawling with sheriff's deputies."

"Not anymore."

"You don't know that."

"Yeah, I do. I make it my business to know everything the cops are doing." Shapiro laughed. "That's how I stay one step ahead of them." He grabbed her hair and pulled her backward, his lips to her ear, his voice husky and threatening. "I'm a wanted man, a dangerous criminal. I've *killed* people. So either tell me where the Broussards are, or I'll force it out of you. I always get what I want. It's just a matter of *how*."

Jude stood at the window in his office and looked down at the Saint Catherine Parish Courthouse. Billowy gray clouds hid the sun, and thunder reverberated in the distance. Maybe the rain would dampen the powder keg of racial tension until they could get a lead on who hanged Remy—and who shot Deshawn Macey in the park.

There was a knock at the door.

"May I come in?" Aimee said.

"Sure. What's up?"

She walked over to him and handed him a folder. "You need to see this. Joe at the lab rushed through the evidence you obtained at the Broussards' apartment as a personal favor to you and hit pay dirt."

"I like the sound of that."

"This was a total surprise, Sheriff. He was able to get viable DNA off a sweat droplet on Zoe Broussard's tank top. It's a match to the blood DNA on Remy Jarvis's shirt."

"You're kidding." Jude scanned the report. And then scanned it again. "So this Cowen character who was involved in Remy's hanging is also the drug dealer who came to collect from Zoe?"

"Exactly. But it makes no sense."

Jude arched his eyebrows. "Not yet. Let's get busy and connect the dots."

"I'm already on it. I'm assembling a team to dig deeper into Cowen's background."

"He told Zoe he was a master of disguises." Jude picked up his cell phone and accessed the photo Aimee had sent him. "It's hard to know who we're dealing with. He could be anybody."

CHAPTER 27

Vanessa trudged through the high grass to the metal shed, her face dripping with perspiration, her shoes suddenly feeling as if they were made of cement. No way was she going in there with Shapiro.

"Stop right there," he said. "Kneel down and put your hands behind your head. I need to get something out of here. If you so much as blink, I'll blow your head off."

Everything in her wanted to run, but she couldn't make her feet move.

"I said down on your knees."

Vanessa complied. She looked out in the distance, beyond the row of live oaks to the sugarcane fields that lay between them and the Langley property. How far was it? Maybe a quarter mile?

She heard a squeaky door slide open. She glanced over at the shed and locked gazes with Shapiro, his arm extended, the gun pointed right at her.

"Don't even think about it," he said.

But she did think about it. Even getting shot sounded better than being tortured or raped or whatever else he had in mind. Images of Ethan and Carter popped into her head, and her vision blurred. Would she ever see them again? Why couldn't she remember what her mother told her to do or not do if she ever found herself in a life-threatening situation?

Lord, I need a way out of here. Unless You help me soon, I'll be seeing You face-to-face.

Was it death that scared her—or just the idea of being murdered? And of leaving Ethan and Carter to fend for themselves?

She heard the metal door slide shut.

"All right, get up. Keep your hands behind your head and walk in a straight line, toward the trees."

Vanessa rose to her feet. "Please. You have to believe me. If I could help you, I would."

"Yeah, I heard you."

"Why won't you believe me?"

"I believe you. Feel better?"

Vanessa was taken aback for a moment. "So why aren't you letting me go?"

"You know too much."

"How can I know too much when I don't know anything?" Vanessa heard the desperation in her voice. "Please. I have a little boy who needs me. Letting me go won't pose a threat to you. You're obviously good at not getting caught."

"That's because I don't leave eyewitnesses behind. Now keep walking until I tell you to stop."

"Please … you don't have to do this!"

"Yeah, I do." He prodded her with the barrel of the gun. "Shut up and keep moving."

Vanessa was curious what it was he had taken out of the shed but was afraid to turn around and look. She found the strength to move one foot in front of the other, her mind racing faster than her pulse. Why didn't he just shoot her and get it over with? What was he waiting for?

She looked out across the cane fields and could barely make out the Langley property on the other side. How ironic that they were this close to Zoe and Pierce, yet Shapiro was clueless. At least they would survive this ordeal. There wasn't anything she could do to save herself. Or was there?

"All right," she blurted out. "I-I haven't been truthful. I'll tell you where the Broussards are." What did she have to lose by making something up? Maybe she could buy some time. "They're staying with Pierce's cousin in New Iberia. Their credit isn't any good, and they're trying to borrow the money from someone in his family. I can take you to them. I know where it is."

"I thought you hardly knew them."

"I was afraid to tell you. I thought you'd hurt them."

He laughed. "You thought right. That's far enough. Stop here."

"I'm sorry I didn't tell you before," Vanessa said. "But I'm telling you now. Please, I don't want to die. My son needs me! I'm begging you. Just let me take you to them! We'll both get what we want."

"Nice try, Vanessa. But you don't know where they are anymore than I do."

"Yes, I do. I'll drive you to New Iberia. Just don't kill me. Please!"

"Kneel down and keep your hands behind your head."

Lord, is this my time to die? She remembered Ethan telling her that he had asked the very same question when he was running from his cousin's killers. Was there still hope? Or was this it?

Vanessa almost bolted, but something inside her held her back.

What was Shapiro doing? He whistled some tune she didn't recognize and seemed perfectly relaxed. Didn't it bother him one bit that he was about to kill a child's mother?

"All right, up on your feet. Keep your hands where they are."

"If you kill me," Vanessa said, "you'll have to answer to God. I belong to Him."

"Well, *I don't.*" He came around and stood in front of her, surgical gloves on his hands, and opened a folding chair and sat it on the ground. That's when she saw the rope.

She sucked in a breath. Terror seized her, and she fought back the tears. Was he going to hang her?

Lord, help me! Don't let him do this!

He flashed a smug grin. "I hung that Jarvis kid on a whim—to distract the cops while I did my business with the Broussards. It's been pretty entertaining. And since the cops think blacks were responsible for lynching Jarvis, they won't have trouble believing blacks hung you in retaliation for the shooting in the park. Especially since this is the tree where Jarvis was hung—and the specific location was never released to the press. Only the killer would know."

"You won't get away with this. My mother's a police chief. She'll make it her life's mission to solve my murder—and track you down."

"Yeah, well. She'll have to stand in line. I'm a popular guy." Shapiro threw the rope over a low branch and tucked his gun in his waistband. "Don't worry. It won't be long before you lose consciousness."

Vanessa homed in on the cane fields behind him and remembered Ethan's stories of how he and Drew would sneak off to the fields and disappear for hours.

Run! The voice was almost audible. *Go hide!*

Vanessa lunged at Shapiro and clawed his eyes with her fingers, then ran as fast as she had ever run in her life toward the cane fields.

Shapiro hollered curses and threats. Shots rang out, and a bullet whizzed past her ear.

She pushed herself until she stumbled and lost her balance, but managed to stay on her feet. *Help me, Lord. Don't let me fall. Don't let him catch me.*

Another bullet grazed her right shoulder, but she kept running, thinking about Carter and Ethan and how she refused to let this maniac steal her from them.

She was quickly closing in on the field. She could do this. She had to do this. She pushed herself until she thought she would collapse, finally bursting through the wall of green, her hands protecting her face as she ran the gauntlet of sharp leaves that whipped and scratched her skin, farther and farther from the mad man who would surely be in pursuit. Finally she stopped, her hands on her knees, and struggled to catch her breath.

Shapiro shouted that he was coming after her. Had he seen where she entered? What would he do if he caught her—shoot her dead and leave her here where she would be cremated when they burned the fields?

There was a road somewhere in these fields for bringing in equipment. Could she find it? Could she find help?

Then it fell quiet. Eerily quiet except for the sound of her panting and the buzzing of insects. Shapiro had stopped shooting. And shouting. She listened for the swishing sound of someone moving through the stalks and heard nothing. Where was he?

※

Jude sat at his desk, looking through the newly created file on the Broussard extortion case. What had Zoe gotten herself into? Normally he wasn't sympathetic to someone who was a thief and a liar. But in the ten years he'd known Zoe, had she ever been anything but gracious? Did she deserve *this?* Did Pierce?

The intercom buzzed.

"Sheriff, there's an Ethan Langley on line one. He says it's urgent, and that he won't talk to anyone but you."

"Okay, Lisa. I've got it." Jude picked up the receiver and put it to his ear. "Ethan, this is Sheriff Prejean. What can I do for you?"

"I think something's happened to Vanessa! She was on her way to pick Carter up earlier this morning and never showed. I left three messages on her cell, and she hasn't returned my calls. I just talked to Pierce and Zoe. They haven't heard from her either, and she told me she was going to call them before she picked up Carter. I'm really worried. Something's wrong."

"When's the last time you spoke with her?"

"At eight forty-five. She was just leaving Zoe B's. Said some male customer had been staring at her—to the point that it gave her the creeps. I stayed on the phone with her until she got in her car and locked the doors. She sounded fine. But I haven't heard from her since. And neither has anyone else."

"Did she say what the guy looked like?"

"No. Just that the way he looked at her seemed threatening."

Jude shook his head but made sure his voice didn't register his grave concern. "You say she was sitting in the car with the doors locked when you last spoke?"

"That's right. She was on her way to use the pay phone at Rouses Market—to check in with the Broussards. And then she was going to pick up Carter at the Corbins'. Ricky's mother, Lindsay Corbin, just called me and said Vanessa still hasn't shown up, and her phone isn't working. Sheriff, I'm worried this has something to do with this Shapiro character. What if he was stalking Vanessa? What if he's trying to get her to tell him where the Broussards are?"

Jude thought for a minute. Didn't he owe it to Ethan to tell him what was going on? "I hate to say it, but that's a real possibility. We just got new information on Shapiro."

"What information?"

"His real name is Reagan Cowen. He's wanted in Texas for aggravated assault and drug trafficking."

"That confirms he's dangerous!"

"Ethan, there's more. We have DNA evidence that puts Cowen at the scene of Remy Jarvis's murder."

"*What?*"

"We haven't connected the dots yet. This evidence has just come out within the past hour—after we went to the Broussards' apartment and retrieved the clothes Zoe was wearing when she was accosted by Cowan. It was his DNA on Zoe's tank top and Remy's T-shirt. No doubt about it."

"Then this guy's a killer!" Ethan said. "What if he has Vanessa? What if he's forced her to tell him where Zoe and Pierce are? They could all be in danger."

"Don't jump to conclusions. Let us check out your apartment first. Do you want to meet us there?"

"I'm at the clinic in Lafayette. It'll take me forty-five minutes to get there."

"Do you have a key hidden somewhere?"

"No," Ethan said. "But go through the Broussards' apartment out to the gallery. We leave our sliding glass door open."

"All right. We'll check it out. I've got your cell number. Is that the best number to reach you?"

"Yes. Call me as soon as you check the apartment. I'm coming back to Les Barbes. I need to pick up Carter."

Jude sat at the desk in his office and dialed the number for the Broussards' prepaid cell phone. It rang once. Twice—

"Hello."

"Pierce, it's Jude. How're you doing?"

"What can I say, other than I'm glad we're safe?"

Maybe not. Jude bit his lip. "Have you heard from Vanessa?"

"No. Ethan asked me the same thing, not ten minutes ago. I got the feeling there was something he wasn't telling me."

"There is. He just called here. Vanessa was supposed to pick up their son at a friend's house where he spent the night—and she never showed. She hasn't returned Ethan's calls. And now her cell phone isn't working."

"That doesn't sound good."

"Is Zoe where she can hear me?"

"I'll get her, hold on … Zoe, Jude's on the phone. He wants to talk to both of us.…"

A few seconds passed, and he heard a rustling sound.

"Okay, she can hear you."

Jude picked up a pencil and started drawing arrows, the way he often did when he was processing. "Zoe, the lab put a rush on the DNA analysis of the clothes you were wearing when you met with Shapiro. They found his sweat DNA on your tank top. And it matches the blood DNA they found on Remy's T-shirt. It belongs to a man named Reagan Cowen. He's wanted in Texas for aggravated assault and drug trafficking."

"Are you saying Shapiro—I mean Cowen—killed Remy?" Zoe said.

"Looks that way. At the very least he's an accessory. Can you receive photos on your disposable cell?"

"No," Pierce said. "Why?"

"I've got Cowen's mug shot in front of me, but it's a few years old. He probably looks different now. Didn't you tell me the man you know as Shapiro was around forty, tall and thin, has a mustache and medium brown hair down to his collar?"

"Yes, that's right."

"And sinister eyes," Zoe added.

Jude made some notes, aware that the clouds were getting darker.

Finally Pierce said, "This isn't good news for us or for Vanessa, is it?"

Jude sighed. "It's hard to say. I want you two to stay put. Keep the doors locked. We've got an APB out on Cowen. He's probably listening to our radio communications and knows we're on to him."

"What if he forced Vanessa to tell him where we are?"

"We don't know that he's even talked to Vanessa. Her being unreachable might be totally unrelated. I still think you should stay where you are. As soon as I can spare them, I'm going to send a couple deputies out there to stay with you—at least until we know more."

CHAPTER 28

Vanessa stood in a jungle of sugarcane stalks that were considerably taller than she, swatting at the pesky bees and flies that tormented her. She was soaked with perspiration, including her hair. All of her exposed skin had been whipped and slashed by the sharp leaves of the sugarcane plants. How badly had the bullet grazed her? She tried to examine it, but the blood had started to dry, causing her sleeve to stick to the wound.

The heat was stifling, and the heavy air seemed hardly breathable. A clap of thunder startled her, and the ground seemed to shake. Would rain help or hamper her ability to get away from Shapiro? How close was he? If she moved, would he hear her? Was he angry enough to kill her with his bare hands?

Lord, You brought me this far. Help me find a way out. Help me get to safety!

Vanessa thought of Ethan and Carter and felt her determination strengthened. Without her car or cell phone, wasn't her only means of escape to cross the field and get to the Langley property? If she could lock herself in the manor house with Zoe and Pierce, she could use their cell phone to call for help.

She took a few more steps, pushing aside the unforgiving leaves of the sugarcane plants, wondering if she had ever been thirstier—or more afraid. She heard a swishing sound behind her and froze, intently listening. There it was again. Something shot out of the green maze, evoking a squeal from her. A dark bird, a glint of red and yellow visible in its wings, landed a few feet in front of her, then clawed through a tangle of leaves and disappeared.

She slapped her hand over her mouth, her heart hammering. Had Shapiro heard her?

⚜

Savannah poured coffee refills for Hebert, Father Sam, and Tex and placed lunch menus on the table.

"*Mes amis*, are you going to have lunch, or do you just want to hang out?" She glanced out the window. "Looks like we're about to get rained on."

"We'd like to hang out here, if that's okay," Father Sam said. "We're hoping to hear any minute that the sheriff has found this Reagan Cowen they think was involved in Remy's murder. It would be some consolation to us all if it happened before Remy's funeral tomorrow."

Savannah nodded. "Sure would."

"I wonder what makes the sheriff think the guy is still in the area," Tex said.

Hebert shrugged. "If he changed his looks, how dey going to find him?"

"He can't change his height," Savannah said. "They said he's six-two and slender."

"I imagine there's some tall fellas around town gettin' double takes." Tex patted his round belly. "I'm not one of 'em. No one's accused me of bein' slim in a long time. Guess I can chalk it up to Zoe B's—and Pierce's cookin'."

"I miss Zoe and Pierce," Father Sam said. "Seems a little strange today, with both of them out."

Hebert looked up at Savannah. "When dey come back?"

"I'm not sure. When Zoe left, she didn't even mention Remy's funeral tomorrow. She sounded … I don't know, almost detached."

"When I was workin' for the oil company," Tex said, "I took on a stress-mode demeanor that my wife said made me seem detached from people. Maybe that's all it is."

"Probably so." Savannah picked up the menus. "Benson is happy to cover the kitchen in Pierce's absence, so we're good to go. If you fellas change your mind about lunch, let me know. Otherwise, stay as long as you like. Coffeepot's on all day."

Zoe sat on her air mattress, hugging her pillow. Was Pierce scared or angry—or both? He hadn't said anything to her since they hung up the phone after talking to Jude.

"I wonder why Vanessa hasn't called," Zoe said, talking more to herself than to Pierce.

"Let's hope there's a logical explanation," he said quietly. "If anything happens to her, it'll be our fault."

"You mean *my* fault."

"All right, *your* fault. I couldn't believe the Langleys were willing to get involved in this in the first place! They have a whole lot more faith in God to get us out of this than I do."

Zoe rocked back and forth. "I thought we had it worked out so that Shapiro—Cowen—wouldn't suspect they knew anything. I would never have intentionally put them at risk."

"There're *a lot* of things you didn't think would put anyone else at risk, Zoe. Yet look at the mess we're in." He shook his head. "I can't believe we're hiding from a drug dealer who'd just as soon carve you up as look at you—all because you lied about who you are."

"There's no way I could've seen this coming. I just wanted a different life."

"Did you honestly believe that changing your name, adopting the Cajun ways, and operating a Cajun eatery would make you Cajun? You're still the same person on the inside. Why didn't you just hold your head high and be proud of who you are?"

Zoe sighed. "Have you heard *anything* I've been trying to tell you? There was nothing worthwhile about Shelby Sieger! I needed to put an end to her and to that part of my life." She paused and composed herself. "I'm sorry for deceiving you, Pierce. I am. And I'm sorry I stole the ring from Mrs. Woodmore. But I'm not sorry I changed my name or that I disowned my family. I deserved to be free."

"*Free?*" His resonant voice went up two decibels. "All you did was trade your secrets for a whole new set of secrets—and shame that you *are* responsible for. You weren't responsible for your father's sick behavior. But you are responsible for using it as an excuse to lie to get what you wanted."

Zoe hung her head and wiped her eyes. Pierce was right. Had she ever been free? Hadn't she, on one level, been in a perpetual state of worry that one day he would find out she was a fraud? Wasn't the reason she confronted Adele Woodmore ultimately about preserving the perfect life she created for herself—and not about remorse?

"Pierce, you wouldn't have given me the time of day unless you thought I was Cajun."

"Don't you dare put that on me!" He combed his hands through his hair. "I fell in love with your heart, not your pedigree. Did the fact that you said you were Cajun have some appeal? Sure. I'm as proud as they get. But it was never a prerequisite to finding a soul mate—though honesty and integrity *were!* Congratulations. You succeeded in faking all three...." Emotion stole his voice, and he turned and stood in the doorway, his back to her.

Lightning flashed, followed by a boom of thunder that rattled the windows. It was as though God agreed with him.

Zoe hugged her pillow tighter. What could she really say in her defense? She thought of Vanessa. What could have happened to delay her phone call?

Vanessa stepped through the tangled weeds on the path between two rows of sugarcane, trying not to lose her sense of direction. It was darker. The wind had picked up and the temperature cooled. The smell of rain was pervasive.

She felt a tickle on her wrist and locked gazes with a hairy spider the size of nickel. Instinctively she shook her arm, a stabbing pain in her wounded shoulder taking her breath away. What if she'd been more than grazed? What if the bullet was lodged? How many times had she heard her mother say that a victim's body would try to reject a bullet, that the person would get sicker and sicker until the bullet was removed—or the person died?

Lord, You're the Great Physician. Help me!

A loud snap, followed by an explosion of thunder, cracked open the heavens. Rain started to come down, and then come down harder and harder—in torrents—rolling down the sugarcane plants and splashing on her from all sides. If Shapiro was combing the field, how could he hear or see her in this downpour? Wasn't this her best chance to pick up her pace and get to the other side? But what if she couldn't find her way out? What if she couldn't escape his clutches? What if she couldn't get home to Carter and Ethan?

Vanessa's gaze fell on the ruby ring on her left hand, and she was, in an instant, transported back to the glider on her parents' screened-in porch....

Ethan got up and knelt on the porch on one knee and took her hand.

"What are you doing?" she said.

Ethan held her hand to his cheek. "Vanessa, it's no secret that I love you. Or that you and Carter are the most important people in my life. You're in my thoughts, on my heart, and in my prayers every hour of every day. I can't imagine living my life without you. Our paths were meant to intersect—and I believe you and I were meant to become one."

Ethan reached in his pocket, took out a ring, and held it between his thumb and forefinger.

"This ruby ring was my great-grandmother Langley's engagement ring. My dad gave it to my mother when they got engaged, and she wore it until their twenty-fifth wedding anniversary. Someday, I want to buy you a diamond ring that we pick out together. But for now, while my money is going to pay for tuition and to keep the old Camry running, would you wear this special family heirloom and let it signify that one day, when the time is right, you'll be my wife?"

A tear trickled down Vanessa's cheek, and she heard herself say, "Yes! I can hardly wait for that day. The ring is beautiful. And it's so special that both your great-grandmother and your mother wore it."

Ethan slipped the ring on her finger and, ever so tenderly, pressed his lips to her hand. "I love you, Vanessa. I can't imagine my future without you and Carter. We were meant to be together—"

A boom of thunder brought Vanessa back to the present. She pictured Ethan taking the ring off her cold, dead finger. Was she going to allow Shapiro to rob Carter and Ethan of the one they loved—or was she going to fight to stay alive?

She took a step forward, and then another, her arms folded in front of her face, shielding her from the sharp leaves. She was either going to make it Langley Manor—or die trying.

CHAPTER 29

Zoe lay on the air mattress in the back bedroom at Langley Manor, her eyes focused on the crystal-globe light fixture on the ceiling, her hearing intent on the rain pelting the windows. Why was she too lethargic to get up and make herself a sandwich, even though it might settle her stomach? She had felt sick all morning and was afraid she might throw up. What then? It's not as though she could flush the toilet. How much longer could her body hold up under this level of stress?

Pierce lay on his side on the other air mattress, seemingly staring at nothing. Their silence was a presence in the room, like some sort of truth police just waiting for a chance to interrogate her. All she needed was another guilt trip. Did she need any more reminders of how miserably she had failed?

A loud ringing startled her, and she realized it was the cell phone. She reached over and grabbed it and put it to her ear.

"Vanessa! Where have you been?"

"Well, well, well. If it isn't Zoe Benoit Broussard."

The voice was unmistakably Cowan's. Her skin turned to goose flesh. She locked gazes with Pierce and put it on speakerphone.

"Surprised to hear from me?" Cowan laughed. "I'd love to see the expression on your face. Did you think you could get away from me?"

Pierce slid his index finger across his throat. "Don't talk to him," he whispered. "Tell him he has the wrong number and hang up."

"Excuse me, who is this?" Zoe said.

"You know exactly who it is. I'm the guy that's going to make a totem pole of you, if you don't have my hundred grand ready to wire before the banks close. I told you I would call you and give you an account number. Get out your pencil and—"

"I'm sorry, you have the wrong number." Zoe disconnected the call and dropped the phone on the air mattress, her hands shaking. "How d-did he get this number?"

Pierce jumped to his feet. "He could only have gotten it from Vanessa or Ethan. And since Vanessa's missing, we have to assume he got her to talk."

The phone rang again. Both she and Pierce stared at it.

"Just let it ring," he said.

"I don't think we should make him mad." Zoe brushed the hair out of her eyes. "I'm sure he recognized my voice. We're not fooling him."

"He's manipulative, Zoe. I don't want you talking to him. I don't like it one bit that he was able to get this number."

"You think Vanessa told him where we are? Maybe we should leave."

"And go where?" Pierce's eyebrows came together. "Cowan wants his money. He's not going to jeopardize that until the deadline. I don't think we have any choice but to wait for Jude's deputies to get here."

❧

Vanessa trudged forward on the narrow path between cane stalks, her shoes getting hung up in the cumbersome weeds, the rain drenching her and making it hard to see. At least Shapiro would be having the same problem. How deep was she into the field? How much farther to the other side? What if she couldn't find her way out? What if she was trapped in here?

Trapped? Vanessa took a shallow breath. And then another. And another. Why did it feel as if her throat were closing off? Why couldn't she get air? Her pulse raced. She could not afford a panic attack. Not here. Not now.

You can do this. You have to do this. Don't give in to claustrophobia. Think about where you're going—not where you are.

Vanessa kept moving, her hands in front of her, keeping the wet leaves from slapping her face.

She had told Ethan over three hours ago that she was going to Rouses Market and use the pay phone to call Zoe. Surely he had called her cell number since, worried that she hadn't returned his calls. And wouldn't Lindsay Corbin have called him when she didn't show to pick up Carter? Was Ethan concerned enough to call the sheriff? Had he figured out that the man whose stares made her uncomfortable was Shapiro?

Lord, it's just You and me.

At least the rain had temporarily stopped the mosquitoes from feasting on her—a welcome relief, considering the other discomforts she was forced to endure. But when the storm was over, wouldn't all her exposed skin become a banquet table for every biting insect?

Her shoes were soggy, and her big toe throbbed. Was she getting a blister? What had made her put on walking shoes this morning and not sandals? How could she have ever walked through this sugarcane field in sandals?

The rain let up considerably, and she picked up her pace and emptied her mind of how miserable she was, trying to stay focused on how much closer she might be to getting out of the sugarcane field and onto the Langley property.

Jude sat in his squad car in the private parking area behind Zoe B's and keyed in the number for Ethan Langley's cell phone. It only rang once.

"Hello."

"Ethan, it's Sheriff Prejean. Vanessa's not in your apartment or at Zoe B's. But Savannah Surette, one of the waitresses, said that just before nine this morning, a customer reported that the back door to the building was left wide open. I've got my deputies dusting for prints and looking for trace evidence. As of twenty minutes ago, Pierce and Zoe still hadn't heard from Vanessa."

"Something's terribly wrong, Sheriff. You have to find her!"

"I will. But don't assume the worst. There could be a logical explanation for Vanessa's not being able to call you."

"I can't think of any. She'd find a phone, unless she was involved in an accident or—"

"Look, Ethan, don't go there. Zoe and Pierce have until the banks close to get the money ready to wire. Right now, we have to assume that Cowan thinks that's what they're in the process of doing."

"Or maybe he forced Vanessa to tell him what they're really doing," Ethan said. "At which point, she becomes dispensable. Sheriff, I've been around Vanessa's mother too long to beat around the bush. Just talk straight with me. I know that's what you're thinking."

"It would be a mistake to try and read my mind, Ethan. I don't like the smell of this either, but there are a number of possibilities. I've been doing this job too long to jump the gun. I've apprised Police Chief Norman of the situation and put out an APB on Vanessa and on Cowen. And we're trying to track her cell phone. The best thing you can do is go home and wait for me to call with updates."

"All right. I'm just pulling up in front of the Corbins' house," Ethan said. "I'll be home with Carter in fifteen minutes."

"I've got to head out to Roux River Park. We've been on the verge of a race riot for days, but with Remy's funeral Mass tomorrow, it's about to blow up. We've brought in officers from New Iberia, Lafayette, Morgan City, and Franklin. I've been asked to do a press conference in twenty minutes. Don't worry. I won't let up on finding Vanessa. And as soon as I can spare them, I'm sending two deputies out to the manor house to stay with Zoe and Pierce. If you hear from Vanessa, I want to know immediately."

Vanessa stopped to rest, her wounded shoulder hot and throbbing. She examined the bleeding scratches on her arms and hands and wondered if she had been able to keep her face from looking as if she'd been whipped.

Rain continued to fall. At least it was cooler and she wasn't bothered by insects at the moment. How much farther could it be until she came out on the other side?

She started to take a step and froze. What was *that* noise? She crouched down and listened intently, rain rolling down her back. Had she imagined it? It almost sounded like a dog's bark—but in the middle of a cane field? Was it a wild animal?

Father, help! You directed all those animals to the ark, surely you can send this one to the opposite end of the cane field.

There it was again—not a dog's bark. A man's hearty sneeze! Did it come from behind her or ahead of her—to the right or to the left? Was it Shapiro tracking her? Or could it have been a field worker? Had she come to the road?

She didn't move. Or breathe. She heard another sound. It was getting louder. Finally she recognized it as the same sound she had been making—shoes sloshing on the wet ground. She crouched lower, hugging her knees, fear boxing her heart like a punching bag. Through the cane stalks, she spotted a glint of blue and a pair of hairy legs—distinctly Shapiro's—about two rows over. Had he been following her? Or was he merely searching?

The Broussards' prepaid cell phone rang. Pierce groped for it and put it to his ear.

"Hello."

"Pierce, it's Ethan. Have you heard from Vanessa yet?"

"No. Jude called and told us she wasn't returning your calls. I'm so sorry, man. We should've never let you get involved in this."

"Hey, it was our choice. We wanted to help. There might be a good explanation for why Vanessa isn't returning my calls. But to be on the safe side, the sheriff put out an APB on her and on Cowen. They're also going to track her cell phone."

"This whole thing seems surreal."

"Sure does," Ethan said.

"Did you pick Carter up at the Corbins'?"

"I did. Poor little guy was ready to come home. He's confused why Mommy isn't here. I really don't know what to tell him."

Pierce heard the angst between the lines and shot Zoe a disgusted look he was sure would remind her that this was all her fault.

"Have you heard anything about the racial problem brewing at Roux River Park?" Ethan said.

"What now? Here, let me put this on speaker so Zoe can hear. Go ahead."

"I don't have details," Ethan said, "but the sheriff has requested officers from three or four departments to help curb the racial unrest. I guess with Remy Jarvis's funeral tomorrow, it's about to go over the top."

"I almost forgot that Remy's funeral is tomorrow." Zoe's eyes filled with tears. "I wonder if we'll even be able to go."

"Not if we're all dead." And the minute Pierce said the words, he wished he hadn't. Ethan must be frantic enough without his stating their worst fear.

There was a long, uncomfortable pause.

Finally Pierce said, "Sorry, Ethan. I really didn't mean that. It's just frustration talking."

"Hey, I'm worried too. I just have to remember that Vanessa and I gave our lives to Christ. Nothing can happen to us unless He allows it for a reason. If I didn't know that, I'd probably freak."

"You have a lot more faith than I do," Pierce said. "I believe it's up to me to take care of myself."

"I'm afraid I'm unequipped for that job—especially now."

Vanessa didn't move a muscle, didn't dare to exhale until Shapiro was yards away from her. If he had known she was there, wouldn't he have grabbed her—or shot her? Maybe now she could follow *him*. At least knowing where he was would ease the fear that he would jump out and grab her.

It was raining harder and the wind had picked up. She rose to her feet and continued walking the same path. How was she supposed to keep the sharp leaves from striking her face—and, at the same time, the rain from running into her eyes? Like taillights in a downpour, the color in Shapiro's clothes stood out and enabled her to focus on him. He was moving faster than she was comfortable with, but she didn't let him out of her sight.

All at once her shoe caught a tangle of vines. She toppled forward onto the ground and landed on her elbows. A silent scream caught in her throat as a bolt of electric pain shot through her wounded shoulder.

She lay on the ground in agony, surrounded by weeds and towering cane stalks. Claustrophobia again consumed her. She took a slow deep breath and exhaled. Then did it again. And again, trying to imagine herself out in a wide-open field.

She forced herself to get up, her shoulder bleeding again, and took a step forward and then another, pushing the wet cane leaves out of her face and struggling to spot the blue cargo shorts. She walked a little faster but couldn't spot him. Had he gotten too far ahead of her—or was he on to her?

CHAPTER 30

Zoe stood at the window in the back bedroom at Langley Manor, the rain coming down so hard she couldn't see where the yard ended and the woods began. Lightning flashed, and she clamped her eyes shut just as thunder boomed and shook the house.

She went over to her air mattress and sat with her legs stretched out in front of her. Pierce lay on his air mattress, facing the wall, and she sensed he was awake. Was he thinking of Vanessa too—and how badly Cowan might hurt her to find out their whereabouts? Could Zoe ever forgive herself if Vanessa ended up dead?

A wave of nausea swept over her, and she closed her eyes until it passed. Would life ever be normal again? Would she and Pierce return home together and work through the lies, or was it over?

Zoe wiped a tear off her cheek and tried to stifle her sniffling.

Pierce exhaled loudly, then turned over, picked up the box of tissues, and tossed it on her sleeping bag.

She plucked several tissues just as the cell phone rang.

Pierce stared at it for a moment, then reached over and put it on speaker, letting go of it as if it were a hot potato. "Hello."

"Well, I see at least one of you is answering."

Cowen's voice filled her with dread.

Pierce glared at her. "How did you get this number?"

"How do you think? I want my hundred grand. Time's running out. Why did Zoe hang up on me?"

"Sorry. She panicked. She wasn't expecting to hear your voice. You said we had until the banks close."

"That's right. But you're not going to get very far without my account number. Grab a pencil."

"Hold on." Pierce picked up the ballpoint Ethan had put in one of the sacks. "All right. What is it?" Pierce wrote the numbers on his hand as Cowen said them, and then repeated the entire account number.

"It would be a huge mistake to double-cross me on this."

Pierce looked over at Zoe and rolled his eyes. "Why would we do that?"

"Now that's the spirit. Because I never forget people who mess with me. I eliminate them—and their friends—with a great deal of *pain*."

The line went dead.

Pierce dropped the phone on the air mattress and shot her a look of disdain.

"At least he believes we're going to wire the money," Zoe said.

"Vanessa must've told him that. But he obviously got to her." Pierce's eyebrows came together. "There're only two ways he could've gotten this cell number, and we know he didn't get it from Ethan."

"I wonder why Vanessa didn't tell him where we are. I know how scary he can be. If he threatened her, she wouldn't have lasted two minutes before she told him."

"I can't answer that. I do know this: He's going to be furious when the hundred thousand doesn't show up in his account. And if he hasn't already killed Vanessa, he will. And then he'll come after us." Pierce threw his hands in the air. "I sure hope getting your *new life* was worth dying for, Zoe."

Vanessa watched her feet as she moved gingerly along the narrow, weed-covered path, barely visible between two rows of sugarcane stalks. How much time had she lost when she fell—one minute— maybe two? Where was Shapiro? How far could he have gone? What if he spotted her and was staying out of sight, waiting for the right time to make his move?

It felt as if she'd been walking for miles. Where was the road? Had the field angled off in a different direction without her being able to tell? Or did the road not come this far south?

Lord, please guide me out of here!

She stopped for a moment and listened carefully, the only sounds the distant rumble of thunder and the *drip, drip, drip* of rain draining from the leaves. Had the storm emptied itself?

Vanessa started walking again, her hands in front of her, protecting her face from being cut by the sharp leaves—and then suddenly, there was nothing but air. She put her hands down and couldn't believe her eyes: She had reached the end of the row and was looking at the log fence that marked the Langley property.

Thank You, Lord!

Wasn't she facing due north? That meant she needed to run to the log fence and climb over it, then turn right and follow the perimeter of the woods around to the open area behind the manor house. She and Ethan owned only fifteen acres. How far could it be to the house?

She stuck her head out just long enough to look to the left and then to the right. Where was Shapiro? If he had come to the end of his row and still hadn't seen her, would he have given up, turned around, and retraced his steps back to her car?

Or would he assume that Ethan had reported her missing, that an APB had been put out on her car, and decided to walk the three miles back to town? Or had he called someone to come get him?

Everything in her wanted to dart out of this cane field and run as fast as she could to Langley Manor. But what if Shapiro was waiting, expecting her to surface—would he shoot her in the back? And if he chased her to the manor house, wouldn't Zoe and Pierce be in grave danger too?

Vanessa sighed. Why was the Lord testing her faith *again?* Why had He allowed this life-threatening situation? Hadn't she passed the test when she stayed faithful to Him, even after she witnessed Drew's senseless murder—and endured those agonizing hours when Ethan was pursued by Drew's killer and she didn't know whether she would ever see him again?

Her thoughts flashed back to that Memorial Day afternoon when she sat out on the screened-in porch with an elderly friend, Tessa Masino, waiting for search and rescue to find Ethan....

"Tessa, why does God have to test our faith?" Vanessa said. "Why do I need another trial? Why does Ethan? Haven't we been through enough?"

Tessa tucked Vanessa's hair behind her ear the way her mother often did. "It seems that way. But is faith really faith until it's tested? It's one thing to claim we have it. It's another to actually put it into practice...."

Vanessa sighed, coming back to the present. Did she have enough faith to believe that no matter what happened, God would use it for good? She looked out at the open space between there and the tree line, convinced it couldn't be more than thirty yards.

Run!

The voice resounded in her head. Was it just her fear talking?

Go!

She hesitated for only a second, then sprang out into the open, running with abandon toward the log fence, the searing pain in her shoulder making her knees weak, but determination giving her legs.

She came to an abrupt stop at the log fence, slipped through it, and kept running, angling to the right and running along the perimeter of the woods.

A shot rang out across the gray Louisiana sky. She heard Shapiro's angry shouts but couldn't make out what he said. Only one voice was distinguishable, and it spoke from within with simple urgency.

Don't stop!

A bullet zinged by her ear and ricocheted off a tree trunk.

Vanessa resisted the temptation to duck into the woods and hide and pushed herself harder than she thought possible, the trees to her left and the cane fields to her right. Judging from the muffled sound of Shapiro's voice, she had a healthy head start. What if she was wrong about where she was? What if she couldn't find the manor house? Or what if Zoe and Pierce were too afraid to answer when they heard banging at the door?

The words from one of the Psalms came rushing to her mind. *God is our refuge and strength, an ever-present help in trouble.*

"Lord, I *am* in trouble. I need You!"

The bullet whizzed by her left ear. Would the next one end up in her back? She didn't want to die, to leave Ethan and Carter. But if she did, was she ready to meet her Savior face-to-face? She decided she was, and the fear left her.

Vanessa kept pushing herself but wondered how much longer she could keep it up before she collapsed. She saw a clearing up ahead. The manor house had to be there. She would run to the back door where Zoe and Pierce could see her from the bedroom. Either they would let her in—or she would be at Shapiro's mercy. Either way, it was out of her hands.

Zoe stood looking out the front windows at Langley Manor, wishing she were out on the gallery at her apartment, watching the activity on *rue Madeline*. She heard the floor creaking behind her, and then Pierce's resonant voice.

"Did you hear *that?*" he said.

"Hear what?"

"Sounded like gunshots."

"I didn't hear anything," she said. "Where were they coming from?"

"Not far."

"Could it be someone hunting?"

"Wrong season."

"What should we do about it?" Zoe moved away from the window.

"I don't know. But we can't ignore it."

"Maybe it was someone poaching."

"Maybe it wasn't."

Zoe studied his somber face. "You're really concerned."

"Of course I'm concerned, Zoe! There's a madman out there who wants you dead—and Vanessa's missing!"

"You think Cowen got Vanessa to talk, that he's coming here?"

"I don't know." Pierce exhaled, the lines on his forehead disappearing. "I guess if he were coming here to get us, he wouldn't fire a weapon and announce his presence. I'm probably being paranoid."

Probably, she thought. But wasn't it nice to see his protective side kick in, especially when he had been so indifferent?

Zoe locked gazes with Pierce and, for a fleeting moment, connected with the man who cherished her. Caught off guard, she looked away, wondering if he felt it too.

A loud banging caused Zoe to jump, her hand over her heart. "Someone's pounding on the back door!"

Pierce grabbed her hand and pulled her into the back bedroom, then picked up the ball bat and stood to the side of the window, his back to the wall, and craned to see out.

"Good grief, it's Vanessa!"

Zoe heard Vanessa's cries and her frantic banging on the door. "We have to let her in!"

"I'll go." Pierce took the key out of his pocket and gripped the ball bat tightly. "Stay here."

"I'm coming with you."

She followed Pierce down the hall and through the kitchen to the back door. He put the key in the bolt lock, opened the door, and pulled Vanessa inside.

"Quick, lock the door!" Vanessa cried. "He's coming! Shapiro's coming! He saw me run up here! We only have a minute before he shoots the lock and gets in here! We have to hide! He hanged Remy Jarvis! He tried to hang me!"

Zoe was rendered mute by the dreadful state of her beautiful friend. Vanessa's long shiny hair was wet and stringy, her face and arms covered with slash marks. Her shirt was blood-soaked, her shoes covered in mud.

"Let's go!" Vanessa took a step, and Pierce caught her, the bat falling on the floor.

"Whoa. Easy, girl."

"My legs are tired," Vanessa said. "I'm not used to running that far."

"What happened to your shoulder?"

"Shapiro shot me when I escaped and ran into the cane field."

"His real name is Reagan Cowan," Pierce said. "The sheriff knows he killed Remy."

"Help me up the stairs. We can hide in the secret tunnel. Hurry!"

Pierce put his arm around Vanessa's waist and draped her good arm around his shoulder. "Okay, let's do this. Zoe, you go ahead of us."

Zoe hurried through the kitchen and up the back stairs to the second floor. She turned around and waited for what seemed an eternity. She heard Vanessa cry out in pain and Pierce apologize for the agonizing climb. The two of them appeared at the top of the stairs just as three deafening shots rang out.

"He's in," Pierce whispered. "Zoe, open the door to the tunnel!"

Zoe ran in the bedroom where sheriff's deputies had discovered the secret door in the closet. She put her hand on the knob, her heart racing, and pulled open the door. She stepped into the inky blackness and took tiny steps, her arms out in front of her, her hands groping the air. How far was it to the stairs?

Cowen's voice boomed. "Your little game of cat and mouse is over, Vanessa. You're going to wish I had strung you up. When I get my hands on you, I'm going to carve you up, piece by piece!"

Zoe stopped about ten feet into the dark void. "I can't see a thing. I don't even know where the stairs are."

Pierce pulled the door closed and helped Vanessa over to where Zoe stood. "Okay, hand me the bat."

Zoe was trapped in a long pause and finally found her voice. "I-I don't have the bat."

"Why not?" His hushed voice sounded angry.

"You just said to go upstairs, and I did. I didn't think about the bat."

"All right," Pierce said, barely above a whisper. "Listen carefully. Our only defense is the dark. Don't anyone move—or even breathe—when he opens that door."

CHAPTER 31

Jude looked down the line of officers that stood between two opposing groups of protestors at Roux River Park. Could they prevent anger from exploding into violence?

He took his cell phone off his belt clip and keyed in Stone Castille's phone number.

"Hello, Sheriff."

"How soon before you and Mike can get out to Langley Manor?"

"We're finished briefing the officers that arrived from Franklin and are ready to head out there now."

"Good. I have a bad feeling that Cowen might go after the Broussards."

"Before the banks close?"

"Just get out there and call me. Gil's beeping in. I've been waiting for him to call back." Jude switched over to the other caller. "So were you able to find the location of Vanessa Langley's cell phone?"

"No. Either the phone's off or it's been disabled. But the last-known GPS coordinates came from the Vincent farm—about two hours ago. I don't like it."

294

"Me either. I think we need to go take a look. I'll meet you at the farmhouse in fifteen minutes."

"You got it."

Jude disconnected the call and keyed in Ethan Langley's cell number.

"Hello."

"It's Sheriff Prejean. Have you heard from your wife?"

"No. And I'm really worried. If there was any way for her to get to a phone, she'd call me. Were you able track her cell phone?"

"There's still no signal. Sorry." Should he tell Ethan about the GPS coordinates? Why add to his worry until they'd had time to check it out?

Ethan sighed into the receiver. "Something bad's happened to her."

"We don't know that," Jude said. "Let's give Vanessa some credit. Her mother's a cop. She must've inherited some of those instincts."

"She's no match for an angry drug dealer, Sheriff."

"We don't know that Cowen has even approached Vanessa. There could be another explanation for why you haven't heard from her."

"I can't think of one."

Jude couldn't either, but he wasn't about to strip Ethan of his last thread of hope.

Zoe crouched in the darkness with Pierce and Vanessa, aware of their shallow breathing and her own racing heart. Would Cowen notice the door in the closet? Would he open it? Would he hear their breathing? Would he smell their fear? Zoe willed away the tears that stung her eyes. Not now! All she needed was to start sniffling and give them away.

Was she ready to die and face the punishment that awaited her? Wasn't her faith as disingenuous as her persona? Her confessions tainted with sins of omission? Wasn't her presence at Mass merely for show—like keeping her rosary in the top drawer of the nightstand? Hadn't she always known deep down that God wasn't fooled by her performance, even if everyone else was?

Wouldn't He expect her to pay for all the lies she told and all the people she deceived—and for the deaths of Pierce and Vanessa, if it came to that? Ethan said that God specializes in messes. But was this one too over the top, even for Him?

"Va-ness-a." Cowen's voice was singsongy and playful. "I know you're in here. I'm following your muddy footprints. You thought you could get away from me." His voice was again low and sinister. "No one gets away from me. *No one.*"

"I don't think he's bluffing," Vanessa whispered. "My shoes are a mess. What do we do?"

"I'll go stand on one side of the door," Pierce said. "Maybe I can surprise him."

"No, that's the first place he'll look." Zoe reached out and found his arm and squeezed. "You'll be safer back here. It's darker."

"I can't just hunker down like a sitting duck," Pierce said. "He's liable to start shooting."

"He's right."

Zoe froze. A stranger's quiet voice had come from behind her, and she felt his breath on her neck. Her skin tingled with goose bumps, her heart nearly beating out of her chest.

Pierce turned toward the voice. "Who said that? Who are you?"

"Carter calls me the candy man."

"How did you get in here?" Vanessa whispered.

"The same way I'm goin' to get you out."

❧

Savannah put a fresh vase of flowers on the table that Hebert, Father Sam, and Tex had occupied since early that morning. The breaking news they had been anxiously awaiting still hadn't happened. Why hadn't the sheriff arrested Remy's killer? The media made it sound as if an arrest were imminent.

"Why are dey dragging dis out?" Hebert said. "Gimme some rope, and I'll end dis ting right now."

Father Sam patted Hebert's arm. "You don't mean that."

"But there are those who do," Tex said. "They wouldn't bat an eye at savin' the taxpayers money by riddin' the town of this scum."

"Let's hope we aren't reduced to that." Father Sam took a sip of coffee. "I just don't understand why the media gets everyone's hopes up before they confirm the information."

"It's all about ratings," Savannah said. "The truth is secondary." She sighed. "I miss Remy so much."

"Dere won't be anudder Remy." Hebert reached over and slipped his hand around hers. "Dat boy was sometin' special to all o' us. Treated me like his *papere.*" Hebert's voice quivered. "I'm trying to accept his death so dat I can be strong for Emile—poor fella is *motier foux.*"

"I'd be half crazy too if someone murdered my child." Savannah sighed. "It's hard enough just being a friend. I want Remy's killer brought to justice—the sooner the better."

"Have you heard from Zoe and Pierce," Tex said, "and whether they're goin' to Remy's funeral tomorrow?"

Savannah shook her head. "They must be really engrossed in whatever business they're doing because I haven't heard from either of them today. I'm assuming Pierce wants Benson to take his shift tomorrow, too."

"I just can't imagine that the Broussards would miss Remy's funeral"—Father Sam took off his glasses and rubbed his eyes—"what with Zoe being so fond of Remy all these years."

"Maybe they wanted to get their business done so they *could* go." Savannah squeezed Hebert's hand and let go. "If you fellas need something, holler. I've got to get these other tables freshened up."

Savannah walked out to the kitchen and opened the refrigerator where she kept the fresh-cut flowers for the vases. Something was going on with Zoe and Pierce. Why had the back door been left wide open? Why had the sheriff come in, asking questions about Vanessa Langley? Why hadn't Zoe or Pierce called today to check in? In the four years she had worked for them, could she ever remember a time when they had gone twenty-four hours without calling an inordinate number of times to see how things were running?

"Hurry," the stranger said. "He'll be here any second. Everybody stand up. I'll shine the flashlight on the stairs. You need to go down quickly and carefully. Move!"

"Zoe, you go first," Pierce whispered. "I'll help Vanessa."

Zoe turned around and saw that the alcove went back another five feet or so to another door. She opened it and waited until the stranger shone the beam of light down a long, narrow staircase. She stepped down, holding the walls on both sides, and quickly made her way to the bottom, instantly hit with the cool temperature and damp, musty smell. A few seconds later the others were behind her.

The stranger shone the light on the far wall. "There's another door behind that empty bookcase."

Zoe hurried over to the bookcase and moved it aside, surprised that it wasn't heavy. She pulled open the door and saw a narrow tunnel, barely high enough for her walk through without bending or touching the sides.

"Go on," Vanessa said. "We're right behind you."

Zoe stepped inside and froze. Were those spider eggs on the ceiling?

"Everybody in the tunnel," the stranger said. "We hafta put enough space between us and the fella with the gun so he won't have light."

"He's got my key ring," Vanessa said. "It has one of those blue lights on it."

"Then we don't have a second to waste!" the stranger said. "Move it!"

Zoe took a couple of tentative steps and stopped, aware of someone nudging her forward.

"Hurry," Vanessa said. "I hear Cowan's voice."

Zoe felt as if she couldn't get air, and her shoes were nailed to the floor. "I-I can't see. Hardly any of the light from the flashlight is getting through."

"Just go straight," Vanessa said. "Hurry! He's on the staircase!"

"Here, let me through," Pierce said. "She's terrified of spiders and small spaces."

Zoe was aware of some shuffling behind her, then felt Pierce's hand on her shoulder and saw that he was holding the flashlight.

"You can't stop to think about this, Zoe. You just have to do it. I'll help you. Come on."

He held the beam of light on the path, and she kept her eyes down, aware of him pushing her down the tunnel at a rapid clip until they reached a wall—and what appeared to be a hatch overhead.

Pierce handed her the flashlight, then climbed the metal rungs that were secured to the wall and pushed up on the hatch until it opened, then jumped down, grabbed the flashlight, and tossed it to the stranger.

"Come on. I'll give you a boost."

Pierce locked his fingers together, and Zoe stepped on his hands so he could lift her onto the rungs. She climbed up to the top, blinded for a few seconds by the outdoor light. She stepped outside, felt the air, like a heavy, wet blanket, and realized she was in the woods.

One by one the others came up. Vanessa. Pierce. The stranger—an African-American man, unshaven and shabbily dressed, who appeared to be about fifty, give or take. Slight build. Kind eyes.

"Thank you for helping us! I'm Vanessa Langley. My husband and I own this house. Who *are* you?"

"Noah Washington. We'll talk later. Right now, we need to spread out in these woods. The fella with the gun is only a minute behind us."

"Can't we sit on the hatch?" Pierce said, "and let the girls go call for help?"

"Not unless you wanna get shot in the behind." Noah glanced around the woods. "There's no time to find somethin' heavy enough to hold him."

Cowen's muffled voice came from the tunnel. It sounded as if he was cursing now.

"Let's pair up," Noah said. "Mrs. Langley, why don't you come with me?"

He looked at Pierce and then Zoe. "You two stay together. Everybody run! Find a place to hide."

Vanessa ran as fast as she could, deeper into the woods, trusting Noah would be able to find the way back. A paralyzing cramp gripped her calf. She hopped over behind a tree and slid down to the ground, her back to the trunk, and started kneading the muscle. The pain in her shoulder made it impossible to press hard enough.

Noah crouched on the ground, facing her. "Relax. Let me do that. Is that a gunshot wound in your shoulder?"

Vanessa nodded and started to cry, then willed away the tears. "You wouldn't believe the day I've had."

"The man who's after you, who is he?"

"A drug dealer named Reagan Cowen. He's mistaken the other lady, Zoe Broussard, for someone who owes him money. Zoe and her husband, Pierce, have been hiding in the house. I guess you know that much. Cowen's dangerous. He's responsible for hanging a man from Les Barbes. He would've hung me, if I hadn't escaped."

"Well, you haven't exactly escaped just yet." He looked at her shoulder, then craned and peeked out from behind the tree. "I think we've gone far enough. Let's rest here. We need to get you to a doctor as soon as possible. At least the blood looks dry. That's a good sign."

"Who are you?" Vanessa said. "Why have you been sneaking into our house? How did you even know about the tunnel?"

Noah gently kneaded her calf and seemed to avoid eye contact. "My great-grandmother G. G. used to tell me stories about this place. Her ancestors were slaves here—bought at an auction by Josiah Langley. Did you know he and his wife, Abigail, were involved in the Underground Railroad?"

"No." Vanessa's mind raced with the implications. "So *that's* what the tunnel was used for?"

He nodded. "Actually there're two tunnels. The cops nailed one of 'em shut. G. G. knew all about this place and the secret tunnels Mr. Langley built so he could bring in slaves and get 'em ready for their journey north. Langley and the Missus were stationmasters, and Langley Manor was one of the key stations for slaves bein' smuggled out of South Louisiana." Noah half smiled. "Hundreds of slaves were hidden in that house. They came in through the tunnels and out through the closet. Stayed in that upstairs room until they were ready to be moved to the next station.

"We had no idea." Vanessa felt her calf muscle start to relax as Noah continued kneading. "The Cajuns in this area resented the Langleys and thought they were snooty."

"The Langleys kept their distance from folks in order to guard the secret. When they built this place, they named it Langley Manor

instead of Langley Plantation so folks would think they were uppity
Brits who had no intention of adaptin' to a new culture. Gave 'em
space to operate."

"What a sacrifice," Vanessa said, "choosing to let others think
badly of them so they could do something good."

Noah gently stretched out her leg on the ground. "G. G. told me
that Mr. Langley tried to free his own slaves, but they didn't wanna go.
He treated 'em so well that they asked to stay and help him with the
Underground Railroad. My great-grandmother's great-grandmother
was one of those slaves. Her Christian name was Naomi. That's really
all I know 'bout her."

"That's amazing." Vanessa's gaze collided with Noah's. "But you
still didn't tell me why you've been sneaking into the manor house."

"Well, I, uh—"

A shot rang out. And then another and another—a staccato of
gunfire echoed in the forest. And then it stopped.

CHAPTER 32

Zoe dug her fingers into Pierce's arm, her heart thumping erratically, and waited in the tension-filled silence for more gunfire.

Seconds passed, the only sound their rapid breathing. She let go of Pierce's arm but remained next to him, hunkered down behind a fallen tree. "Who do you think Cowan was shooting at?"

"I don't know," Pierce said, "but someone returned his fire. Maybe Jude's deputies finally made it. I think we should stay here until we're sure."

She studied his expression. The indifference was gone—at least for now. She relished the moment and wished she could hold on to it.

"Thanks for taking charge in the tunnel," she said. "I was having a panic attack."

"I know how scared you are of spiders. I was surprised you even went in."

"Me too, but I didn't have a choice." She shuddered, remembering the spider eggs so close to her skin. "I knew you'd understand. I'm not sure the others did."

"The important thing is we made it out. But it's not over yet."

Zoe sat on her heels, afraid to end their undeclared truce by saying something that might set him off.

A couple minutes passed. The only sound she heard was the cawing of a crow.

Finally Pierce said, "Zoe … what are we going to do when this is over?"

"Go home?" Had she said the words out loud, or was it just wishful thinking?

"And then what?" His eyes glistened. "How do we reconcile all the lies?"

"I never lied about loving you. Falling for you was the most honest thing I've ever done." Zoe ran her thumb across the diamonds on her wedding band. "But when we met, I'd already become Zoe Benoit. I'd already used the money I got from the stolen ring to start up the eatery. I hated lying to you." She glanced up at him. "But it was either lie or lose you—some choice."

"Did you ever consider that maybe I didn't want to lose you either?"

"I figured you would, once you found out I started Zoe B's with dishonest money—and that my family was just poor white trash."

"Will you please stop referring to yourself that way?" Pierce bopped her on the arm with his palm. "Did you honestly think I wouldn't marry you unless you were Cajun? I fell in love with your heart, Zoe. Your family tree doesn't matter. What *does* matter to me is honesty. And everything I know about you has been a lie."

"Not anymore." Zoe cupped his face in her hands. "Now that you know the truth, there's no reason for me to lie."

"How could I ever be sure? I never suspected you were lying before. What does that say about *me?* I feel like a complete fool."

"Don't. My new identity became so real to me that I almost believed it myself."

Pierce rolled his eyes. "Is that supposed to make me feel better? How can we have a future together as long as I know you have the power to deceive me?"

"But why would I want to? I'm relieved I don't have to lie anymore."

"Well, good for you, Zoe," he said sarcastically. "It's great that you're *relieved*. It's a whole lot more complicated than that for me—"

"Zoe and Pierce Broussard. Vanessa Langley. This is Sheriff Jude Prejean." His booming voice echoed, as if it were coming through a bullhorn. "Cowen is dead. Please return to the manor house immediately. Repeat: Please return to the manor house immediately. The threat is over."

Over? Zoe could almost hear the door to Pierce's heart slam shut. One life-altering crisis had ended, but another was just beginning.

Zoe sat across from Jude Prejean and Aimee Rivette at the oblong table in interview room one, going over and over the details of her involvement with Reagan Cowen.

"Are we about finished?" Zoe looked from Jude to Aimee and back to Jude. "I'm exhausted. I'd really like to go home."

"We appreciate your helping us piece this thing together," Jude said. "When my deputies took him out, Cowen was wearing a size ten and a half Columbia Newton Ridge hiking boot, an exact match to one of shoe prints we cast at the scene of Remy's hanging. Vanessa told us that Cowen admitted he hanged Remy to stir things up and distract law enforcement while he came after you. He took some serious risks, trying to get his hundred thousand."

"This was about more than just the money." Zoe glanced up at the black-and-white clock on the wall. "He wanted to teach Zoe Benoit a lesson for disappearing with her inheritance and not paying him what her parents owed. If it hadn't been for the feature in the newspaper, he would never have found me—and assumed I was the Zoe Benoit he was looking for. It was totally a case of mistaken identity."

"Yes, I'm satisfied it was. I believe we're done here." Jude looked over at Aimee. "Would you give us the room?"

"Sure." Aimee gathered her notes, then got up and left the room, closing the door behind her.

Jude turned his pencil upside down and bounced the eraser on the table. "I'm sure you don't need a lecture to know how lucky you are that you never went to jail for stealing the ring—or that Cowen didn't slit your throat or put a bullet through your head."

"Believe me, I don't. At least I've arranged to make monthly payments to Mrs. Woodmore until I've paid back the value of the ring."

"I respect you for doing that. Legally, no one can force you to since the statute of limitations has run." Jude let half a minute pass, and then said, "How're you and Pierce doing?"

"Not so great. As soon as Gil and Stone are finished questioning him, he's going to drive down to Houma and stay with his parents. I think it's over between us."

Jude winced. "I'm sorry, Zoe."

"Who can blame him? I'm not the woman he married. I'm a thief and a liar. He's better off without me."

"Do you really believe that?"

Zoe blinked to clear her eyes, and a tear spilled down her cheek. "I don't know."

"I think you do." Jude tilted her chin. "We've known each other for ten years. I admit I'm surprised and disappointed. I don't condone the choices you made, but I'm not going to throw you under the bus either. There's a lot more to Zoe Broussard than her mistakes."

"I'm not so sure."

"I am." Jude made a tent with his fingers. "What you and Pierce have together is worth saving."

"What is it we *have*, since the woman he fell in love with never existed?"

"Well, that's what the two of you need to figure out." Jude leaned forward on his elbows and looked her in the eyes. "He's in love with *someone*. Don't you think it's time you accepted her?"

"What if I don't like her?"

"What if you do? It's not just your name and where you were born and who your parents are that defines you. All that's just background noise. The real deal is the person Pierce fell in love with. Deep down, he knows that. And so do you."

Savannah rushed out of the kitchen at Zoe B's and over to the table by the window, where Father Sam, Hebert, and Tex were still seated.

"I just got off the phone with Zoe." Savannah set a carafe of fresh coffee on the table. "She wanted me to tell y'all that she and Pierce are down at the sheriff's department. They'd been hiding out at Langley Manor—from the suspect that was shot and killed by sheriff's deputies!"

"The man suspected in Remy's murder?" Father Sam said.

Savannah nodded. "Vanessa Langley tried to help them and was shot in the shoulder. She's been taken out to the medical center."

"Mercy," Tex said. "How did those three get involved with someone like *that?*"

"All I know is that he was a customer here."

"That's disturbing," Father Sam said. "Zoe didn't tell you his name?"

"No. She said he wasn't from this area and to watch the news."

"Langley Manor?" Hebert stroked the stubble on his chin. "What's dat about?"

Savannah shrugged. "I'm still in shock. Zoe wanted us all to know that she'll be at Remy's funeral tomorrow. But that Pierce was going to Houma and stay with his mom and dad. She asked if Benson would take his shift for a few days."

Hebert sat back in his chair, his lips pursed, his head cocked. "Pierce had to rush off, wid Remy's funeral tomorrow? Dat's peculiar."

"Very," Savannah said.

"Especially since Pierce was so fond of Remy—and Emile." Father Sam pushed his glasses up higher on his nose. "He wouldn't miss the funeral if he could help it."

"Dat's fuh shore," Hebert said.

"He wouldn't give up his kitchen that long either." Savannah folded her arms across her chest. "Whatever business he has must need his immediate attention."

"What business you tink is more important dan Remy's funeral?" Hebert said.

Savannah arched her eyebrows. "Maybe Pierce's parents need help. It's not like Zoe to be so private, though. She's definitely not volunteering anything on this."

⚜

Vanessa hung up the phone and looked out into the parking lot at Hargrave Medical Center. The shot of Demerol she received was starting to wear off.

"Well?" Ethan squeezed her hand. "It sounded like your folks took the news better than we thought they would."

"Probably because they can't see how awful I look."

"Your injuries *are* awful." Ethan brought her hand to his lips. "But you, my love—alive and safe—are the most beautiful sight I've ever seen."

Vanessa smiled in spite of herself. "This from the man who thought I was beautiful when I was nine months pregnant and looked liked a hippo."

"You were, undoubtedly, the loveliest hippo I'd ever seen. Still are." Ethan laughed and ducked, his hands in front of his face.

Vanessa grabbed the extra pillow, giggling all the while, but didn't have the energy to throw it.

"This really isn't a laughing matter." Ethan lowered his hands. "Finish telling me about your conversation with your folks."

"You heard my side of the conversation. They're just glad the bullet wound was superficial and I'm alive. Mom said Cowen practically signed his own death certificate when he held a sheriff's deputy at gunpoint. They had no choice but to take him out."

"It's unfortunate it came to that," Ethan said, "but it's hard to feel too bad, knowing he'd kill again."

"I think Mom's feelings are hurt that we didn't call and ask her advice before we got involved in something this risky. But even though neither of them said it, I think Mom and Dad are proud of us for being Good Samaritans."

"I never thought of it that way. I'll have to use that angle when I tell *my* parents about the first guests we hosted at Langley Manor." Ethan picked up her hand and brought it to his cheek. "I can't believe how close I came to losing you. Now I understand how you felt when Drew's killer was after me and all you could do was pray and trust the Lord."

"That was the longest day of my life."

"I think this was the longest day of mine."

Vanessa sat with Ethan in the stillness for a few moments and then said, "I wonder how Zoe and Pierce are doing. You think they'll go home together?"

Ethan shook his head. "I doubt it. Pierce said something about going to stay with his parents. I wish he'd stay here with Zoe and work it out. Separating might be the beginning of the end."

"That would be sad." Vanessa sighed. "They really do love each other."

"Zoe's betrayal was pretty serious, honey. Pierce might not be able to get through this by himself."

"Are you thinking of counseling him?"

"I'm certainly willing, but he might not open up with me."

The nurse pranced in the room. "How are you feeling, doll?"

"I'm starting to hurt again."

"Well, it's time for another shot of Demerol. I've got it right here." The fifty-something bottle redhead washed her hands with sanitizer and put on plastic gloves, then came over to Vanessa's veno-cath and injected the pain medicine. "This should take the edge off in no time. By the way, if you're still doing well in the morning, the doctor is going to release you."

"That's great news," Ethan said. "Our four-year-old will be so glad. He really misses his mom."

"I just hope the sight of me covered with scratches doesn't scare him to death."

"Okay, doll. That'll probably make you drowsy. Get some rest. Use your call button if you need something." The nurse left as quickly as she had come.

"Before I get too sleepy," Vanessa said, "tell me what the sheriff is doing about Noah Washington."

"Nothing, since we decided not to press charges. They were going to get his statement and let him go."

"What else could we do?" Vanessa said. "He saved our lives."

Ethan arched his eyebrows. "He's also guilty of trespassing. I don't think we should let that go unaddressed. I'd like to hear his explanation."

"Me too. But I also want to hear everything his great-grandmother told him about Langley Manor. Those tunnels are your family's legacy, Ethan. Langley Manor can be so much more than a bed-and-breakfast now. It's a memorial to the brave souls, black and white, who manned it as a station on the Underground Railroad. Our guests will love knowing that."

Ethan smiled. "*I* love knowing that. My dad and uncles are

going to be amazed. I don't think there's any written record of this. Noah Washington may be our only link to the past."

"How will we get in touch with him?"

All of the expression left Ethan's face. "I have no idea. I hope the sheriff does."

CHAPTER 33

Jude followed Aimee into interview room three, where Noah Washington had been with his deputies for the past couple hours, answering questions.

"Mr. Washington, I'm Sheriff Jude Prejean and this is Deputy Chief Aimee Rivette. I know you've talked to my deputies at length about what happened today at Langley Manor, but I'd like to talk with you myself."

"Yes, sir. What else do you need to know?"

Jude sat next to Aimee and opposite Noah, his hands clasped on the table. "Vanessa and Ethan Langley have opted not to press charges against you for trespassing."

"I'm grateful."

"You should be."

Noah lifted his gaze, his dark eyes wide. "No harm came to anyone because I stayed in that empty house. I jus' needed a place to light for a while."

"How'd you even know it was vacant?"

"I didn't till I got there. My only plan was to see the place I'd heard so much about. I've pretty much lost everything. I was lookin' for some kinda connection."

"You told Vanessa that your great-grandmother's great-grandmother, Naomi, was a slave at Langley Manor. And that the Langleys were involved in the Underground Railroad."

"That's true, sir."

"Is that a matter of public record?"

"I couldn't say. I learned it growin' up. My great-grandma G. G. learned it when she was growin' up. But why would my people put the slave owners in a good light, if it wasn't true?"

"Did you think that because your ancestors lived at Langley Manor you had the right to let yourself in?"

Noah hung his head. "No, sir. I just didn't have any place else to go. I didn't hurt anything by comin' and goin' through the tunnels. I was amazed they were still there, jus' like G. G. said."

Jude noticed the lettering on Noah's dirty T-shirt—*Bourbon Street*. "Why don't you have anywhere else to go? Where are you from?"

"New Awlins. Lost my home in Katrina. Didn't have flood insurance. Lost my job, too."

"Why didn't the government relocate you?"

"I didn't ask 'em to."

"Do you have family?"

Noah's eyes were suddenly dark pools, and he seemed far away. "Uh, no. Not really. My wife and teenage daughters were swept away before rescuers could get to us. I don't really have anyone."

"I suppose you know you have resources that can help you get on your feet—like the Red Cross or the Salvation Army or Catholic Charities?"

"I do. But mostly I try to make it by myself."

"I can appreciate that," Jude said. "But since you don't have anywhere to stay, you're *not* making it by yourself. You really need to reach out and let one of these agencies help you before you do something unlawful and the other party does press charges. Or maybe that's what you want—to end up in jail? I promise you there are better ways to find food, clothing, and shelter."

"If I was lookin' to go to jail, I'd have been there a long time ago. I'm just down on my luck at the moment."

Jude leaned forward on his elbows. "Why'd you decide to help Mrs. Langley and the Broussards? You could've stayed hidden in the tunnel and let things play out."

"I figured Josiah Langley helped my ancestors, I should help his. I knew the tunnel was their ticket out. I couldn't just let 'em get shot."

Jude studied Noah's relaxed demeanor. Was he telling the truth—or was he just a practiced con man?

"I'd like to shift gears and talk about something we found on the property adjacent to the Langleys'. Seems a shoe print we cast near the scene of a murder turned out to be a size nine Sears and Roebuck loafer like the one you're wearing."

"I know about the hangin'. I was on that land a couple days before."

"Really?" Jude laid today's mug shot of Reagan Cowen on the table. "Do you know this man?"

"No, sir."

"Name's Reagan Cowan. Ring a bell?"

"Sure does. He's the fella who was chasin' after Vanessa Langley and who followed us through the tunnel. I never did see his face."

"And you never heard his name before today?"

"No, sir." Noah scratched his chin. "I overheard the Broussards say his name after they talked with someone on the cell phone this mornin'."

"But you never met the man?"

"No, never did."

Jude picked up a pencil and bounced the eraser on the table. "What possible reason would you have for being on the Vincent property?"

"I was searchin' for a house. G. G. mentioned that Abigail Langley's brother had built him a house a couple hundred yards down the bayou from the manor house. Some of my ancestors were slaves there, too, but he wasn't sympathetic to the Underground Railroad. Didn't know his sister was either. I just wanted to see it."

"Are you referring to that old farmhouse?"

"No, that place is nothin' like G. G. described. She said it was a two-story plantation house with a porch all around. I'm guessin' it's been tore down. I walked all over the property and didn't see it."

Jude mused. "So, just to be clear, you're saying you were *not* on the Vincent property Wednesday morning, July twenty-seventh and had no knowledge of Remy Jarvis's hanging—or the note left on Deputy Castille's windshield?"

"That's exactly what I'm sayin', sir. I'm guilty of trespassin' at both places, but I don't know this Cowan fella, and I sure wasn't involved in any hangin'."

Jude glanced over at Aimee. The look on her face told him she believed Noah and didn't think they were going to get any new information from him.

"All right. I think we're done here. Mr. Washington, you're free to go. But I want you to stay in Les Barbes until we sort this out. Monsignor Robidoux at Saint Catherine's has already made room for you at Haven House. You can shower and shave and get some clean clothes. The place is cool and comfortable. And the food's not bad either."

Noah gave a nod. "Thank you, sir. Sounds mighty good 'bout now."

"Wait here and I'll have one of my deputies take you over there." Jude stood. "Oh … I could tell when I spoke with the Langleys that they're eager to talk to you about Josiah Langley's involvement in the Underground Railroad."

"I really don't know much else."

"Well, they felt a connection. Maybe you have more to offer than you think."

Zoe stood at the railing on the gallery outside her apartment, trying not to think about Pierce packing his bags.

She looked out at the crimson sky and inhaled the sweet aroma of caramel corn coming from Kernel Poppy's. She heard Cajun music playing at Breaux's. And the street vendor chanting his mantra, "Andouille corn dogs. Best in da bayou."

Across the street, on the gallery above the Coy Cajun Gift Shop, Madame Duval waved from a wrought-iron table, where she sat sipping a mint julep, her cat, Juniper, curled up next to the glass pitcher.

Was this special community that had received her with open arms about to turn its back? Could she manage Zoe B's without Pierce? Could she afford to hire a chef and, at the same time, pay Mrs. Woodmore a thousand dollars a month? Did it even matter? How long would it be before some ambitious reporter found a "source" in the sheriff's department, willing to reveal details of her past? Or before Pierce, disillusioned and angry, was willing to tell his story?

A horse-drawn carriage stopped in front of the Hotel Peltier, and a bride and groom stepped off the carriage and walked hand in hand through the revolving door. Was their reception taking place there—or were they checking in to spend their first night as husband and wife? Her mind flashed back five years, to the evening of June fifth....

Pierce lifted her into his arms, bunching her long, lacy wedding veil in her lap, and carried her across the threshold of the bridal suite at the Hotel Peltier. He closed the door with his foot, then set her down and positioned the veil so it draped down her back.

He looked adoringly into her eyes, his hands cupping her face. "I give you my heart, Zoe Broussard. I promise there will never—ever—be anyone else. You are everything my heart desires. Now and forever."

As their lips melted together, her conscience squirmed with the knowledge that she had won his love by pretending to be someone she wasn't. She quickly dismissed it. Wasn't her love genuine, her devotion sincere? Why should she let the past rule the present or the future?

She pulled her lips back from his just far enough to say, "I never knew I could love any man the way I love you. You are my soul mate. The one—the only one—I will ever love."

As Pierce slowly unleashed the passion he had restrained during their engagement, she responded freely and eagerly, feeling none of the fear or revulsion she had associated with her father's abusive advances. Why should she? Shelby Sieger no longer existed.

The next day, she and Pierce flew to Grand Cayman, a wedding gift from his many aunts and uncles. They spent their days bathed in the warm, shimmering green waters of the Caribbean Sea, their nights enchanted by the showcase of dazzling diamonds spilled across the black velvet heavens—and the ecstasy of two becoming one....

"I'm leaving now." Pierce's voice startled her, and she remembered where she was and what was about to happen. "I'll call and let the phone ring once when I get to Mom and Dad's—so you'll know I made it."

"I wish you would stay—and work this out together."

"I can't, Zoe. Not now. I need to be by myself and think."

Zoe swallowed the fear and sadness that threatened to steal her voice. Did this man who had once declared she was his heart's desire now feel so betrayed by her that he would never recover? She breathed in slowly, then turned around, trying not to look as desperate as she felt.

"At least you're willing to think about it," she said.

"It's not like I asked for this, Zoe. How are we supposed to live together when I can't trust you? It was humiliating enough to realize I'd been duped. Do you really think I can allow myself to be that vulnerable again?"

Zoe took a step closer to him. "I wouldn't blame you if you didn't trust me again. But I want you to know that you *can*. You know everything now. I have no secrets to protect."

He rolled his eyes. "Like I could tell if you did. I just wanted you to know I'm leaving. Don't call me, Zoe. When I've got something to say, I'll let you know." He turned around and disappeared through the living room. She heard the front door open and close and listened to his footsteps as he walked away.

"I love you, *cher*," she whispered, salty puddles clouding her vision. "You're never coming back to me."

CHAPTER 34

Zoe opened her eyes, realizing that the obnoxious buzzing in her head was actually her alarm blaring. She groped the nightstand on Pierce's side of the bed and hit the snooze button—something *he* always did. She hugged his pillow and relished the masculine, woody scent of his Tuscany cologne. She pictured him lying in the brass bed in the guest room at his parents' house. Was he awake yet? Had he ever gone to sleep? Had he missed her for even a fleeting moment? Then again, why would he? All he wanted to do was get away from her.

Zoe struggled to sit up. Did she have the emotional strength to push off the weighty guilt that seemed to have her pinned down and get up and face the day—and the probing questions she would get from employees, friends, and customers? One thing she didn't have was the luxury of nursing her own heartache—not with Remy's funeral this afternoon.

She threw her legs over the side of the bed and lowered her bare feet onto the floor and headed for the shower. At least she wasn't camping out at Langley Manor without air-conditioning or running water. Wasn't that something she could be grateful for?

She turned on the shower and thought of how pitiful Vanessa had looked, covered in bloody scratches, a bullet wound in her shoulder. Poor thing probably couldn't wait to shower—to cleanse herself of Cowen. Hadn't that been Zoe's reaction on Saturday night after Cowen grabbed her and cut her face, threatening to do worse if she didn't do what he said? She must have stood in the shower for thirty minutes, as if soap and water could wash away her memory of it.

Zoe stepped into the tub and pulled the shower curtain, the pulsating water hitting her back, feeling both soothing and therapeutic. She poured conditioning shampoo onto her head and worked up a luxurious lather, the massaging motion of the warm water making her long for the sleep she never got.

She rinsed and dried off, then slipped into her terry bathrobe and saw Pierce's matching robe still hanging on the back of the door. Her thoughts immediately raced in reverse to those special days when they took off work together and stayed in bed—talking, reading, listening to music, watching movies, making love … no commitments at the eatery and no interruptions. Weren't those times alone with him pure bliss?

She stood in front of the mirror and dried her hair, then put on waterproof mascara, anticipating the emotional impact of Remy's funeral. She put on her black dress and fastened her favorite strand of pearls around her neck. Why did she look so pale? She brushed a little blush on her cheeks and put on lipstick. Better. At least she looked alive.

Robotically she went into the kitchen and made a single cup of fresh-brewed coffee, then sat at the breakfast bar, staring at the collage of photographs held to the refrigerator with heart magnets. Would these end up in the bottom of the shoebox with the photos of her parents and her brother, Michael?

She took a sip of coffee. How was she going to get through this day without letting on that her heart was broken? Guilt taunted her with biting sarcasm. How hard could it be for someone as practiced as she—the queen of pretense, the lady of lies?

She glanced at her cell phone and noticed she had a message. Had Pierce called her while she was in the shower? She keyed in the numbers to retrieve the message.

"Zoe, this is Adele Woodmore. It's eight o'clock on Tuesday morning. I called several times Sunday and Monday and can't seem to reach you. I decided to leave a message this time. My attorney has drawn up the papers, hon. You indicated that you'd prefer to come back to Alexandria to sign them so let me know when. I have them here at the house. I've been praying for y'all. I do hope things are working out the way you hoped. Let me hear from you soon."

Zoe blinked the stinging from her eyes. How could she renege on this agreement after she had made such an issue of it? But if she signed the papers and Zoe B's profit took a nosedive because of her personal life, Adele wasn't going to get her thousand dollars a month. Should she take tomorrow and drive to Alexandria and just tell Adele the disappointing truth? How could she? How could she not?

Zoe stood and dumped her coffee in the sink. She didn't have to decide today. Today was reserved for Remy.

⚜

Vanessa waited in her hospital room with Ethan for someone to bring her discharge papers. Outside her window, the morning haze looked ghostly as it hovered above the damp ground and caught the rays of sun.

"I'm glad you got a good night's sleep," Ethan said.

"I really did. But I'm so anxious to get home to Carter. I miss him so much."

"He misses you, too, honey. I'm just glad it's over."

"So am I."

Ethan pulled a chair up next to her bed and sat. "I called Southern Pride and told them about the door in the closet, the hidden staircase, and the tunnels, and they're going to come out next week and take a look. They'll probably make some adjustments to the new blueprints."

"Did you have a chance to call Haven House and talk to Noah?"

"I did. Noah said he would love to talk with us anytime. I told him I would call him there as soon as you're up to it. Apparently, Sheriff Prejean asked him not to leave town for a few days."

"Was he planning to?"

Ethan shrugged. "I didn't get that impression. But the guy doesn't have anywhere to go."

"I wonder what his story is. I've always wondered why someone would choose to stay homeless when there are so many agencies willing to help them."

"Honey, you can't ask him such an intrusive question."

Vanessa rolled her eyes. "He's the one who intruded on our lives. I'm not letting that man get away without finding out every detail he's willing to tell us. If I'm a little intrusive in the process, he'll have to forgive me. I have a million questions."

"Which I'm sure you'll ask."

"Oh, come on, Ethan. You're just as curious as I am about Josiah Langley's involvement in the Underground Railroad."

He smiled. "You bet I am. But I'll tell you whose curiosity is over the top—my dad's and uncles'. Dad's going to dig out the original blueprints. But he's almost positive the tunnels aren't on there."

Vanessa mused. "After this new discovery, I wonder if the three Langley brothers might regret their decision to give us the family heirloom as a wedding gift."

"Are you kidding? They're more excited than ever to let us bring the place back to life. And I'm sure we're all just a little prouder now to have the name Langley."

CHAPTER 35

Pierce sat in the glider on the screened-in porch at his parents' home, the ceiling fan going round and round and rustling the pages of today's issue of the *Houma Courier*. He folded the newspaper and set it on the seat next to him. Could he remember anything he'd read?

He picked up his mug and took a sip of coffee, focusing on a lone white ibis meandering through the back lawn, picking through the blades of grass in search of a tasty breakfast. Glints of sunlight filtered through the sycamore trees that shaded the yard. How relieved he was to be home—in the house he grew up in—ninety minutes from Les Barbes. He wondered if he would feel as relieved when one o'clock rolled around and he couldn't go to Remy's memorial Mass.

He thought of Zoe, and an image of her pretty face popped into his mind. Wouldn't he be smart to just walk away? It's not as though he needed the job at Zoe B's. Wasn't he experienced enough now to get hired as a chef almost anywhere in South Louisiana—or go back to teaching history?

The Church would probably annul the marriage. The woman he promised to love "for better or for worse," and to whom he pledged his faithfulness, didn't exist.

Pierce sighed. Would an annulment really change the reality that he had loved Zoe with all his heart—and still did? At least the Zoe he knew. How could she have been carrying around all those secrets without him picking up on it? So much for being soul mates!

He heard someone cough and realized his dad was standing next to the glider, dressed in his gray coveralls.

"How're you doing, son?" Burke Broussard said.

"I'm alive."

"Mind if I sit?"

"Not at all. I'm lousy company, though." Pierce picked up the newspaper and set it on the end table.

Burke sat on the couch next to him, his arms folded across his chest. "I've got to get out to the sugar refinery. Just wanted to check on you first. Did you sleep?"

"Not really. I've got a lot to sort through."

"Yeah, you do. I just got on the computer and read today's headlines in the *Les Barbes Ledger*. The article focused on that drug-dealing creep who hung your friend Remy, and his threats against Zoe and Vanessa—not so much on you."

"No, I'll just be stuck with the stares and the unspoken questions—like what kind of dupe falls for a woman like *that?*"

Burke rubbed his red and gray beard and seemed pensive. "Zoe does love you, son. She didn't lie about that."

"Didn't she?"

"You *know* she didn't. She got herself in over her head and made some really bad mistakes. But I've known her for six years. Five of those years she's been my daughter-in-law. I've seen how the two of you are together. I know love when I see it."

"Yeah, well, I thought I did too."

Burke pushed with his foot and made the glider go faster. A minute passed without either of them saying anything.

"Don't worry, Dad. If I decide to petition the Church for an annulment, I'll be quiet about it so I don't humiliate you and Mom."

"Is that what you think we care about? We're not worried about you humiliating us. We're worried about your well-being—*and* Zoe's. She's family. If the two of you split up, we lose someone we love too."

"I can't be married to someone I don't trust."

"You're feeling betrayed right now. That's understandable. But I wish you'd take some time to consider everything before you act in haste." Burke seemed nervous and kept glancing at his watch. "I've still got a few minutes before I have to leave. I'm going to step out on a limb and tell you something I've never told anyone, except your mother."

Pierce glanced over at his dad and noticed his face was flushed. "What is it?"

Burke cracked his knuckles and looked straight ahead. "After your mother and I had been married a year, we talked about buying a house and having a baby. We were both working our tails off, saving every penny we could. Making a baby was the easy part. The house was another matter." Burke pursed his lips, his eyes squinted. "Wouldn't you know, the perfect house came on the market and your mother went nuts over it. We only needed another three thousand dollars for the down payment, but there was no way we could borrow it. She *really* wanted that house."

Pierce shifted his weight. Did he want to hear the rest of the story? His dad was his hero.

"Stay with me," Burke said. "I'll get to the point here in a minute. Seeing your mom's excitement about the house made me want to get it for her more than anything in the world. At the time, I was a painter. And a guy named Jacob Daigle hired me to paint the inside of his lake house. Big job—eight thousand square feet. The man had an amazing collection of artwork—oils, charcoals, pastels, pencil sketches—you name it. Daigle had one large oil painting of pelicans on a marina—really an amazing piece. I remember thinking it was a shame that he had hung it in an obscure room that looked like a library for paperback books."

"I'm not sure I like where this is going, Dad."

"Just hear me out. I'll never have the guts to bring this up again. One night after I sent my crew home for the day, I took the painting and put it in my van. I hadn't planned to do it. My justification was that Daigle had hundreds of thousands of dollars tied up in artwork, and he wasn't going to miss one painting that meant nothing to him, but it might enable your mother and me to get the house. The next morning, I took it to a dealer and found out the artist was some big shot down the bayou. The dealer gave me a money order for thirty-five hundred, and I didn't haggle with him."

Pierce shook his head. "Weren't you afraid of getting caught?"

"Sure. But no one could prove it. I figured I'd just deny everything with a straight face. I mean there were paintings all over that house. I hung a different painting in its place and doubted Daigle would even miss it right off. And when he did, there wouldn't be any way for him to prove I took it."

"Did you tell Mom?"

"How could I? She would never have let me keep the money. And I wanted to get that house for her more than anything." Burke's eyes brimmed with tears, his chin quivering. "So I came up with a plan. I told your mother that a guy I used to work with on the oil rig bought a boat and wanted to take me deep-sea fishing. I went down to Grand Isle for the weekend. I went fishing all right, but only from the pier. I wanted to get some sun so I looked believable."

Pierce couldn't believe what he was hearing. His dad was a thief? And a liar?

"I came home from fishing and told your mom that my friend had also taken me to the race track—and that my horse won big. I picked her up, spun her around, and told her how much it was. I'd never seen her so happy. We bought that house, son. You're sitting in it right now."

"I grew up in a house you bought with dishonest money?"

"Part of the down payment was. I'm not proud of it." Burke put his face in his hands. "Five years ago, right after you and Zoe were married, I went back to Mr. Daigle's place with a check for the thirty-five hundred. I was ready to tell him the whole truth."

"What'd he say?"

"He had passed away the year before. His daughter owned the house. I told her my story, and she was shocked that I came back to make it right. She didn't even call the cops or ask me to pay what the painting was worth at that time. She just thanked me, took the check, and said she hoped that cleared my conscience."

"What about Mom? Did you tell her the truth?"

"Yeah." Burke whisked a tear off his cheek. "That was the killer though."

"How'd you do it?"

"I took her for a drive and just told her outright. She was horrified. She felt I had betrayed her by deceiving her that way. She
wondered what else I hadn't told her. She questioned how I could say
I loved her, then look her in the eyes and lie."

"Well? How could you?" Pierce tilted his father's chin and forced
him to meet his gaze.

"I don't know, son. I loved your mother with all my heart. I
just saw the joy in her eyes when we found the house, and I wanted
to make her happy." His eyes turned to dark pools and tears spilled
down his cheeks and onto his beard. "What I did was terribly wrong.
It wrecked my relationship with God until I made it right. I passed
over it every time I went to confession. Ignored it when I went to
communion. The only way I could live with it was to justify it and
then forget it. I knew I wasn't a bad person. I wasn't a common
criminal. I just wanted something that was out of my reach—and I
compromised to get it."

"Are you trying to tell me that Zoe loves me? And that she did
the same thing?"

"That's exactly what I'm doing. Was she wrong? Big time! Is she
lucky she didn't go to jail? Absolutely. But you've got to give her some
credit for trying to make things right with Mrs. Woodmore."

"Why? The only reason Zoe tried to square things with her
was because of the anonymous notes she was getting. I'm not sure
she even thinks what she did was that wrong. The lady's filthy rich,
Dad. Zoe knew Mrs. Woodmore didn't need the ring. And that
the money Zoe could get by selling the ring could make her dream
come true. She wanted to be able to support herself. She wanted

to start an eatery. She stole in order to get it done. She's not sorry. Why should I give her credit for anything?"

Burke gripped Pierce's wrist. "Listen to me. I'm not making excuses for Zoe's behavior. What I'm saying is that just because she didn't have the courage to tell you things she's ashamed of doesn't mean she never loved you. Or that she lies to you about other things. *I* didn't. Maybe she doesn't either. Don't you owe it to yourself to find out? I know you love Zoe. Can you really let her go that easily?"

Pierce's throat tightened with emotion. He didn't want to lose it. Not here. Not now. "Dad, I don't know how I feel. I haven't begun to come to grips with the fact that everything I believed about my wife is a lie. And now my father tells me essentially the same thing. What am I supposed to do with that? Am I supposed to just forgive you both and pretend none of this matters?"

Burke shook his head. "No, son. What you're supposed to do look deep inside us for the part you *know* to be true—the part your very soul can't deny. Zoe and I stole something to get what we wanted most. And we lied to protect the secret, for fear of losing the one we love. That was cowardly and morally wrong. And for that I am deeply sorry and hope you can forgive me. Your mother has, and we've managed to move on. I've worked hard to earn her trust. But we're happy again."

Pierce felt as if he had a wad of peanut butter in his throat. Even if he had known what to say, could he have formed the words and pushed them out?

"I suspect that Zoe has wounds deeper than even she knows. After being sexually abused by her father, I can only imagine the torment she lives with—made worse by her silence all these years. She doesn't need rejection from you right now. She never said what she did was right,

and she doesn't expect you to condone it. She just needs to know that
you still love the part of her that you *know* to the depth of your being
is authentic, regardless of the name she chose or where she came from.
She needs to know that the 'for better or worse' part of your vows can
withstand this test. And that good is stronger than evil."

Pierce felt as if his head would burst with all the thoughts bouncing off his brain. "*Is* good stronger than evil, Dad? Because I see evil
everywhere tearing people's lives apart."

"Evil can only do what we give it permission to do." Burke
sighed. "Son, look at me. I'm still the same dad who's always loved
you—and your mom. My mistake and my attempt to hide it didn't
negate that. I feel sure that Zoe's didn't either. That girl loves you. I
know you're hurting. I just don't want you to lose sight of that."

Pierce put his fist to his mouth and coughed instead of letting
out the sobs just below the surface. What had it cost his father to
come to him and admit such a failing?

Burke patted Pierce's knee and then stood. "I've got to go to
work. I know I laid a lot on your heart. And I don't want to add to
your burden. My point in telling you what I did is that this *can* have
a happy ending. It just depends on how much grace you're willing
to give Zoe."

"You're putting this on me? She's the one who messed up."

Burke nodded. "But you're the one with the power."

CHAPTER 36

Zoe sat at her desk in the office at Zoe B's and wiped the tears off her cheeks. Shouldn't she get this over with? It wasn't going to get any easier.

She folded the *Les Barbes Ledger* and tucked it under her arm, then got up and left the office. She walked through the alcove and out into the dining room, where Father Sam, Hebert, and Tex sat at the table by the window.

They looked up, wide-eyed and silent, as she walked toward them and stopped at the table.

"May I sit with you?" she said.

Father Sam fumbled to grab the back of the chair. "Please do."

Zoe sat next to the priest and across from the other two men, her hands folded on the table, her pulse racing.

A second later, Savannah was standing at the table, a white carafe in her hand. "Are we ever glad to see you!" She filled Zoe's cup with coffee and set the carafe on the table. "What an ordeal."

Zoe wasn't sure how to respond. Had they all read the *Ledger*? Had they watched the morning news? "I-I don't know what to say. I was shocked and horrified to find out this Cowen who came looking for me was behind Remy's murder."

"We were too," Savannah said. "Sheriff's deputies came in to talk
to us, and I gave the sketch artist a description of the man who was
with Cowen."

The others shook their heads.

Zoe's eyes brimmed with tears. "I can't stop thinking that it
would never have happened if I hadn't lied to that reporter, who
wrote the feature story on Zoe B's."

"Lied?" Savannah said.

Zoe nodded, moving her gaze around the table at four pairs
of questioning eyes. "Yes. There's something I need to tell you. My
parents didn't die in a house fire. I made that up when I moved here.
I'm sorry I let you think it all this time. It was just easier than getting
into matters I was uncomfortable with. The truth is: I grew up in
an abusive home. When I was old enough to leave, I walked away.
Eventually, I changed my name from Shelby Sieger to Zoe Benoit,
and then Broussard when I married Pierce. I'm not even Cajun."

"Why didn't you just tell us this before?" Savannah said. "Who
cares if you're not Cajun? We like you the way you are."

Shame scalded Zoe's face. "It's complicated. I was starting a
new life and *really* wanted to fit in here. I didn't think people would
support a Cajun eatery unless the owner was Cajun. I apologize for
misrepresenting myself. There's more I have to work out—most of
it with Pierce—but it's a private matter. I hope you all will respect
that."

"Of course, we will," Father Sam said. "We're just so happy
you're safe, Zoe. You seem to be all right. But are you?"

"I will be. It's going to take time. Vanessa endured the worst of it."

"What about Pierce?"

"He wasn't hurt physically." Zoe sighed. "But he didn't know I lied about my past until after Cowan accosted me and demanded money. He needs some time to think. He's staying in Houma at his parents'."

Half a minute went by without anyone saying anything.

"Don't feel like you have to talk about your ordeal"—Savannah kept glancing at the Band-Aid on Zoe's cheek—"but just tell me this: Was the article in the *Ledger* accurate?"

"About what happened with Cowen, yes. But you're the only people besides the sheriff, the Langleys, and Pierce who know I lied to the reporter about my past. None of this would've happened if I hadn't. Cowen was in Lafayette the weekend the feature story was in the newspaper. When he read it, the details all fit. He was convinced he had found the Zoe Benoit whose parents had owed him money." Zoe shook her head. "Why did he have to kill Remy? It hurts me so much to think he killed Remy for nothing more than to distract the authorities."

"You're not responsible for anything Cowen did," Tex said.

"I know that in my head. But my heart is broken. Remy would be alive if I hadn't lied." Zoe wiped a tear off her cheek. "How do I get past that?"

Hebert patted her hand tenderly. "*Un jour a la frou.*"

"Hebert's right," Father Sam said. "One day at a time. We'll help you."

She knew they would. Not that she deserved it. "Enough about me. This day is about paying our respects to Remy. How's Emile?"

Hebert shook his head. "I tink he'll do better after we get Remy's funeral overwid. Later on, he's going to carry his ashes down to da Roux River and let 'em go."

Father Sam looked at his watch. "Which reminds me, I need to get over to Saint Catherine's. I want to spend some time going over Remy's eulogy. One o'clock will be here before we know it."

At twelve-thirty, Zoe walked in the front door of Saint Catherine Catholic Church and took a memorial folder from the usher. She dipped her fingers into the holy water and crossed herself, then walked up the side aisle until she spotted Tex's bald head in the third row. She bowed her head, made the sign of the cross, and moved into the center of the pew and knelt next to him.

Tex kept his eyes focused on something straight ahead. She wondered if this Texas Baptist felt like a foreigner in a Catholic church—or if he was just succumbing to the sobering heaviness of the moment.

Zoe bowed her head for what seemed a respectable length of time, and then looked up at the altar. So *that's* what Tex had been staring at! In spite of Emile's appeal that, in lieu of flowers, donations be made to Catholic Charities, the sanctuary was lavishly adorned with flower arrangements of every shape and size—all red flowers, the color of the cap Remy always wore. For a split second she pictured him standing there, smiling like an angel, his red cap backward on his head.

Zoe's eyes burned with tears. That beautiful human being would still be alive if Cowen hadn't come to Les Barbes looking for her. How many other people were thinking the same thing? She could almost feel the stares.

She turned her focus on her hands and didn't look to her right or to her left. After a few minutes she eased back and sat on the pew.

God, I'm sorry. I'm so sorry.

She heard a man coughing. Sounded just like Pierce. She'd already done a double take twice today, thinking she had seen him. Would she ever adjust to his absence? It was as though half of her had been stripped away and she was exposed and vulnerable.

She heard shuffling and realized everyone was standing. She rose to her feet just as the organ began to play a song she didn't recognize. She waited as Remy's relatives walked slowly down the center aisle and into the first two rows, not surprised to see Hebert with them.

Emile looked a decade older. Father Sam, dressed in white vestments, walked behind the cross bearer and up the steps to the altar. It occurred to her that she had never seen him outfitted for Mass before.

"'I am the resurrection and the life.'" Her white-haired friend spoke with gentle authority. "'Whoever believes in me, even if he dies, will live, and everyone who lives and believes in me will never die....'"

She felt Tex slip his arm around her. His show of tenderness so touched her that she could restrain the tears no longer. She took a handkerchief out of her purse, held it to her mouth, and quietly wept.

Pierce sat at the far end of the back pew at Saint Catherine's, wearing sunglasses, and with enough mousse in his hair that no one should recognize him. He waited several minutes until the congregation, row by row, came down the center aisle and exited the church.

Zoe had looked broken, her face red and swollen, her gait wobbly and frail. At least Tex Campbell held her by the arm and seemed to steady her. Was he aware that she and Pierce were thinking of separating? Or had Zoe kept that secret, too?

It was disturbing to see Emile Jarvis look so devastated. Would he ever recover from this? Would he ever be able to accept that his sweet, innocent son was hung from a live oak, his head bashed in?

Pierce put his hand on the back of his neck and massaged the muscles. He felt at the same time fury and compassion for Zoe's plight. She had lied about herself. She would have to live with the consequences. But could there be any doubt that she cared deeply about Remy and would have never put him in danger? She wasn't the monster; Cowen was. If there was any justice at all, Cowen was in hell.

One by one the stragglers left the church until Pierce was the only one left. He got up and walked down the side aisle and up to the front of the church where the statue of Mary stood, vases of flowers at her feet. He put an offering in the box and lit a votive candle, then knelt and said a prayer for Remy.

Finally he stood, a lump in his throat, and whispered, "Rest in peace, bud. You're in a better place."

Was he? Pierce wasn't sure what he believed anymore. If God was so good, why had Remy been murdered? Why was his own life falling apart? He'd been faithful. He'd done exactly what the Church had required of him. He never missed Mass on Sundays and holy days. He went to confession regularly. Communion every Sunday. He kept the Ten Commandments the best he could. Said the rosary. He tried to be a good husband. He was faithful to Zoe and loved her with all his heart.

Did he deserve to have his marriage fall apart? Or to find out his father wasn't his hero after all—that he was capable of doing something so dishonest?

Pierce glanced over at the altar and saw Father Sam, now dressed in black slacks and his black clerical shirt, reading the note cards on the flowers.

He turned around and walked quickly down the side aisle and exited by the side door. Most of the people who had populated the pews had left now. The parking lot was almost empty—like his heart and soul.

His father's voice seemed to echo in the void. *Just because she didn't have the courage to tell you things she's ashamed of doesn't mean she never loved you. Or that she lies to you about other things. I didn't.*

Pierce sighed. How was that even possible? Should he get in his car and drive back to Houma? Or should he go find Zoe and take the first step to save their marriage? There was little chance he would change his mind about going back to her. But unless *little* chance became *no* chance, didn't he owe it to himself to at least be open?

You're the one with the power....This can have a happy ending. It just depends on how much grace you're willing to give Zoe.

Pierce started the car and turned on the air conditioner. He adjusted the side mirror and heard laughter. He caught a glimpse of a young couple walking into Louie's, one of the man's arms around a pretty brunette, the other holding a curly-headed blond baby.

His heart felt as if it had gone limp and was lying in a heap. Could he bear to spend the rest of his life without Zoe—without any chance at his dream to raise a family with her? He was thirty-seven.

How many years would it take him to start over? To find a woman
he loved the way he loved Zoe?

Who was he kidding? He could never love any woman the way
he loved her. He blinked to clear his eyes and swallowed the tightness in his throat, then pulled out of Saint Catherine's onto Church
Street, still not sure what to do.

His dad said he had all the power. So why did he feel so lost?

CHAPTER 37

Vanessa sat on her living room couch, cuddling Carter and soaking in the wonder of being alive—and being *home*.

"When is Daddy bwinging the candy man to our house?" Carter hugged Georgie and looked up at her with those deep blue eyes that reminded her of her own.

She stroked his thick strawberry-blond hair with her fingers. "Any minute, sweetie. Daddy had to drive to the Haven House to pick him up. That's not far from the courthouse. You know where that is."

Carter gave a nod.

"But I think it's time we called the candy man by his real name."

"What is it?"

"His name is Noah Washington. I think maybe Mister Washington is a little long. Why don't you just call him Mister Noah?"

"Mister Noah?" Carter smiled with his eyes. "Is he bwinging us animal cwackers?"

Vanessa chuckled at her son's developing sense of humor.

There was a knock on the door, and then it opened. "It's just us," Ethan said.

Ethan showed Noah around the apartment, then took him into the living room and seated him in the most comfortable chair and brought him a glass of raspberry tea.

"This place is somethin'," Noah said. "Kinda nice bein' able to go outside on that big gallery and enjoy watchin' the people on the street."

"It is for now," Vanessa said. "After the renovation is done, we'll move into Langley Manor and operate it as a bed-and-breakfast."

"That's what Ethan said on the way over here. Sounds like you have big plans for that place."

"We do," Vanessa said. "We'll have to make some modifications now that we know about the two tunnels. We want to preserve them."

"Tell us a little about *you*." Ethan put his arm around Vanessa. "We're so grateful you helped Vanessa and Zoe and Pierce escape from Cowen. We'd like to know you better."

"Not much to tell. I lived in New Awlins all my life. My folks have passed away now, and my brothers live in Detroit. Made my livin' as a landscaper. I built a clientele and eventually had a crew of six workin' for me. Married a beautiful woman named Rachellyn, who was a nurse at Children's Hospital. We didn't have kids for a long time, but the good Lord finally blessed us with two daughters born a year apart—Tasha and Teena." Noah smiled at Carter. "We sure did enjoy those girls."

"Where's your family now?" Vanessa felt Ethan nudge her with his elbow. "I'm sorry. Maybe that was too direct. It's just that I feel a connection since both our families once lived in Langley Manor and worked together on the Underground Railroad. I find that intriguing."

"So do I. Josiah Langley was a fine man. None finer. From all G. G. told me, I'd be honored to shake his hand. But let me answer your question." Noah laced his fingers together. "I lost Rachellyn and the girls after Katrina. We lived in the ninth ward. Flood waters took 'em before rescuers could get to us. The house is abandoned. I didn't have flood insurance."

"I am *so* sorry, Noah." Vanessa hated that her words sounded rote. What else could she say?

"Me too," he said. "My girls were fifteen and sixteen. I've missed out on their teen years and can't seem to get my groove back. Most of my clients never came back after Katrina. My crew either. I'm just too tired to start over. The experience has me whipped."

"Couldn't you get help from the government?"

Noah shrugged. "Some. But I'm just kinda lost, if you know what I'm sayin'. I know I gotta pull myself up. But it's been hard. Rachellyn would be ashamed if she could see me bummin' it like this. I used to have more clients than I could get to."

"What kind of gardening did you do?" Ethan said.

"You name it, I did it. Landscaping. Maintenance. I did a lot of commercial lawns. Loved it. I'm happiest when my hands is in the dirt."

"Any ideas on what we could do at Langley Manor?"

"It wouldn't be hard for you to make *those* grounds a show place. You just need to trim the live oaks and let more light in. Put in blossom trees—dogwoods, magnolias, crepe myrtles. Some azaleas. Bougainvilleas. A rock garden in the middle of the front lawn would look mighty nice, especially with a waterfall. You'd need Saint Augustine grass that can handle the shade. It depends on your budget. But that place could spruce up real nice."

Vanessa squeezed Ethan's hand, and he squeezed hers back.

"Noah, I realize I'm stepping out here," Ethan said, "but would you consider drawing up a plan we could look at? We'd pay you, of course. The truth is, we're going to need to hire someone to do the landscaping. We can't really do much until the renovation is done because of the workers coming and going. But would you have any interest in tackling it?"

Noah's eyes grew wide and animated. "Are you serious?"

"Why not?" Ethan said. "It seems fitting since we both have a family history at Langley Manor. But those times have changed, and we'll gladly *pay* you for your services."

"I-I don't know what to say."

"Say yes."

"It would be a privilege to help get that place lookin' beautiful again. But it's goin' to be a long time before the renovation's done. Can't just sit on my thumbs all that time. I've got to find a place to stay. Get work to tide me over."

Ethan smiled. "We can make some inquiries. Surely there are businesses and private residents who are looking for a landscaper. You're practically famous after saving Vanessa and the Broussards."

For the first time, Noah smiled like he meant it. "Actually the monsignor down at Haven House told me he would help me find work when I was serious about it. Said I could stay there as long as I'm workin' and tryin' to improve my situation. They don't ask for rent, but expect everybody to pitch in with the chores—cookin', cleanin', maintenance, yard work, and such. Sounds like a good way to find my way back."

Vanessa locked gazes with Ethan, marveling that a descendent of Josiah Langley and a descendent of a slave named Naomi had not only met, but were going to work together to restore the manor house their ancestors had secretly used as a doorway to freedom for hundreds of slaves.

"It's just starting to hit me how historic this is," Ethan said. "I mean, think about it. This is really something."

"Actually"—a slow grin spread across Noah's face—"it's somethin' *else!*"

CHAPTER 38

Pierce turned his Toyota Prius onto *rue Madeline*, the traffic bumper-to-bumper and moving at a snail's pace. He glanced over at the gold building with black trim and the new sign suspended from the gallery just above the entrance:

Zoe B's Cajun Eatery
Pierce and Zoe Broussard, owners

Owners. And partners. Something inside him stirred. He and Zoe made a great team. Hadn't the past five years been the happiest of his life? Hadn't he walked away from teaching without ever looking back—with little thought to the tenure and benefits and summers off? Teaching had been his profession, but cooking was his passion. Being able to bring that passion into a business partnership was a win-win for both of them.

Something caught his eye, and he looked up on the gallery above Zoe B's. A man holding a toolbox stood outside the door. Zoe must have finally called someone to fix the broken bolt lock. That's all he needed—a repair guy hanging around when he wanted to talk to her in private.

The cars ahead of him picked up speed, and he drove to the end of the block and turned right, then made a sharp right into the alley. He drove up behind Zoe B's and spotted Vanessa's Honda Odyssey. He wondered when the sheriff had released it, and if she would want to sell it after being forced by Cowen to drive it to the Vincent farm.

Pierce parked next to Zoe's car and turned off the motor. Did he really want to do this? If he chose not to, and just drove back to Houma, would he ever be able to muster the courage to confront Zoe? To deal with the emotional wounds he felt right now? Or would he shut down?

He got out of the car and walked to the back door and unlocked it, then went inside and up the steps. He stopped in front of the door to his apartment. Should he knock? It's not as though he was a guest.

He put the key in the door and slowly pushed it open. He started to call Zoe's name when he heard voices in the bedroom and noticed the door to the gallery was left open a crack. His pulse raced. Was she entertaining a man? He dismissed the thought just as the man raised his voice.

Pierce walked ever so softly down the hall, slipped into the bathroom, and put his ear to the wall.

"You got my partner killed. Now you can pay *me*."

"We d-don't have that kind of money. I told Cowen we would have to borrow it. It would take time."

"He gave you time. You stiffed him—*again*. Now you're gonna pay with your life—but not till your husband pays me somethin'. I'm not walkin' away from this with nothin'."

"Please, I'm not the Zoe Benoit you think I am."

"I don't believe you. But I don't really care. Let's see how much that husband of yours can scrape up if he thinks he's got two hours before I gut you like a catfish and throw you in the river."

Zoe squealed. "You're hurting me."

"Trust me, I'm not. When I start hurting you, you'll be beggin' me to stop." He laughed. "Now call your husband's cell phone."

No! Pierce started to pat himself down, trying to find his cell phone before it could ring. He pulled it out of his back pocket and it slipped out of his hand and dropped onto the floor, his lively ringtone version of "The Sting" echoing in the bathroom. It was several more seconds before he could grab it and turn it off. He stopped breathing and listened.

"What was that?" the man said.

"Pierce's cell phone. That's his ring. He must have forgotten to take it with him."

"Has your call gone to voice mail yet?"

"No."

"Then why'd it stop ringing?"

Jude hung up the phone and turned to Aimee Rivette and Gil Marcel.

"We've got an ID on Cowen's sidekick from the artist sketch we released to the media. The manager of an adult bookstore remembered him coming in a few days ago and pulled his credit card receipt. Suspect's name is Jag Jones. He did time for robbery, aggravated assault, and drug possession. The Fort Worth PD had him under surveillance for drug trafficking, but he disappeared before they could move on him. Sure sounds like our guy. I'm thinking that the third set of shoe prints we cast at the scene of Remy's murder belong to him."

Gil raised his eyebrows. "Jones probably high-tailed it out of here after we took down Cowen."

"Well, I just put out an ABP on him," Jude said. "We're going to get this creep."

Aimee smiled knowingly. "Why don't I call the Broussards and the Langleys and let them know about the new development?"

"Do it. Thanks." Jude folded his hands on his desk. "Boy, what a difference a day makes. Once news got out that a white man was behind Remy's murder—and that we took him out—the racial unrest came to a halt. Of course, it didn't hurt that Deshawn Maccy pulled through." Jude's mind flashed back to those fragile moments in the park when he was afraid the boy was bleeding to death.

"I'm glad we got it done before Remy's funeral."

"We all are." Jude moved his gaze from Gil to Aimee. "But what we did between the time we found Remy murdered and the time we took out Cowen was equally important. We managed to keep a powder keg of racial violence from exploding. I have you two to thank for that. You did a brilliant job of putting deputies and police officers where we needed them—and with the pressure of the whole world watching. I'm proud of you."

"Works both ways, Sheriff," Gil said. "The way you represented this department in front of the cameras and behind the scenes makes me proud to be a part."

Aimee nodded.

Jude felt his face flush and brought his palms down on his desk. "Okay, we've still got work to do."

"I'll go get ready for the afternoon briefing," Gil said. "It's great that we have an ID on this Jag Jones. Cowen got off easy. I want to catch this dirtbag and make sure he stays alive and goes to trial."

Aimee rose to her feet. "I'll go call the Broussards and the Langleys."

The assailant forced Zoe down the hall, gripping the back of her collar with one hand and holding the knife to her neck with the other. He stopped her at the bathroom door.

"Where's the light switch?" he said.

"Just to the right of the door."

"All right, turn it on," he said. "*Slowly.*"

Zoe reached to the right and flipped the switch, shocked to see Pierce standing with his back flat against the wall, his index finger to his lips.

"Do you see the phone?"

Pierce nodded at her.

"Yes," she said. "It's here."

The assailant pressed the tip of the knife between her shoulder blades. "Slowly pick it up and give it to me."

Zoe's mind went into high gear. Did Pierce want her to lead the guy into the bathroom or away from the bathroom? He put the phone in her hand and gave a nod.

"Okay, I'm passing it back to you." Zoe handed it over her shoulder to the assailant.

"All right, slowly back out of the bathroom, and keep your hands where I can see them."

Zoe did as she was told.

"Now slowly turn around and walk into the living room and sit on the couch."

Zoe made an about-face, her legs feeling wobbly as a colt's, and moved toward the living room as the assailant prodded her with the knife. What was Pierce going to do? Surely he wouldn't try to overtake this man? Was he any challenge for a criminal wielding a knife?

God, please don't let him get hurt.

Pierce's eyes searched the bathroom for something he could use to disable the assailant. He might get only one chance. Failure was not an option.

He opened the mirrored cabinet above the sink and quickly scanned the glass shelves. Pill bottles. Tweezers. Toothpaste. Dental floss. He picked up a tiny pair of scissors. Too small.

He pulled back the shower curtain. A bar of soap. Zoe's disposable razor. Back scrubber. Nothing that would serve as a weapon. Hurry!

He spotted a can of bathroom spray. He grabbed it from the back of the toilet, his heart racing, adrenaline almost oozing from his pores. He would have to do this just right. If he missed, he could end up dead. Zoe, too. He peeked out of the bathroom. The creep had his back to him and was prodding Zoe across the living room.

Pierce took a deep breath. Gripping the can so hard his knuckles were white, he crept ever so quietly across the hall and came up behind Zoe's assailant. It was now or never.

Pierce let out a battle cry that seemed to rock the walls. He grabbed the assailant, put him in headlock, and sprayed the aerosol in his eyes and nostrils until he dropped the knife. Pierce kicked it over to Zoe.

"Call 9-1-1!"

Seconds later, there was a loud pounding on the door.

"It's Ethan. Are you all right?"

"No!" Pierce said. "Come help me hold this guy until the police get here."

Ethan flung the door open and came rushing in.

Pierce held the assailant with pit-bull-like tenacity, not loosening his grip, though the guy screamed obscenities and clawed at his eyes.

Ethan, his hands on his hips, looked from Pierce to the assailant and back to Pierce. "I don't know why you need *me*, man. This guy's not going *anywhere*."

CHAPTER 39

In the wee hours of the next morning, Pierce sat on the couch in the moonlit living room and listened to the *tick tick tick* of the grandfather clock, the events of the past few days racing through his mind.

It had been just one week since Remy Jarvis was murdered. How many lives had been dramatically changed by the two men responsible? At least Zoe was safe now. And Vanessa was on the mend. His mind flashed back to the image of Emile leaving the church after Remy's memorial Mass. How would Pierce have dealt with it if Zoe had been murdered? The thought of living his life without her was unbearable.

Yesterday's conversation with his father wouldn't leave him alone. Burke Broussard was about the finest man he knew. How could he be flawed? Flawed like Zoe and saddled with the same kind of secret—a secret so shameful that he chose to hide it from his wife for over thirty years? Still ... could there be any doubt that his parents were totally committed to the relationship? That they had managed to work through the betrayal?

You're the one with the power.... This can have a happy ending. It just depends on how much grace you're willing to give Zoe.

Pierce's eyes burned with tears. *Grace.* What did that even mean? Was he supposed to forget Zoe fabricated her life's story? That she was capable of deceiving him on that level?

"Can't you sleep either?" Zoe stood in the hallway, wearing the lacy pink nightgown he bought her for their anniversary weekend.

"No. I'm wide awake."

"Have you decided whether you're going back to Houma in the morning?"

"I honestly don't know what I'm going to do."

Zoe turned and started to go back into the bedroom.

"Wait!" Pierce heard himself say. "Come sit with me."

She hesitated for a few moments and then walked over to the couch, barefoot and childlike, and sat next to him.

It was all he could do not to pull her into his arms. Instead, he folded his hands in his lap.

"The truth is, I need to make a decision, and I'm torn."

"I lied to you. How can you trust me now? I get it."

"I don't think you do." Pierce blinked the stinging from his eyes. "You are half of my heart...." His voice failed, and he paused to pull himself together. "If I leave you, I leave a part of myself. When we got married, we became a new creation. That's what the priest said—a new creation. We're one. You can't separate that creation ... without ripping it apart...." Pierce stopped and swallowed the emotion that stole his voice again.

"I know I did a lot of things wrong," Zoe said. "Please believe that I never intended to hurt you. I just didn't want to lose you. I've never loved anyone the way I love you."

His father's voice resounded in his head. *She got herself in over her*

head and made some bad mistakes.... But I've seen how the two of you
are together. I know love when I see it.

"Can you ever forgive me?"

Pierce sighed. Could he? "I'm working on it, babe."

Zoe cocked her head and looked up at him. "You said *babe.*"

He reached over and took her hand. "It's going to take time to
sort this out. But I just realized something: I'd rather suffer through
it with you than suffer alone without you."

Zoe's eyes brimmed with tears that soon spilled down her cheeks.
"I don't know what to say. I never expected this. What changed your
mind?"

"Some things Dad said." Pierce took his thumb and wiped away
her tears. "I've touched your soul, Zoe. There's a part of you that no
one else has been privy to but me. It has nothing to do with the name
you had. Or what family you were born to. *That's* the part of you I
don't want to lose."

"Thank God," she whispered.

"I can't promise you this is going to be easy. Or that there won't
be times when I'm overwhelmed by it. But whatever we have to do
to fix this can't be any harder than living without you."

Zoe let out a sob and then another and another until it seemed
a dam of emotion had broken and the tears could not be stopped.

Pierce pulled her into his arms, trying for the first time to imagine all the pain *she* had been carrying, beginning with the horrible
abuse she suffered in her parents' home, to the helplessness of being
dependent on Mrs. Woodmore, to the theft of the ring, the fabrication of Zoe Benoit, the dishonest money that bought Zoe B's. Then
living the past five years with the fear that Pierce might leave her if

he found out. Her pain became his pain, and he let his tears fall and mingle with hers.

After a few minutes, his tears stopped, and he just held her. Finally he said, "We should get Ethan's advice. Maybe he can hook us up with a counselor. You open to that?"

Zoe nodded, her sobbing softer.

"I already know he's going to say we need to get God involved," Pierce said, "though God must be helping us already or we'd both be dead. Vanessa, too."

Zoe stopped crying and rested her head on his chest. "I'd give anything to be as comfortable with God as Ethan and Vanessa seem to be. They pray like He's right there with them and they know He's going to answer."

Pierce took the bottom of his T-shirt and dried Zoe's face. "And He did answer. More than once."

"When I saw you in the bathroom, I prayed you wouldn't get hurt. But I had no idea what you were going to do." Zoe cupped his cheek in her hand. "That took courage."

"More like fear. I overheard what the creep said he was going to do to you. I knew I had to act while I could." The corners of Pierce's mouth twitched. "Maybe there's some poetic justice here. Whatever happens to this Jones character, the thing he'll be remembered for is that he was captured by a Cajun with can of bathroom spray."

CHAPTER 40

Two weeks later on a Wednesday morning, Zoe watched Savannah model the new black skirt and white blouse "uniform" for Hebert, Father Sam, and Tex.

"Sure looks classy," Tex said. "When you said uniform, I envisioned something entirely different. Of course, the young lady modelin' it would make anything look good." He winked.

"Thank you very much." Savannah curtsied. "I do like the idea of not having to spend money on different outfits for work, especially when this one is so cute."

Zoe felt her cell phone vibrate and looked at the screen. She walked out of the dining room and into the alcove.

"Hello, Mrs. Woodmore."

"Hello, Zoe. I hope I didn't call too early. But I wanted to catch you first thing."

"Not at all. We open at six. I've already put in a couple of hours. Pierce and I signed the repayment agreement papers your attorney dropped by and will be sending them back today."

"Well, hon, it just so happens I have to make a trip down your way and thought if it was all right with you two, I'd stop by

359

Zoe B's this afternoon and pick them up myself. It'd save y'all the postage."

"Sure, that'd be fine." *Oh my heavens! She's coming here!* "What time?"

"Around two-thirty? That should give you time to get through the busy lunch hour. Will that work?"

"Yes, perfectly. Do you need directions?"

"No, Julien can use the GPS." There was a long pause, and the only sound was Adele's breathing into the receiver. "How are you doing, hon? Ever since you called after your ordeal and asked if I could send the papers instead of your making a trip here, I've been wondering how things are. You know I'm praying that the Lord would help you get your marriage back on track."

"He is. I won't pretend there are no bumps. But in a strange sort of way, those terrifying encounters with the drug dealers have brought us closer. We both realize how close we came to losing each other."

"Yes, indeed," Adele said. "I read the articles you sent me several times. Made me shudder."

There was a long moment of dead air. Had she lost the connection?

"Mrs. Woodmore, are you still there?"

"I'm here, hon. I just want to say how proud I am that you and Pierce are working things out—and that you told him the truth. I never felt good about going forward with our arrangement until he was fully apprised of the situation."

"I know." Zoe sighed. "I wish I could say that I told him before Cowen threatened me and left me no choice. But I did tell him *everything.*"

"Your life can only get better from here, hon. You did the right thing."

"I can't tell you how much I appreciate your attitude," Zoe said. "You have every right to be furious with me. Instead you've showed me nothing but kindness."

"Well, I've been on this earth more years than I'm willing to admit, and I've never once seen a grudge bring about positive results. I've forgiven you, Zoe. There's nothing to be gained by dwelling on the past."

"That's so gracious of you. I'll go tell Pierce you're coming. I know he'd like to meet you."

"I'd like that too. I'll see you both around two-thirty."

Zoe waited until the lunch crowd thinned out and then hurried to prepare a table for Mrs. Woodmore. She unfolded a red and gold fleur-de-lis print tablecloth, shook it, then spread it evenly across the table by the window, smoothing out the wrinkles. She set a vase of fresh flowers in the center.

She saw the kitchen door open, and Pierce came out, still wearing his apron and his chef's hat.

"You'll be happy to know that the lemonade bread pudding came out perfect today."

"Oh, good." Zoe put her hand to her heart. "Thanks for making it. It's one of the recipes I created while I worked for Mrs. Woodmore. It was one of her favorites."

"I know, babe. You've reminded me at least a dozen times. Why are you so nervous?"

"I just want everything to be perfect for her visit here."

"Zoe …" Pierce walked over to her and tilted her chin. "Don't make this into something it isn't. Mrs. Woodmore is picking up a legal agreement that's allowing us to pay back the value of the ring you stole. And will squeeze our budget for the next thirty months. This is not a social visit."

"I still want it to be nice."

"I do too. I just don't want you to set yourself up for a big disappointment. This woman sounds wonderful. But somehow I don't see us swapping life stories over dessert. This is a serious business arrangement, regardless of how gracious she is."

Zoe sighed. "You're right. I'm just so fond of her, and I realize how much I've missed her. For six years, she was the only family I had."

"I understand that. I do. But you owe this woman a great deal of money. And right now, you need to keep your business hat on." Pierce looked over her shoulder. "Take a deep breath, babe. I think that might be her now."

Zoe turned around and saw a familiar silver Rolls Royce sitting out front with its flashers on. The chauffeur, dressed in a charcoal gray uniform, got out and walked around to the passenger side and opened the back door.

"That's Julien," Zoe said. "He was her chauffeur when I worked for her. I saw him when I drove to Alexandria."

Julien helped Adele out of the backseat. She said something to him and then started walking toward the front door, a brown envelope tucked under her arm.

"Attractive lady," Pierce said.

"Always."

Adele was dressed in a powder blue skirt and jacket that complemented her snow-white hair. She wore sandals instead of pumps and took small steps instead of strides. But she was as classy as ever.

The bell on the front door jingled as Adele came inside. Through the window Zoe saw Julien drive away in the Rolls Royce, evoking double takes from several people on the sidewalk.

"Hello, hon." Adele smiled with her eyes. She took Zoe's hand and kissed her on the cheek. "You're looking well."

"Thanks. So are you."

"And this must be Pierce."

"Hello, Mrs. Woodmore." Pierce took a step forward and shook Adele's hand. "Nice to meet you."

"I hear you are a marvelous chef."

"Thanks." The corners of Pierce's mouth twitched. "Your source is undoubtedly partial. But I do enjoy it."

"He made a surprise dessert for you," Zoe said. "After we're finished with business, maybe you can stay a while longer and enjoy it with us."

"I'd like that." Adele glanced around the dining room. "Charming."

Zoe felt guilt jab her conscience. Was Adele thinking that it was the anniversary diamond Zoe stole from her that had made this place possible?

"Why don't we walk to the office and take care of business," Pierce said. "Then we can come back out here, and I'll serve you dessert. Right this way."

Zoe accompanied Adele and followed Pierce out of the dining

room into the alcove and stopped at the office door. He put the key in the lock and pushed open the door, then flipped the light switch.

"Ladies first."

Zoe filed in after Adele. "Let's sit there at the table. Can I get you something to drink—a soft drink, juice, bottled water?"

"Nothing for me, hon."

"I'm good," Pierce said.

Pierce held out a chair for Adele and seated her, then joined Zoe on the other side of the table.

Adele set the letter-sized brown envelope on the table, the gold cross around her neck reflecting the fluorescent lights overhead, her blue eyes the kindness in her heart.

"Before y'all give me the contract"—Adele folded her hands—"there's something I want to say. I don't believe in coincidences. I believe that everything happens for a reason. Our Creator knows the plan He has for each of us, and somehow He makes it all come together in His perfect timing. He knew Shelby Sieger was going to steal my ring long before my sweet Alfred got the idea to have it made for our fiftieth anniversary. Everything I have belongs to the Lord. And whatever happens to any of it is His business."

Adele looked into Zoe's eyes. "I forgive you for taking the ring, Zoe, and for lying about it. That's not to say I condone what you did. It was more hurtful than you'll ever know. But like I said, whatever happens to anything the Lord has given me is His business. I do thank you for owning up to it and wanting to make it right. Legally, the time has passed for anyone to hold you accountable."

"I can't do anything about the pain I've caused you," Zoe said. "But I really do want to pay back the money. We both do."

"I know you do. But I've given a great deal of thought to our agreement and have decided *not* to go through with it." Adele held up her palm. "Hear me out. It's for your own good."

Zoe's heart sank. What was she talking about? How could she do this?

Adele slid the brown envelope across the table. "I think it's important that you understand my reasoning. I didn't decide this without a great deal of thought—and prayer. Open it, hon."

Zoe opened the envelope and pulled out the contents, then perused the document. "This is the deed to our building. How did you get this?"

"Look at the other document."

Zoe skipped to the next document, the words "Paid in full" stamped across the front. "What in the world…?"

Pierce put his arm around Zoe and took a closer look at the document she was holding. "These are the mortgage papers on this building." His jaw dropped, and he looked over at Adele.

"Yes," she said. "I paid it off—just before I came over here. The building is yours free and clear."

Zoe stared at the papers. "But I stole from you. I lied to you. I don't deserve this."

"I didn't expect you to deserve it, hon. It's a gift. Actually it'll help me to move forward too."

Pierce nodded as if he knew what Adele meant. "It's grace, Zoe."

"Just like that?"

"*Especially* like that." He looked over at Adele, his eyes glistening. "This is very generous—on every level."

"Listen, hon. I've amassed a fortune in my lifetime. I'm not taking a cent of it with me into glory. It's my pleasure to do this for you two."

"It goes beyond the money." Zoe looked into Adele's eyes and saw complete and utter acceptance. "Saying thank you doesn't seem like enough, but I don't have words to express what I'm feeling."

Adele took Pierce's hand and joined it with Zoe's. "A day will come when someone you know is in desperate need of grace. Remember how this moment feels and pass it on. Healing comes as much in the giving as in the receiving."

No one said anything for half a minute.

Finally Adele rose to her feet. "That completes our business. Now I want to taste this surprise dessert. Do I get a hint?"

Zoe smiled, wiping the tears off her face. "Something I used to make for you with fresh lemons. It was your favorite."

"Lemonade bread pudding?"

"Yes! You remembered."

"How could I forget? It was so scrumptious."

"Well, knowing Pierce, he probably added a little something to it and made it even better."

Adele walked out into the hallway and locked arms with Pierce and Zoe and strolled through the alcove and into the dining room.

"Where would like me to sit?"

"Right here." Zoe hurried over to the table by the window and held the chair. "This table is reserved for our special friends."

"I'll go get our dessert," Pierce said. "I'll be back in a minute."

Zoe got Adele seated and situated at the table and then sat across from her, noting the gold cross that she had worn as long as Zoe had known her.

"Mrs. Woodmore, you're close to God," Zoe said. "I can tell."

"Well of course, hon. He lives in my heart. I invited Him in and asked Him to run things. I've been much happier since."

"That's because you're such a good person."

Adele threw back her head and laughed. "Wrong."

"I think you are."

Adele's face was suddenly bright pink. "There's so much you don't know about me. I haven't always been agreeable, hon. I've said and done things I'm ashamed of and would be embarrassed for people to know. I suppose we all have."

"So did someone give *you* grace?"

Adele smiled, a faraway look in her eyes, her fingers touching the gold cross. "Yes … someone did. A King. But that's a story for another day."

CHAPTER 41

On a Monday afternoon in mid-November, Zoe sat with Pierce, Vanessa, and Ethan on an old quilt on the grounds at Langley Manor, enjoying a picnic lunch and watching the work crew busily going about the renovations at the manor house. The air was nearly rung dry of humidity, the temperature balmy, the breeze scented with pine.

"The new roof looks great." Ethan slipped his arm around Vanessa. "My dad and uncles were pretty fired up over the pictures I emailed. None of them wanted to move here and tackle this, but they were very willing to help fund it. They spent a lot of time here when they were kids. They want to see it come back to life."

"The place is going to be fantastic." Pierce popped a chicken nugget. "And now that everybody in town knows that Josiah Langley wasn't a British elitist who snubbed the Cajuns, but a selfless man who gave himself to the task of freeing the slaves, the attitude has changed."

"It's obvious in the way people have opened up to us." Vanessa looked at Ethan and smiled. "At first I thought we were always going to be outsiders. But now I almost feel Cajun, *cher*." She laughed. "It's probably all that Cajun food we're feasting on at Zoe B's."

A big red plastic ball bounced on the blanket and into Zoe's lap. A few seconds later Carter dropped down on the blanket between Zoe and Pierce, sounding out of breath.

"I like this big, big, *big* yard!" Carter said. "I can kick the ball weally far."

"That's because *you* are the soccer star." Pierce tickled Carter's ribs, evoking boyish shrieks and husky giggles. "The champion kicker of all four-year-olds in the whole world."

Pierce tickled Carter mercilessly until they were both belly laughing so hard they ran out of wind.

"Will you boys settle down?" Vanessa's playful tone betrayed her. "Or I'll have to give you a time out."

"Well, *someone's* a party pooper." Pierce put his index finger to his lips, the corners of his mouth twitching with restraint.

Carter pressed his lips tightly together, his eyes animated, his arms folded across his chest.

No one said anything for a minute, the sound of the buzz saws in the house filling the quiet.

Zoe ran her fingers through Carter's mound of strawberry-blond hair. "I think you're going to like living here when it's all finished. I have a feeling you'll be entertaining the guests. You're such a little character."

Carter cocked his head and flashed a wry smile. "What's that?"

"Character is a grown-up word that can mean a lot of things. But in your case, it's an adorable little boy who makes people smile."

"Oh."

"Pierce and I will miss having you living next door. What will I do when I need a little-boy hug?"

Carter shrugged. "Maybe you hafta get a little boy of your own."

Zoe glanced over at Pierce and smiled, and then smiled broader.

"Why are you laughing?" Vanessa said. "That's a *great* idea. We won't be moving out for a while. You should plan ahead."

"Gee, I wish we had thought of that," Pierce said.

Ethan looked over at them, his eyebrow arched. "What's going on with you two? You've been sending nonverbal messages all day."

"Spoken like a true shrink," Pierce said. "What do you think, babe? Shall we tell them? It's your call."

Zoe felt radiant and wondered if she looked that way. "I think we should." She moved her gaze from Carter to Ethan to Vanessa. "Pierce and I are going to have a *baby*."

Vanessa sucked in a breath, both hands over her mouth.

"That's terrific!" Ethan said.

Carter leaned his head back and looked up at Zoe. "A boy baby?"

"We don't know yet, sweetie. It might be a girl baby."

"When's your due date?" Vanessa said.

"May twenty-first." Zoe reached over and took Pierce's hand. "We're ecstatic—and surprised. We're still trying to catch our breath from the summer. We had postponed this idea for another year."

"But I love being surprised," Pierce said.

Vanessa picked up the red ball. "When did you find out you were expecting?"

"Friday." Zoe glanced over at Pierce. "We snuck off to Houma to tell his parents. That's where we were over the weekend. Needless to say, there was a lot of hooting and hollering going on at the Broussards'."

"Do you think you'll stay in the apartment?" Vanessa said. "It may seem smaller to you after the baby starts walking."

"We've already talked about it." Pierce squeezed Zoe's hand. "After you move into Langley Manor, we can knock out walls and have the two apartments connected. We'll double our space and have three-bedroom apartment with two full baths, two half baths, and a study. The full gallery will make a nice big play area outside, and Cypress Park is just down the block. I think we'll just stay where we are and raise our family. We really like having our business downstairs."

Ethan nodded. "Sounds like a plan."

"When you get a baby," Carter said, "you won't need me to give you little-boy hugs anymore."

Zoe cupped Carter's face in her hands and looked into his clear blue eyes. "That's absolutely not true. There will never be another little boy just like you, and I will *always* need hugs from you—even when you're a big boy."

Carter raised his arms high. "Even when I'm *this* big."

Zoe smiled. "Even then. You will always be special to me. And I'm going to need your help taking care of the baby."

"I'm the goodest helper."

"Yes, you are." Zoe pulled Carter closer and gave him a gentle squeeze.

"So have you told Adele yet?" Ethan said.

Pierce shook his head. "We're driving up there this weekend. We didn't want to tell her over the phone."

"Your friendship with her is a miracle," Vanessa said. "It's so exciting what God has done in your lives through her."

"It really is."

Zoe looked up at the cloud puffs that dotted the crisp blue autumn sky, quietly fingering the gold cross around her neck, at peace with the

King of Kings who had given Adele grace and who now lived in her own heart—and Pierce's.

Would she ever cease to marvel at how grace had transformed her life on every level? Could she ever have imagined that the broken and abused young woman from Devon Springs who covered her shame with lies would discover that Jesus had sacrificed Himself so that she could be born again, adopted into His royal family—cleansed, forgiven, restored? A new creation. A child of the King.

"Miss Zoe?"

Carter's voice brought her back to the present.

"How come you're cwying?"

Zoe smiled and tapped his nose with her finger. "These aren't sad tears, sweetie. I'm just so full of joy it doesn't have anywhere else to go."

CHAPTER 42

On a clear cool morning in mid-February, Zoe stood at the table by the window at Zoe B's, talking with Hebert, Father Sam, and Tex.

"Mardi Gras is next Tuesday already," Hebert said. "Les Barbes will start filling up wid tourists for da parade dis weekend."

Father Sam nodded. "I'm glad our parade is family oriented. That's good for businesses."

"*We're* ready," Zoe said. "We've got two crates of beads to give out to customers. And we're going to put up our decorations this afternoon. We've got some beautiful masks we bought at the gift mart."

Hebert took a sip of coffee, his mousey gray hair sticking up where he'd slept on it. "Can you believe dat in ninety-four years, I've never missed da Mardi Gras parade in Les Barbes?"

"That's really amazing," Father Sam said. "I think you're the only one in town who can say that."

Hebert gave a nod. "Probably so. Emile's coming wid me dis year, now dat Remy's gone. It's good he's finally getting out some."

"That *is* good," Zoe said. "Though I doubt it's much consolation that Jag Jones isn't getting out of prison until he's an old man."

Hebert looked at her bulging middle. "How you feeling, young lady?"

"Great. I've been walking every day like my doctor told me to. I'm getting more and more energy."

"Dat's real good, Zoe."

"Tex, you're awfully quiet," Father Sam said.

"Yep. I guess I am."

Hebert flashed an impish grin. "Why do you *make a bahbin?*"

"I'm not poutin'," Tex said. "I'm mentally gearin' up for a rematch."

"Ha! Bring it on."

Father Sam looked up at Zoe, the amusement in his eyes magnified by his thick lenses. "Hebert has won the last twelve checker matches."

"Ah, so that's it."

"Tex don' like being beat by a man old enough to be his pop. Isn't dat right?"

Tex sat back in his chair, his thumbs hooked on his suspenders. "I don't like bein' beat—period." A smile spread across his face, his bald head flushed. "I'm not the first fella to lose to Hebert, and I suspect I won't be the last."

"When you want anudder match?"

Tex laughed. "You kiddin'? Let's go."

Hebert reached in his bag and pulled out the checkerboard and the box of checkers and started setting it up.

"I'll see you guys later," Zoe said. "I'm rooting for both of you."

She walked into the kitchen and spotted Savannah. "I'm going to take my morning walk. I'll see you in an hour." She waved to

Pierce, who was up to his elbows in flour. "I'm going down to the park, *cher*."

He smiled and blew her a kiss.

Zoe walked through the dining room and out the front door and was instantly hit with the crisp February air and warm sunshine—a combination she loved. She walked on the sidewalk under the galleries, shoulder to shoulder with tourists, peering into shop windows and enjoying the delicious smells of warm pastries, ground coffee, and something spicy wafting under her nose.

The postman, his leather pouch strapped to his shoulder, waited for the horse and carriage to pass by, then zipped across *rue Madeline*.

Zoe strolled to the end of the block and crossed the street into Cypress Park, savoring the sunlight that filtered through the trees thick with Spanish moss.

She ambled around the duck pond, her hands tucked in her sweater pockets, and walked up on the wooden bridge. Below her, six black-necked stilts waded in water a few inches deep, their red legs catching the sun. On the far side of the pond, a lone great egret high-stepped through the shallow water, stalking its prey.

The bells of Saint Catherine's began to toll as she looked up in the bluebird sky and watched a flock of white ibis flying in a V formation, southward toward the rookery. How close she had come to losing this amazing place that she had fallen in love with a decade ago.

She glanced at her watch. Where had the time gone? She felt a tiny thud as if a finger had flicked her tummy. And then another.

She fumbled to pull her phone out of her sweater pocket and punched in Pierce's speed-dial number.

"Hey, babe. What's up?" he said.

"Grace finally kicked! There was no doubt this time. It was more than a flutter. It was a thud. Two thuds actually. It was so amazing!"

Pierce laughed. "I love it. Where are you?"

"At Cypress Park. I'm on my way back."

"Hurry. Maybe it'll happen again."

"I'm coming."

Zoe started walking briskly. She crossed the street and headed up the sidewalk on the south side of *rue Madeline*, this time zigzagging around the people and hoping she didn't run into anyone she knew.

She was vaguely aware of the clip-clop of a horse's hoofs, the street vendor's mantra, and Japanese tourists posing for pictures in front of the Peltier Hotel. Finally she spotted the hanging sign above the front door of Zoe B's.

She broke free of the crowd, laughing out loud when she saw Pierce standing out front, still wearing his chef's hat and dusted in white flour. She ran to his arms, and he picked her up off the ground, then set her back down.

Zoe grabbed his hand and pressed it tightly to her abdomen. "My heart's beating so fast." She was almost out of breath and giggling like a schoolgirl. "I'm not sure you can feel her kicking."

"That's okay. Relax. We'll have plenty of chances." Pierce brushed her cheek with the back of his hand. "To tell you the truth, babe, I'm getting a bigger kick out of seeing the wonder on your face."

... a little more ...

When a delightful concert comes to an end,
the orchestra might offer an encore.
When a fine meal comes to an end,
it's always nice to savor a bit of dessert.
When a great story comes to an end,
we think you may want to linger.
And so, we offer ...

AfterWords—just a little something more after you
have finished a David C Cook novel.
We invite you to stay awhile in the story.
Thanks for reading!

Turn the page for ...

- **A Note From the Author**
- **Discussion Guide**

A NOTE FROM THE AUTHOR

*"Therefore, if anyone is in Christ, he is a new creation;
the old has gone, the new has come!" (2 Cor. 5:17)*

Dear reader,

Does anything we think, say, or do escape the notice of the God of the universe? I imagine few of us have a story of deception as extreme as Zoe's. But have we ever been guilty of pretending not to see a sin area in our lives, as if ignoring it will make it invisible to God? Is there anything, past or present, we're so ashamed of that we lie to cover up? Something that would make our faces burn with shame if it were published on the front page of the newspaper?

Shelby Sieger was not a horrible person. She was wounded, her spirit crushed, her self-image malformed. The shame she bore from her abuse was intensely painful. But the lies and the deception she employed in an attempt to "escape her past" were ineffectual and destructive—and ultimately resulted in even more shame.

Zoe tried to justify her deceptive methods as necessary to ensure her survival and happiness. She cleverly managed to avoid going to jail but was instead locked in an *emotional* prison. Changing her name to Zoe Benoit didn't erase the ugly truth of her past. Disowning her family, stealing from Adele, and marrying Pierce under false pretenses didn't set her free. Nor did it heal her wounded spirit or change who she really was. Ultimately, Zoe came to understand that only in Christ could she find her true identity.

I didn't know until the last few chapters that Pierce's father, Burke Broussard, would teach his son about the importance of extending grace, or that Adele Woodmore would be the one to bring Zoe and Pierce to the real Source of all grace. I love it when my fingers receive those "pearls" from above.

Well … we certainly haven't heard the last of the Broussards, their little Grace to come, or the Langleys and the rest of the cast of characters in Les Barbes. Join me in book two, where we will discover more secrets of Roux River Bayou. Prepare to stay up late. It promises to be page-turner.

I would love to hear from you. Join me on Facebook (www.facebook.com/kathyherman) or drop by my website at www.kathyherman.com and leave your comments on my guest book. I read and respond to every email and greatly value your input.

In Him,

Kathy Herman

DISCUSSION GUIDE

1. Why do you think our family of origin is so important to our self-image? What elements go into forming a healthy self-image? When those elements are missing in a child's life, who is responsible? When those elements are missing in an adult's life, who is responsible? Where do we find our true identity?

2. At what point in time should an adult take responsibility for dealing with the wounds of his or her childhood? Do you agree or disagree with this statement: "It's not your fault if you grew up dysfunctional, but it is your fault if you stay that way." Explain your answer. Were Zoe's parents responsible for the choices she made?

3. Do you think people who carry around the wounds of childhood are handicapped in their decision-making ability? Zoe's "victim mentality" allowed her to justify helping herself to Adele's ring in order to achieve her financial independence. What was wrong with that thinking? What, if anything, might Zoe have done differently to achieve the same goal? What options might she have had? Would it have made any difference in the right or wrong of her actions if no other options were available to her?

4. In your opinion, what constitutes a lie? Why do you think lying is offensive to God? Zoe told some whoppers, but do you think "white lies" are acceptable? Is deceiving the same thing as lying?

Can you name some biblical characters that got into trouble by deceiving others? How far-reaching were the consequences? Have you ever been deceived by someone you trusted? Were you able to forgive the person? Were you ever able to trust that person again?

5. What do you think is meant by 2 Corinthians 5:17, "Therefore, if anyone is in Christ, he is a new creation; the old has gone, the new has come"? When God pours out His saving grace, which is it that is paid in full: the penalty of one's sin or the consequences? Will the "new creation" be set free from the earthly consequences of past sins?

6. One definition of grace is *unmerited favor*. What are some ways that Zoe received grace from people in this story? Which touched you the most and why? Without the grace Zoe was shown, what might have been different in her life?

7. Since the garden of Eden, humans have tried to hide their sin from God. Why do you think that is? Are we sometimes guilty of hiding our sin—or justifying it—even after we're saved? Why do you think someone might do that instead of claiming the promise in 1 John 1:9, "If we confess our sins, he is faithful and just and will forgive us our sins and purify us from all unrighteousness"?

8. James 5:16 tells us, "Therefore confess your sins to each other and pray for each other so that you may be healed." Do you think

confession is good for the soul? Which do you think took more emotional energy for Zoe: carrying her bag of lies or opening it? Does confessing to each other mean opening up your bag of sin to every believer? Is there a case to be made for using wisdom and discretion in choosing whom we tell? Are there times when confessing our sin might inadvertently cause someone else great pain or embarrassment? Can you think of examples?

9. Do you think a person can come to faith in Christ and make a true confession and not even be aware of sin areas still to be dealt with? When you trusted Christ for your salvation, did you know the full extent of the sin in your life? If not, why do you think the Holy Spirit didn't reveal it all then? Do you think God forgives us for sin we don't yet recognize? Once we become aware of our sin, what should be our response?

10. What do you think Jesus meant in Matthew 18:21–23 when He said we should forgive seventy times seven? When is it hardest to forgive? Does the gravity of an offense have any bearing on the command to forgive? Though judging someone else's heart in real life is not our job, let's take a close look at the characters in the story. Who are the people in this story who either forgave someone or who still need to? Which would be the most difficult for you, were you in his or her shoes? Based on this line from the Lord's Prayer in Luke 11:4, "Forgive us our sins, for we also forgive everyone who sins against us," is forgiveness an option? Would that apply also to Zoe's forgiving her parents for the horrible abuse she suffered?

11. Is forgiveness in any way intended to mean that the offense didn't matter or that it didn't hurt—perhaps even deeply? Why do you think God commands us to forgive? Who benefits most when forgiveness occurs? Have you ever received grace from another person when you knew you didn't deserve it? How did it make you feel? Have you ever extended that kind of grace to someone else who didn't deserve it? What was your motivation for doing so? How did it make you feel?

12. If you could meet one character from the story, who would it be? What would you like to say to that person? What did you take away from this story?